To "
from Roberto
Aug 2010

ROBERTO DE HARO

FOR NADINE'S LOVE:

A WARRIOR'S QUEST

BOOKS
By
Roberto de Haro

Twist of Fate:
Love, Turbulence and the Great War

The Mexican Chubasco

Intermezzo of the Longing Hearts

Jolene's Last Gasp:
A Novel of Dreams Denied

Camino Doloroso

Assassins' Raid:
Killing Admiral Yamamoto

Murder at the Villa Museum

DEDICATION
To Nancy and my family

ACKNOWLEDGMENTS

I am indebted to numerous librarians, scholars, and military historians for their generous support and assistance. Librarians occupy a soft spot in my heart. They are resourceful and helpful professionals often willing to do extensive research to assist a writer. They can be invaluable in learning as much as possible about an event or topic. Museum curators specializing in aircraft developed before and during the Second World War were generous with their time, and shared important information that helped me prepare this book. In particular, the curators and experts at the Smithsonian Institution provided valuable information and support.

Numerous books were consulted to secure factual information for use in this novel. A few that were particularly helpful include: *Air Force Combat Units of WWII*, edited by M. Maurer (Edison, NY: Chartwell Books, 1994); *B-17s Over Berlin*, edited by Ian L. Hawkins (Washington: Brassey's, 1990); Pierre Clostermann's *The Big Show: The Greatest Pilot's Story of World War II* (London: Cassell, 2004); Ed Cray's *General of the Army: George C. Marshall, Soldier and Spokesman* (New York: Cooper Square Press, 2000); Robert Dallek's *Franklin D. Roosevelt and American Foreign Policy, 1932-1945* (New York: Oxford, 1995); John Keegan's *The Second World War* (New York: Penguin, 1989); Alex Kershaw's *The Few* (Philadelphia: Da Capo Press, 2006); and, Mark A. Stoler's *George C. Marshall: Soldier—Statesman of the American Century* (Detroit: Gale, 1989).

Overlooked in many historical accounts of World War II are the contributions of American women. I talked with several female historians and pilots who encouraged me to mention the role of American women pilots during World War II. Through them, and other sources, I learned to understand, admire, and appreciate the job these women did during the war, and afterward.

I extend sincere thanks to scholars and faculty colleagues who listened to me talk about my plans for this novel, and offered valuable advice and suggestions to strengthen the manuscript. And finally, sincere praise for the editors at CreateSpace, and special thanks to Nancy Henning, my partner, for reading the text to make recommendations and corrections.

Roberto de Haro

INTRODUCTION

The story of Nadine Desnoyers and Quentin Norvell began in Paris during December 1916. Theirs is a romantic tale, entwining the two from a chance meeting when the nascent spark of mutual attraction kindled strong emotions within each of them. Against the backdrop of the Great War, the dangers and intrigues that filled each day the conflict raged, a remarkable affinity develops between them. For Nadine, a young aristocratic woman of extraordinary beauty, married to an older man in the French Diplomatic Service, the convalescing American pilot serving with a French fighter squadron unlocks a hidden passion. Quentin, an Ivy League-educated Cajun American from Louisiana, is captivated by the aristocratic beauty, even though she is married and the mother of a young daughter. They gradually explore the allure that compels each to reach out to the other and find a bliss that neither could have imagined. Impelled by their passion, the two become secret lovers.

When the Great War ends, Quentin returns to America, brokenhearted because he has left the true love of his life. Unknown to him, Nadine gave birth to their son in 1918. Once Quentin is gone, Nadine separates from her husband and gradually becomes a highly respected and influential woman of enormous wealth in France. Quentin attends law school at Columbia University and becomes an attorney. He meets and falls in love with Ione Vandersteel, a lovely and musically gifted heiress from a wealthy family. The two marry and have a little girl, Florence. Ione dies shortly after childbirth, and Quentin retreats into a shell, convinced his actions have hurt Nadine deeply and caused Ione's death.

When Bernice, Quentin's mother, contacts Nadine and informs her about his hermetic behavior, the French woman's love for the Cajun cannot be denied.

She visits New York and rekindles their deep love and commitment. After Nadine's husband dies of a serious illness, she informs Marlon, their son, that Quentin is his father. The boy is stunned. When Quentin learns that Marlon is his son, he is perplexed and sullen until Nadine explains why she had to keep secret that Quentin is his father.

During the 1930s, Nadine draws Quentin into her world of finance and arranges for him to handle her investments in America and Canada. The two lovers see each other regularly as Quentin crosses the Atlantic in his Lockheed Electra. In 1939, Quentin asks Nadine to marry him, and, just when it appears the two will wed, the Germans attack Poland.

America in 1939 is not willing to consider any foreign military adventures. The effects of the Great Depression are still felt, and memories about the Great War and the number of American lives lost in that conflict reinforce a strong mood of isolationism. This is a time when America looks back at the Roaring Twenties as a time of change and excitement. Women finally gained the right to vote. But, Prohibition, enacted as part of a moral crusade, creates a new and unexpected development: the rise of organized crime. Some criminals are glamorized by the media, and the romantic legend of the "bootlegger" results in a new mythical antihero. A disenchanted segment of American society, known later as "the lost generation," leaves what they consider a corrupt and vacuous way of life, most fleeing to Europe. Nadine then introduces Quentin to the American literature of "the lost generation."

Quite by accident, Quentin becomes involved with a dangerous criminal, a chieftain in Lucky Luciano's New York gang. He meets and befriends a beautiful dancer enslaved by the gangster and finds a way to free her.

While Nadine adds to her family's fortune, Quentin expands his horizons, is soon financing motion pictures, and capitalizes on new technologies such as sound and color in films. During his trips to Southern California, he meets the leaders of Hollywood film studios and develops a rapport with Howard Hughes, a film mogul and a famous flyer.

The Great War dramatically changed the face of Europe and destroyed four long-lived empires. Once freed from their serfdom, many Europeans immigrate to America for a better life. But, the international depression and the seeds of discontent contribute to the rise of fascism in Europe and Japan. Fascist dictators ensconced themselves in Italy, Germany, and Spain, while a totalitarian communistic state developed in Russia. In the Pacific, Japan emerges from a feudal society as an aggressive militaristic nation building a modern army and navy.

In spite of the many warnings offered by progressive thinkers and leaders in the United States and elsewhere, most Americans remain committed to isolationism. The aftermath of the Spanish Civil War is viewed by a few informed thinkers as a prelude to more hostilities between fascism and democracy. While Europe teeters on the verge of war, Nadine and Quentin face an uncertain future.

It is against this backdrop that the story of Nadine and Quentin continues. The two lovers, ready to marry and find happiness with each other, now look with trepidation at the prospects of renewed hostilities in Europe. As Quentin is flying home from Europe on a fateful day at the beginning of September 1939, a tragedy begins to unfold.

PART I

❖

THE COMING OF WAR

CHAPTER 1
WAR, AGAIN

So faithful in love, and so dauntless in war,
There never was a knight like the young Lochinvar.
Sir Walter Scott, *Lochinvar, st. 1*

The drone of the Lockheed Electra 10's engines soothed Quentin as he sat at the controls of the *Amelie*, the name he'd given his plane in memory of Amelia Earhart. Quentin admired Amelia Earhart and had contributed to her campaign to fly around the world. All he asked for the money he sent was an autographed photo of her which he framed and gave to Florence, his daughter. He methodically scanned the instrument panel to ensure that everything was working smoothly before checking the compass and their heading. The rhythmic vibrations given off by the engines were an important sensory transmission Quentin felt through the plane's yoke. It was another form of sensual stimulation that translated messages to his mind, letting him know when everything was copasetic.

Quentin, copilot Hardy Chappelle, and Mark Waterman, the navigator and radio operator, left Paris early on the morning of September 1, 1939. Nadine was there to see them off. Hardy and Mark often commented that Nadine was a real looker. Now in her mid forties, she was still slender with firm muscle tone and a body fit from regular exercise and a careful diet. She was blessed with the right bone structure and genes and continued to be a beautiful woman regardless of her age.

When Nadine and Quentin first met in Paris that fateful night in December 1916, both of them succumbed to an irresistible attraction, destined to alter their lives substantially. But, so much had transpired since that time. Now, some twenty-three years later, the constraints that kept them apart no longer existed. Quentin had asked Nadine to marry him and she had accepted. No date had been discussed for the marriage, even though Quentin (aka the Cajun) wanted it to be as soon as possible.

As Quentin guided the Amelie on a westward trajectory, with several hours of flying over the expanse of the North Atlantic remaining, he thought about Nadine. The lovely French woman was brilliant and headstrong. She'd taught him so much, especially about love. He remembered their first sexual encounter. It was 1917, and that splendid experience waited as they went to bed. But, his hurried and lustful approach toward sex, typical of a young man lacking knowledge and the finesse to satisfy a woman, almost undid him. Without sophistication in such matters, he gave scant attention to foreplay and penetrated her roughly and with little regard to what she might want or enjoy. She resisted and pushed him away. Crushed, Quentin was confused and dejected. But, to his surprise, Nadine pressed her naked breasts against his back and asked if she could teach him how to make love properly. Most of what he knew about sex was from experiences growing up along the bayous of southern Louisiana and among the Cajuns. The rough and calloused men in the bayous cared little about whether their partners enjoyed sex. Some of this had been tempered when he attended Princeton University. But, still, the young Cajun was an ingénue in dealing with women and satisfying them sexually. Nadine taught Quentin marvelous ways of lovemaking, especially how to please and satisfy a woman. Together, they shared an exquisite passion.

Quentin felt a tap on his right shoulder and turned to see Mark holding a thermos with coffee. Mark tapped the thermos, a signal to learn if the "skipper" wanted coffee. Quentin shook his head. Instead, he nudged Hardy and pointed at the thermos. The copilot nodded, and Mark poured some coffee into a thick mug. Quentin motioned for Mark to come close and spoke loudly into the navigator's ear.

"Have you picked up anything on the radio about the fighting in Poland?"

"All I've gotten is stuff from the Brits. They claim the Germans have attacked the Poles on several fronts. Keep hearing the Soviet army is massing on the eastern border of Poland," Mark reported.

"Damn!" exclaimed Quentin. "Let me know if you hear anything else." He shook his head and scanned the instrument panel again before looking toward the horizon. It was a clear day, the warmth of summer still lingering from when they'd left Paris that morning. But, over the North Atlantic, the weather was unpredictable and frequently cold, especially at twelve thousand feet. There were a few high clouds, but no indications of a weather front moving toward them.

After looking at the clock and the compass and checking their bearing, Quentin made a slight course correction to compensate for a two-point drift. *Headwinds*, he thought. Out the window of the plane, only the expanse of a dark blue-colored Atlantic was visible in every direction. Their last landfall was Ireland, where the fuel tanks were filled. Several hours of flying remained before reaching St. John's on Newfoundland. After refueling, they would fly south toward Long Island where Quentin kept the Amelie.

Extended flights over water were often boring, with nothing to see but the expanse of empty ocean. Now and then, when they flew over a shipping lane, a ship, little more than a speck trailing a wake on the sea below, was visible. The monotony encouraged Quentin to share the controls with Hardy, the copilot, which allowed him to walk back to stretch his legs and chat with Mark. Hardy and Mark were in their late thirties and hired as the crew for the Amelie when Quentin purchased it a few years before. Both men were licensed pilots and employed by an airline company that allowed them to join Quentin on long flights, often to California and Paris, and occasionally on short hops to Washington, D.C. On some of the flights, Quentin's family joined them. Both of Quentin's children were trained and reliable pilots, especially Marlon, the older son. But, Hardy and Mark favored Florence, the daughter. The lovely teenager was rapidly becoming an accomplished flyer, and Quentin did everything he could to encourage her as a pilot. Marlon and Florence adopted Hardy and Mark and treated them like extended family.

As the Amelie powered westward, fighting a headwind, Quentin could not avoid thinking about the hostilities between Germany and Poland. *Hitler must be crazy,* he thought. *The Brits and the French will never allow him to attack and conquer Poland. Maybe his generals and advisors will get him to back down and avoid a war,* he thought, hoping for the best. *I'll call Ruben when I get home. Maybe he'll have something good to share with me.*

Ruben Valderano was one of Quentin's legal clients and a close friend. The Mexican was born in Sonora, educated in Spain and France, and served with distinction during the Mexican Revolution, eventually becoming a key military aide to Alvaro Obregon, a former president of Mexico. President Obregon was assassinated in July 1928, and, after the fallen president's funeral, there was an attempt on Ruben's life. He was injured severely, left Mexico, and relocated to New York City with his son Kendall and later became an American citizen.

Valderano was an internationally recognized expert on modern warfare. His books on mechanized warfare were international bestsellers and earned him numerous invitations by foreign governments, like Finland, to consult on military strategy and armaments. Tiring of the cold winters in New York City, Ruben moved his family to Santa Barbara, California, in the late 1930s. Through Julia, his American wife, he met Eleanor and Franklin Roosevelt and became a strong financial backer of the president. The Mexican became a close friend of George C. Marshall, soon to be the head of the Joint Chiefs of Staff. The two men enjoyed each other's company, and, whenever Marshall visited Ruben, they would ride horses together. Ruben had given Marshall a beautiful and spirited Arabian stallion that became one of the general's favorite mounts.

Ruben and Marshall often consulted with Quentin Norvell about the development of air power. Quentin, a celebrated World War I fighter pilot and ace, was an expert flyer, and knowledgeable about military aircraft and their uses. Through contacts in Germany and England, Quentin learned about the development of jet propulsion and its possible adaptation to aircraft. He considered the refinement of jet engines and their application to military aircraft the next important step in air power. Through one of Nadine's informants, the Cajun learned that on August 27, 1939, Flight Captain Erich Warsitz had flown the first German jet plane, the Heinkel He 178. He knew it was just a matter of time before the Germans developed a jet fighter. He shared this information with Marshall, but others in the U.S. Department of Defense dismissed the German efforts to build a jet plane.

Mark's voice on the intercom snapped the pilot out of his reverie.

"What's up?" he asked Mark.

"We're closing on Newfoundland. We should be approaching St. John's in about an hour," said the navigator. "I'm getting their signal, and we need to make a slight course correction," he told the pilot.

"OK, give me the new heading." Quentin made the adjustment and told Hardy to take over and follow the new course.

"I'm going back to talk with Mark and find out what's happening in Europe," he told the copilot as he left the cockpit and walked to where the navigator was sitting.

"Anything new about Poland?" he asked. Mark shook his head.

"We'll know more when we land at St. John's," Mark told him. "Up here, we don't have access to wire service news that travels through the telephone lines. But, folks at St. John's will have all the latest news."

When they landed at St. John's, they deplaned, each with a specific task. Hardy did a careful examination of the *Amelie's* exterior, and the engines. Mark checked the weather and adjusted their flight plan. Quentin arranged for the refueling and purchased food for the three of them, along with a fresh thermos of coffee. He sat and talked with the radio operators at St. John's and drank a cup of fresh, strong coffee laced with cream and sugar.

"Anything new on the fighting in Poland?" asked Quentin.

"Not good," replied Arno, the Canadian radioman, glumly. "We got word over the wire that the Germans knocked out the Polish air force. The Brits are calling on Hitler to stop their invasion or else. Guess we'll be at war with the Germans in a few days."

A few minutes later, Hardy, Mark, and Quentin ate dinner at the airport. Quentin always insisted on buying his crew a hot meal after the long flight over the North Atlantic. "You think the Brits and the French will declare war on the Heines?" asked Mark.

Quentin nodded and played with his food.

"Think we'll get into it?" asked Hardy.

Quentin looked up at them and said, "I don't think so; real strong sentiments in the U.S. against any involvement in a war in Europe, or elsewhere." But his thoughts focused on American isolationism and the harm this policy would probably cause Europe and America. "Besides," he added, "if the Brits and the French stand up to Hitler and threaten to invade Germany, the fighting may stop."

"But what if Hitler decides to continue fighting?" asked Hardy.

"I hope that doesn't happen. If Hitler doesn't back down, then heaven help all of us," said Quentin with a serious expression.

The three men finished their food in silence; each worried that the fighting in Poland would escalate into a deadly conflict.

Half an hour later, they were in the Amelie as Quentin turned the plane into the wind, added power, and sped down the runway. The silver Lockheed Electra 10 lifted off the ground and quickly gained speed and altitude. The remainder of the flight was routine, but Quentin asked Mark to monitor the radio for any news about the fighting in Europe.

As they approached Islip on Long Island, Quentin called the tower and asked for wind and landing instructions. He identified himself by using the number of his plane, but the operator working in the tower recognized his voice. He gave the pilot the wind direction and what runway to use.

"Mr. Norvell," said the radio operator from Islip, "someone here wants to say hello."

"OK, put them on."

"Daddy, it's Florence," said his lovely sixteen-year-old daughter. "We came to meet you."

"Who's with you?" asked the Cajun.

"What's your name again?" Florence teased to someone with her.

"Give me that, you brat," Quentin heard Marlon say more out of jest than anything else.

"Hi, Dad," he heard Marlon, his son, say over the radio. "What's your ETA?"

"We should be on the ground in about fifteen minutes."

"Flo and I decided to meet you," said Marlon. "We'll be waiting for you."

Twenty minutes later, after Quentin taxied the Amelie to her hangar and turned off the engines and switches, he slid open the pilot's window and waved at his children. Marlon was twenty-one and about to start his last year at the Massachusetts Institute of Technology (MIT) where he was majoring in architecture and engineering. At almost six feet one, he was just as tall as his father. Marlon was handsome, trim, and muscular, with hazel eyes and large, straight teeth. He had inherited the best qualities of Nadine, his mother, and Quentin. Florence was five feet seven and still growing. She was willowy but starting to fill out in the right places. Florence was a gorgeous young woman with golden blonde hair, flashing blue eyes, and teeth as white as pearls. She reminded Quentin of Ione, her mother. A pang of sadness momentarily engulfed him as he thought of Ione. She had died shortly after giving birth to their daughter. More and more as his daughter matured, the Cajun saw so much of Ione in her. Florence was in her last year of prep school, where she excelled in music, mathematics, and anything athletic. Her musical talent was incredible, a gift inherited from her mother. Ione had been a nationally recognized cellist with a promising musical career until her unexpected death. Florence had mastered the violin and the cello by age twelve and was an outstanding pianist. The Julliard

School of Music in Manhattan had already recruited her.

My children are special, thought Quentin. While he had grown up around the bayous of Louisiana amid the Cajun culture, Marlon and Florence were the products of his liaison with Nadine and marriage to Ione. They were the children of privilege, and their lives were insulated from harsh conditions in American society at the time. But, a remarkable thing had happened. Even though they were half brother and sister, they were very close. Marlon was Florence's strongest fan; whenever he was home from MIT, they sat next to each other while she played the piano. Marlon was Florence's dream hero, someone she thought infallible.

When Hardy and Mark stepped out of the plane, Florence hugged them, something that made each man beam. Marlon shook their hands and patted them on the back while asking about their trip. When Quentin emerged from the plane, Florence leaped into his arms and showered him with kisses.

"What did you bring me, Daddy?" asked Florence with a sly smile on her face.

"What makes you think Dad would bring you anything, Funny Face?" Marlon teased.

"Oh, hush, you jealous preppy."

Before responding to his daughter, Quentin asked Hardy and Mark if they needed a ride into town. Both men thanked him and said they had rides. After saying good-bye to Quentin and his children, they walked to their lockers in the hangar to stow their flight suits and gear.

"OK," said Quentin, "let me get my bags and we'll be on our way."

As they were driving from Long Island to Manhattan, Marlon mentioned the news about the German attack on Poland.

"Do you think the fighting will continue?" he asked his father.

"We'll know tomorrow or the day after," answered a pensive Quentin.

"We won't be involved, will we, Daddy?" asked Florence, concern evident in he voice.

"I don't think so, honey," replied the Cajun. But he was not certain what would happen in Europe.

"Will Nadine be OK?" asked Florence, while Marlon looked on intently.

"She'll be OK, honey." His expression betrayed him as Marlon locked eyes with him. He wondered what Marlon was thinking.

Quentin changed the subject and said he had surprises for them, along with gifts from Nadine. Florence pleaded to learn what Nadine had sent, but the Cajun smiled and said, "Wait 'til we get home."

The driver stopped in front of their residence, in an exclusive part of midtown Manhattan, and Ben, the doorman, immediately came out to greet them. He and the driver removed the bags from the trunk and put them on a cart while Quentin, Marlon, and Florence took the elevator up to their top floor residence.

* * *

In Paris, after watching Quentin's silver plane disappear into the western sky, Nadine was driven home. She worried about the fighting in Poland and wondered what the French government would do about the German invasion. France and Great Britain were pledged by a defensive treaty to support Poland against foreign aggression. *Unless Hitler relents*, thought a pensive Nadine, *there will be war*. She gave a slight shiver at the thought of another major war in Europe.

Nadine was the eldest of two daughters by Arlene and Edmund la Fleche de Beauvais. Her family had a long aristocratic heritage and great wealth. After Quentin left France in 1918, Nadine separated herself from Henri Desnoyers, her husband. Henri was from an old aristocratic family that had fallen on hard times and eventually lost their wealth. He dropped out of the university after less than two years and, with the political intercession of close family friends, was offered a position with the French Diplomatic Service. With funds from marriage to a wealthy girl and guile, the suave diplomat gained promotion. After his first wife died, he returned to France and was assigned to a circumscribed midlevel position. His career was stagnant until he met Nadine. She had just turned seventeen. Even though she was a remarkable and talented dancer, the prestigious Parisian ballet company rejected her as a prima ballerina because she exceeded the height and bust size requirements. Crushed by the rejection and unwilling to be restricted to dancing in the chorus, she abided by her family's encouragement to marry. Henri, almost thirty years her senior, courted Nadine relentlessly. He was suave and worldly, and he impressed Nadine at a time when she was dejected, disillusioned, and vulnerable. They married; almost a year later, Nadine gave birth to Christine, a lovely little girl.

Nadine's marriage to Henri Desnoyers was an essential element in the diplomat's plans to enhance his career. Linked to a family from the old nobility with enormous wealth, he used Nadine's family influence and financial resources to gain advancement in the diplomatic service. Henri was a cold, devious, and self-centered man, and he soon began to enjoy Nadine's wealth and use it to purchase the attention of attractive courtesans. Whenever the French diplomat traveled abroad on diplomatic missions, he sought the company of native women, especially in Indochina. It was the man's cunning, questionable financial dealings, and unfaithfulness that eventually motivated the lovely French woman to restrict their relationship.

When Nadine arrived at her elegant home in an exclusive part of Paris, she told Moira Todd, her personal and social secretary, to hold all calls and cancel any appointments for that day. Then, she called Noel DeCloux, her executive assistant, and told him she would be in the office after 2:00 p.m. She telephoned Louis Bondurant, her uncle, at his estate near Limoges in the south of France. Louis was Edmund's cousin and a surrogate uncle for Nadine and Desirée, her younger sister. Louis had served as a general and senior member of the French air command during The Great War. He retired to his large estate near Limoges, which he called La Croisiere, but continued to keep an apartment in Paris and visit with Nadine and her parents often. He enjoyed escorting Nadine to the opera, the ballet, the theater, and the symphony. And it was not unusual for him to be in the company of Arlene and Nadine at social functions.

When Louis came on the line, she asked him about the fighting in Poland.

"I doubt the Boche will stop their aggression," he said. "That madman and his Nazi henchmen have made a serious mistake."

"Do you think we'll go to war with the Boche?"

"Yes," he said, "but I worry about our chances." She detected pessimism and a dark premonition in his words.

"Uncle Louis, will you come to Paris soon?"

"I need to tend to the harvest," he replied, "but I'll be there in a few days."

"Bon," she said in an upbeat voice. "I'll have Denis (her chauffer) pick you up at the *gare* (train station)." He mentioned sending a telegram with the train number and its arrival time in Paris.

They chatted for a few minutes before saying good-bye. When she hung up the receiver, disquietude settled over the lovely woman. *Will France fight?* she wondered. *And if we fight, can we win?*

Nadine went to her office near the center of Paris that afternoon and worked until almost seven in the evening. Instead of going home, she went to her parents' home. Edmund and Arlene were waiting, and the three of them sat in the parlor to talk before having dinner.

"This fighting in Poland is worrisome," said Edmund, sipping on some Dubonnet. "I tell you our inept government will not handle this crisis well."

"Oh, Edmund," said Arlene, "must you be so pessimistic? What does Louis think?" she asked, turning to look at her daughter.

"I spoke with him earlier, and he was noncommittal," said Nadine, unwilling to share her uncle's pessimism. "He'll be here in a few days. Perhaps by then we'll know more about what will happen."

"Nothing good," said Edmund, looking out the window of their home.

"Papa," said Nadine, sitting next to her father and taking his free hand in hers, "we must trust in God and hope for the best."

"Yes, Edmund, listen to your daughter."

He kissed Nadine's hand and, looking fondly at Arlene, said, "France cannot stand another war like the last one. And now with all these horrible weapons of destruction…" His voice trailed off as he suppressed emotions on the verge of surfacing.

"If war comes," said Arlene, "what will become of Desirée (their daughter) and Bertrand (her husband), and Christine and Armand (her husband)?" Nadine let the question linger for the longest time before saying it was too soon to speculate about war and how it might affect their family. Instead, she changed the subject to discuss other matters until dinner was served. It was almost nine in the evening when the three of them sat down to eat.

That evening, as she was driven home, Nadine was preoccupied with concerns about her parents, her sister and Bertrand, and her daughter Christine and Armand if war broke out. Would Bertrand and Armand have to fight? She put such unpleasant thoughts out of mind and, instead, remembered her first encounter with Quentin.

When Nadine met Quentin in December 1916, she was surprised by the strong emotions the young Cajun stirred in her. There was something sincere and refreshing in the recuperating pilot that was appealing and compelling. She made a decision that night to see him again. In the months that followed, she and Quentin became lovers. And, unknown to the American, she allowed herself to become pregnant with his child in 1917. After Quentin returned to America in December 1918, Nadine separated from Henri. By the spring of 1919, she forced Henri to sign an agreement that denied him access to her family's wealth, and she closed her bedroom door to him. The solicitor she retained had investigated Henri secretly and presented Nadine with a hefty dossier about his illicit activities: consorting with loose women and profligate expenditures. As both were Catholics and married in the church, divorce was not desirable. A public divorce would lead to scandal, which would reflect badly on Nadine's family's name. Instead, she forced Henri to accept terms that allowed them to remain married in name only. In return, he received access to some of her property and could see the children as often as he wanted. Aware that any public airing of his lifestyle and liaisons with women of ill repute would damage his career in the diplomatic service, Henri accepted Nadine's agreement. He continued to believe that Marlon, the son born to Nadine in

1918, was his. He died of complications associated with a venereal disease in 1929.

After separating from Henri, Nadine became a highly successful business leader and gradually expanded her family's fortune. With the great wealth available to her, she was a key benefactor of the arts, especially ballet, opera, and the symphony.

She recalled the tensions that arose after Henri's funeral. Only then did Nadine tell Marlon that Quentin was his real father. The boy was stunned and in a state of disbelief about his mother's revelation. He could not believe that she had betrayed Henri and committed adultery. Gradually, he understood and accepted why Nadine had kept secret his true father's identity. Had Quentin known the truth, he would never have left France without Marlon. A duel would have ensued, and the American might have killed Henri. Marlon's grandparents and then Louis Bondurant helped the boy accept and appreciate his mother's decision. Nadine remembered how difficult it was to tell her lover about his son. Quentin was surprised and angry. But the lovely Frenchwoman pressed him to understand her motives in keeping the secret. Slowly, the Cajun relented and accepted her actions and rationale. Only then did she encourage him to meet with Marlon. Once the two met as father and son, their lives changed, and Nadine knew that Marlon must move to New York and live with Quentin. Instead of losing a son, Nadine saw the strong bond that developed between Quentin and Marlon. As time passed, she was overjoyed by the strong filial attachment between Marlon and Florence; now, the outbreak of war threatened everything.

That evening, before she retired, Nadine sat and wrote an entry in her journal. It was laced with concerns about the fighting and fears that Marlon and Quentin would be involved. The last line expressed the deepest affection for her lover and son and worries about them if the fighting in Poland escalated. She closed the journal, went to bed, and slept fitfully, her dreams filled with images of war, fighting, and death.

* * *

Across the Atlantic, Quentin shared the presents he'd brought for Florence, Marlon, and Camila, his daughter's governess. Camila was originally from Cuba and had married into a wealthy family in Havana. A marital indiscretion resulted in her expulsion from her husband's family and exile to the United States. Through a mutual acquaintance, Camila met Quentin, and he hired the attractive and talented woman. She played the piano beautifully and worked with Florence to enhance her musical talents. In addition, she taught Florence to speak Spanish and French. When Marlon moved to New York, Camila taught him and Quentin to speak Spanish until they were fluent in the language.

"Oh, Daddy, the gloves are perfect," exclaimed Florence as she tried on the handmade leather gloves. "And the perfume is so light and fragrant," she said excitedly.

"Just don't use it instead of bathing," teased Marlon.

"Oh be quiet, you jealous preppy," she shot back.

"Dad, the scarf is beautiful. Thank you," he said, admiring the handsome polka dot silk scarf. "And the leather satchel is marvelous," he added while running his fingers over the fine leather carrying case.

"Your mother sent that," said the Cajun, nodding his head in the direction of the leather carrying case. "It has a handle and a strap for your shoulder."

"Funny face, will you play something for us?" asked Marlon, looking directly at Florence.

"I don't know," she said, playing with the soft leather gloves. "I might for Daddy, but for you...," she said, shaking her head and trying to act cross with her brother.

"If I apologize and tell you how beautiful you are, will you forgive me and play?" he pleaded in a playful manner.

"Yes!" she exclaimed. "See, Daddy, he thinks I'm beautiful, but he needs to be forced to tell the truth!"

"Please play," said Quentin, relaxing on the plush sofa and looking toward the baby grand piano in the room.

"What would you like to hear?" she asked.

"Chopin," said Marlon.

A brilliant Polish composer and pianist, thought the Cajun. *It's a message for me.*

Camila rose from her chair, opened the leaf to the piano, and motioned for Florence to sit and play.

Florence sat and began to play the lovely *Polonaise in A-Flat Major.* She played flawlessly, with verve and passion. The way she played the romantic piece by the Polish composer revealed an extraordinary musical talent. As the classic melody filled the room, Quentin looked at Marlon. Their eyes locked, and the Cajun knew he and his son needed to talk in private.

It was almost eleven thirty when Marlon and Quentin were alone. Camila and Florence had gone to their rooms, leaving the two men alone with the lights dimmed in the living room.

"What are you thinking?" Quentin asked his son.

"I'm worried about the fighting in Poland."

"Why?" asked the Cajun.

"I don't think the Germans will back off," said Marlon. "And if the fighting continues, France and Britain will have to honor their commitment to help Poland," he added. "What do you think?"

There was a silence in the room as Quentin contemplated his son's question. Finally, after what seemed like a long time, but was perhaps less than a minute, he replied with carefully chosen words. "It's too soon to tell how far the Germans will go. It all depends on what France and Britain do."

"What do you mean, Dad?"

"If the French and British attack Germany at a key point like the Rhineland, it may persuade the Germans to back away from what they're doing in Poland. But, if they just threaten the Germans and take their time preparing for war…" His voice trailed off. For Quentin, the worst-case scenario in Europe was if the British and the French dragged their feet and did little to compel the Boche to withdraw from Poland.

"I don't know, Dad," said Marlon, looking directly at his father. "From everything I've read about Hitler and what you and Ruben have told me, I don't think he'll stop the fighting, especially if the German army defeats the Poles."

Quentin carefully considered Marlon's words before responding. "It'll take a few days to know how the fighting in Poland is going. I'll call Ruben tomorrow and find out what he thinks. When do you have to be back at MIT?"

"In about a week," replied Marlon, continuing to look at his father.

"It's too soon to tell what might happen, son," said the Cajun. "Best not to speculate unnecessarily. But, one thing's for sure—if this develops into a war, I'll do everything possible to get your mother out of France."

"That's what I wanted to hear," said Marlon, rising to pat his father on the shoulder. "I'm going to bed. You coming?"

Quentin nodded and stood. *Marlon must know that I'll move heaven and earth to keep Nadine out of harm's way,* he thought.

* * *

The next day when Quentin arrived at his office, Sarah Katzmann, his secretary, greeted him with a smile.

"Welcome back," she said politely, her eyes betraying mixed feelings.

He could sense discomfort within the young woman and wondered what was bothering her. *Something's wrong*, he thought. *I'll set aside some time to talk with her this afternoon.*

"I've sorted your mail and phone messages. They're in priority order," she told him. "The senior partners are meeting at four o'clock today."

"Do we have an agenda?" he asked while examining his messages.

"Mr. Barston would like to discuss that with you."

"Call Lois (Barston's secretary) and find a time for us to talk this morning. I'm going to clear away my mail and then return some calls." Glancing at his watch, he told Sarah to call Ruben Valderano in California and arrange for them to talk before the noon hour. Then, he went to his desk and began sorting through the memos and correspondence. It was almost 10:30 a.m. when Sara knocked on his door.

"Mr. Barston would like to have lunch with you today if that's convenient?" He replied affirmatively and inquired about the time and place. "One-thirty at his club; he'll come by to meet you," she said, handing him some files. "Mr. Valderano will expect your call at noon." As she turned to leave, he asked if she could stay a few minutes after work. She nodded and asked how long the meeting with the senior partners might go.

"I'll be out no later than 5:30 p.m.," he told her.

"I'll be at my desk," she said and left the room.

Quentin went through his correspondence and dictated three letters before making several telephone calls. The last one was to his in-laws. He arranged to have dinner with the Vandersteels the following evening, saying the children would be with him.

It was just past the noon hour when Quentin asked Sarah to get Ruben on the telephone. A few minutes later, she said Valderano was on his private line.

"Ruben," he spoke into the receiver.

"*Hombre, como te va* (My good man, how are you)?"

"*Estoy bien, mi general* (Well, my general)," replied the Cajun in very good Spanish to tease the Mexican. His comment elicited a laugh from Valderano. They chatted for a few minutes, catching up on their respective families and activities. Then, Quentin turned serious and asked Ruben about the fighting in Poland.

"Too soon to tell; but I'm worried that Hitler will start another 'big' war," he said pessimistically. The Mexican changed the subject, saying that he and Julia (his wife) would be in New York in about ten days. "We're taking the girls and Kendall east for their fall terms." Quentin knew that Kendall, Valderano's son, was entering Harvard, and the two girls from Julia's previous marriage, Edda and Lina, were attending exclusive boarding schools in New England.

"Are you coming by train?" Ruben replied affirmatively. "May I send my plane for you?" asked Quentin.

"Are you sure?" asked the Mexican.

"*Como no* (Of course)!" said the Cajun, using a phrase Ruben had taught him. The Mexican thought for a moment and replied affirmatively. Quentin said the plane would pick them up at the Santa Barbara airport in two days.

"Hardy Chappelle will call you when he and Mark arrive," mentioned the Cajun. "The plane trip will give us time to be together for a few days."

"*Bueno*," said Valderano. "I'm in your debt. Oh, by the way, our friend Healy is on her way to Germany."

"I thought Healy [Rohwer] was in North Africa." The Mexican said she had been, but sent a wire indicating she was catching a plane to Switzerland and then on to Germany to do a story on the fighting in Poland.

"She wants me to join her," said Ruben. *Of course,* thought Quentin. *Ruben is an authority on warfare, and Healy would just love to do a story on the fighting in Poland with Ruben's exclusive commentary.* He asked Ruben if he planned to join her.

"I'm thinking about it," he heard the Mexican say. "We'll talk more about this when Julia, the children, and I get to New York." They talked for a few more minutes before ending the call. *If anyone can convince Ruben to go to Poland and observe the fighting, it's Healy!* thought the Cajun.

Healy Rohwer was a tall, attractive, blue-eyed, strawberry blonde photojournalist that just turned forty-five. She started her career as an illustrator for *The Herald Tribune* during the First World War. Gradually, she became a nationally and internationally respected writer, illustrator, and photographer. Her stories were syndicated, and many of her photographs and illustrations were carried in the most popular magazines and journals. She'd won numerous awards including two Pulitzers for stories about Mexican president Alvaro Obregon, and the Japanese intrusion in China. *Always near the action,* thought the Cajun about Healy.

After his meeting with the other senior partners, Quentin met with Sarah in his office for privacy. It was a little after five in the afternoon, and some of the office staff were still at their desks. He asked her to sit on the small couch while he sat opposite her.

"Something wrong?"

She hesitated to respond, but the Cajun pressed her.

"Tell me," he encouraged.

Finally, Sarah looked down at the floor and held her hands together on her lap. "We have family in Poland," she said slowly, trying to control her voice.

"Where do they live?" he asked.

"Near Kalisz. It's to the south and west of Warsaw."

He stood and walked to his bookcase and withdrew an atlas of the world and found the town.

"My parents are afraid the Nazis will overrun it and send all the Jews there to a camp."

"A concentration camp?"

She nodded, and said more like a death camp, her eyes becoming moist.

"Sarah, please do something for me."

She looked up at him surprised, unsure what he wanted.

"I want you to get me their names and addresses. I might be able to help."

"I don't understand," she said, puzzled by his comments.

"Get me their names as quickly as possible and where it might be possible to reach them," he insisted. She sobbed, but quickly caught herself and looked away.

Quentin approached and put his arm around her shoulders. "Better go home, Sarah. Talk with your parents, and get me the names of your relatives and their addresses in Poland."

After Sarah left the office, the Cajun finished some correspondence and prepared to leave. Tomorrow, he would send Nadine the names and addresses of Sarah's family members in Poland and find out if anything could be done to help them.

After his two trips to Germany in 1934 and 1936, Quentin experienced firsthand the brutal way the Nazis treated Jews, Gypsies, and others they considered undesirables. He wanted to believe that Nadine would find a way to help Sarah's relatives near Kalisz, especially if the Germans conquered Poland.

The following day, September 3, 1939, America learned that first the British and then the French had declared war on Germany. Hitler had no intention of withdrawing from Poland and ignored the Allied threat of war. The wire services provided bits and pieces of information about the rapid advances by the German Heer (army) units in western Poland. Nazi Panzers (tank units) supported by the Luftwaffe (air force) were slicing through Polish defenders and moving rapidly toward Warsaw. Quentin worried that the Poles could not stop the rapid German advances.

Meanwhile, in the offices and corridors of Barston, Marwick, Fowler and Peterson, the fighting in Poland and the declarations of war against Germany by the British and the French were the major topics of discussion. Sarah's face showed anxiety and worry when she gave Quentin the names and addresses of her relatives in Poland. He quickly prepared a cablegram for Nadine and sent her the information. His message was brief: *can you do anything to help these people?*

That evening, Quentin, Marlon, and Florence drove to the Vandersteels' residence to have dinner with Fiona and Harold. The Cajun asked Kathleen O'Meara, a close friend of the family, to join them. Kathleen was a nurse Quentin had met in December 1918 while on a combination troop and hospital ship returning to America after the First World War ended. They became close friends, and the nurse was adopted as a family member by the Norvells and the Vandersteels. Kathleen was almost sixty-two, but she was still trim, youthful, and energetic. She worked as a nursing supervisor for a university hospital in Manhattan and had been with Quentin and the Vandersteels when Ione gave birth and later died. She was a surrogate auntie for Florence.

The Vandersteels' home that evening was filled with nervous chatter about events in Europe, especially the Allied declaration of war. There was much speculation about what might happen in Europe, but almost everyone in the room knew that war meant fighting, bloodshed, and loss of life.

"I hope the fighting can be contained and that hostilities end soon," said Harold. It was more a prayer than anything else. Marlon, wanting to change the subject, whispered to Florence, and the two of them walked to the grand piano. He lifted the leaf as she sat and opened the lid to the keyboard. Marlon sat next to Florence on the piano bench as she played Mozart's *Rondo in D*. Then, she played *Liebestraum* by Franz Liszt. Quentin marveled at the way Florence coaxed sounds from the piano, each note full and clear, blending together to form a melodic stream that created a tranquil mood. Ione had done the same thing when she played the cello. Within his daughter lived the soul and gift for music that his wife had passed along. *Ione, I hope wherever you are you can hear our daughter playing. She has the gift you gave her,* thought Quentin.

Before they all sat down for dinner, Quentin noticed Marlon put his arm around Florence and whisper something to her. A moment later, Florence played a selection from *An American in Paris* by George Gershwin. As she played the spirited tune, Marlon looked at his father intently. It was a special message between the two of them. Kathleen noticed the eye contact between them and thought the nonverbal message had to be about Nadine.

CHAPTER 2
THE FOUR HORSEMEN OF THE APOCALYPSE

*Outlined against a blue-gray sky, the
Four Horsemen rode again. In
dramatic lore they were known as
Famine, Pestilence, War,
and Death.*
Vicente Blasco-Ibañez,
The Four Horsemen of the Apocalypse, [1916]

In Paris, Nadine received Quentin's urgent telegram with the names and addresses of a family in the general vicinity of Kalisz, Poland. His message was terse, but clear. She called him immediately and learned that they were Jews and relatives of one of his employees.

"I'll see what I can do," she told him on the phone.

"Thank you. Have I ever told you how much I appreciate you?"

"And…"

"And how much I love you."

"Cherie, I can never hear that enough from you."

"I'm worried about the fighting in Poland, especially now that France is at war with Germany."

"So am I," she said softly. "Louis will be here soon, and I will share what he says. I wish you were here too."

"Give Louis my best. Tell him I'll try to be in Paris in about three weeks. Marlon and Florence will be back in school by then," he mentioned. "Have you and Marlon talked?"

"Yes, Cherie, he called yesterday. He's worried and wanted to know what would happen to us if the Boche attacked France."

"I just hope it doesn't get as bad as the last war," he told her softly. "Neither France nor England can stand another war like that."

They talked for a while longer before ending the call. She told the Cajun how much she loved and missed him. "Come back to me soon," she encouraged him.

In the following days, the news from Poland was discouraging. The Germans broke through the western border defenses of the Poles and advanced rapidly on Warsaw. Their plan was to encircle Warsaw and force the Poles into a pitched battle and destroy or capture the Polish Poznan army. The Germans were using new tactics, mechanized units working in concert with their Luftwaffe (air force). The speed of their advances into Poland was surprising. Among a few military experts like Ruben Valderano, there was growing concern that the Poles would be crushed in a matter of weeks.

When Ruben Valderano and his family arrived in New York, Quentin met them at the airport. They drove to the Cajun's residence on Manhattan in a two-car caravan. Quentin had received a call from President Roosevelt asking him to attend a meeting in Washington. He suspected that Ruben had also been called and asked to attend. The Cajun waited until he and the Mexican could be alone to discuss the war in Poland and the Washington meeting.

Late that evening, after the children and Julia had gone to bed, Ruben and Quentin sat in the large living room in front of the fireplace.

"I've been called to a meeting in Washington by the president," said Quentin. "I think you've been asked to attend also."

"Yes," said the Mexican as he lit up an expensive Cuban cigar. "It's scheduled for the eleventh. Do you know who else will be there?"

Quentin mentioned Secretary of State Cordell Hull and Secretary of War Harry Hines Woodring.

"Maybe Harry Hopkins and General Marshall will be there," he added. The Mexican nodded and puffed on the aromatic cigar.

"Will you travel to Poland to observe the fighting?"

Valderano nodded. "Yes, the Associated Press (AP) has invited me to join Healy and do an analysis of the fighting in Poland," Valderano confided.

"I thought Healy was working with Reuters."

"She was," said Ruben, as he checked the length of the ash on his cigar, "but Reuters is headquartered in England, and with the British now at war with the Germans, it's prudent for her to be with a news service located in a neutral country."

Quentin nodded. "Does Julia know you're planning to go to Germany?" asked Quentin.

The Mexican nodded again. After a pause, he said, "She's not happy about my going. I've assured her that Healy and I will not be in any danger. Perhaps by the time I meet with Healy in Germany, we'll be able to predict the outcome of the fighting."

"When do you plan to leave for Europe?" asked Quentin.

"A few days after our meeting in Washington," replied the Mexican. "Why do you ask?" Quentin told him about his plans to visit Paris in a few weeks. "Good. We'll compare information," said the Mexican with a smile. The two men talked until a few minutes after eleven when both went to their respective rooms.

Quentin and Ruben flew to Washington and checked in at the Mayflower Hotel. Brook Hamilton Stoner at the State Department knew of their arrival and arranged to have dinner with them the night before their meeting with the president.

When the three men sat down to eat, Stoner surprised them by saying he would be at the meeting the next morning.

"Who else will be there?" asked the Mexican.

Stoner replied, "Cordell Hull, Harry Woodring, and Harry Hopkins (a chief advisor to President Roosevelt)."

"Why Hopkins?" asked the Cajun.

The diplomat was noncommittal.

"I presume," said Ruben nonchalantly, while cutting a piece of his fish, "you're not to reveal any more than instructed."

Stoner chuckled and made eye contact with Quentin, realizing that the Mexican appeared to pay more attention to his fish than anything he might say. After a pause, Stoner spoke up. "General (his way of addressing Valderano), I've heard that you plan to visit Germany as an observer."

"Perhaps," replied the Mexican, toying with the American diplomat.

Stoner smiled politely and said he had heard from a reliable source.

But Ruben cut him off and said, "Stony, you should disregard speculation that comes from a secondary source when you have the principal in front of you."

At this, Quentin chuckled and said, "Stony, I'd say Ruben has put you in your place."

The diplomat smiled and agreed with him.

"I'll be candid with you about my plans," said Ruben, "but you must reciprocate, or else we'll just have a friendly dinner. Remember, Stony, what you tell us stays here," he said, before sipping some of his white wine.

"All right," said an amused Stoner. "I'll tell you all I know." In the next fifteen minutes, Stoner revealed the concerns Roosevelt and Hopkins had about the fighting in Poland.

"The boss (Roosevelt) is worried that the Germans will carve up Poland. If that happens, the Brits and the French are on their own." He paused to let them consider what he'd shared. But, he was surprised by how quickly the Mexican spoke up.

"The Soviets will invade eastern Poland, perhaps in a week or ten days," Ruben stated. "The question now is how Britain and France will choose to proceed against the Germans."

Quentin realized that Ruben was privy to information the diplomat was not. He also suspected that the Mexican knew more than he was telling them. When Stoner asked Valderano a few questions, Ruben parried them and winked at the Cajun, careful to ensure that the diplomat could not see the signal.

The three men talked for almost an hour before Ruben said it was getting late and he had things to do. Stoner thanked both of them for dining with him, shook their hands, and left. When they were alone, Quentin asked Valderano about going to Germany.

"I have to go," said the Mexican. "The Germans are employing new tactics, some mentioned in my books. And, thanks to you, the coordinated uses of air power and tanks. Obviously people in the German high command have read my treatises, as well as those of others like de Gaulle," he said almost casually. "There is, sometimes, genius in the way people apply theory in practice," said the Mexican. "I must see and learn firsthand the new German methods in warfare."

Quentin nodded. They talked until 11:30 p.m. and then walked to their respective rooms.

"Tomorrow will be an interesting day," said the Cajun.

"Yes, my friend, perhaps more interesting than you or I can imagine," said the Mexican with a smile.

Early the next morning, Ruben and Quentin were greeted at the White House and taken upstairs to where Roosevelt and the others waited.

"Good morning, gentlemen," said the president, motioning the Cajun and the Mexican to where he was seated. The president looked tired. Quentin was about to say something when Ruben caught his sleeve and whispered they should get something to eat.

"Thank you for coming," said Roosevelt. He turned to look over his shoulder and said, "George, bring me a small pillow, please." George was Roosevelt's black valet, and someone the president relied upon to assist him because of his impaired mobility. Roosevelt had been afflicted with polio earlier in his life and was unable to walk without braces and crutches.

After Roosevelt was comfortable, he introduced Cordell Hull, Harry Woodring, Harry Hopkins, and Brook Hamilton Stoner. They exchanged handshakes and sat around the table. Food was brought to them, along with strong, hot coffee.

The president began by explaining the purpose for the meeting. He was worried about the fighting in Poland. "It seems, Ruben, that you have intelligence about the Germans and the Russians," said the president. Ruben nodded.

"Care to share some of it with us?" asked Roosevelt.

Ruben finished munching on some bacon before speaking. He said the Germans and the Soviets would overwhelm the Poles before the end of September, maybe sooner. He indicated the two had a pact and would divide Poland between them. He shifted quickly to the military advances, saying the Germans had control of the skies, and their Panzers were striking deep into Poland and had already surrounded Warsaw.

"It's only a matter of when the Poles capitulate," said Ruben as he held out his cup for Quentin to fill it with coffee. The others sat solemnly, waiting for him to continue.

"With that in mind," he said, adding cream and sugar to his coffee and looking at the Cajun with a smile, "my concern is how the British and the French will react to the Polish defeat."

"I can help on that matter," said the president. He nodded at Secretary of State Cordell Hull.

"Well," said Hull, playing with the watch chain on the vest of his three-piece suit, "the British are sending an expeditionary force to Northern France composed of infantry, mechanized units, and several fighter squadrons. The French are mobilizing and ready to probe the German defenses across the border."

Quentin asked if the French had decided to attack the Germans. Hull replied negatively.

"Unless the Allies attack Germany on its western front, there will be no reason for Hitler to stop his advances in Poland," said the Cajun. "If Britain and France don't move before October to press the Germans, Poland will be lost and most of the Whermacht transferred from the eastern front to the west," Quentin told them.

"Correct," said the Mexican, nodding and smiling at Quentin.

The president looked perturbed and finally said, "There's not much we can do, except encourage the British and the French to take bold steps against Hitler and his Nazi thugs. But I doubt that will do much good," he said, shaking his head. "And that's why I invited you here. I've decided to appoint Stony as a special envoy to England and France. He'll serve as a liaison with our diplomatic officers in both countries and report back to me on matters where we might be of assistance to the Allies," said a worried Roosevelt.

"Mr. President," Secretary of War Harry Woodring said, "I remind you that the people of this country will not condone anything that might lead to our becoming a combatant in this conflict."

"Yes, yes, Harry, I know," said the president, visibly disturbed by Woodring's remarks.

Quentin learned from Forrest Marmion, his cousin and a senior member of the House of Representatives from Louisiana, that Harry Woodring was a strong isolationist. *Roosevelt might not like what Woodring is saying,* thought Quentin, *but he needs reminding about the popular sentiment in favor of isolationism.*

"Ruben, George Marshall (recently appointed by Roosevelt as chairman of the Joint Chiefs of Staff) tells me you're going to Germany to observe the fighting in Poland. When are you leaving?"

"In two days."

"I'd like you to find out what the Germans are doing, militarily, and if possible, anything you might learn about their future plans," he said, looking directly at the Mexican.

"You want me to spy?" asked the Mexican with a sly smile.

"Of course not," said Roosevelt, chuckling. "Just some educated guesswork on your part will do nicely."

At this, Ruben started to laugh and nodded his head.

"And, you, Quentin, I'd like your views on what the French will do if Poland falls," said the president, smiling at the Cajun. "I know you have influential friends in the government and the military there. We need to know what they may be thinking and how they may respond to any Nazi moves along their border."

Quentin shot a glance at Ruben, and the Mexican winked.

"Gentlemen," said the president, fitting a cigarette on his long holder, "the information we're getting through normal diplomatic channels is mixed. I'm asking for your help to sort the wheat from the chaff. Of course, all of this is unofficial," he added, with the hint of a smile as he lit the cigarette. "But you would be doing me and this country a great service by gathering reliable intelligence."

There was silence in the room as Quentin and Ruben exchanged eye contact while the others waited for their answer.

"Mr. President," said Ruben, standing to stretch, "may I confer with my colleague before we respond?"

Roosevelt threw back his head, laughed, and said, "Why not? I think a bathroom break is in order anyway."

In the hallway, Ruben asked Quentin to share his thoughts.

"I don't think we have a choice," said the Cajun. "It's in our best interest to know what the Nazis are up to and how the Brits and the French will respond."

"I agree," Ruben said, "but no one must know our true intentions. The Nazis will 'liquidate me' if they suspect I'm spying on them. In your case, some in France will welcome you with open arms." Quentin chuckled at Ruben's pun.

"Best if I share my information with you only," said the Mexican. "There can be no direct links between me and any official U.S. representative."

Quentin nodded in approval and said, "*D'accord.*"

"*Muy bien* (OK)," replied Ruben, taking the Cajun's arm and walking back into the room where Roosevelt and the others waited.

It was agreed that Ruben would leave for Spain in two days; from there, he'd go to Switzerland where he would cross into Germany and join Healy Rohwer. The AP, at

Healy's request, had offered Ruben a job as a military observer and consultant. Moreover, Valderano's added purpose was to gather firsthand observations for a new edition of his book on modern warfare. Quentin would visit Paris in three weeks to gather information on how the French planned to deal with any German threats to their border.

Before the meeting ended, Ruben asked Roosevelt if he might share something with him and the others. Roosevelt, intrigued by the Mexican's request, nodded.

"Watch developments in the Far East carefully," he said with a serious expression. "Don't take the Japanese lightly," he warned. Roosevelt frowned, but nodded for the Mexican to continue. "Japan has a modern, well-equipped, and trained navy, and its army has already proved its potential in China and Manchuria."

"Are you saying that they pose a threat to us?" asked Hopkins.

Ruben nodded.

"Why?" asked Hull.

"Look to their military leadership," said the general. "They have in Hideki Tojo, a smart and aggressive general." He commented that Tojo was a very capable military leader and responsible for the initial successes of the Japanese army in Korea, Manchuria, and China. "He's now the vice minister of war, and the inspector general for army aviation."

"What are you trying to say?" said Hull, uncertain where Valderano was going.

"I'm saying that Tojo served as a military observer in Germany and favors strong ties with the Nazis. And he has a rather poor image and regard for Americans. He's ambitious and a proponent of territorial expansion. If he becomes a leading political figure in Japan, we might face a confrontation with him," he warned.

Hull and Woodring were uncomfortable with the Mexican's remarks, but Quentin and Stoner were fascinated.

"Thank you, General," said Roosevelt, "we'll look into this."

After the meeting, Quentin and Ruben left the White House together. As they walked toward their hotel, Ruben spoke softly to the Cajun.

"Bright men are often blind to a peril, especially if biases are involved," he told Quentin.

"You mean underestimating the Japanese," said Quentin.

The Mexican nodded. "Roosevelt and his closest advisors believe that Hitler and the Nazis are our major concern. But, Japan and the Soviets will pose problems unless we deal with them," he cautioned.

The two men checked out of the Mayflower and flew back to New York. Two days later, Valderano was on his way to Germany, while Quentin would visit Paris at the end of September.

* * *

The situation in Poland deteriorated. On the seventeenth of September, Warsaw was completely surrounded, and the Germans began to bomb the city relentlessly. At the same time, two Soviet armies invaded Poland from the east to help the Nazis crush the Poles. On 27 September, Warsaw capitulated. Poland as a country would cease to exist in a few days.

In Paris, the news about Poland's defeat was stunning. Nadine could feel a siege mentality pervading her country. Lights were dimmed at night, and traces of worry and concern were evident in the faces of people throughout Paris.

It was late in the afternoon when Louis Bondurant came to her parents' home, red faced and barely able to contain himself. He'd met with people in the military and other government offices.

"The fools," exclaimed the old general, his eyes cold and staring into space, perhaps seeing a horrible premonition. "We are leaderless," he blustered, "and doomed because of petty men afraid of their own shadows."

"Uncle," said Nadine, going to Bondurant's side and reaching for his arm.

At her touch, the old warrior softened, and in a low voice said, "France must stand alone against an enemy that will stop at nothing to humiliate us."

"Please, Louis," said Arlene, her face ashen and anxiety noticeable in her voice, "you frighten me."

"Sit here, Uncle, next to me," said Nadine, her voice calm and relaxed. The old soldier took in several deep breaths and finally smiled at his favorite niece before sitting next to her, his head bowed a bit as he stared at the exotic Persian carpet on the floor.

"Louis," said Edmund, his voice controlled and friendly, "tell us what you've learned."

In the next fifteen minutes, Louis Bondurant spoke about meeting with members of the high command, and then leaders in the French government responsible for national defense and security. He ran slender fingers through his silver hair, and then used the thumb and index finger on his left hand to smooth a well-groomed moustache as he spoke. Nadine knew these as signs of annoyance in her uncle. The French military, he continued, was simply going to wait for the Germans to attack the Maginot Line, the long and heavily fortified defensive barrier built by France along its border with Germany.

"They are insane to believe the Boche will hurl themselves against our fortifications, like ignorant barbarians," he told them. "The Boche will find a way to bypass our fortifications and flank our defensive lines." When Edmund asked him to elaborate, Louis said the Germans would probably attack from the north by overrunning Belgium and Holland as they did during World War I. Then, he said there were no reliable defensive fortifications in the Ardennes.

"There [the Low Countries and the Ardennes Forest]," Louis said emphatically, "is where the Boche will strike," he hissed.

"But why there, Uncle?" asked Nadine.

"Because there is where I would attack," he replied, shaking his head in disgust.

"But won't the English help us stop the Boche in the north?" asked Edmund.

"Speed and encirclement," said the old general, "a new kind of warfare. I don't believe the English will be able to cope with a sustained aerial and tank assault by the Boche." He paused for a moment, realizing he had shocked Arlene and Edmund, while Nadine sat silently looking at him with those expressive eyes, eyes that looked deep into his soul. *She knows,* he thought, *that France and England are not prepared for the kind of war the Boche will wage.*

"I've said too much. Forgive the ramblings of an old soldier," he told them. Nadine placed her hand on Louis's left shoulder and kissed him tenderly on the cheek.

Nadine remembered telling Louis that there was nothing to forgive. *He was honest with us,* she thought. *But, now, I think it best to prepare for the worst.*

* * *

The next few weeks passed slowly as Nadine waited for Quentin's arrival. The news from Poland was tragic and depressing. Germany and the Soviet Union had destroyed most of the Polish resistance. Warsaw had fallen on September 27. Nadine knew that Poland would be partitioned and her territory and citizens absorbed into Nazi and Soviet enclaves.

On the 29 she received a message from Quentin telling her that he would be there the next day. In spite of the worrisome news about Poland, knowing that her lover would be at her side brightened her disposition. She called her parents and Louis and let them know Quentin was expected and asked that they come to her home for dinner in two days. Then, she called Raoul Mendeville and Etienne de Gavrelac and invited them and their wives.

When the Amelie landed at the Paris airport (Le Bourget), Quentin taxied the Lockheed to a predetermined place. He had been delayed by several hours because of new regulations. He had to file a flight plan in St. John's, noting that he was from a neutral country with his final destination: Paris, France. Then, he had to get permission to fly over England while in Ireland and receive approval for the flight to Paris. The delays to get clearance, because of the war, meant that he arrived in Paris on October first. Nadine was waiting for him, even though it was early in the morning.

Nadine made arrangements for Mark and Hardy to stay at a small hotel close to Victor Hugo Place. Accommodations in Paris were tight because of the influx of foreign journalists and people leaving areas near the German border.

"It is an excellent hotel, and there are several good restaurants nearby," she told Hardy and Mark. "And I have tickets for you and your escorts to a new revue tomorrow night," she said with a smile. The two men were impressed and expressed their gratitude.

When Nadine and Quentin were alone, she hugged and kissed him, and he could feel the tension in her body.

"What is it?" he asked.

"I'm very concerned about the war," she told him. "I'm worried about our leadership and my country's resolve to prevail against the Boche."

He held the lovely woman in his arms, contemplating her comments.

"Have you spoken with Louis about this?" he asked.

"Yes, Cherie. We are of a mind," she said, burying her head into his shoulder.

"It'll be all right," he told her. "The British will help." He wondered if he sounded convincing about the war with the Germans.

"Bon, enough of this sad talk, Cherie," she said, regaining her composure. "I've invited a few friends for dinner tomorrow. Tonight, we should go dancing."

That evening, as Nadine and Quentin went out to dinner and then dancing, he noticed an increase in the number of men in uniform and early precautionary signs like the dimming of lights and new signs that alerted people to the nearest air raid shelter. *It's happening again*, he thought, *just like during the last war*. But, something deep inside of him was less encouraging than before. He decided to share his feelings with Nadine that evening.

The two of them arrived at Nadine's elegant home well after midnight. Their lovemaking early that morning was passionate and prolonged. The uncertain circumstances caused by the war promoted intensity in their sexual activity.

"May we talk for a few minutes?" he asked his lover after they made love.

"What is it, Cherie?"

"If the war goes badly for the French, will you leave and come to America with me?" he asked, holding the beautiful woman in his arms.

"I don't know if that will be possible," she said softly.

"Why?" he asked. She leaned on one elbow, propping herself up so that in the dim candlelight she could look directly at him. He marveled at the way her naked breasts, still firm and appealing, were revealed. The sepia tones from the candlelight bathed her body in a soft hue and stimulated a feeling of excitement as he drank in the loveliness of her undraped upper body. *My God, she's so beautiful*, he thought.

"I have my parents, friends, and employees to consider," she told him. "I cannot, in good conscience, abandon them."

He considered what she told him, but remained silent.

"Cherie, if the worst should happen and the Boche overrun us, I will not be able to leave until my parents, my sister, and my daughter and their families are safe."

He said he understood, but did he really? "Nadine, if the worst happens, the Nazis will occupy France and seize all of your assets," he told her.

"Yes, I know that, but I have already transferred substantial portions of my family's wealth to Switzerland and England. I need your help to send other parts of our financial resources to your country."

"So you're expecting the worst," he told her. She replied affirmatively. He rolled over onto his back and looked up at the ceiling.

"What is it?" she asked.

He said he could help her invest whatever sums of money she wanted in the United States. "If the war is long and America begins to sell arms and military materiel to the Allies, your investments in my country could be very profitable," he said dryly. "But, I'm more concerned about the way the Nazis operate. They're ruthless, darling, and will do anything to capture and control your holdings and financial resources. Don't underestimate them."

She was silent for a few moments before saying that other things factored into her decision to remain in France.

"Like what?" he asked.

"Cherie, there are different ways to fight a war. Sometimes, wealth can be used to purchase important human resources and valuable information."

"You're not thinking of setting up a spy network, are you?" he asked.

"Oh, Cherie, it's too soon to say. But, I love my country and my people and will not abandon them in a time of crisis," she said, her voice firm and determined. He did not reply. Instead, he took the magnificent French woman in his arms and pressed their naked bodies together while stroking her back with his hands. He found her lips and kissed her passionately.

That morning, he made a pledge to do whatever he could to protect his lover from an enemy that would use every sinister method imaginable to eliminate whatever threat it developed.

The day passed quickly for Nadine and Quentin. The two went shopping for food and then walked along the Seine where venders exhibited their wares. Quentin bought things for Florence, Kathleen, and Sarah. He was searching for something to give Marlon when Nadine told him she had something in mind.

"I know a place where they make fragrances for men," she told him.

"Cologne?" he said.

"No, Cherie, something else, for his face and hands."

He was puzzled, but didn't say anything. The Cajun had long ago learned that Nadine was clever and creative when it came to selecting presents for family and friends.

At a shop specializing in fragrances, Nadine selected two containers of lotion for Marlon. She had both scented. "Hmmm," said an appreciative Quentin, "what are these?"

Nadine explained that both lotions were made with aloe and other substances that helped to moisten and protect the skin. "One is for him to use as an aftershave. The other is for his hands," she told him.

"But what are the scents?" he asked.

She smiled and said the aftershave was gardenia and the hand lotion bay rum.

"He will like them, n'est-ce pas?" He nodded his head, and the two of them laughed.

* * *

The guests arrived for dinner at Nadine's home and were ushered into a spacious living room that was elegantly furnished. She had exquisite taste and had collected impressive pieces from around the world. As they sat and talked, Louis Bondurant was in a good mood because Quentin was with them. The two were inseparable. Arlene and Edmund sat next to Raoul Mendeville, Quentin's former squadron leader when they flew together with the Twenty-seventh French Escadrille during the Great War, and his wife Eunice. Etienne de Gavrelac and Argentina, his lovely Mexican wife, were a handsome couple and very outgoing. Etienne was Quentin's closest friend when they flew together with the Twenty-seventh Escadrille. The group chatted and sipped excellent French champagne. The warmth from the blaze in the fireplace helped to enliven the mood. However, talk about the war surfaced, and the conversation turned serious.

"Louis," said Raoul, "I went to the air service to volunteer."

"And?" said Louis, perhaps privy to information that made him suspect what Raoul would say.

"They thanked me and said they would contact me later," he said with annoyance in his voice. Louis, Raoul, and Quentin looked directly at Etienne, sitting quietly and smiling.

"I too approached our military and was told they had a nice desk for me to fly," he said with a smirk.

Argentina, his wife, poked his shoulder and said that, at his age, that was about all that he could navigate safely. Everyone laughed at her comment.

But, it was Quentin who turned to Louis and asked his opinion about the war. The old general examined his champagne flute carefully, watching the tiny bubbles rise to the surface of the amber-colored liquid in the glass. After a moment of silence, Louis spoke up.

"The war in Poland is over. The Nazis and the Soviets have destroyed that nation and enslaved the Poles. God help them," he said. "But the misfits and cowards here in France will betray us," he said solemnly.

"Why do you say that?" asked Quentin, puzzled by the old warrior's comments.

"I think I know why, my friend," said Raoul, looking directly at Quentin. "We are not prepared to fight the kind of war the Boche will wage. Our military's plan is to defend France as if this war will be like the first one."

"Precisely!" added Louis emphatically.

"But, surely, our military leaders understand the changes in warfare and learned from what the Boche did in Poland," added Etienne, sitting on the edge of his chair.

"There are a few, like de Gaulle and Leclrec (Phillippe Leclrec, a strong supporter of de Gaulle and an advocate of mechanized warfare), who understand what France must do," said Louis. "But, unfortunately, they do not enjoy the confidence of the spineless functionaries in our high command."

At Louis's last comment, the room erupted in questions and comments by the men. This prompted Nadine to stand and attract the attention of those in the room. "I do not consider it appropriate to merely criticize our leaders. We must find a way to impress upon them the dangers for France if the Boche are not repelled."

Immediately, Argentina spoke up. "Nadine is right. Quentin, Ruben is in Germany at this moment. Have you heard from him?" she asked.

"Why yes," he replied. "He sent me a couple of wires before I left the U.S. He's met with Gerd von Rundstedt, a senior general in the Wehrmacht and Erich von Manstein, his chief of staff."

"How did he manage that?" asked Louis, a troubled expression on his face.

"He met with Baron Nicholas von Kleist, a friend of mine. His uncle is Ewald von Kleist, a senior general in the Wehrmacht. Through them, he's met General Walther von Brauchitsch, commander-in-chief of the Wehrmacht, and plans to interview General Heinz Guderian," said the Cajun.

"Isn't Nicholas von Kleist the Boche pilot you captured?" asked Etienne.

"Yes, he's now a general in the Luftwaffe," said Quentin.

"Maybe you should have killed him when you had the chance," Argentina remarked bitterly. Louis looked at the attractive Mexican woman and smiled.

Etienne chuckled and explained that his wife was not one to miss an opportunity. "It's in her blood," he said with a smile. But, it only provoked Argentina.

"I fought during the Mexican Revolution and learned some bitter lessons," she told them. "And one was never to allow a dangerous adversary a second chance to harm you!" she added emphatically.

Louis looked at her again, clapped his hands, and, in a loud voice, said, "Bravo. You should be the commander-in-chief of our military."

At this, the room was still until Nadine smiled and stood, clapping her hands and repeating the word "bravo." Then, everyone laughed and said Argentina was right.

"Time for dinner," said Nadine, taking Quentin's arm and leading the group to the dining room.

After dinner, they returned to the living room and sat to talk. Argentina spoke up and said that what Nadine had told them about doing something positive required action.

"I think we should consider asking Ruben Valderano to 'enlighten' the military high command about what he's learned in Germany. Can that be arranged?" she asked, looking directly at Nadine.

"Why yes," said the Nadine. "My father and I have good contacts within the newspapers. Louis, would you be willing to help me host Ruben at meetings with people from the press and key people in our high command?" Louis looked at Edmund, who smiled at him and nodded his head in approval.

"Cherie," she said to the Cajun, "your cousins here are still well regarded by people in the government. Could you persuade them to help?"

He smiled and nodded.

They talked until midnight. Edmund looked at his watch and said it was late. He and Louis stood, and both men walked to Nadine and kissed her on the cheek. Raoul and Etienne did the same. The women were gracious and hugged and kissed each other before leaving. As Louis Bondurant was preparing to leave with Edmund and Arlene, he took Quentin's arm and said, "I pray your country will come to our assistance again. I'm uncertain that France and the English alone can defeat the Boche."

"I'll do everything I can to convince American leaders to join France and England to end the Boche aggression," he told the old warrior.

Raoul and Etienne spoke briefly with the American before leaving. Then, Nadine and Quentin were alone.

"They are all marvelous people," said Quentin, holding Nadine and looking at the still hot embers in the fireplace.

"Yes," she said softly, "and we will need your help to prevent a calamity." He understood what she was saying, but he worried that America would refuse to go to war against Germany.

* * *

Quentin stayed in Paris with Nadine for almost a week. During that time, he met with several members of the French high command. Through contacts his cousins had arranged, he met with key leaders in the government. His impressions, based on the anecdotal information gathered, were troublesome. French leaders were indecisive and waiting to see what the Germans would do and whether diplomacy might still avoid a war. Among a few important leaders he sensed indecisiveness. Louis had been right; the leadership in France was weak and unable to agree on the best course of action against the Boche. *This is not good,* he told himself.

The last night they were together, Nadine and Quentin discussed what he had learned and his perceptions about what might happen if the Boche invaded France.

"There is a lack of resolve to go on the offensive," he told Nadine.

"Among our leaders?" she asked.

He nodded.

"I pray the English will help us to resist any invasion by the Boche," she told him.

Again, he nodded, and they were silent for a few moments before the Cajun spoke up.

"I'll be interested to hear from Ruben what he learned in Germany," he said.

"Will he come to Paris?" she asked.

He shook his head and said, "No, Ruben will go to Switzerland, then through Portugal on his return to America."

"Give him my love when you see him," she told him. He smiled and nodded.

Quentin took Nadine's hand and led the lovely French woman to her bedroom. That night, they explored each other's bodies with a newfound passion. Their lovemaking, afterward, was torrid.

Early the next morning, October 10, 1939, Hardy, Mark, and Quentin boarded the Amelie and prepared to leave. After the engines were warmed sufficiently, Quentin blew the beautiful woman a kiss, closed his window, and taxied the Lockheed Electra to the runway. He turned the plane into the wind, added power, and in a matter of minutes was airborne and gaining altitude rapidly. Nadine waited until the silver plane was out of sight before going home. As she was driven home, the blue eyes of Amelia Earhart's image that Quentin had painted on the side of the Amelie stayed in her mind.

Quentin's return trip to America was slowed by a large weather system moving east from Canada. They arrived late at St. John's and in a driving rain. They waited there until the weather ahead cleared before resuming their flight to New York. It would be a little over two months before Quentin returned to France.

On his return to New York, Quentin called Julia and asked if she had heard from Ruben.

"He's on his way here," she told him. "He sent me a cablegram from Barcelona where he stopped to be with his family. I expect him here in two or three days."

He thanked Julia for the information and arranged for her to join him for dinner at the Vandersteels' the following evening.

The fighting in Poland ended on October 7, 1939. The Soviets, encouraged by the Nazis, had entered the conflict and defeated the remnants of a Polish army fleeing to the east. They proceeded to occupy what was once eastern Poland. The Germans garrisoned Warsaw and key cities in western Poland and quickly began redeploying Wehrmacht units to the border with France. Meanwhile, the French continued to wait while the English deployed their expeditionary forces in Belgium. Quentin doubted whether the Germans would mount a winter campaign. Instead, there was a lull in the war. While the Allies waited to find out what the Germans would do, the Germans began massing troops and vehicles on their western borders with Belgium, Holland, and France. The hiatus in the fighting became known as the "Phoney War."

CHAPTER 3
ANTICIPATION

*Wild, dark times are rumbling toward us, and the
prophet who wishes to write a new apocalypse will
have to invent entirely new beasts, and beasts so
terrible that the ancient animal symbols of Saint John
will seem like cooing doves and cupids in comparison.*
Heinrich Heine, *Lutetia: or, Paris* [1842]

The daylight shortened in Paris, and Nadine felt a nip in
the air as the temperature in mid-October slowly dropped.
The leaves had turned, and on the long and solitary walks
or horseback rides, she drank in the fall foliage resplen-
dent in splashes of yellows, ochers, and scarlet. The riot
of colors was beautiful and memorable. These sensory experiences sustained her in difficult times. It was difficult
for her, and others, to believe that a state of war existed
between the Allies and the Germans. But, somewhere
over the eastern horizon, she knew a dark ogre waited,
angry and determined to punish France for the Treaty of
Versailles. If the Americans were allied with England and
France, she could cope with the demons that lurked in
her mind. *Oh, Quentin, please be there when I need you,* she
thought as a prayer.

During the third week of October, a delegation of
leaders within the arts community of Paris approached
Nadine. She met with them on a gloomy Thursday
morning.

"Madame Desnoyers," said Monsieur Drancy, the polished and poised spokesperson for the group. He was

a slight man, dressed in a well-tailored three-piece suit. He had a pointed face with a well-trimmed goatee and strands of silver visible in his dark hair. "We come to you with an urgent request." There was an insistence in the man's voice that alerted Nadine.

When she asked what they wanted, Drancy told her about three projects the group wanted to complete before the spring of 1940. The first was to move priceless works of art that might be damaged in the event of shelling or bombing to a safe hiding place. Nadine asked him to elaborate. Drancy told her about rare and valuable artifacts at important museums and galleries in Paris.

"They should be carefully packed and sent to a secret facility where no harm will come to them," he said. She nodded and motioned for him to continue. "There are items in the Louvre that must be moved, and perhaps taken out of the country for safekeeping until the war is over," he told her.

"Why?" she asked.

"If France is attacked and Paris bombarded, we must not allow our national treasures to be destroyed," he replied.

"But aren't most of the items you mention well protected in the Louvre?" she asked.

"Yes," he replied. "But there is another precaution, one that pains me to mention."

"Speak up, monsieur," she encouraged.

"If France is defeated, and I hope that will not happen, it is only prudent for us to safeguard precious items that we do not want confiscated by the Boche." There was a twinge of sadness in his voice.

Nadine looked carefully at the others in the room and detected the insecurity in their faces. *They're afraid France will be defeated by the Boche,* she surmised. "We need courage and determination at this time," she told

Monsieur Drancy and the others in the room, "not talk about defeat."

"Yes, Madame Desnoyers," said a portly man she recognized as Monsieur Claude Berault, a prominent art critic and collector. "But, we dare not risk our national treasures by doing nothing and hoping for the best."

She nodded, aware of the deep concern he and the others in the room had for priceless works of art that none of them wanted damaged or lost. "Continue," she told Drancy.

"Our third concern is the stained glass in Notre Dame. It should be removed and replaced with opaque glass. The stained glass can be cataloged and moved to a safe location." He paused to let his words take effect.

"What is it you want of me?"

"Madame," said Drancy, "we need a benefactress and someone to plead our case before others with wealth."

"You mean others with wealth and willing to support your projects, n'est-ce pas?"

Drancy bowed his head politely and said, "Absolument."

"Very well," she said without hesitation. "I'll pledge the following amount and will raise similar sums from six or seven others." She took a piece of paper and wrote five hundred thousand Francs on it before handing it to Drancy.

"You are a rare individual and a patriot," said Drancy, as he shared the amount she pledged with the others.

After the delegation departed, Nadine called Noel and had him make appointments with seven wealthy men. Most of them had large personal fortunes, and three were the heads of large and successful industrial concerns in France. By the end of November, Nadine had raised more than four million Francs for the projects. She told the wealthy men that their contributions were an investment in the future of France and protection for their nation's priceless artistic heritage. She established a not-for-profit foundation and channeled the funds into it. This, she told the other benefactors, would provide them with a tax advantage. She convinced the contributors to serve on the board of directors for the foundation. All of them agreed with her plans for the foundation and praised her dedication and leadership to protect and preserve priceless French national treasures.

* * *

It was mid-October when Quentin returned from Paris. Ruben was waiting for him in New York. The two men met for lunch at an exclusive club. The Mexican insisted they not arrive together and meet in a private area where they could not be observed or heard by strangers. When Quentin asked him about this, Ruben said he would explain later. After finishing their meal, they exchanged information about what they had seen and heard. Ruben began the conversation.

"I'm indebted to you, *hombre*, for arranging my meeting with General Nicholas von Kleist in the Luftwaffe. He sends you his best wishes...and this letter." He handed Quentin a large envelope, which the Cajun let sit on the table. Ruben continued. "Through your friend, I met his uncle, Ewald von Kleist, in the Wehrmacht. Both men are brilliant military leaders." Ruben drank some water and handed two file folders and a book to the Cajun. "Keep these files confidential. You must not let anyone know you have them. The book was written by Heinz Guderian," said the Mexican. He added that Guderian, a brilliant German tactician in armored warfare, had developed a new form of mechanized warfare

Quentin examined it and read the title, *Achtung— Panzer*. He noticed that it had been published in 1938. "May I keep this for a while?" he asked the Mexican.

"It's yours," said Ruben. "And it's autographed by Guderian. You'll find numerous passages in it about the coordinated use of tanks and airplanes. When I read it, I thought the three of us were having a conversation," the Mexican said with a smile.

"I'm impressed with Guderian and two other German officers." Quentin nodded, a signal for the Mexican to continue. "General Gerd von Rundstedt and Erich von Manstein, his chief of staff, are professional soldiers and very capable military leaders. They were instrumental in the rapid defeat of the Poles."

"Hmm," said the Cajun, looking at the book by the German general, "you seem to admire Guderian."

"Yes. He's clever and has initiated something the German's call *blitzkrieg,* their term for 'lightning war.'" Ruben briefly explained the Wehrmacht blitzkrieg battle tactics. "The Germans had little difficulty defeating the Poles," said the Mexican. "Their battle plans were well crafted and methodically executed. I'm impressed with General Heinz Guderian. I had dinner with him one evening."

The Cajun looked at the Mexican and finally said, "And?"

"He's brilliant...and not very fond of Hitler. His tactics for mechanized warfare and coordinated air support will vex the Allies when the fighting continues," said Valderano.

"So you're saying the war will go on," Quentin said, resigned to the developments.

"I'm afraid so," said the Mexican, "and I'm worried that the French cannot withstand the German blitzkrieg." He looked away from the American and played with his water glass.

Quentin sensed that Ruben was waiting to hear about his trip to France. Quentin began by mentioning what he learned in Paris. His concern was that the French would not take the offensive against the Germans.   "If the French wait for the Germans to come at them, it will go badly for them."

"And the English?" asked Valderano.

"I think they will hold their ground. But, unless they have adequate ammunition and supplies, their situation will be compromised," Quentin continued, saying that morale in the French army was low and that their leadership was divided on numerous matters, and probably unable to wage the kind of modern warfare to cope with the Nazi blitzkrieg. They continued to discuss the level of military preparation in Germany and France, with Quentin gradually becoming convinced that unless the British offered strong military and diplomatic support, the Allies might be defeated.

"I believe the RAF (Royal Air Force) can hold its own against the Luftwaffe. But, I haven't talked with any senior air ministry personnel," he told the Mexican. "Any German offensive in the spring will certainly involve large numbers of armored units. If the Germans can keep the RAF from attacking their tanks, the Allies will be outmaneuvered."

"You suspect the worst, don't you?" Ruben asked.

The Cajun nodded and did not say anything.

"Well, the English and the French have a few months to prepare for what the Germans might do in the spring," he told the Cajun.

"Yes, that's true, Ruben," said Quentin. "But I worry that the French high command is not up to the task," he pondered aloud.

"*Quien sabe* (who knows)," said the Mexican, drinking the last of the water in his goblet. "But one thing is certain. If the Allies don't go on the offensive and attack the Germans, they will be on the defensive and lose ground. The Germans will try to divide the Allies. If they succeed and cut off the main French forces from the British, the Germans will prevail."

Their conversation had turned sober and depressing. Each man could see what the Allies needed to do. Any failure by the British and French to prevent the Germans from launching their form of lightning war would be disastrous.

"I must warn you about this information," said Ruben, touching the two file folders and the envelope from von Kleist. "Keep it confidential. When you visit Washington, do not read from my notes or mention anything about von Kleist's letter."

"Why?" asked the Cajun.

"The Nazis are very suspicious," Ruben told him. "They are methodical and leave nothing to chance. Even now, I suspect we are under surveillance by Nazi operatives."

"Are you sure about this?" asked a surprised Quentin. "Nazi spies...here!"

"Yes," replied the Mexican. "I cannot visit Washington and must not come near a U.S. government employee, especially one in the military."

"But we're a neutral country," said the Cajun.

"The Nazis don't trust us. They know Roosevelt is pro English. I've asked Healy to meet with you. She will corroborate my comments about being followed," he told Quentin. "Read over what I have written in my reports carefully and take notes. When you talk with Roosevelt and his people in Washington about what I learned, do it from your notes and don't mention my name. Use a code name for me," he warned the Cajun. "After you convey the information, destroy my reports."

"Why do you want me to destroy them?" asked Quentin.

"The security in the White House is lax. General Marshall mentioned that a top secret army memorandum was found in the trash that had been tossed into a garbage truck. The Germans are resourceful and will do everything they can to learn what the U.S. plans to do now and when the fighting resumes."

The Cajun shook his head at Valderano's warning. He remembered being under surveillance in Paris during World War I before the United States entered the war on the side of the Allies. The British and the French followed him whenever he was in Paris.

"Very well," he told the Mexican. "I'll do as you ask."

"Gracias," said Ruben. "Julia and I leave for Santa Barbara tomorrow."

"Would you like me to fly you home?" asked Quentin.

"No," said Ruben. "I appreciate the offer, but remember that we are being watched. Best not to provide the Nazis with anything that will corroborate their suspicions about our working together. Remember, my friend, the Germans don't believe in coincidences."

That evening, Quentin read Nicky's letter. Von Kleist swore the Cajun to secrecy and shared his dislike and mistrust of Hitler and his cronies.

The man is a super patriot, a dangerous form of politician capable of leading
a nation on a ruinous path. I fear for the welfare of my country and my family.

Von Kleist provided information that confirmed the Cajun's suspicions about Hitler's plans to continue the war against France and England, and aggression elsewhere. The German general finished the letter by asking the American to visit him in the near future. He professed his friendship and wished the Cajun and his family the best of health and good fortune. After finishing the letter, Quentin destroyed it, as the German requested, and contemplated what von Kleist had shared. *If what he wrote to me ever got out,* thought the Cajun, *Nicky would be in serious trouble.* More and more, the Cajun realized the danger Hitler posed, not just for Europe, but for the rest of the world.

Three days later, Quentin visited Washington and met with Roosevelt, Cordell Hull, Harry Woodring, and George C. Marshall, now a full general and the head of the Joint Chiefs of Staff. He requested a stenographer be present.

"For security purposes, I prefer to make an oral report and not transmit anything in writing," he told them. When Roosevelt asked why, Quentin said he and "the general" (his code name for Ruben Valderano) were probably being followed by Nazi operatives.

A surprised Roosevelt asked, "Are you certain about this?"

Quentin nodded. "I spotted a man following me to the train station where he spoke with another man who got on the train. When we arrived here, another man was waiting and followed me to my hotel."

"Damn!" exclaimed Roosevelt. "Well, I'll see that something is done about this. Go on with your report."

After Quentin relayed what he and Valderano had learned in France and Germany, he noticed that Marshall was looking intently at him. *George wants to talk with me in private,* surmised the Cajun. He nodded at Marshall while the others were busy talking about his report and mouthed the word, *later.* When the others were not paying attention, Marshall nodded at Quentin.

"You're absolutely certain about this information?" asked the president.

"Yes," replied Quentin. "Our good friend the general and I are not optimistic about France's ability to overcome a German blitzkrieg."

"I've been informed that the British have a well-trained and equipped force in Belgium. Surely, they will be able to counter any Nazi attack," said Harry Woodring.

"The Nazis will try to split the lines of communication and supplies between the French and the British. If they succeed, the British will have to fall back. Otherwise, the Germans will encircle them," Quentin said forcefully to make his point.

"But how can this be?" said Woodring. "The combined French and British forces exceed those of the Germans."

"That's true," said the Cajun, "but don't be fooled by numbers. Too many French troops are committed to the Maginot Line. The general told me that if the Germans open a breach in the French line of defense, their mechanized units will pour through and race to divide the Allies." He looked at Marshall and knew the American general understood.

"That's a big if," said Woodring.

Roosevelt let Woodring and Quentin debate the issue while Cordell Hull and General Marshall listened intently. Finally, the president said he had another meeting.

"Quentin, thank you for the information that you and the general have gathered; I'll study it carefully. I promise that it will be factored into whatever policy we develop toward the Germans and the Allies. George," said Roosevelt, turning toward General Marshall, "I'd like to see you later. Harry, you and Cordell wait."

Quentin shook hands with Roosevelt, Woodring, and Hull before leaving the room. Just ahead of him was Marshall. They met in the hall and Marshall asked Quentin to walk with him.

Meanwhile, Roosevelt told Woodring and Hull that Quentin's report was sobering. "I will, of course, confirm what Quentin and the general have learned," he told them. "Cordell, I need you to talk with our ambassadors in London and Paris. Keep Stony in the loop," he said. "We need to apprise them of this new intelligence." They talked for a few minutes before the two men left the president.

When he was alone, Roosevelt buzzed for his secretary. "Get J. Edgar Hoover over here as soon as possible."

* * *

In mid-November, Nadine received news from her contact in Switzerland about the status of the Jewish family from Kalisz, Poland. She was told that five of them had made it to Zurich.

"Only five," she said incredulously over the phone.

"Best if we do not discuss this on the telephone," said her contact in Zurich.

"When can they be in Paris?"

"Perhaps ten days," he told her.

"No sooner?" she pressed. He replied that the group was exhausted and had suffered greatly in escaping from Poland.

"Just the paperwork will take a few days."

"Very well," she said. "Do what is necessary. I want them in Paris as soon as possible."

Eight days later, Nadine, Moira, and a Polish-speaking interpreter were waiting at the gare for the train from Switzerland. When it arrived, the interpreter held up a sign in Polish with the name of the family. Nadine and Moira were stunned to see two thin adults and three nervous children come toward them. *My God,* thought Nadine, *they look so emaciated. What must they have experienced!*

That evening, through a Polish interpreter, Nadine and Moira learned about the hardships suffered by the Kazminsky family. Nine of them fled south to what remained of Czechoslovakia, then to Hungary, and from there to Austria where they traveled with a group of

Gypsies using back roads and trails until they crossed into Switzerland. Two of the adults in the original group became very ill and stayed in Hungary. A teenage boy and a young woman were arrested in Austria. The two adults, Josef and Maya, cared for the three children, often going without food so that the little ones could eat. Their clothes were worn and torn in places from crawling through thick brush and wading across small streams to avoid capture. It seemed to Nadine that the dark and hollow eyes of the two little girls and the small boy were evocative of a painting of children suffering from famine and the plague in the Middle Ages.

Nadine contacted friends in a Jewish refugee group and notified them about the two adults and the three children. The next day at around ten in the morning, a Jewish man and woman arrived at Nadine's home and spoke with the Kazminsky adults. Nadine told the two Jewish workers that she wanted the Kazminsky family to go to America to be with their relatives in New York City.

"That might take time and money," said Lech Milosz, the worker from the Jewish refugee group.

"I have contacts in America who will help," said Nadine. "As for the money, that will not be a problem."

Early in the afternoon, Nadine called Quentin and informed him about the Kazminsky group. She asked him to work with the American immigration service to bring the Kazminsky family to the United States as political refugees. Quentin said he would make all the necessary arrangements and begin the formal process for visas.

"Contact Brook Hamilton Stoner at the U.S. Embassy in Paris," he told Nadine. "And let him know that we're working to get the Kazminsky family to the U.S. Have him contact me if he has any questions."

Before they ended the call, Nadine asked when Quentin would visit Paris again.

"I'll be there the second week of December," he told her. "Marlon will be with me."

"Magnifique!" she exclaimed. "I will have my two favorite men with me."

They chatted for a few more minutes before ending the call. Nadine hung up first while Quentin listened for the sound of the click that signaled the end of the call. The silence that followed always tugged at his heart and made him feel lonely. Slowly, he returned the receiver to its cradle.

After talking with Nadine, Quentin called Sarah into his office. He told her about the escape of five Kazminsky family members. She was stunned, and her eyes filled with tears.

"Nine left Poland. Two became ill and remained in Hungary, and two were arrested in Austria. We're trying to find out what has happened to them." He handed Sarah a piece of paper with the names of the five Kazminsky family members. She sobbed, and Quentin handed her his handkerchief. "Mrs. Desnoyers and I are arranging for your relatives to be brought to New York. I'm sorry we couldn't get the others out of Poland."

The next day, Sarah told the Cajun that her parents invited him for dinner the next evening, or as soon as he could. He checked his calendar and said he could join them for dinner the following evening.

When Quentin arrived at the Katzmann home, Ari, Sarah's father, and two other men greeted him warmly. This was not the first time the Cajun had visited the Katzmann home.

"Welcome to our home," said Ari. "Iz good to see you again." He motioned for the attorney to join him in the living room of the spacious apartment.

"Sarah has told us vhat you've done to help our family in Poland. Zis is a bad time," he said in a sad voice.

"I'm sorry we could not get more of your relatives out of Poland," Quentin told Ari and the others.

"You're not to blame," said the slender Jewish man, his large, expressive brown eyes looking at the attorney with kindness. "Ve can never repay you for your kindness. But, come; let us have a little something to drink before supper."

After dinner, the men sat in the living room and talked. Mainly, the men asked Quentin questions about the condition of their relatives. Quentin shared what he knew.

"Ven can ve expect zem?" asked Jacob, a short, balding man with a full beard wearing gold-rimmed glasses.

"I'm making arrangements for them to come to New York as political refugees," he told them. "I hope we can have your relatives here by the middle of December, maybe sooner."

"Ve vill pay you for your time," said Mathias, an elder.

Quentin shook his head and said he would not take any money.

The men in the room tried to persuade the Cajun to change his mind and take a fee for his services, but Quentin refused.

"Vhy do you do zis for us?" asked Jacob.

"Because it's the right thing to do," replied the Cajun. "And we are friends."

Later, when Sarah walked Quentin down to the front of the apartment building, she took his sleeve gently and said, "You have been wonderful to my family. We can never repay you for your kindness."

"I'm certain you would do the same for me." She turned away as if to hide her emotions from him, but Quentin held Sarah's shoulders and looked into her moist eyes. "Don't worry, Sarah. Your relatives will be here soon. I'm sorry that only five of them could make it out of Poland."

"The Nazis are not just arresting Jews," she said sadly. "We've heard they're killing them." Her words stayed with Quentin as he wondered what the Germans were doing to the Jews.

That evening, on his way home, Quentin was pensive, preoccupied with thoughts about the Kazminsky family in Poland unable to leave, and the ones that remained in Hungary. But, most of all, he worried about the two young Kazminskys that had been arrested in Austria. *What will happen to them?* he wondered.

* * *

Try as he might, it was not possible for Quentin to see Florence daily. She was an active and studious teenager and busy with school and extracurricular activities, especially her music. His attendance at social functions to represent the firm and his occasional late hours working on special contracts preoccupied him. Moreover, his trips to Canada and the West Coast on business often lasted several days. He made it a point to be with his daughter as much as possible. He had season tickets for them to attend the symphony, the opera, and the ballet. While Quentin loved to take Florence to the symphony, he preferred the opera and especially the ballet. She liked theater, and, together, they attended many enjoyable off-Broadway performances. Now and then, when Marlon was in New York, he would join them. Marlon was a movie fan, something that he and Florence delighted in doing together.

Quentin witnessed a remarkable metamorphosis in his daughter. She was sixteen and now resembled Ione. She had Ione's facial features: the slightly turned up nose, the intense blue eyes, the lovely classic jaw line, and lips that were a delicious shade of pink. Although he could not see it, Carmela and Kathleen pointed out that Florence had so much of him in her.

"She's self-assured and strong," said Kathleen, "and knows her own mind."

"Yes, the señorita has much of you in her," said Camila. "She laughs like you and is athletic like you and *señorito* (master) Marlon."

Quentin nodded and pondered what Camila had said. Florence was a terrific athlete and an accomplished sailor, like her grandfather and mother. She loved to swim, play tennis, and golf. At her prep school, she was the captain of the field hockey team and enjoyed playing basketball and volleyball. Quentin and Marlon had taught Florence how to throw a baseball and football. She grew up a tomboy, but she was rapidly maturing into a bright and beautiful young woman. Florence's love of flying brought her closer to him. The girl was a natural pilot and would beg the Cajun to let her fly whatever plane they were in. Mark and Hardy encouraged her and said Amelia Earhart would be proud of Florence's flying abilities.

Next year, thought Quentin, *Florence will be a debutante. I wonder what she'll look like then.* His daughter was maturing rapidly and, at times, seemed to change as he was observing her. He wanted so much for her to be happy. Lately, he'd noticed an intriguing behavior in Florence whenever she was with Marlon. They were close and usually walked arm in arm, smiled, and whispered to each other at social functions. When Marlon was home, they went sailing when the weather permitted and would be gone for the entire day. *I wonder what they do and talk about,* thought Quentin. Perhaps one of these days, he'd ask Marlon.

* * *

The next few weeks passed quickly for Quentin. He flew to California on business in November and met with Ruben Valderano at a movie studio in Hollywood. They arrived in separate cars and made certain they were not followed. Quentin shared new information he'd learned about diplomatic efforts by the Allies with the Germans. He also shared his plans to visit England and meet with persons in the air ministry.

"Good," said Valderano, as he sipped the strong coffee. They sat in an outdoor garden that was sheltered from the wind and enjoyed the bright California sunshine.

"I've news about Japanese activities in the Pacific," said Ruben.

"Oh?" said Quentin, his interest piqued.

"Yes," continued the Mexican, "it seems they're very interested in French Indochina and want to build air bases from which to strike into southern China."

"The French will not give them permission to do that," said Quentin.

"The French and the British are moving troops from the far east to strengthen their reserves in Europe. The Japanese are clever and opportunistic and will intensify their military efforts in China and perhaps elsewhere in Southeast Asia."

"If you don't mind, Ruben, how do you know all this?"

"You've met my brother, Luis," said Ruben with a sly smile on his face.

"Yes, he's a Jesuit priest and works in the Vatican."

"He's part of the Vatican diplomatic corps, and we met on his way back to Rome from a trip to China and Indochina. The Church has an excellent intelligence service with many eyes and ears," said the Mexican with a smile.

"So that's it!" Quentin was quick to understand what his friend was sharing. "Have you mentioned this to anyone in Washington?"

"About my brother's information?" asked Ruben.

The Cajun nodded.

"No, it's best to keep secret this source of information," he cautioned.

"I understand," said Quentin. "But, surely, this intelligence is critical and important for people in Washington."

"Yes, but I don't think Roosevelt and his people will pay it much attention," he said ruefully.

"Why?" asked the Cajun, taken aback by his friend's remark.

"Europe is their main concern," said Ruben, as he finished his coffee. "Share what I've told you with General Marshall. I promised to keep him informed." Quentin nodded and agreed to do so. They talked for a while longer before Quentin said he had a meeting with the heads of another studio.

"I see you continue to dabble in the movie business," said the Mexican with a smile.

"It's good business," replied the Cajun, "and profitable." The two men laughed and agreed to talk on the telephone in a few weeks. Quentin mentioned that he and Marlon would fly to France in December.

"Will you be flying to England first?" asked the Mexican.

Quentin said yes and asked Ruben what he had in mind.

"Will you take Kendall with you so that he can be with his mother in London for a few days?"

"Of course," said the Cajun. "I'll have Marlon call him. We'll make all the necessary arrangements."

"Gracias," said Ruben. "I'm indebted to you."

Before the two men parted, they discussed their next meeting. Ruben and Julia would visit New York in December to be with their daughters and relatives for the holidays. They agreed to celebrate the New Year together in New York.

For Thanksgiving, Quentin, Marlon, and Florence flew to Louisiana to be with the Norvells. Bernice and Roland, Quentin's parents, were delighted to have them visit. It proved to be a festive and enjoyable time for them. They were joined by Quentin's cousin, Forrest Marmion, and Forrest's wife. Forrest was recently reelected to the House of Representatives, and a distant cousin had just been elected the junior U.S. senator from Louisiana. Before dinner on Thanksgiving Day, Forrest, Rene (Quentin's older brother), and Quentin went for a walk.

"I'm worried about what's going on in Europe," Forrest told them.

"You mean the war?" Rene inquired.

"Yes," said Forrest. "I'm afraid of what Hitler might do."

"But there hasn't been any further fighting," said Rene, trying to sound reassuring.

"The Germans are busy moving troops to the border with France. No telling what they have in mind," Forrest told them, a tic of nervousness in his voice.

"Cousin," he said, turning to look directly at Quentin, "you haven't said anything, and that bothers me."

Quentin glanced at his cousin and looked down while shaking his head. He had nothing positive to say and wondered how much he should share. Finally, he relented and decided not to withhold information from his blood kin. "I'm afraid of what the Boche might do," he told them.

"Why?" asked Rene.

"I was in France recently and talked with leaders in their government and several key military persons," he said somberly. "Their war plans are flawed, and I worry that the French defensive strategy will fail."

"Why do you say this?" asked Forrest.

Quentin explained what he'd learned in France, and, without mentioning Ruben Valderano, related the waiting strategy favored by the French.

"You mean they're just going to wait for the Germans to attack?" asked an incredulous Forrest.

Quentin nodded.

"But that's absurd," added Rene. "Surely, the English will push them to go on the offensive."

The Cajun shook his head and looked at the ground in disgust.

Rene and Forrest glanced at each other, unspoken thoughts passing between them. A moment later, Rene asked, "What will Marlon do?"

"What do you mean?" replied a surprised Quentin.

"I mean he will most certainly want to fight against the Germans, just like you did," said his older brother.

Quentin had considered what his son might do if the fighting continued in Europe. But, Rene's comment caught him off guard. He shook his head and said he'd not discussed the matter with Marlon.

"Well," continued Forrest, "he's your son and will follow in your footsteps. After all," he said, looking directly at Quentin, "you went to France and fought against the Germans well before we entered the war."

Quentin nodded in agreement. He remembered his decision. He'd just graduated from Princeton in 1916 and went to France to enlist. He'd been encouraged to join the Lafayette Escadrille like other Americans, especially a few Ivy League types. The Escadrille enjoyed a romantic aura and was supported by prominent Americans like Norman Prince and Cornelius Vanderbilt. Instead, Quentin enlisted in the French Foreign Legion, but not before emphasizing he was a trained pilot and extracting a written agreement to be commissioned an officer. The French had, at first, been reluctant to meet his demands, but they relented. He suspected that someone in the foreign legion contacted his cousins in France, Marcel Couvres and Albert Navralette, prominent businessmen in key governmental positions. He went to France and, after a few months of training, was commissioned a lieutenant and assigned to the French Twenty-ninth Escadrille commanded by Raoul Mendeville.

Quentin knew that Marlon had learned from Nadine and others about his decision to fly with a French fighter squadron in 1916. Shortly after Henri Desnoyers' death, Nadine told her son about Quentin's numerous accomplishments during the Great War. Marlon's strong affection for his mother, the desire to protect her no matter the cost, and his father's military activities during the Great War bolstered the young man's resolve to join the French military. Aware that Marlon was contemplating enlisting, he decided to speak with him about it.

It was not until early Saturday morning after brunch that Quentin was alone with Marlon. The two of them got into a small boat with an outboard motor and went into the bayou. Quentin remembered the waterways well, and the two of them finally landed on a small island where they sat to fish and talk.

"Marlon," said Quentin, "care to share your thoughts about the war in Europe?"

Marlon looked at his father, and a slight smile crossed his face. "You're worried that I might enlist and fight for the French like you did."

Quentin nodded.

"I'm thinking about it," he told his father.

"Can I get you to wait until we know more about what might happen?" said the Cajun.

Again, Marlon smiled and said, "It's hard to know what's going to happen over there. But, one thing is sure, if the Boche invade France, I'll find a way to volunteer and fly for the French just like you, Dad."

"I hope it doesn't come to that," said Quentin, considering carefully his son's words. "I was hoping you'd graduate from MIT in the spring. I waited until I finished at Princeton."

"I'd like to do the same, Dad" said Marlon, "but it all depends on how the war goes."

"I see," said Quentin, giving a quick tug to his line to set the hook in a fish.

"Dad, you've got one," said an excited Marlon.

After landing the large catfish, Quentin spoke to Marlon about volunteering to fight for the French. "Promise me you'll wait until we have a better idea of how things develop in Europe. I'd really like you to graduate from MIT," he stressed.

Marlon smiled and said he would wait. "But, if France is invaded by the Boche, I'll join the Allies," his son said in a determined voice.

"Have you spoken to your mother about this?"

"Yes, briefly," he told his father.

Quentin raised an eyebrow before speaking. "We'd better have this conversation next month when the three of us are together in Paris." Marlon nodded and smiled at his father. The Cajun nudged him and pointed at a nibble on his line.

That evening, Florence, Marlon, Louis and his wife, and three of their cousins went into New Orleans to make the rounds of the jazz clubs. Normally, Quentin would not have allowed Florence, because she was only sixteen, to go to the jazz spots. However, his younger brother Louis and his wife, along with Marlon, promised to look after her. The Cajun finally relented, but insisted that Florence be home before midnight. He thought about going with the group, but he decided against it and stayed with Bernice and Roland. Ever since their arrival in Baton Rogue, his parents communicated discreetly their desire to discuss something with him. This evening seemed like the right moment for them to chat.

Bernice, now in her sixties, her once raven hair heavily streaked with silver, was still a handsome woman. She peered at Quentin, her middle son, over her reading glasses. Finally, she asked, "Does Marlon want to go to France and enlist?"

Quentin looked at his mother. A barely perceptible frown crossed his face that made him look inquisitive and not unlike when he was young and she had asked him a question that involved a careful answer. "Yes, he might," he replied. "Nothing is definite at the moment."

"Have you talked with Nadine about this?" she followed up.

Now Quentin smiled, realizing that very little escaped his mother's attention. It made him love her all the more. He noticed that Roland had put down his newspaper and was waiting for his response.

"I'm going to Paris with Marlon next month. The three of us will discuss his choices," said Quentin. Roland made a soft snorting sound and resumed reading the paper. He recognized his father's gesture as an indication of approval.

Bernice, meanwhile, spoke in a soft voice and pursued the matter. "You went to war when you were young and were almost killed. I pray to god that Marlon will not have to endure the same," she told him.

"If he decides to enlist and fight, he'll be all right," Quentin replied, while observing Roland out of the corner of his eye for anything he might say or do. But, his mother was not satisfied with his response.

"Marlon's not like you, Quentin," she said. "You were born and raised in these bayous and have the Cajun blood. It made you hard and strong. But he's different."

"What do you mean, Mother?" he asked, waiting for her to continue.

There was a special rapport between the Cajun and his mother. He admired and trusted Bernice. She had been his strictest tutor and taught him to shoot, fish, and survive in the swamps. Roland loved Quentin, but he focused much of his attention on Rene, the oldest, and Louis, the youngest son. As the middle son, Quentin was often left to make do on his own. Rather than let Quentin drift, Bernice devoted herself to educate and prepare her middle son. She did everything possible to help him become strong and self-reliant. She raised him to understand and tap into the strong Cajun blood and the "ways" of her people. With her help, he learned the Cajun culture and developed into a resourceful and independent young man. It was Bernice who had encouraged and helped Quentin attend a prestigious military preparatory academy from which he graduated with distinction before entering Princeton. Now, she was concerned about her grandson and wanted to know what Quentin was going to do to help Marlon.

"If he goes to war," she told him, "you must prepare him."

"I understand," he replied, cognizant of what she was asking of him.

"He will never be like you, my son," she warned. "He is much like his mother, bless her," said Bernice. "Nadine has done much to make him the fine young man he is, but, in war, other preparation is needed. You must do what you can to protect him," she instructed her son.

Quentin saw his father drop the newspaper and nod at him. He understood what his parents were telling him. They were concerned about the war in Europe and knew that eventually Marlon would fight to protect his mother and the land where he was born. It was his responsibility to train Marlon to survive. *If Marlon decides to fight for the*

French in Europe, I will prepare him, the Cajun promised himself.

* * *

On the flight back to New York, Marlon flew the Amelie with Florence in the copilot seat. Quentin watched his two children carefully, noticing the way they exchanged looks and worked together to fly the plane. They exchanged glances and mouthed words with hidden meanings. They were exceptional children, he thought, but something about the way Florence looked at her brother intrigued the Cajun. It was a conundrum that puzzled him. *Sooner or later,* he thought, *I will find the answer to that riddle.*

Before his flight to London and Paris, Quentin met with President Roosevelt and two of his top advisors. Harry Hopkins was there, along with Secretary of State Cordell Hull.

"Quentin," said Roosevelt, sitting in his wheelchair and brandishing a long cigarette holder like a baton, "I need you to do something when you visit London. I know you're planning to meet with Sir Cyril in the air ministry. I can't make any public commitments to support the British, but I want to help them. As long as we're neutral, my hands are tied. I've learned that you're sympathetic to our British friends."

Quentin remained silent, aware of the way the three men were looking at him.

"You can be very helpful to the British," continued the president.

Quentin understood what Roosevelt was saying, but he decided to elicit something precise about what role, if any, he might play to help the British. "What do you have in mind?" asked the Cajun.

Roosevelt glanced first at Hopkins and then at Hull before continuing. "I know you have business associates who feel like we do about helping the British. There are many in America who dislike the Nazis."

Quentin nodded and remained quiet, waiting for the American leader to vocalize a course of action to assist the English.

"There must be a way for some of our 'friends' to send funds to the British that need not flow through normal governmental channels," said the president, waiting to learn what the Cajun might say or do. "I can't order you to do this," he said, "and I'll deny ever having this conversation," he added. "But your help is needed."

Quentin could see the sincerity and determination on the faces of the president and his advisors. *This is no time to be coy*, thought the Cajun.

"There are ways to help the British and the French," said the Cajun.

"Yes?" asked the president, eager to learn what Quentin had in mind.

"I can meet with business leaders who might be willing to assist the Allies with money and credit. But, it will take time to explore and cultivate the right people," he said. "Then, a mechanism must be developed, such as an investment group, and accounts where funds can be deposited anonymously and then channeled to the British," said Quentin, making eye contact with Roosevelt. "The investment group must be established secretly as a numbered account in Switzerland. Loans from it, with a modest charge for interest, can be arranged for the British," he added. Quentin waited for the reaction of the three men. Convinced that they were interested, he continued. "The third leg of this financial stool will be to contact the appropriate people in the British government and present this proposal to them. I'd recommend we focus on the air ministry," said the Cajun.

Hopkins whispered something to Roosevelt that caused the president to encourage his aide to speak up.

"Why the air ministry and not their admiralty?" asked Hopkins.

"It takes vast sums of money to affect naval development," said the Cajun. "And, the British already have a large capital fleet. But, smaller sums can be critical to improve air operations. This war will require air power and control of the skies for the Allies to prevail. Also," he continued, "there is the matter of profits. If I am to convince businessmen to invest in this venture, they must see a profit as well as victory in it."

"Very well," said Roosevelt, taking a drag on the cigarette in his long holder. "If you think it's best to assist the British Air Ministry, that's how it will be. So, will you do this?"

Quentin smiled and said, "Nothing would give me greater pleasure."

"Bravo," said Roosevelt, while Hopkins and Hull approached Quentin and shook his hand. "But, remember," Roosevelt warned, "this conversation never took place. If anyone inquires about this arrangement, the trail will never lead here," he said, looking directly at the Cajun.

"I'm comfortable with that," said Quentin. They continued to talk about "the arrangement" until Roosevelt said that Quentin should share his progress and activities with Hopkins. Quentin nodded and smiled at Hopkins. The two men locked eyes and silently agreed to what the president had recommended. Then, the Cajun looked at his watch and said he had a train to catch.

As Quentin was about to leave, Roosevelt took his hand and said, "I can't tell you how much I appreciate what you'll be doing, Quentin. This assignment can be dangerous. If the Nazis ever find out you're behind this, there's no telling what they might do."

Quentin smiled and said, "You forget, Mr. President, the Germans have shot at me before."

"All that aside," said the president, "be careful."

CHAPTER 4
THE GATHERING STORM

And blood in torrents pour in vain—
always in vain,
For war breeds war again.
John Davidson, *War Song*

The flight to Paris was delayed by stormy weather over the North Atlantic and then by increased scrutiny at the London airport. The war, even though there was no appreciable fighting between the Germans and the Allies, had resulted in tightened security and an intensive examination of all flights over Great Britain and into France. Florence was with them, even though Quentin initially objected to her joining them. However, Marlon and Kendall Valderano had supported her pleas and finally convinced the Cajun to relent.

Quentin liked Kendall Valderano, Ruben's attractive and charming son. The Cajun had taught Kendall to fly, and it was something of a relief for him, Hardy, and Mark to sit back and watch the three young flyers pilot the Amelie.

Kendall was eighteen, tall, handsome, with wavy dark brown hair and engaging green eyes. He had been born in England. Glinda, his mother, was a beautiful and talented British actress and singer in London. When Ruben first met her, she was a sensual dancer with ambitions to become a leading singer and actress in the theater. Her first encounters with Ruben Valderano were filled with awe because of his savoir faire and wealth. When they became intimate, the Mexican's lovemaking triggered intense stimulation that unlocked hidden passions in the young Englishwoman. Glinda became pregnant by accident, and, when Ruben proposed marriage, she consented, and they were wed. During her fifth month of pregnancy, she had to put aside her work in the theater. Soon after Kendall was born, tensions developed between her and Ruben. The young Englishwoman was not prepared or willing to be a full-time mother. She told Valderano that her goal was to become a top actress in the theater. Glinda became obdurate and rebuffed Ruben's efforts to reach a mutual accord. Her stubbornness resulted in an impasse and they finally decided to end the marriage. When they divorced, Ruben managed to gain custody of Kendall. He spared no expense to make certain that his son was tutored to be highly educated and cultured. Kendall attended the best preparatory schools and was privately tutored, learning to speak four languages flawlessly: Spanish, English, French, and German. He was a bright, charming, and considerate young man and part of the 1939 entering freshman class at Harvard University.

As a boy, Kendall traveled everywhere with his father. They moved to Paris temporarily, and it was there that Kendall and Marlon met and became good friends. Later, Ruben and Kendall relocated to New York City where, in time, the elder Valderano married Julia Geldersman, a wealthy widow and a close friend of Eleanor Roosevelt. When Quentin brought Marlon to New York, the two boys renewed and strengthened their friendship. Although they were almost four years apart in age, the two were close, and Kendall deferred to Marlon as if he was an older brother.

When the Amelie touched down at the airport near London, Quentin taxied the plane to a hangar where a dark sedan was waiting. The Cajun turned off the engines and switches and had Mark and Hardy do the ground check and clearance for their flight to Paris while he,

Marlon, Florence, and Kendall walked toward the waiting sedan. A chauffer dressed in dark livery opened the car's back door, and a handsome woman stepped out and opened her arms to receive the embrace of her only son. Glinda Pennington was a beguiling woman, attractive and alluring, with raven-colored hair cut short to accentuate delicate facial features. She was tall and slender with a beautiful face and large, expressive eyes. She fought back tears as she hugged Kendall. They whispered to each other, and then she kissed her son on the lips.

"Hello, Glinda," said the Cajun.

"Quentin," she replied, "how kind of you to bring me my son." She extended her arm to the Cajun, who took it and kissed the back of her hand.

"Marlon and Florence, my how you've grown," she said with a smile. "Florence, you're lovely," she said, her voice full and expressive, embracing the young blonde and kissing her on both cheeks. "And, Marlon, you are more handsome every time I see you," she said before kissing him on the cheek. "Will you stay awhile?"

"I'm afraid not," said the Cajun. "Perhaps on the way back," he told her.

"Please do," she said sincerely. "I'll have tickets for all of you to attend my show."

"Daddy!" exclaimed Florence. "Please say we will."

The Cajun smiled and said he could not refuse. They talked awhile longer, Glinda holding her son's arm before Mark approached them with Kendall's bags.

"We need to get going, boss," said Mark.

Quentin nodded and told Glinda when they would return. After saying their good-byes, Marlon, Florence, and Quentin joined Mark and Hardy in the Amelie. Kendall and Glinda watched as Quentin started the engines and waited for them to warm. He received clearance from the tower and taxied away slowly from the hangar as Glinda waved at them with one hand, holding Kendall's hand with the other. The silver plane was airborne quickly and disappeared into the twilight headed east for Paris.

* * *

Nadine was waiting at Le Bourget Airfield, northeast of Paris. It was an emotional moment for Marlon and Florence as they watched the gorgeous French woman approach them. Nadine hugged and kissed both of them, her eyes moist from the encounter. *How marvelous,* thought the Cajun, *that she loves both of them so much and that Florence is like her own daughter.* Nadine kissed the Cajun on the lips and whispered something to him, which evoked an enormous grin. She turned and greeted Hardy and Mark and told them the name of their hotel, which made both of them smile with genuine satisfaction. They had mentioned to Quentin that their previous stay at the hotel Nadine selected had been very comfortable and enjoyable. She said that a car would take the two crew members to the hotel and be available for their use. Then, she took Quentin and the children to her sedan where their bags had been loaded.

"Let's go home," she said to the driver, who put the large sedan in gear and moved away from the private hangar toward the central part of Paris. "Tonight, we will celebrate," said Nadine as she ran her slender fingers through Marlon's hair and looked affectionately at Florence.

"I'm either the luckiest man in the world," said Quentin, "or a forgotten wretch."

At this, Florence punched her father on the arm affectionately and huffed that he was being a pill, while Marlon turned to look and smile at his father.

Nadine reached across, took his face in her hands, and said, "Patience, Cherie, your time will come."

At this, all of them laughed.

That evening, after they had dinner, Marlon encouraged Florence to play the piano.

"Yes, my dear, please do," said Nadine.

Florence beamed and nodded. Marlon took her by the hand, and, together, they walked to the lovely grand piano in the music room.

"Please play Chopin," Marlon whispered, his soft breath lingering in Florence's ear.

She turned and smiled at him in a sly way and said, "*Mais oui.*"

* * *

The day after they arrived in Paris, Nadine asked Moira and one of her friends to take Florence shopping and sightseeing. After they departed, Quentin, Marlon, and Nadine sat to talk. Nadine, looking directly at Marlon, asked if he was considering enlisting in the French military.

"I've been thinking about it," he said while looking into his mother's eyes.

"When?" she asked.

"I'm not certain," he replied, a barely perceptible frown visible on his young face.

"You should complete your studies at MIT," said Quentin, glancing at Nadine.

Did the two of them talk about this last night? thought Marlon, looking first at his mother and then at the Cajun. He waited for Nadine to say something, but, instead, she remained quiet, waiting him out.

After what seemed like an eternity, Marlon finally spoke. "I'll finish up at MIT before enlisting in the French air service," he told them.

"You'll graduate in May," Quentin commented, knowing the date would be of interest to Nadine.

"Around the beginning of May," he replied.

"Bon," said Nadine, "there is still hope that diplomatic efforts might prevail. There may not be any more fighting," she said, trying to sound upbeat. They could see that Marlon was unconvinced.   "Uncle Louis will be here tomorrow," said Nadine. "Maybe you should wait and talk with him."

Marlon nodded and smiled, looked away from his mother and waited for his father to add something. When Quentin remained silent, he decided to be forthright. "It'll be good to see Uncle Louis. But, if the Boche invade France, I'll volunteer," he said with resolve.

"Very well," said Quentin. "I trust you'll want to be a fighter pilot?" he inquired. Marlon nodded. "Then promise that before you volunteer to fly for the French, you'll let me prepare you for combat."

Marlon didn't respond, contemplating his father's request.

Nadine held her tongue until she could be alone with Marlon. She wanted to try to appeal his decision about volunteering. While she was proud of Marlon for wanting to enlist in the French air service, something deep within her feared a negative outcome. Hostilities between the Allies and the Boche would lead to casualties. They continued to discuss the situation between Germany and the Allies before Marlon decided to go shopping for Christmas gifts.

When they were alone, Nadine looked at Quentin and, in a serious voice, asked what he was thinking.

"You mean about Marlon's decision to join the French military?"

"Oui," she said, waiting for him to speak up.

"Well, of course I don't want him going off to war, but we must consider a few things," he said.

"Such as?" she asked.

"It might be difficult for him to go through normal channels to enlist," he stated. "He is, after all, an American citizen, and the U.S. does not approve of her citizens enlisting in and fighting for a foreign nation."

"But you did," she shot back. "And he was born here and is French," she added adamantly.

"Yes, he does have something akin to dual citizenship," said the Cajun before continuing. "But, the French might have more than enough pilots ready for combat duty. If so, there will be little demand for volunteers, especially those from another country," he told her.

"And?" she asked expectantly.

"Even if he does enlist in the French military, he'll have to go through training, especially if he wants to be an officer and fly. That could take months. And there may be a priority for bomber pilots over fighter pilots," he told her.

"Why is that important?" she queried.

"Marlon wants to be a fighter pilot. He doesn't want to fly bombers," said the Cajun.

"So if he is not promised service as a fighter pilot he might not enlist?" she asked, her large expressive eyes focused on the Cajun, eager to hear something positive, any possibility that might prevent her son from joining the French military and going to war.

He nodded at her before saying that it would be best for Marlon to speak with Louis and others such as Raoul Mendeville.

"Oh, Cherie, I'm so afraid for our son," she told the Cajun as he embraced her.

"Then pray that diplomacy prevails and war with the Boche is avoided," he whispered in her ear. But, deep inside, Quentin believed the Nazis would attack France and the British Expeditionary Force (BEF). *I hope the Allies can defeat the Boche when hostilities start,* he thought.

The following afternoon, Louis Bondurant arrived in Paris. Quentin and Marlon were at the *gare* to meet his train. When the old soldier emerged from his coach,

Marlon noticed stiffness in the way the old soldier walked. Bondurant was into his eighties, but he looked remarkably fit for his age, except for the way he was walking. As they drove to Arlene and Edmund's home for dinner, Marlon asked Louis how he was doing. The old soldier, proud and composed, said he was well. That was when Quentin inquired about his walk.

"It's nothing," said Louis brusquely, "just a mild strain." But Quentin sensed otherwise. They talked about Louis's estate, La Croisiere, near Limoges. The old soldier seemed preoccupied with something but managed to answer their questions about his crops, the production of his vines, and the ceramics plant that he and Nadine owned in Limoges. By the time they arrived at the la Fleche de Beauvais home talk of the war monopolized their conversation. Marlon, in particular, asked questions about military preparations by the French, and the old general replied with restraint that France's future was in the hands of "weak and indecisive" functionaries who were little more than addlebrained bureaucrats.

"If the Boche attack," asked Marlon, "will we prevail?"

"It's all in God's hands," said the old soldier evasively.

Marlon then suspected the worst. He turned and looked at Quentin and saw annoyance in his eyes, not for what Louis had said, but for what Marlon believed was the truth. *Dad and Louis don't think the French will do well against the Boche*, he thought.

By the way Marlon was looking at him, Quentin decided to talk privately with his son about what might happen if the Boche invaded France. Just before they arrived at the home of Nadine's parents, Quentin changed the subject.

"Louis, you cannot imagine how much Florence has grown and how she has changed," the Cajun said.

"Really," said the old general, a twinkle returning to his blue eyes. "Tell me about her."

"She's a beautiful young woman, and her musical talent is constantly improving," he said, looking at Marlon for confirmation. "Wouldn't you say, son?" the Cajun pressed Marlon.

After a pause, Marlon knew what his father expected and complied. "Uncle Louis, she's special. You won't recognize her. But," he warned in a playful way, "we don't want to spoil her."

At this, the three of them laughed aloud. A moment later, they entered the la Fleche de Beauvais driveway and were soon welcomed into the large foyer of the elegant old home.

As the three men shed their coats, hats, and gloves, Florence appeared with an enormous smile. She went straight for the old soldier and hugged and kissed him on both cheeks with gusto. The old general stood straight and smiled in a way that made him feel twenty years younger.

"My dear girl," said Louis, "you're a lovely creature."

Florence smiled, took the old soldier by the arm, and said he was her favorite chevalier.

"Be careful with her, Uncle Louis," said Marlon, "she's still a freckled-faced little girl trying to masquerade as a woman."

"Hush, you boorish boy," chided Florence as she led Louis to where the others were seated. "We've had enough of your adolescent envy."

But, as she did so, Quentin noticed the wink she gave her brother. *They love each other,* thought the Cajun, pleased that his children could be so charming and still find ways to tease each other.

Nadine, waiting at the doorway to the sitting room, hugged and kissed Louis.

"You continue to delight this old soldier with your timeless beauty," said Louis, as Nadine took his arm.

The three of them walked into the sitting room where Arlene, Edmund, Raoul, and Eunice Mendeville were seated. Next to them were Desirée and Bertrand. Seated across from them were Christine and Armand. They all rose to greet Louis. Desirée and Christine embraced and kissed the old general while Bertrand and Armand greeted him.

The conversation livened up as Nadine asked Louis about the new estate bottled wines from his vineyards. He smiled and said several cases of the latest vintage were put aside for all of them.

"It is an excellent vintage," he told them with a smile. "But it will need to mature for about five years."

They talked about different things until Bertrand mentioned the war.

Christ, thought a quiet Marlon, *I hope talk about the war doesn't turn ugly.* He shot a quick glance at Quentin and noticed that he was staring at the blaze in the fireplace.

The Cajun also wanted to avoid a long discussion about the war. Yet, he needed to learn about any new French preparations or diplomatic activities. Raoul mentioned a few things he'd learned at the air service, along with the offer of a senior staff position with the rank of full colonel.

"Will you take it?" asked Bertrand.

"I'll consider it, but not before February," he replied.

"Why then?" asked Louis.

"I've business matters to attend before joining the military," said Raoul.

"What exactly will your duties be at the air service?" asked Armand.

Raoul answered that it would be mainly planning and logistics.

"Good for you," said Louis. "They need a fresh voice and someone of your caliber."

After some further discussion about the war, Quentin whispered something to Nadine.

"Florence, would you mind playing something for us?" she asked.

"Yes, please do," said Marlon, relieved that his mother had done something to end the discussion about the war.

"Of course," replied the young blonde. "What would you like to hear?"

"Mozart," said Marlon.

This elicited a smile from his sister, and she extended her arm toward him. He stood, and the two of them walked into the music room to the grand piano. Nadine, holding Louis's arm, with Quentin in tow, walked with the others to the music room. Marlon lifted the leaf and propped it open while Florence opened the lid to the keyboard. She patted the seat next to her, and Marlon sat beside her.

Florence played a lovely rondo by Mozart and then a sonata by Chopin before playing a lively song by an English composer. During the third piece, Arlene's maid appeared and whispered that dinner was ready. Arlene stood and clapped after Florence finished playing and announced that dinner was ready.

During the meal, the conversation was lively and enjoyable. Bertrand did a few sleight of hand tricks to amuse them. Even Louis got into a festive mood and recited some poetry. When dinner was over, Nadine spoke to Florence and asked if she would mind playing again.

Nadine led all of them to the music room where, once again, Florence motioned for Marlon to sit next to her on the piano bench. Once he was seated at her side, she began playing. Florence played several Christmas carols, and Nadine and Christine handed out small leaflets with the lyrics to the carols. As they sang or hummed the familiar songs, each one pondered the future. It was almost midnight when Nadine informed her parents and Louis that they were leaving. The others thanked Arlene and Edmund for a delightful evening and praised Florence for her flawless and enjoyable piano playing.

After they arrived at Nadine's home, Quentin mentioned that he was tired and ready to retire. Nadine smiled and glanced at her lover and said she would escort him to prevent his becoming lost. He loved it when she teased him. Florence and Marlon looked at each other and giggled.

"It's been a long day. Don't stay up too late," the Cajun chided them in a friendly way.

"I'll be along in a few minutes," said Marlon, before turning to look at his sister, seated in a large overstuffed chair in the sitting room, her eyes focused intently on him.

She's so beautiful and mature, he thought as he gazed at Florence.

Quentin too noticed how lovely and grown up his daughter appeared. It was hard to believe she was just sixteen. Sitting in the shadows of the sitting room, the low light added an air of mystery that momentarily transformed Florence into the image of Ione. Quentin turned away, took Nadine's arm, and walked upstairs with her. But, his thoughts were of Ione and how much Florence resembled her. He felt as if Ione was present, and the thought caused a shiver. Try as he might, the Cajun could not erase Ione's image from his mind.

Nadine sensed something in Quentin. When they got into bed, she asked if anything was wrong. "Please, Cherie, I know you're preoccupied with something. Won't you tell me what it is?"

"It's Florence," he confessed. "She looks so much like Ione."

"Why does that disturb you?" she asked.

"I don't know," he replied evasively.

"Ione was a beautiful woman and very talented," Nadine told him softly. "You should be happy that she gave life and beauty to Florence and a marvelous gift. But, Florence is like you too," she added. "I see so much of you in her," said the lovely French woman.

They talked about Florence and Marlon briefly before Nadine lit a candle and turned off the lights. Then, she touched the Cajun in a way that she alone knew and aroused him.

After Nadine and Quentin left the music room, Marlon sat next to Florence and told her how grown up she looked and praised her piano playing. "You played beautifully tonight," he told her.

"Did you really think so?" she said in a low voice with inflections that sounded different to him.

Her voice was strangely appealing. It didn't sound like his little sister speaking. To change the subject, he said she was changing before his eyes.

"You mean I'm not Funny Face anymore?" she teased. He shook his head and chuckled. She laughed before extending her hand, which he took in his. They sat not saying anything to each other, her eyes probing his face. Finally, Florence spoke to him softly. "You're going to join the French army, aren't you?" she asked tenuously.

"Maybe," he replied elusively.

"I don't want you to fight," she said in a low, serious voice.

"Why?" he asked.

"Because you might be injured or killed," she shot back.

"I'll be OK," he said, trying to be reassuring. "Dad went off to war and came through it all right."

"Oh, Marlon, I wouldn't know what to do if something happened to you," she said, her voice suddenly filled with anxiety.

He stood and motioned for her to stand and embrace him. "I don't want you to worry. Nothing bad will happen to me," he said as she buried her head into his shoulder.

"Promise me that if you go to war, you'll come back in one piece," she pleaded.

"Don't worry," he told her. But, his sister's behavior elicited mixed emotions within him.

Florence did something that surprised Marlon. Taking his head in her hands, she kissed him on the lips before rushing away to hide the tears that burst forth. Her emotional outburst perplexed Marlon, confused by nascent feelings of arousal within him. *She's my sister,* he thought, *but there's something else.* He stood alone in the doorway to the sitting room for the longest time, contemplating what had transpired between him and Florence. Try as he might to analyze and understand the incident, an attraction to Florence overrode his attempts at a logical assessment of what had transpired. Slowly, he turned off the lights and walked to his bedroom, lost in thought about his sister's behavior. But, what disturbed him most were his feelings and desires toward Florence. *Christ, what's wrong with me?* he thought to himself.

In her bedroom, Florence fell on her bed sobbing. Why did Marlon want to go to war? *It's not his war,* she thought. *Oh, Marlon, please, please don't join the army. I can't bear the thought of your dying.* She cried for a while before sitting up and thinking, *I'll talk to Daddy. He'll listen and maybe do something to stop Marlon from going to war.*

* * *

The next few days in Paris passed quickly. Nadine and Moira took Florence shopping, while Marlon and

Quentin visited extended family and friends. The next day, Quentin met with key personnel in the French air service while Marlon and Florence went shopping together and visited museums and attractions in Paris, including trips to Versailles and Fontainebleau. Two days before leaving for England, Quentin called Stoner at the American embassy. Prior to this trip, the two of them had agreed to meet and compare notes. They met for lunch at a pleasant restaurant near the opera house.

"Why so glum, sport?" asked the indefatigable Stoner.

"Something's wrong, Stony," replied the Cajun.

"Come again?" said the diplomat.

"I mean people on the street are scared. They're trying not to show it, but I can feel it," he told Stoner. "And as for the bureaucrats, some of them are hedging their bets."

"You mean prepared for war, but not for victory," said Stoner with a wry expression.

"Yes. But maybe it's also a sense of false hope that hostilities can be avoided and some kind of compromise reached," said Quentin before sipping his wine.

"Well, there's not much movement on the diplomatic front," Stoner said dryly. "The Germans are stalling. I think they're waiting for good weather."

"Any inside intelligence on what the German army is up to?" asked Quentin.

"Some. We get bits and pieces of information, mainly that they're moving troops and mechanized units toward the border with France," said the diplomat as he bit into a piece of tender veal. "What have you heard?"

Quentin shared what he knew and his impressions that the French were waiting for the Boche to attack rather than take the offensive. "It's not a good strategy," he told Stoner.

The two men talked until they finished their meal. Stoner asked Quentin if he had heard from Healy Rohwer.

"No," he replied. "Why do you ask?"

"Well, sport, she came through here recently, on her way back from Berlin. I think she's in Italy now. But, while in Germany, she wined and dined some senior military officers and learned a few things. We missed each other, but she left me a message. She'll be in New York at the end of the month and wants to see you."

"Really?" said the Cajun, trying to mask his curiosity. He knew Stoner wanted to know what Healy had learned in Germany. Rather than pursue the topic, the Cajun looked at the diplomat, nodded, and smiled.

Stoner got the nonverbal message and changed the subject by asking about Nadine, Florence, and Marlon. Quentin told him they were all well. In turn, he asked Stoner if he had spoken with Nadine recently.

"Why yes, as a matter of fact," said the diplomat. "She's sponsoring a Polish family that escaped the Nazi invasion."

"How's that going?" asked the Cajun.

"Well, we've (State Department) done our share, and the five of them are leaving for New York as soon as we can book passage for them," he said.

"If it's a matter of money," said Quentin.

"No, it's finding space for them on a U.S. liner. We don't want them going on a French or British ship."

"Why?" asked Quentin.

"We're neutrals. So far, the Germans have kept their distance from us. But we don't want Polish refugees on an Allied ship that might be engaged by a German U-boat or raider."

Quentin nodded.

When their coffee was served, a dark, rich, fragrant brew, Stoner asked when Quentin was returning to the United States.

"We're leaving day after tomorrow, but we're stopping in London before heading home," he told Stoner.

"Business or pleasure?" asked the curious diplomat.

"Both," said Quentin. "I'm meeting with people in the British Air Ministry. Geoffrey Barries-Cole Hawkins has promised to introduce me to Sir Cyril Newall, chief of the air staff, and Air Marshal Hugh Dowding."

"Ah, yes, Dowding is air chief marshal and in charge of fighter command for the Brits. Geoff went through Camberley (the United Kingdom's army senior staff officers college) and came out a brigadier general," said Stoner. "By the way, did you know his wife died recently?"

"I didn't know," confessed the Cajun, a pained expression crossing his face.

Stoner nodded and looked away before saying, "She died a few months ago of cancer. When you meet with him, pass along my condolences." He paused a moment before changing the subject. "You did say something about personal matters?" inquired the diplomat.

"Yes," replied the Cajun, still absorbing the news of Geoff's wife's death. He felt a twinge of sadness and remembered what it had been like to lose Ione. Putting aside that thought, he said, "I'm picking up Kendall Valderano. He's been staying with his mother."

"Glinda Pennington, a lovely successful actress and singer," said Stoner, "and a very charming woman. I still find it hard to believe that she and Ruben were married and then divorced. She's never remarried," mused the diplomat. "But how is Kendall?"

"He's eighteen and in his first year at Harvard," replied the Cajun while looking at his watch.

"Well, give Kendall and his mother my best wishes," said Stoner as he stood up. He noticed Quentin reach for the check. "Thank you, sport, for taking care of the bill. I suspect you'll manage to take it off your income taxes…a business expense no doubt," he teased.

"Of course," said the Cajun casually.

Nadine was with Quentin at the airport when his family boarded the Amelie. The December weather was cold, and the dark skies threatened rain.

"Oh, Cherie, it looks so ominous," said Nadine as she looked at the dark clouds to the north.

"Yes," replied the Cajun, taking her in his arms. "But the storm is staying to the north. We'll get into London without any problems." He kissed the beautiful woman on the lips. She asked when he would return; his reply was perhaps in late February or early March. The Cajun kissed her again, turned, and climbed into the Lockheed.

Through the windows of the plane, Nadine saw Marlon wave while Florence blew her a kiss. A moment later, Quentin extended a gloved hand through his window and gave a thumbs-up. Then, she saw him close the window and heard the engines roar. The Amelie moved away and taxied to the end of the runway. In a few minutes, the silver plane lifted from the ground, gained altitude, and dipped its wings as it passed overhead and headed west. She watched until it was out of sight.

"Come back to me soon," whispered Nadine before turning away.

* * *

The weather in London was cold and damp when Quentin and his family arrived. Kendall was at the airport to greet them. The Cajun booked rooms for Hardy and Mark at a comfortable inn on the west side of London. He, Marlon, and Florence stayed at an elegant hotel close to the theater district. That evening, Kendall, Florence, Marlon, and the Cajun had a pleasant dinner and discussed plans for the following day. While Quentin met with senior staff and officers at the air service, Kendall volunteered to take Marlon and Florence on a sight-seeing tour and then shopping for clothes and Christmas presents. Kendall told them that his mother had invited them to the show in which she was starring.

After dinner, a message was delivered to Quentin that Brigadier Sir Geoffrey Barries-Coles Hawkins had called and left his number. When he returned the call, a man's voice answered and asked his name.

The Cajun identified himself and said he was returning the brigadier's call. The man asked Quentin to hold for a moment. In less than a minute, Geoff's voice came on the line.

"Quentin, how good of you to return my call."

They exchanged greetings, and Quentin expressed his condolences on the death of Lydia, the general's wife. The Cajun noticed Geoff's subdued tone when he thanked the American for his sympathy. He asked about Quentin's family and invited all of them to dinner the following evening.

"We can't," said the Cajun. "We're going to the theater as guests of Glinda Pennington."

"Can't top that, old boy," said Geoff. "But how about the following night?"

Quentin replied affirmatively. Then, they talked about the meetings that Geoff had arranged.

"I'll send my car for you," said Geoff. "I'm afraid we'll monopolize your time for most of the day. You will be my guest for lunch. But, rest assured, transportation to your hotel will be arranged for no later than four in the afternoon."

"That'll be fine," said Quentin.

The next morning, a driver met Quentin and drove him to the air ministry. Geoff greeted Quentin warmly, and they walked arm in arm to his office. The Englishman walked with a limp and used a cane. Quentin remembered his first meeting with Geoff. It was early in 1917 before America entered the First World War. Geoff had been a pilot in the Royal Air Corps and had been wounded, a severe hip injury that ended his combat flying. They worked together and became friends, especially after the United States joined the Allies. After the war, whenever the American was in London, he'd call Geoff.

They sat in Geoff's office and chatted. Quentin volunteered information about France's preparations to repel a German attack, and the French air service. Even though the Cajun tried to be positive, Geoff could sense the American's reservations.

"We're a bit concerned about our French allies," said Geoff, to test his hunch about the American's incertitude.

"Why?" asked the Cajun.

The brigadier mentioned lack of cooperation between the two militaries, particularly regarding air support. Quentin pursued the matter and learned that the British wanted France to join them in a series of offensive thrusts against the Germans.

"On the ground or in the air?"

"On the ground," replied the general.

"I gather that won't happen," tested the Cajun.

The Englishman nodded and looked away for a moment.

"You know the Germans are preparing for an offensive in the spring," he told the brigadier.

Again, Geoff nodded silently.

Quentin changed the subject and asked how Frank Whittle was doing with his jet engine.

"Actually, quite well," said Geoff. "Your financial support for his research is appreciated. Air ministry funds for Whittle's project are limited."

"If he needs more money, let me know, and I'll make the necessary arrangements for the added funds."

"That's grand of you," said Geoff. "I'll ask Whittle what he may need and let you know."

Quentin asked if any plans were under way to adapt it to a plane.

Geoff looked intently at his friend and shook his head.

The Cajun smiled. *Geoff knows more than he's willing to share,* thought the American. He decided to share the intelligence he'd received about the successful flight of a German jet plane. He mentioned the collaboration between Dr. Hans von Ohain, a German pioneer in jet engine technology, and Ernst Heinkel, the airplane manufacturer.

"Really!" exclaimed Geoff, reacting to Quentin's news. "Have they got a prototype?"

Quentin told him that Flight Captain Erich Warsitz had flown the Heinkel He 178 successfully on August 27, 1939. "The Nazis are moving ahead with plans to build a jet fighter."

"Is this information reliable?" asked the Englishman.

Quentin nodded and said the information was accurate and that he had verified the story.

"Well, that does put matters into a different perspective," said the brigadier. "We've heard rumors that Jerry (Germans) is dabbling with jet propulsion."

"I think they're doing a little more than dabbling," said the Cajun with a smile.

Just then, there was a knock on the door, and a uniformed staff officer poked his head into the room and announced that Sir Cyril Newall, chief of the air staff, was expecting them.

"Jolly good," said Geoff, standing and extending his arm to the American. "Let's not keep Sir Cyril waiting."

Sir Cyril Louis Norton Newall was born in India in 1886. He fought in World War I as a pilot in the Royal Air Corps (later becoming the Royal Air Force), eventually becoming a wing commander. After the war, he was promoted to senior roles in the British military, and, in 1937, he was appointed to chief of the air staff, the military head of the Royal Air Force (RAF). Newall had been briefed on Quentin Norvell and was impressed by the American's victories in the air during the Great War. They'd met briefly on three occasions, but this day he looked forward to talking with the American at length about the war and the role of airplanes in combat.

"Good to see you again, Norvell," said Newall, extending his hand in a friendly greeting.

"Always a pleasure to see you again, Sir Cyril," said the Cajun, smiling at the other man.

"Please, be seated," said Newall, motioning to a comfortable-looking overstuffed leather chair. "Will you have some tea?"

"I'd prefer coffee," said the American. Newall chuckled and asked an aide to bring them some tea and coffee. Newall motioned for Geoff to sit next to him.

"What brings you to England?" asked Newall.

"Business and pleasure," replied the Cajun.

"It seems he has the attention of Glinda Pennington. He's attending her show this evening," said Geoff.

"Well," said Newall with a big grin, "that alone makes the trip worth it. Have you seen her perform?"

Quentin mentioned that he knew Glinda and had brought Kendall, her son, on his plane.

"I didn't know she was married," Newall said, a puzzled expression on his face.

"Actually, Sir Cyril, she's divorced," he volunteered. "Her former husband is General Ruben Valderano."

"Then General Valderano is the boy's father?" asked Newall. Quentin nodded. "Valderano is quite an authority on modern warfare. I've read his books," said Newall, canting his head to a shelf where Quentin saw three of Ruben's books.

"He mentions you in his recent ones," said Geoff.

Quentin smiled modestly.

They talked for a while about Ruben Valderano, Glinda Pennington, and their son Kendall.

"I've seen Miss Pennington perform," said Newall. "She's damned talented and a lovely woman."

"Yes," said the Cajun, "she is a beautiful woman. Would you like to meet her?"

"By Jove, I'd like that," said Newall.

"I'll make the arrangements," said the American. He turned toward Geoff and said, "I can arrange for the two of you to meet her. Interested?"

"Of course!" exclaimed the Englishman, a huge smile on his face.

Quentin knew that both Newall and Geoff were widowers and was positive Glinda would enjoy meeting them.

Newall smiled briefly before lifting his head a bit and saying, "I do appreciate your offer to introduce us to Miss Pennington. Thank you. But, now, you mentioned something about business. May I inquire in what capacity you are visiting?"

"Do you mean am I here officially, or something less formal?" replied the Cajun.

"Are you here officially?" asked Sir Cyril.

"Let's say that I am here as an unofficial observer, but I able to transmit information about my visit to senior members of my government," said the Cajun.

"High-level elected officials?" teased Newall.

Quentin nodded. "Let me be candid, Sir Cyril. Senior leaders in our government are very interested in the welfare of Great Britain. Let us say that, even though we are neutrals, I and others in the United States would like to find ways to be of assistance to your country. Our support, however, must be confidential and any transmittal of resources kept secret," said Quentin, shooting a quick glance at Geoff, who was nodding his head and smiling.

"I understand," said Newall. "And what kind of support might we expect from you and your friends?"

"Credit and large sums of money when needed; and an alternative communications conduit that can operate, when necessary, without bureaucratic entanglements," said the Cajun.

"I take it this kind of arrangement will not involve political apparatus?" tested Sir Cyril.

"Correct," replied the Cajun.

"I'll need to think about this," said the Englishman.

Quentin nodded to indicate he agreed.

"But what advantage will there be in such an arrangement for you?" he asked.

Quentin smiled and looked at Sir Cyril and Geoff before saying, "I'm a businessman and interested in a profit. But, I also want to be a good friend to your country. We have common goals. Shall we leave it at that?"
Newall looked at Quentin for the longest time before a big grin appeared on his face. "I rather like your approach, Norvell. I'm certain we can do 'business.'" Newall rose, approached Quentin, and extended his hand.

They talked for a while about military matters, then aircraft, and the squadrons of Hurricanes that were sent to France.

Geoff praised Quentin's support for Frank Whittle's research on jet propulsion but didn't mention anything about the flight of the German jet plane in August.

Quentin was convinced the two of them would discuss it later.

At a little after twelve noon there was a knock on Sir Cyril's door, and an aide informed the chief of the air staff about a luncheon engagement.

"Very well," said Newall. "I hope we see each other again soon, Norvell. Anything I can do to help while you're here, just tell Geoff. I hear you're meeting with 'Stuffy' and Keith Park."

Stuffy? Who's that? wondered the Cajun.

"Yes, we're having lunch with Air Chief Marshal Dowding and Air Vice Marshal Park," said Geoff.

"Splendid," said Newall. "I wish I could join you, but two MPs and their committee chairs insist on hearing me report what they already know," said Newall dryly. "Good to see you again, Norvell. Don't be a stranger." He turned and walked out of the office with Quentin and Geoff.

Newall's aide appeared with the chief of the air staff's hat, coat, gloves, and silk scarf.

Geoff took Quentin's arm, and the two of them walked back to the brigadier's office.

* * *

As Quentin and Geoff walked to the Englishman's office, the brigadier whispered how intrigued and pleased he was by the American's proposition.

"Care to fill me in on what you have in mind?" asked Geoff.

"Sure," said the American with a smile, "but you'll have to buy me lunch."

"Deal," said the Englishman enthusiastically.

"By the way," asked Quentin, "who's Stuffy?"

Geoff chuckled and said it was a friendly nickname given to Air Chief Marshal Dowding by his loyal subordinates.

Half an hour later, Geoff and Quentin entered an elegant private dining room in a facility near the British Air

Ministry. Waiting for them were two RAF officers. Geoff introduced the American to Air Chief Marshal H.C.T. Dowding and Air Vice Marshal Keith Park of the RAF. Quentin had met Park before when he visited England and flew test flights in a Hurricane and a Spitfire.

"Good to see you again, Norvell," said Park extending his hand to the Cajun.

Dowding appeared reserved, but he smiled politely as he shook the American's hand. They exchanged greetings before sitting down to have lunch.

Quentin asked Dowding about his service with the Royal Flying Corps during the Great War. The older man did not smile, but the American noticed a twinkle in his eye.

"Yes, I flew during the war, but I didn't have as distinguished a career in the air as you did," commented the air chief marshal, his features softening a bit. "I recall reading about your exploits, especially how you captured a German pilot, a chap by the name of von Kleist. Highly commendable."

"Yes," said Geoff, "he was a celebrated ace and had earned the Blue Max (highest honor and medal that a German pilot could earn during World War I).

"Baron Nicholas von Kleist is now a general in the German Luftwaffe," the American informed them. The three Englishmen glanced at each other quickly before Geoff asked the question Quentin expected.

"Have you seen von Kleist recently?"

"No," replied Quentin, sipping on his water. "But maybe I'll get a chance to meet him next year."

"Planning a trip to Germany, are you?" asked a curious Dowding.

"I'm trying to get permission to visit Germany early in the spring," he replied, looking directly into Dowding's clear blue eyes.

"Business or pleasure?" probed Dowding.

"A bit of both," said the American. "But, I'd rather talk about the friendship and support I, and a group of Americans, can offer the air service." Dowding and Park glanced at each other furtively while trying to appear nonchalant.

"Let me be direct," said the Cajun and shared parts of his discussion with Sir Cyril. Price listened attentively and did not move a finger, while Dowding pretended to pick at his food. However, Quentin noticed that when he mentioned the possibility of providing large sums of money for use by the air service, Dowding stopped what he was doing and looked directly at him.

After Quentin finished talking, Geoff, to change the subject, asked a question that began a lively discussion. They discussed the capabilities of the Hurricane as a fighter.

Quentin quickly mentioned his preference for the Spitfire. "It's the most impressive fighter I've ever flown."

"How do you think it will match up against the Messerschmitt Bf 109?" asked Price, while Dowding anticipated the American's reply.

"I think the Spitfire is a superior fighter. Its limited range is just a minor issue," said Quentin, a sly grin on his face.

The American's comment was exactly what Dowding and Price wanted to hear. There followed numerous questions and chatter about the Spitfire and other British fighters. As their time together lengthened, Quentin felt a warm friendship developing between him, Dowding, and Price. Every now and then, the American would glance at Geoff and see the twinkle in the brigadier's eyes. It was almost three in the afternoon when Geoff announced that Quentin had to leave.

"You will be back soon?" said Dowding, grinning.

"Yes, by all means," added Price. "There's so much we need to discuss."

Quentin mentioned he would try to return at the end of February or early in March. The four of them stood and shook hands. Price praised Quentin, the meal, the conversation, and Geoff for bringing them together. Something about Dowding, even though the air chief marshal was reserved, communicated a developing bond with the Cajun. It was the beginning of an enjoyable friendship.

* * *

The Amelie powered westward on the return trip to the United States. Quentin sat in the navigator's seat while Mark snoozed next to Hardy Chappelle. Marlon was flying the plane while Florence and Kendall took turns in the copilot seat. Quentin was jotting down some notes from the trip, especially his conversations with important RAF leaders like Sir Cyril, Dowding, Price, and Geoff. He talked with Glinda after her impressive performance and asked if she would meet Sir Cyril and perhaps one or two others in the air ministry. The charming woman smiled graciously, mentioned she was delighted, asked for their names and numbers, and promised to set up a luncheon with Geoff, Sir Cyril, Dowding, and Price. The evening before they departed, Glinda met with Quentin and Kendall. She told the Cajun to look after Kendall and give her love to Ruben.

Quentin saw a fleeting sadness in the attractive woman's eyes. *She's still in love with Ruben. Perhaps she regrets not being with him,* he mused.

CHAPTER 5
POINT OF NO RETURN

Wherever Germany extends her sway,
she ruins culture.
Friedrich Wilhelm Nietzsche, *Ecce Homo*

Rain and high winds delayed the flight of the Amelie in Newfoundland. The next day, now the middle of December 1939, they were airborne again and on their way to Long Island. Nineteen thirty-nine was rapidly coming to a close, and Quentin wondered about the New Year.

The holidays came and went quickly, with several parties and social events occupying the Norvells. Healy Rohwer's presence somehow made the holiday season of 1939 seem so alive and festive. The attractive and talented writer and photojournalist accompanied Florence, Marlon, and Quentin to several parties and social functions. When she and Quentin were alone, Healy shared somber stories about the German army's brutality in Poland.

"They (the Nazis) despise the Poles," she told him. "They'd just as soon shoot them as look at them," she commented dryly. "They treat the Poles almost as badly as they do the Jews. I can't begin to tell you what I saw over there," she told him angrily. "They took away my camera and exposed all the film I'd shot. Bastards!"

"What was their rationale for doing that?"

"Oh, some bullshit story about how what I had shot was sensitive military information. Yeah, as if watching them slaughter Polish soldiers and civilians indiscriminately was military information. They just didn't want the world to see what they're really like," she hissed.

"Did you happen to mention this to Herr Goebbels?" asked Quentin, curious about the response his question would elicit.

"That mealy mouth sniveling snake," she spat. "He's got to be the biggest liar in the world."

Quentin smiled and teased, "Now, now, Healy, we need to be kind to our fellow humans."

"Not that miserable shit or his delusional boss," she shot back angrily. "I know you dislike Hitler and his gang of creeps, so don't give me any crap about being charitable."

Quentin nodded and said, "Yes, I don't care for Hitler and those around him. But, I do worry about Nicholas von Kleist."

"Well," said the journalist, "he's the exception to that gang of thugs. Von Kleist has scruples and a sense of right and wrong. I know he dislikes Hitler and thinks this war is going to get out of control. He gave me something for you," she said, handing him a letter. "He'd like to see you as soon as you can manage it."

Quentin took the letter and did not open it.

They talked about von Kleist, the war, and what might happen if the Germans attacked the French.

"Well, I'm worried about that," she told the Cajun. "I dislike Hitler and his goons, but we shouldn't underestimate their military leaders."

"Care to elaborate?" said the Cajun, intrigued by the writer's comment.

"Hell, I'm not a military expert. Shit, I wish Ruben was here," she said pensively.

"Never mind Ruben," said Quentin, "tell me what you think."

"The Germans are massing troops along the Belgian border and moving large numbers of tanks and other mechanized equipment near a place called Trier across from Luxembourg. The Krauts wouldn't let me anywhere near Trier, but I managed to photograph several trainloads of tanks and heavy guns in the Rhineland on their way west. What do you make of this?" said the curly haired, strawberry blonde handing him some photographs to examine.

Quentin looked at the black-and-white photos, counted the number of tanks, and estimated that there were perhaps ten or twelve on each train that Healy had photographed.

"How many trains per day do you think are carrying tanks and going toward Trier?" asked the Cajun.

"I don't know for sure," said a pensive Healy, her bright, periwinkle blue eyes focused on Quentin, "but I'd say three or four a day, and maybe the same number at night."

Not good, thought the Cajun. *The Boche seem to be massing armored units for a quick strike through Luxembourg. I'd better talk with Ruben. He'll know what to make of this,* he thought apprehensively. "May I keep these?" asked Quentin.

Healy nodded and said, "I can blow up any of them."

Quentin said he wanted Ruben Valderano to look at the photos and hear what she had just told him.

"If you want my opinion," she said, looking intently at the Cajun, "the Krauts are getting ready to invade France through Luxembourg and Belgium. If they do, it's going to get ugly for the Allies," she said, frowning.

"Did you happen to get any information about their Luftwaffe?" asked Quentin.

"No," replied the blonde, "but maybe von Kleist has written something about that in his letter," said Healy, pointing at the unopened letter from the German.

They talked awhile longer, Quentin trying to calm down the irate photojournalist. But, Healy would not be restrained.

"Quentin, if you'd seen what I did in Poland. It was despicable! The Nazis are a bunch of sick bastards."

"Are they any worse than the Japanese?" he asked, knowing that Healy had been in China and had seen some of the atrocities by the Imperial Japanese army.

She shook her head and looked away for a moment, recalling what she had witnessed in Nanking and other parts of China. "I don't know if I'll ever forget what I saw..." She could not finish the sentence and instead started to cry.

"OK," said the Cajun, moving close to embrace and console Healy. "It's all right," he told her softly.

"I hate the Japs and the Nazis," she blurted out between sobs.

* * *

That evening, Quentin opened and read von Kleist's letter. The German wished him and his family well and asked when the American might visit Germany. The overall tone of the German's letter was friendly and positive, but there were passages in the letter that piqued the American's curiosity. He was now a general in the Luftwaffe and responsible for fighter pilot training and tactics, but he indicated he would be given a new assignment soon. The German repeated his invitation for Quentin to come to Germany.

Von Kleist wouldn't repeat himself like this unless there was something he wanted to share without others around. Guess I better go to Germany, decided the Cajun.

The next day, Quentin contacted the White House and requested a meeting with the president. A week later, he was in Washington and joined Cordell Hull, Harry Hopkins, and Stoner in Roosevelt's office.

"I need to visit Germany," said the Cajun, "as quickly as possible." When Roosevelt asked him why, Quentin said he had received an invitation from a friend in the German military.

"Anyone we know?" asked Stoner.

"I'd rather not answer that," he replied, and would say no more.

"Is this a personal matter?" asked Secretary of State Hull.

The Cajun nodded.

"You may not be welcome in Germany," said Hull. "After all," he continued, "they must know you've been to England recently and maybe that you've met with people in the British Air Ministry."

"I'll have to take that chance," replied the Cajun.

"What excuse will you use to visit Germany?" asked Hopkins.

"Synthetics," said Quentin. "The Germans are doing remarkable things with synthetics and combining them with cotton and wool. They've done wonders with rayon and have an improved form of nylon that intrigues DuPont. We don't know how far they've gotten with their new fabrics and chemistry, but our people are interested in different uses for rayon that the Germans have developed. If what the Germans are producing looks promising, a group of backers I've put together is prepared to buy some of their patents."

"Sounds good," said Stoner with a sly smile. "The Germans would like nothing better than to sell us something and improve trade with them, but do you think this will be enough to make you welcome in Berlin?"

"I've got another proposition for them, a link with the German movie industry where we'll purchase some of their films for distribution and viewing here," he told them. "There's a good market for foreign films in parts of the U.S., and I'm certain the Germans will be delighted to share some of their 'best' films with us."

"Propaganda films?" asked Hopkins, while Hull looked at the pilot intently.

"Maybe," said the Cajun, "but we'll take those along with others by Fritz Lange, Karl Hartl, Leni Riefenstahl, and Carl Boese."

"I've heard of Riefenstahl," said Hull, "but not the others you mention."

"They're all top directors, and many are eager to have some of their films distributed here," said the Cajun.

"But the films are in German," said Hull. "Won't that be a problem?"

"We can do subtitles for them."

"But won't some of the studio heads in Hollywood chafe at distributing films that may be anti-Jewish?" Hull asked.

"Those films can be conveniently held without immediate release," said Quentin with a smile. "Besides, the studio heads are looking for stars like Marlene Dietrich and Hedy Lamarr and directors like Fritz Lang. The best way to get them to come to the U.S. is to market some of their films here."

"Hedy Lamarr's German?" asked a puzzled Harry Hopkins.

"Actually," said the Cajun, "she's Austrian and was married to Friedrich Mandl, the Austrian arms dealer. She's really quite bright and a whiz at mathematics."

"Really?" said Roosevelt with a big grin. "But, she's certainly one of the most beautiful women in Hollywood."

The Cajun mentioned that Lamarr divorced Mandl and went to London where Louis B. Mayer met and signed her to a film contract.

"Hedy Lamarr has stiff competition in Hollywood from Ingrid Bergman and Katherine Hepburn. However, she's more intelligent than either Bergman or Hepburn."

"Hmm," muttered Stoner, "you certainly know the movie business and some of its leading personalities."

"Well, it does look like you have legitimate reasons to visit Berlin," said Hopkins. "But, you said something about meeting with someone in Berlin. Care to share who it is?"

The Cajun wanted to protect von Kleist and replied carefully that he had a reliable contact who was also a senior officer in the German military. At this, Stoner and Roosevelt looked at each other before the president spoke up.

"Is your contact in Germany willing to help you meet the people you need to while you're over there?" he asked.

The Cajun smiled and nodded at Roosevelt. "All right," said the president, "what do you need from us?"

Quentin mentioned having someone in the American embassy in Berlin work with him. "It would help if people in the embassy there (Berlin) speak to the appropriate people about my visit."

"I'm certain their textile people and scientists will welcome your visit, especially if they see a possible profit," said Hull. "But, for the film things, you'll have to go through Goebbels."

"I've met him," said Quentin. "He's bright, ambitious, and very suspicious." The Cajun mentioned his previous interaction with Goebbels and the German's amorous interest in Lida Baarova, the beautiful Czech actress. "I tried to get her to come to the U.S.," said Quentin, "but it didn't work out."

"Anything happen between Goebbels and Baarova?" asked Stoner.

The Cajun said they had an affair until Goebbels' wife found out and went to see Hitler. "Hitler told Goebbels to break it off with Baarova," said the Cajun.

"Tough to fight city hall," said Hopkins.

"All right," said Roosevelt. "Quentin, go and get back here as quickly as you can. While you're over there, anything—"

"Yes, Mr. President, I'll do whatever I can to gather intelligence while I'm in Germany and share what I learn with you."

Roosevelt smile and wished Quentin good luck.

* * *

The day after returning from Washington, Quentin was greeted by Sarah with a smile. His secretary looked on the verge of tears.

"Thank you so much for what you did," said a misty-eyed Sarah. "My relatives from Poland arrived yesterday. They would like to meet you and thank you for what you did."

The Cajun smiled and said he would be delighted.

A few days later, Quentin, Florence and Kathleen visited Sarah at her parents' home and met Josef and Maya Kazminsky and the three children. They could not speak English, so it was necessary for Ari, Sarah's father, to translate. The adults shared some of their experience escaping from Poland and the hardships they'd endured in Czechoslovakia and Austria before reaching Switzerland. They also mentioned how kind the beautiful Mrs. Desnoyers was. Florence played the upright piano in the Katzmanns' apartment and later encouraged one of the Kazminsky children to play *Chopsticks* with her.

Why would anyone want to harm these people? the Cajun wondered.

As Quentin, Florence, and Kathleen were leaving the Katzmann apartment, Sarah walked them to the front door and thanked all of them for coming. She noticed a sad expression on Quentin's face.

"Anything wrong?" she asked the Cajun.

"I'm just sorry we couldn't get the rest of your family out of Poland," he told her with sadness in his voice.

She hugged him and said, "We're forever in your debt, Mr. Norvell."

"Quentin," he corrected her softly.

"Old habits are hard to change," she told him with a smile before leaving them.

Florence took her father's hand and looked up at him, her bright blue eyes moist. "Daddy, you're the best."

Kathleen kissed Quentin on the cheek, and, together, the three of them walked to the car. It was starting to snow. A few days later, Quentin left for Europe.

* * *

It was bitter cold when Quentin arrived in Berlin at the end of February. His trip had gone smoothly until he reached the German border with Switzerland. There, he was questioned extensively about the purpose of his trip, even thought he had earlier been granted permission by the German Embassy in New York to visit Berlin. He was asked where he would be staying and who he would be seeing. He noticed armed guards everywhere, and military personnel monitoring the border crossing. His interrogation at the border took almost twenty minutes before he was allowed to enter Germany. It helped that he had diplomatic support to conduct business with German manufacturers and that he was meeting with Herr Goebbels. However, once he mentioned meeting with General Nicholas von Kleist, his entry to Germany was expedited.

Waiting for Quentin at the Berlin train station was Eric Kohler from the U.S. Embassy. "Good to see you, Mr. Norvell," he said, extending his hand to shake the pilot's. "I've a car waiting for us," he said, and then inquired about the Cajun's luggage. After collecting the luggage, they drove to the Cajun's hotel. "You realize you've been followed from the moment you left Portugal," said Kohler.

"Yes, I knew I was under surveillance," said the Cajun. "Good thing I didn't come through France."

"Yes," said Kohler. "I don't think the Germans would have liked that." Kohler changed the subject and mentioned appointments with people and chemists working with the new synthetics, especially the industrial uses of rayon. "They're quite anxious to meet you," said the diplomat. "They're very interested in dollars and raw materials."

"What about the film matter?" asked the American pilot.

"Ah, yes, Propaganda Minister Goebbels is *very* interested in meeting you," said Kohler. "I believe he wants 'certain' films from Germany distributed in the States. By the way," said Kohler with a smile, "Hitler and some of the Nazi brass are still smarting because of Marlene Dietrich."

"How about Hedy Lamarr?" the Cajun inquired.

"Double for her," said Kohler with a smile. "She's sure a beautiful woman. The ambassador would like to see you after you check in and freshen up."

"Good," said Quentin. "I'll catch a cab to the embassy as soon as I get settled."

"We can send a car," offered the diplomat. Quentin shook his head and said he wanted to take a taxi.

Quentin's hotel was a very elegant and tastefully appointed establishment frequented by well-to-do businesspeople and some diplomats. There was a message waiting from General Nicholas von Kleist. After checking in and unpacking, Quentin called the German.

It took a few minutes for the American to get through to von Kleist. Quentin's German was passable, but the call was screened by several people until at last the American spoke with the general's aide.

"Ah, yes, Herr Norvell, the general is expecting your call. I'll put you through," said Major Kalkenstein.

"Well, Norvell, I see you finally made it to Berlin," said the German. "Are you free for dinner tonight?" he asked.

"Yes," said the Cajun.

"We're having a few guests, some you might enjoy meeting. I'll send a car for you at 7:30. Lorelei will be delighted to see you," he said dryly.

"How is your beautiful wife, Nicky?" asked the American, baiting the German with the nickname von Kleist's wife and closest friends used.

"Frivolous as ever," replied a nonplused von Kleist. "She's anxious to see you. Why, I cannot imagine. Perhaps there is something in her Swabian background that enjoys the plebian," the German told him sardonically.

At this, the American laughed out loud and said, "Perhaps it's because I'm a better dancer than you."

"How common," replied the German, trying to affect disdain.

"Well, Nicky, Lorelei and I will have to put our heads together and find a way to loosen you up."

"How boorish," replied the general with a chuckle. "But, your ribald behavior might yet prove amusing. We dress for dinner," said the German. "I take it you've brought suitable clothing," he teased. "Otherwise, I can suggest a good tailor."

"I'll manage," said Quentin, laughing into the telephone.

It was almost six in the evening when Quentin returned to the hotel after meeting with the ambassador and some of the embassy staff. After a private conversation with the ambassador and one of his aides, he was escorted to a room where four other embassy staff personnel waited, one the military attaché and the other a military observer. Quentin surmised that the other two were intelligence personnel. The discussion at first centered on the Cajun's visit to Berlin and the people he was scheduled to meet. After a while, the military attaché changed the subject to discuss the war between Germany and the Allies. Quentin mentioned the concentration of German troops near Trier.

"If hostilities start in the spring, the Germans will probably attack the Allies by going around the Maginot Line," said Major Conklin, a military observer.

Quentin asked if there were any new developments on the diplomatic front. The ambassador smiled and said it appeared the Germans were stalling. "Perhaps in the spring we'll know more about their intentions," said the ambassador tactfully.

So, the Germans are stalling, thought Quentin. *Hitler's going to attack the Allies in the spring.* Quentin looked at his watch and mentioned an appointment he had for that evening.

"Of course," said the ambassador. "Do you need a ride back to your hotel?" he asked.

"If it's not too much of a bother," said the Cajun.

The ambassador had Quentin driven to his hotel. As they drove to the hotel, Quentin noticed the number of men, boys, and even young girls in uniforms. *Hitler youth,* thought the American. He noticed that the Germans were going about their activities as if there was no state of war. It was quite different from what he'd seen in France, where there was a collective nervousness among the Parisians.

Quentin was waiting in the hotel foyer when a large, black Mercedes sedan pulled up. A Luftwaffe captain emerged from the car and walked into the hotel. Quentin caught his eye, and the German approached and asked if he was Herr Norvell. He nodded and greeted the captain in German, whereupon the German clicked his heels, bowed, and said he was Flight Captain Klaus Maria Stembeiler. He motioned for them to walk toward the sedan. As he entered the sedan, Quentin noticed the driver was a sergeant and also in the Luftwaffe. Once seated in the back, the captain said something to the driver, and the powerful sedan pulled away from the curb smartly and headed east. About ten minutes later, they arrived at a familiar, large and impressive home in an exclusive part of Berlin. A tall doorman wearing a heavy coat opened the car door and greeted the American politely. Stembeiler walked with the American to the door and joined him in the foyer. A moment later, Lorelei, von Kleist's Bavarian wife, greeted Quentin with a hug and a kiss.

"You are more handsome every time I see you," said the lovely German woman.

"And you are more beautiful than ever," he replied in German. She gave a radiant smile, took his arm, and they walked toward the sound of voices.

When they entered the large room, Quentin noticed that all but four of the men in the room were in military uniforms. There were several generals, three colonels, two majors, and two captains counting Stembeiler. He learned later that the other men were a military attaché, a military observer, and two intelligence personnel. The women were seated in two groups and chatting. But, when the Cajun entered the room, he felt several of them study him very carefully. The females were scrutinizing him.

"Ah, I see you made it, Norvell," he heard the familiar voice of Nicholas von Kleist address him.

"Good to see you, Nicky," said the American, teasing the German. Von Kleist, wearing the uniform of a generalmajor in the Luftwaffe, cleared his throat disapprovingly and raised an eyebrow. He stood tall and stiff and appeared to have gained some weight, and his hairline was receding slightly.

"Nicky," said Lorelei, "he told me I was beautiful. Why don't you tell me that anymore?" she teased.

"His type," said the baron with an air of insouciance "is given to flattery. It masks a common background."

Quentin laughed at the German's comments, but Lorelei said, "Really, Nicky, where are your manners! Quentin is a guest in our home. Behave yourself!" The German shook his head, clicked his heels, nodded at the American, and managed a barely perceptible smile, a hidden message passing between friends.

"Very well," said von Kleist, "let me introduce you."

"You'll do nothing of the kind," said Lorelei, taking the Cajun's arm. "If you can't be civil, I'll do the honors."

"You're too kind," said the American. "And I appreciate a lovely woman escorting me instead of someone dressed like a Brummagem doorman," teased the Cajun.

"Touché," Lorelei told the American. "It's good for Nicky to be put in his place now and then," she said with a mischievous smile. She took Quentin by the arm to meet the other guests. "By the way, what does Brummagem mean?" she whispered.

He stopped her and explained the term softly so only she could hear.

"Wunderbar!" she exclaimed, turning to glance at her husband and giving him a smug look.

The first officer that caught Lorelei's attention was Ernst Udet, a German World War I fighter ace and now a general in the Luftwaffe. Udet and Quentin had met before, and the two greeted each other as old friends.

The Cajun mentioned several of Udet's recent exploits, such as purchasing American Curtis aircraft to promote the German's strong support for dive bombers.

"Yes," said the German, "they are serviceable aircraft and will yet prove my theories about dive-bombing. But, enough of that," said Udet, as he took the American's arm and walked him to where a Luftwaffe officer was standing, listening to others talk.

"Werner, allow me to introduce Herr Quentin Norvell from the United States," said Udet.

The German officer bowed politely and momentarily appraised the American.

"This is Werner Mölder, our top ace with the Condor Legion in Spain," Udet told the Cajun. "The two of you should get on famously."

"Yes, I've heard of your victories in Spain," said the American, "congratulations."

The German smiled at Quentin, and the three of them began talking about fighters and fighter tactics. *He's bright and certainly knows his stuff,* thought the American about Mölder.

Udet mentioned that von Kleist had recruited Mölder, Günther Lützow, and Adolf Galland to work with him to develop new fighter tactics. As they talked, Quentin memorized the names of Galland and Lützow. He was impressed with Mölder and his ideas about fighter tactics. *I need to learn more about Mölder,* thought the Cajun, *and his ideas.*

Quentin noticed that Udet was holding a glass of brandy, which he refilled regularly. When the Cajun casually mentioned Udet's consumption of liquor to Lorelei, she took him aside and said, "Ernst is not particularly happy working for Erhard Milch (head of the Third Reich's Aviation Ministry RAM). Nicky can tell you more about it," she said before taking his arm and introducing him to another German general.

That evening, Quentin met Generals Albert Kesselring, Heinz Guderian, and Ewald von Kleist, Nicky's uncle. Kesselring was a bright and congenial person who grinned often and had a good sense of humor. He asked Quentin if he had met Willy Messerschmitt.

Quentin said no.

"Well, then," said Kesselring, "he's over there with the Countess von Falkenberg. Let me introduce you."

When Messerschmitt greeted Quentin, he praised the American for his knowledge of aircraft and for his victories during the Great War. They were soon chatting about airplanes and especially about Messerschmitt's Bf 109 fighter plane.

"It's a formidable fighter," said the American, "and the use of fuel injection is very creative."

"Yes, it is," replied Messerschmitt, pleased by the American's praise, "but the head of RAM is slow to realize the potential of similar engineering advances," he said with disdain.

"I gather you don't think much of Milch," said the Cajun. Messerschmitt nodded, swallowed hard, and held his tongue. *Milch is obviously someone who has frustrated Willy Messerschmitt,* thought the Cajun.

"By the way," said the Cajun, "I hear that you've mated a jet engine to a plane."

"Nein, not I," replied Messerschmitt. "You must be referring to Ohain's vacuum cleaner. You know about this?"

Quentin nodded, without revealing his precise knowledge of the flight in August 1939 by the Heinkel He 178.

"You are interested in jet propulsion?" asked Messerschmitt, his curiosity aroused.

Quentin nodded and said jet propulsion would be the basis for future aircraft engines. Messerschmitt smiled and told the American that he was a very progressive thinker. He was just about the say something else to the American when Lorelei approached.

"Willy, I must take our guest away from you," said a radiant Lorelei as she locked arms with the American and led him to where a tall, attractive general was listening to a conversation by two other officers.

"Heinz," she said with a charming smile, "I'd like you to meet Herr Quentin Norvell from the United States of America."

The German focused on Quentin and paused a moment before a hint of recognition crossed his face. Then he smiled. "I'm delighted to meet you," said Guderian.

The German was a charming man, tall, with clear blue eyes that missed nothing. He praised the American for his exploits as a fighter pilot in the Great War.

"I've read General Valderano's books on modern warfare," he told the American. "I was particularly impressed by your contribution on the coordination of tanks and airplanes," he said. "You must have had those thoughts during the Great War," he said.

Quentin nodded. "I've read your book," said the American pilot, smiling at Guderian.

"And?" asked Guderian.

"Brilliant," said the American.

Guderian chuckled, patted the Cajun on the shoulder, and said, "We must talk. It seems so few of us realize the importance of close coordination between panzers and air support."

The dinner was long and filled with numerous conversations, mainly about the German victory over Poland and the diplomatic detent with the Allies. While Quentin's German was good—he could speak and understand it hesitantly—in a social setting where conversations were rapid and new terms involved, he needed assistance. He was seated on Lorelei's left, and she helped him understand some of the conversations. From time to time,

Kesselring, sitting across from the Cajun, would smile and ask the American questions. When Quentin hesitated, Lorelei interpreted. Von Kleist looked on bemused at what Lorelei was doing. Now and then, he would answer for Quentin, something that seemed to please him.

How like Nicky, thought Quentin, *to help a poor, struggling American to understand.*

Toward the end of the dinner, after much wine had been consumed, there were numerous references to settling matters with the Allies. When Quentin asked about this, a wealthy industrialist said that Germany had regained the lands in the east it had lost under the Treaty of Versailles.

"The Fuhrer only wants what belongs to Germany," he told Quentin and the others at dinner. "And now we should recapture Alsace and Lorraine and bring them into the Third Reich where they belong," he said after draining his wine glass. There was cheering at the long table, and several officers rose and offered a toast to the inevitable victory of Germany over the Allies. Everyone rose, except Quentin. The American's action caused some murmuring, and tenseness developed among the men present.

"Ladies and gentlemen," said Nicky, "our guest is from a neutral country. He is not required to take sides. But he is a friend and someone to whom I am beholden. Anyone who questions his behavior must answer to me. Is that clear?"

Quentin noticed that Ewald von Kleist stood, along with Guderian and Kesselring, to support the baron. There was a hush in the room and nothing more about Quentin's behavior was said. After dinner, Quentin thanked Ewald von Kleist, Heinz Guderian, and Albert Kesselring for their support.

Before Quentin left, Nicky asked if he would go walking with him the next day, or the day after.

Quentin replied that he would be delighted and promised to find a suitable time for them to get together. Lorelei kissed him on the cheek and apologized for any rudeness that her guests might have exhibited toward him.

"I'd like to make this up to you," she said demurely. "Please dine with me and Nicky before you leave Berlin." The Cajun said he would be delighted to do so and kissed the baroness's hand.

* * *

Over the next two days, Quentin met with businessmen and chemists in German firms working with synthetics. He was impressed with the extensive research done on rayon and especially some of the synthetic bonding fibers developed to blend with rubber. He learned that the synthetic filaments introduced into rubber compounds added to the product's strength and gave an elasticity that was not possible with just the natural product. It prompted him to offer to purchase some of the synthetics patents. The German businessmen, while eager to do business with the American, indicated they had to discuss his offer with a senior minister in the Nazi apparatus.

"*Gleichshaltung?*"* Quentin asked tactfully.

"Ja," replied the spokesmen for the businessmen.

"Very well," said the American, "let's leave it in the hands of the Fuhrer."

There was nervous smiling and subdued approval for the American' suggestion.

The following day, Quentin met with Goebbels to discuss increasing the marketing of German films in the United States. The minister of propaganda was in rare

---

* The term means a centralizing process to bring every organ of German life directly under Nazi control.

form. Not only did Goebbels give the impression of interest in what the American proposed, but he volunteered to assist in any way possible.

"After all," said a smiling Goebbels, "we have very good friends in America who welcome the opportunity to see our films."

"Are you referring to people in the German American Bund?" asked the Cajun.

"Well," replied the sly Goebbels, "we'd like to enhance our approach to the American market."

And not have to publicly associate with either Fritz J. Kuhn or Gerhard Kunze, thought Quentin. The Cajun remembered that Kuhn and Kunze had been heads of the German American Bund, a right wing neo-Nazi political group in the United States. The organization was considered a front for the Nazi party in the United States, and two of its leaders were ardent pro-Nazis. Later, Kuhn and Kunze were discredited and indicted for crimes by the American authorities.

"Yes, I'm certain many Americans would welcome the opportunity to see German films and learn about your talented directors and actors," said the Cajun with a thin smile.

"Splendid," said Goebbels. "We will prepare a list for you, or do you have some films in mind already?"

"How kind of you," said the American. "I have a list of German directors and actors, but I will rely on you to select their best works for viewing in my country."

"Excellent," said a grinning Goebbels.

They talked about the details, and he agreed to have a list of films with their availability in Quentin's hands the next day. Then, Goebbels asked if Quentin was free for lunch that day.

Quentin nodded.

"Marvelous," said Goebbels. "I know just the place. Let me arrange it," he said, pressing a button on his desk.

An assistant appeared at the door, and Goebbels told him to make a reservation at a restaurant.

"Now," said a smiling Goebbels, "perhaps you would answer a few questions for me?" In the next hour, Goebbels tactfully asked about America's position regarding the war. Quentin replied that the United States was firmly committed to neutrality.

"My country is in an isolationist mood," he told the German. When Goebbels pressed him, Quentin smiled and said most American newspapers and conservative radio announcers didn't want the United States involved in a foreign war. Goebbels grinned and changed the subject.

"Tell me, how is Marlene Dietrich?"

The Cajun smiled and said she was doing well in America and was dating Gary Cooper. Quentin knew that Dietrich's leaving Germany was a sore point for the Nazis because she objected to the Third Reich and its brutality. But, Goebbels' question puzzled him until the German said that the Third Reich wanted Dietrich and other actors, actresses, and directors who left Germany to consider returning.

"They will be received with open arms," said Goebbels with a smile that masked something sinister. When Quentin did not comment, Goebbels moved on.

He asked about several other movie personalities; then, in a clever way, he inquired about the bias against Germany by studio heads in Hollywood. Quentin knew that Hollywood movie moguls disliked German anti-Jewish activities, but, rather than engage Goebbels on this matter, the American merely nodded and changed the subject.

At lunch, Goebbels introduced Quentin to several German industrialists and Nazi party leaders. The Nazis were polite and indicated they wanted the United States to have a good impression of Germany. Quentin managed to parry many of their questions and dealt with the others as tactfully as possible.

After lunch, Goebbels had scheduled meetings with some of the leading people in the German cinema. The talented artists Quentin met were, for the most part, upbeat about their work in cinema. However, a few were visibly nervous and cautious about saying anything to agitate the Nazis. *Poor souls,* thought the American, *to live in fear and not be able to do other than what your master wants.*

It was late in the afternoon when Quentin called von Kleist on the general's private line. Again, he heard the voice of Captain Stembeiler say, "Ah, yes, he's expecting your call." A few minutes later, the general came on the line and asked if Quentin could join him and Lorelei for dinner that evening.

"It will only be the three of us," mentioned the German.

Quentin replied affirmatively.

"Good," said the German. "Dress comfortably, but not shabbily."

The American chuckled at the friendly reproach and indicated he would wear something suitable.

"I'll send my car to your hotel. Otherwise, you might not be able to find our home," teased the German.

* * *

When the Cajun arrived at von Kleist's home, he met their eldest daughter who was just about to leave.

"Heidi," said Lorelei, "this is Herr Quentin Norvell from the United States." The lovely young woman smiled and extended her hand to the American. She was tall, perhaps five feet seven, with white teeth, large bright blue eyes, and ash-blonde hair. Quentin complimented her on being a charming young woman, and she blushed.

They exchanged pleasantries for a few moments before Heidi left.

"She is married to a lieutenant in the Kriegsmarine (German navy)," Lorelei informed the Cajun. "He is expected home in a few hours. Come," she told him, taking the American by the arm and leading him to a sitting room. "Nicky is on the telephone."

A few minutes later, von Kleist appeared, slightly annoyed.

"Anything the matter?" asked the American, but the German just waved it off and whispered something to Lorelei. She smiled and left the two men alone.

"How is your son?" asked Quentin.

"Manfred's well," replied the general. "He's enrolled in the *Kriegsakademie* (prestigious Prussian war college) and wants to train to become a fighter pilot."

"Following in your footsteps," said the American.

The German nodded before speaking. "You realize the fighting will begin anew," he told the American. Quentin nodded and waited for von Kleist to continue.

"There is little disagreement about engaging the French and the British," said the German. "But, beyond that, some of us worry that the war will escalate and involve other nations."

"Like America?" the Cajun asked.

The German shook his head. "The Soviets," replied the general. "The Fuhrer does not trust the Bolsheviks. We are at cross-purposes with them."

Quentin remained quiet.

"You should not be surprised when hostilities resume in the spring," said the German. "A diplomatic solution to our differences with the Allies is remote. You see," he said, offering the American some champagne from a chilled bottle, "we must force the Allies to accept our terms to end the war. The Fuhrer has no intention of giving back any conquered territory."

"So, Germany will attack the Allies in the spring?" said Quentin.

The German nodded and said, "Sooner."

"I don't understand," said the American, perplexed by the German's remark.

Just as von Kleist was about to say something, Lorelei entered the room and said it was time to eat. The five-course dinner that evening was beautifully presented and delicious. Quentin ate modestly, leaving parts of his meal uneaten.

The American watched his diet carefully and tried to limit his daily caloric intake. However, he noted that Nicky finished large portions of food.

After dinner, the three of them moved to a comfortable sitting room where the fireplace filled the room with warmth. They sat and talked about Quentin's trip, his appointments with the industrialists, and other meetings. However, Quentin's thoughts were elsewhere, puzzled by the German indication that an attack against the Allies would take place soon. *I wonder what he meant,* thought the Cajun. Von Kleist asked about Quentin's other appointments, and the American mentioned Goebbels. There was a disapproving look on the German's face.

"I gather you don't care for Herr Goebbels?" asked Quentin, as Lorelei looked at him over her glass of sherry.

The German didn't respond, an indication that the Cajun's assessment was correct.

"Tell us about your children?" asked Lorelei to change the subject.

Quentin mentioned that Marlon was in his last year at MIT, and Florence was finishing her final year at a preparatory school and had been offered a place in the entering class for the fall of 1940 at the Juilliard School of Music. Lorelei said she'd heard about a famous conservatory of music in New York and asked if it was Juilliard. Quentin replied affirmatively and said the Institute of Musical Art in New York City had merged with the Juilliard graduate program.

"It is one of the most competitive musical academies in my country," said the Cajun.

"We've heard your daughter play the piano," commented von Kleist. "She has a unique talent."

"Do you have a recent photo of her?" asked Lorelei. Quentin opened his wallet and produced pictures of Marlon and Florence.

"My, but your son is very handsome," said Lorelei. "And your daughter is beautiful."

"That she is," said the German. "She's inherited her beauty and talent from her mother."

At this, Quentin chuckled, which elicited a smirk from the German. However, Lorelei would not let the jab pass without comment.

"Nicky, behave yourself. Quentin's our guest. Besides, I see much of Quentin in his handsome son *and* in his charming daughter."

"So there," said the American to tease the German. The three of them laughed at the American's comment. They chatted until well after eleven o'clock when Quentin said he had to return to his hotel.

"When are you leaving?" asked von Kleist.

Quentin replied he would leave for Switzerland the following day.

"Can you join me for a walk tomorrow morning?" asked the German.

Quentin asked what time, and the general said at eight thirty. "I'll come by your hotel," said von Kleist.

Lorelei hugged and kissed the American before he left, and von Kleist reminded him of their walk the following day.

The next morning was clear but crisp, with a freshening northwest wind that warned of an approaching cold front and possibly snow. As the two men walked, von Kleist said that only in the open could he be candid.

"Colleagues of mine have been reprimanded for comments that disagreed with the foolish notions of the Fuhrer."

"Does that mean that your conversations are monitored?" asked the Cajun. The German nodded.

"Even as we speak, we are under surveillance," said von Kleist.

"I can understand why my activities in Germany are monitored," said Quentin, "but has that affected you?"

"My dear man," said the German, as they walked briskly, "all senior-level officers are under surveillance, especially those who may not agree completely with the Fuhrer."

"Have you said anything to displease Hitler?" asked the American.

"Let us say that my lack of enthusiasm for some of his ideas has not been well received by the Fuhrer or his lackeys."

"Are there others who think like you?" Quentin asked.

The German nodded.

"Kurt Tank and Willy Messerschmitt are not favored by Milch," said von Kleist with annoyance. (Kurt Tank was a brilliant aviation engineer and was designing a new potent fighter.)

"I met Werner Mölder and learned he's working closely with you."

"Yes, he's a brilliant fighter pilot," said the German casually, looking toward the sky as if to test the weather.

"But he's also a tactician," said Quentin.

"Of course," replied von Kleist. In the next few minutes, he told Quentin about Mölder's ideas and tactics.

Von Kleist is surrounding himself with very capable pilots and developing experts on fighter tactics, thought Quentin.

Rather than pursue what the German was doing and impose upon his friendship, Quentin decided to change the subject.

"Tell me about Ernst Udet?" asked the American.

The German shook his head before speaking. "I'm worried about Ernst," said von Kleist sourly. "He's drinking too much. He complains in confidence about Nazi bureaucrats and their political pandering. They're a scourge." The general was quiet for a few moments, collecting his thoughts. "While we are able to speak freely," he said, "I want to share some things with you." In the next fifteen minutes, the German told Quentin about the buildup of the Wehrmacht and particularly its panzers. He then talked about the increases in the Luftwaffe. He stressed that Goering wanted a large air force capable of extensive offensive activity. He paused for a moment, and, sensing no questions from the American, continued. "But, first, look for activity in Scandinavia," said the German.

"Germany plans to attack the Swedes?" asked the American incredulously.

"Closer than that," said the general, "then the Allies. We will prevail against them; however, the Fuhrer has aspirations in the east."

"The Soviets?" asked the American.

The general nodded and glanced at Quentin.

"But you're allies," said Quentin, surprised by von Kleist's comment.

"Try to understand," said the German, "that the Fuhrer's ambitions are misguided. He and his sycophants did not believe the British and the French would go to war over Poland. And now that we're at war, he's convinced that France must be defeated and the British forced to sue for peace."

"That will not happen," said Quentin.

"Time will tell, my friend," said von Kleist, as they approached the hotel.

"I wish you well," said the German, as they stood in front of the hotel.

"I hope all goes well for you," said the Cajun.

"Perhaps my assessments about the Fuhrer are incorrect," said von Kleist skeptically. "Deep inside, I feel a terrible tragedy about to unfold."

When Quentin returned to America, he could not forget von Kleist's last words. *Deep inside, I feel a terrible tragedy about to unfold.*

PART II

❖

THE DOGS OF WAR

CHAPTER 6
STORM SIGNALS

*And for the season it was winter, and they that
know the winters of that country know them to
be sharp and violent, and subject to cruel
and fierce storms...*
William Bradford, *Of Plymouth Plantation*

At the beginning of March 1940, Nadine received a progress report on the projects to preserve and relocate French art treasures and artifacts to safe locations. Numerous priceless paintings and smaller artifacts were already stored in safe locations, and the work of removing the stained glass from Notre Dame was well over half done. She inquired about the completion of the project at Notre Dame and learned that with added workers it could be finished by April 1940.

"Very well," she said, "make it so. Hire the necessary people, and I will cover the cost."

The following day, she met with Moira, Noel, and Millard, the latter a strong and rebellious man in his early forties. He had been recommended to her by Noel as someone loyal to France who could be trusted. She began by saying that their conversation was to remain strictly confidential.

"I've called you together because there is a way for us to fight the Boche," she said. "Regardless of the outcome of the war, we must find ways to fight the Nazis."

At this, Moira smiled, while Millard raised an eyebrow and gave his undivided attention to the lovely French woman.

"What do you propose?" asked Noel.

"We must do three things," she told them. "First, develop a secret and secure escape route from Allemagne into France and beyond."

"Where beyond France?" asked Millard.

"England, Canada, and the United States," she told them.

Millard nodded.

"Second, we must establish an intelligence network in Allemagne that will provide us with reliable information about engineers, scientists, and technicians doing military research. Third, and I hope it will not come to this, the names of men and women in France we can count on to help if France falters."

The room was silent as the others stared at Nadine. It was Millard who finally spoke up.

"I gather you suspect the Boche may defeat the Allies," Millard remarked declaratively.

"I pray we will defeat the Boche, but it is only prudent to prepare for any eventuality."

"You can count on me," Moira spoke up.

Noel was silent. He nodded to signal Nadine of his support.

She looked at Millard, waiting for him to speak. He contemplated carefully what she had said, and replied resolutely, "Madame, if the Boche invade France, I will fight them with whatever weapons are available. I'm too old to serve in the regular military, but I'm not too old to fight."

"Then we are all agreed," said Nadine. "This is what I propose."

The three of them listened carefully to the lovely French woman's strategies and plans. When she completed her comments, Millard looked at Nadine and smiled.

"Madame, you should have been a general."

A few days later, Nadine received a cablegram from Quentin. He would be in Paris around the middle of April before going to Switzerland on business. She consulted her calendar and cleared away any appointments and meetings. *Perhaps I will join Quentin in Switzerland,* she mused. *It will be good for the two of us to travel together.* A warm smile crossed the French woman's face as she made a mental note to entice her lover with a joint trip to Switzerland.

The next week when Quentin and Nadine spoke on the telephone, their conversation was mixed with sadness and anticipation.

"I'm delighted that we will travel to Switzerland together, but I'm worried about the German advances against Denmark and Norway."

"Yes, the news is troublesome," she replied. "Do you think the Boche will prevail?"

"The Danes don't have much of an army, and the Allies cannot help them stop an invasion."

"And Norway?"

"It may be difficult for the Germans to invade and conquer them," he said, anticipation in his voice. "Let's not dwell on that. Let's think about the trip to Switzerland. We'll have a grand time."

* * *

The Germans easily overwhelmed the Danes and by April 9, 1940, were in control of the country. Norway proved a challenge for the Nazis, especially with the assistance the British provided. After talking with Ruben about Norway, Quentin accepted that the Germans would prevail there too.

Von Kleist was right, he thought. *Hitler is dangerous and demonic.*

By the time Quentin departed for Paris early in April 1940, the Danes were ready to surrender. His trip across the Atlantic was uneventful, and he decided not to land in England but fly directly from Ireland to Paris. The weather cooperated, and the Amelie landed in Paris just a little behind schedule. Nadine was waiting and greeted Quentin with a passionate kiss that caused Hardy and Mark to grin in awe.

The boss was a lucky man, they told each other.

The following day, Quentin and Nadine caught the train to Geneva. They tried to put aside news about the collapse of Denmark and the German advances in Norway. As they sat in their compartment reading and enjoying the scenery, Quentin mentioned that Marlon was at the top of his class at MIT and would graduate *summa cum laude.*

"He's so bright and talented," said Nadine. "Does he still want to become an architect?"

Quentin nodded and said Marlon was contemplating graduate school at Yale to combine a program in business administration with a master of fine arts in architecture.

"How wonderful," said Nadine, gently putting her head on Quentin's shoulder. "We are so lucky to have such wonderful children. Tell me about Florence?"

The Cajun did not speak up immediately, causing Nadine to look up at him and notice a slight frown. She smoothed his forehead with her long delicate fingers and said, "Something troubling you about Florence?"

"Yes and no," said the Cajun slowly.

Nadine sat up and looked into his eyes. "A musical talent agency wants her to do a tour playing the piano."

"As a soloist or part of a group?" she asked, her curiosity piqued.

"I'm not certain," he replied. "Either way, I'm unsure about this."

"Why?" she asked. "Will it interfere with her schooling?"

He told her about the agency wanting her to sign a one-year contract that was renewable for another year. "I think she should continue her schooling at Juilliard and play recitals as part of her class assignments or program for performances," he told the lovely French woman.

She asked if he had discussed this with Florence, and the Cajun shook his head.

"Why?" she asked.

He indicated wanting to speak with her principal instructor at the preparatory school and also someone at Juilliard.

"I see," said Nadine. "Cherie, consult those people quickly and then discuss this with Florence immediately," she advised. "The decision must be one that is rendered by the two of you. After all, she is only sixteen."

"Hmmm, that's true, but she will be seventeen in June and is already acting very independently."

Nadine clicked her tongue and said, "Poof," with a smile, "one day a girl, and the next day a woman!" She concurred that Quentin talk with her instructors as soon as possible and then with the appropriate person at Juilliard.

"There's something else," he added. In the next few minutes, he mentioned how tactile Marlon and Florence were. His comments puzzled the French woman. She inquired about the nature of the attachment between the two.

"It's nothing I can put my finger on," he said tentatively. "But they're close, and Florence has strong affections for Marlon." He went on to explain how they touched each other, and how Florence always wanted Marlon to sit next to her. "I see them holding hands often. And when they're flying the Amelie, they're openly tactile, smile at each other as if sharing something private and special. She's also very afraid he'll enlist in the French army and fight against the Boche."

Nadine stiffened a bit and was quiet for a moment while she digested Quentin's remarks. "It may be nothing," she said.

But, the Cajun saw the lovely woman become pensive. "I guess it's nothing, just the affection between a son and daughter."

"Perhaps," said Nadine. "But, remember that Florence has been without a mother and may be substituting an attachment to her brother to fill the void left by Ione's death."

She's so beautiful and so smart, thought Quentin, as he looked admiringly at Nadine.

"You may be right," he finally said and decided to let the matter drop.

Nadine considered carefully what Quentin said about Florence and Marlon and tried to recall moments when she observed them together and how they behaved toward each other. It captured her attention and she determined to learn more about the relationship between her son and his half sister.

The days Nadine and Quentin were together in Geneva were a welcome respite from their normal routines. News about the fighting in Norway was not good. Rather than worry about the war, they focused on enjoying their time together in Geneva. Business obligations were handled expeditiously to allow maximizing their time together. Geneva was an idyllic place. The charming city, the lovely lake, and the surrounding mountains refreshed and invigorated them. Even though it was just the first week in April and still cold and rainy, they strolled through the old town and visited points of interest like the Palace du Bourg-de-Four, the Place Neuve, and the

Conservatory of Music. They attended a musical recital at Victoria Hall. During their stay, the lovers dined at elegant establishments before departing for France.

In Paris, the climate was warmer than in Switzerland. Nadine could sense the tension in her lover as he paid close attention to the fighting in Norway and the improving weather.

"You're worried about the war," she finally told Quentin during dinner on his last night in Paris.

He looked away for a moment, contemplating the changing weather. The snow and rains of winter were gone and already there were buds in the trees and shrubs. With the improving weather and the lack of progress on the diplomatic front between the Allies and the Germans, the Cajun knew hostilities would begin soon.

"The Boche control Denmark, and soon Norway. Unless there's a diplomatic solution, the war will intensify," he told Nadine.

"Cherie, you think the Boche will attack soon?"

"Yes," he replied. "France will have to fight on her own soil."

He grew sullen for a moment before the lovely woman reached for his hand and told him to hope for the best. Nadine too felt uneasy but tried not to show it.

The next day, when Quentin, Hardy, and Mark were preparing to leave La Bourget, a light drizzle was falling.

"Will you be all right?" she asked the pilot, glancing at the gray overcast sky and slight misting.

"We'll be OK," he reassured her. "I'll let you know when I get home."

They embraced, and he kissed her passionately. The sweet taste of the kiss lingered on his lips as he entered the plane, closed the hatch, and made his way forward. Once in the pilot seat, with the engines warmed, he called the tower for clearance, waved at his lover, and taxied to the end of the runway. The Amelie lifted off the ground and soon disappeared into the misty sky. Nadine's eyes were moist as she lost sight of the plane.

"Be safe and come back to me, Cherie," she said softly.

* * *

In April, business responsibilities and personal matters kept Quentin busy. He visited Washington for a few days and met with Roosevelt and Marshall. Then, he flew to California to meet with key movie industry leaders to finalize the agreement for German film distributions. Ruben Valderano joined him in Beverly Hills where the two of them discussed the situation in Europe at length.

"You realize, now that the Germans control Denmark, they will attack the Allies as soon as the weather improves," said Valderano.

The Cajun nodded and looked away for a moment before speaking. "I worry that the Allies will not contain the Germans."

The Mexican nodded and said it all depended on how quickly the Wehrmacht moved. "If they are able to divide the Allies and cut off the British supply lines, then the French will bear the brunt of the attack," said Ruben soberly, his mind already playing out possible military scenarios.

They talked about the coming hostilities and promised to meet with Roosevelt and General Marshall in Washington the following month.

When he returned to New York, Quentin met with Florence's mentor in her preparatory school. She suggested that Florence not accept the invitation to go on tour but continue her studies, and she encouraged Quentin to meet with the dean of instruction at Juilliard. She handed him a card with the dean's name and telephone number. When Quentin met with the dean he too expressed reservations about Florence going on tour.

"If you can," he told the Cajun, "try to convince your daughter to continue her studies. If you like, we can arrange for a tutor to work with her during the summer. We have an excellent facility in upstate New York that is ideal for intensive musical instruction."

The next day, Quentin and Florence talked about her plans for the summer and the fall of that year. At first, Florence toyed with the idea of doing a tour, but only during the remainder of 1940. When the Cajun told her the talent agency had specifically stipulated a one-year commitment, with another follow-up year, the teenager looked nonplussed.

"Honey, would you like to take summer music classes?" he asked. She said getting away from New York during the summer would be nice. "Why don't we call the people at Juilliard and ask them to recommend something for you?" he told her.

She nodded and said that sounded fine. Then, she changed the subject.

"Daddy, I've decided to attend the debutant cotillion with Kris Dekker."

"That's splendid," said Quentin. He knew the boy. Kris Mortensen Dekker III was the youngest son of a wealthy Knickerbocker family. He was about to enter his sophomore year at Yale and had dated Florence a few times in the last year. Kris was a well-mannered young man, an excellent hockey player, and an accomplished sailor. He was charming and urbane.

"We'll need to get you a nice dress."

At this, Florence kissed her father on the forehead and forced him to hug her. "I know a swell place to order a gown," she told him.

It will be expensive, thought the Cajun. *But the hell with the cost,* he thought. *She'll only be a debutant once.*

The evening when Quentin saw Florence in the new gown with her hair combed up, it took away his breath. She was Ione reincarnated. "Darling," he told her, "you're beautiful, just like your mother."

"Really! Thank you, Daddy."

"We need to take some pictures of you. Camila, please bring the camera."

The Cuban American governess returned with the camera, and she and the Cajun took turns taking pictures of Florence, some with Camila with Florence, and others with Florence and Quentin.

As he looked at Florence, images of Ione were paramount in his mind. *She's so much like you, Ione,* he thought.

Late that evening, Quentin sat alone in the living room in front of the large fireplace as the glow from the still hot embers cast eerie shadows. *It'll be May in a few days,* he thought. *I can feel the war coming.*

* * *

The beginning of May was a time of numerous obligations for Quentin. Marlon was completing his studies at MIT, and graduation ceremonies were scheduled for the end of the second week in May. Nadine planned to be at the ceremony with Quentin and Florence. Meanwhile, Florence was completing her final assignments at the prep school and would participate in commencement ceremonies during the first week in June. The Cajun's busy work schedule and obligations with his children left little time to follow developments in Europe, although he continued to skim the newspaper accounts of the German advances in Norway. He talked often on the telephone with General Marshall in Washington to get precise information about the fighting in Europe. The Wehrmacht was moving relentlessly northward, engaging and defeating a British brigade and elements of the Norwegian army. In spite of British naval support for the Norwegians, it appeared Norway was doomed.

Quentin arrived early for a breakfast meeting with the other senior partners on May 10, 1940. It was almost eight when Mrs. Jordan, the office manager, knocked on the door, opened it, and stood in the doorway, a look of dismay on her face.

"The Germans have invaded Holland," she said in a tremulous voice.

The room was still, news of the Nazi attack coming as a surprise to all but the Cajun. Gradually, the senior partners turned toward Quentin. Surely, he understood what was happening and would explain the attack on Holland.

"It's started," was all the Cajun said soberly. He was about to leave the meeting, but Everett Barston, a senior partner, told him to stay and share his thoughts.

"What can you tell us about this attack on Holland?" he asked Quentin, while the others looked attentively at the Cajun.

Quentin sat down and began by saying that the Germans were probably planning to attack Belgium to cut off the British Expeditionary Force (BEF) from their source of war material and other support. He explained in general terms the German strategy to strike through the Low Countries to cut off and defeat the BEF.

All at once, the room was abuzz with comments and questions, until Barston spoke up and asked for their attention.

"Gentlemen," said Barston, "from what Quentin has told us, this is just the beginning. I propose we cancel this meeting and attend to our concerns. There will be more news about the German invasion of Holland later today and tomorrow."

The other senior partners nodded in agreement and picked up their portfolios. Barston motioned for Quentin and another senior partner to stay behind.

"Quentin," said Barston, "we have important investments in Europe. We need to know how these hostilities will affect them. I'd like you and Mel (another senior partner) to examine our European portfolio and determine our best course of action."

The Cajun mentioned that he had already transferred substantial resources and funds from the Low Countries and France into secure accounts in Switzerland. He smiled and said, "Your suggestion is a good one. We'll know more about the fighting in the next few days. Mel and I will look into our investments over there and provide some options for the firm to consider."

Mel nodded in agreement.

"Very well," said a solemn Barston. "Let me know if you need help."

Quentin said he would and huddled with Mel for a few minutes before returning to his office.

It was almost nine in the morning when Quentin reached his office. Sarah was waiting.

"You have several calls," she said, looking pale and uncertain. "One is from General Valderano, and another is from Washington."

"Get me Ruben on my private line," he told the tense, raven-haired secretary and walked into his office. A few minutes later, he was talking with Ruben Valderano.

"Ruben," said the Cajun, "this doesn't look good. Can you come to New York?"

"Actually," said the Mexican, "I think we'll meet in Washington. The president called. He wants to meet with us."

Quentin was silent for a moment, digesting his friend's remarks. "I'll send my plane for you—"

"No need, George (Marshall) is flying me to Washington."

They talked for a few minutes and agreed to stay at the Mayflower Hotel in D.C. Quentin said Sarah would make the reservations. Ruben thanked him and said they would see each other in Washington.

"Before we sign off," said the Cajun, "what do you think will happen?"

"If the British cannot stop the Germans, they will have to fall back and try to link up with the French army. It all depends on how quickly the Germans move through Holland and Belgium. We'll know more tomorrow or the day after," he said cautiously.

"If I know the Germans," said a worried Quentin, "they have a well-thought-out plan of attack and may be hard to stop."

There was silence on the other end of the line as the Mexican considered his friend's remarks.

Finally, Ruben repeated that they would know more about the fighting in the next day or two and said, "Hope for the best."

After ending his call to Valderano, Quentin called Nadine. However, the heavy telephone traffic across the Atlantic prevented him from getting through. He walked to Sarah's desk, where she was talking on the telephone, and whispered that he was getting coffee and asked if she wanted some. She nodded and handed him three messages. One was from the White House, another was from Marlon, and the third was from Florence.

When he returned with the coffee, Sarah put down the telephone, only to have it ring again. She took a quick swallow of her coffee and answered the call. She put the person on hold, looked up at Quentin, and said, "It's General Marshall."

He smiled and said he'd take it in his office.

"Quentin," he heard the familiar voice of George C. Marshall say, "the president wants to meet with you and General Valderano day after tomorrow. An early morning meeting would be best. Can you join us?"

Quentin responded affirmatively and said he'd make a reservation at the Mayflower.

"Don't bother," said Marshall, "we'll handle it from our end."

"George, what do you think will happen in Holland?"

"Too soon to tell," said Marshall. "But, I hope French morale is high and that the British can hold their own against the Germans." They chatted for a few minutes before Quentin said he had other things to do. "Yes, of course," said Marshall. "Call me if you have any problems or need help."

Just as the Cajun hung up the phone, Sarah poked her head into his office and said that Mrs. Desnoyers was holding on the other line.

"If my son calls again, tell him to sit tight while I talk with his mother. Get his number so that I can call him right back," he told her.

She nodded and pointed at the line on which the French woman was holding.

"Nadine," he said somberly, worried about her and the renewed fighting.

"Cherie," he heard her strained voice, "the Boche have invaded La Hollande and are preparing to move on La Belgique. There is much anxiety here." Her voice was filled with sadness.

"It's too soon to tell how the fighting will turn out," he replied, trying to be upbeat. "The French and the British have more troops and tanks than the Boche. Their combined air strength should be able to check the German advances in Holland and Belgium," he added.

"I pray you are correct."

"Are you still planning to be here for Marlon's graduation next week?" he asked.

"I don't know." Her voice seemed distant and uncertain.

"I'll send the Amelie for you."

"Yes, yes, of course. But who will fly it?"

He mentioned sending Hardy, Mark, and Cliff Lachlan (an Irish American pilot Quentin had befriended through Mark and Hardy). "I'll make all of the arrangements and let you know when they'll arrive. If they're delayed, they'll call."

The two talked awhile longer, the American trying to assuage the lovely French woman's fears about the German invasion of the Low Countries.

"Don't worry about Marlon," he told her. "I'll talk with him and make certain he doesn't do anything until after he graduates."

"*Merci,*" Nadine said softly. "We'll see each other soon." She professed her love and ended the call.

Quentin walked to Sarah's desk and noticed she was still on the telephone. She handed him several messages, tapping the top one with her index finger. It was Marlon's number. Once back in his office, the Cajun dialed it; after a few rings, he heard his son's voice.

"Dad, thanks for calling back. What's happening in Europe? Have you talked with Mom yet? Flo called; she's really upset. Have you talked with her?" He was about to ask another question when Quentin cut him off.

"Marlon, slow down; I'll share as much as I know." He mentioned the German attack on Holland and the impending advance into Belgium through Luxembourg. So far, the Germans had not pushed directly into France. "It's too soon to know anything definitive about the Boche advance. I'll know more tomorrow or the day after. I want you to graduate from MIT. Your mother will be here. I'm sending the plane to pick her up."

"When will she be here?"

"In about four or five days," answered Quentin.

Marlon paused, considered his father's comments. "OK, I'll hold on until Mom gets here. But, if the fighting over there continues, I'll enlist."

"In the French air force?" asked the Cajun.

"Yes," replied Marlon. "Why do you ask?"

"I want to help you get ready for combat flying."

"What do you mean?" asked Marlon, curious about his father's comment.

"After you graduate from MIT, I'll show you what I mean."

"OK," replied Marlon, uncertain what his father had in mind. "Flo called. She's really upset and started crying. Did you say anything to her about my enlisting?"

"No," replied the Cajun. "But, she knows you want to. I'll talk with her when I get home." *There it is again,* thought Quentin, that nagging feeling about the relationship between his two children.

"If you think it'll do any good, I'll call Flo after you talk with her," Marlon offered.

Quentin thanked him and said they'd talk after he called Florence.

The remainder of Quentin's day was filled responding to urgent telephone calls from clients worried about the hostilities in Europe and what effect the war might have on their investments. The steady stream of calls and impromptu visits from people in the law firm made the day long and fatiguing. It was almost seven that evening when he got home. Waiting for him was Florence, her eyes red and swollen.

"What is it, honey?" he asked.

"Daddy, Marlon's going to war, isn't he?"

"Why do you say that?" He could tell how distraught she was.

"Because he said he would," she told him before starting to sob.

It pained him to see her so tense and worried. He took her in his arms and, for the first time, noticed she was wearing a familiar but elusive fragrance. He searched his memory for the source of the fragrance. Was it something Nadine had given to her?

"Honey," he told Florence as he lifted her chin and gazed into her large blue eyes, "I'll do what I can to persuade Marlon to wait before enlisting. I doubt whether he'll be able to enlist in the French army. He's a U.S. citizen, and there's a policy against fighting under another flag."

"Daddy, you have to stop him," she said between sobs.

"I can't do that," he told her. "He's a grown man and will do what he wants."

"No, Daddy, he's just a boy."

He saw fear visible in her eyes. "Florence, your brother is twenty-one. He'll graduate from MIT in a few days. He's not a boy, and he knows his mind. I'll do everything I can to persuade him to stay with us as long as possible."

Florence gave out a low wail and pressed her face into his shoulder.

"Daddy, please help him. I don't want to see him hurt or killed."

"Yes, honey," he told her softly. "I'll do everything possible to help."

"Promise?" she said between sobs. He looked at her and nodded.

To change the subject, he asked about the fragrance.

She stopped crying for a moment and took the handkerchief he handed her to dry her eyes.

"Grand mummy gave it to me. She said it was the kind Mommy used."

Quentin turned away from his daughter to hide the tears forming in his eyes. Memories of Ione flooded his consciousness; for a moment, he thought of nothing but the painful moments before she died. "I've got to change my clothes," he finally told Florence, "and I need to call your brother."

She looked up at him and was surprised to see his eyes moist. She wanted to listen in on his call to Marlon, but she decided against it. She'd talk to Marlon later. All she wanted at the moment was for her father to persuade Marlon not to go to war.

It was just after nine that evening when Quentin and Marlon talked on the telephone. He urged Marlon not to do anything until after the graduation ceremonies at MIT. "We'll know more about the fighting by then. Besides, day after tomorrow I'm going to Washington and will get reliable information about the fighting."

"Will General Valderano be with you in Washington?" asked Marlon.

Quentin replied affirmatively.

"All right," said Marlon. "But keep me informed."

"I will," said the Cajun. "Your mother and I are very proud of you. We want to see you graduate." They talked for a while before Quentin said it was late. When he put the phone back in its cradle, his mind was filled with so many concerns. *I need to call Mom and Dad,* he thought, *and Kathleen. God damn you, Hitler!*

* * *

Quentin met Ruben Valderano at the Mayflower Hotel on May 14. The news from Holland was distressing. The German Luftwaffe had destroyed the Dutch Air Force by May 13. On the ground, elements of the BEF and the French army had tried to support the Dutch but could not check the advancing Germans.

"The Germans have achieved air superiority," said a solemn Valderano. "They're pounding the Dutch and Belgian armies. They've marched through Luxembourg and are pinching in on the Belgians at critical points. It's not going well for the Allies."

"Can the Allies counterattack and stop them?" The Mexican looked down, hunched his shoulders, and shook his head.

"Well, I hope the president has some good news for us," said Quentin, as they approached the White House.

After clearing the security gate and entering the White House, Ruben and Quentin were met by Brook Hamilton Stoner, who took them upstairs where Roosevelt, Secretary of War Woodring, Secretary of State Hull, and George C. Marshall were waiting. It was almost 7:30 in the morning.

"Welcome," said the president. "You all know each other. Get something to eat," he said with a sweep of his hand in the direction of food on a side table. "Coffee's hot and fresh."

When the Mexican and the Cajun sat down to eat, Quentin wondered what Roosevelt and the others in the room had been discussing. He glanced at the Mexican, who winked and began working on some pancakes and bacon. Quentin took a few bites of his food, drank some orange juice, and looked directly at the president, who was whispering to Cordell Hull. When Roosevelt noticed that the Cajun was looking directly at him, he spoke up.

"Gentlemen, thank you for coming. I have news to share about the situation in the Low Countries. George," he said, indicating Marshall should speak.

Marshall opened a file and began to report on the German advances in the Netherlands. The Wehrmacht had struck through Luxembourg and advanced into Holland. Their Ninth Panzer Division reached Rotterdam on the thirteenth. The Dutch army had been badly mauled and was in danger of collapse. The situation in Belgium was deteriorating. German armor had gained the upper hand in central Belgium. The Nazis were about to break through the combined French and Belgium forces. Marshall looked up and scanned the faces of the men at the table. The mood in the room was somber. He continued by saying that the most recent intelligence received placed the Germans at Sedan.

"Gentlemen," said a dispassionate Marshall, "the Germans will probably cross the Meuse River in force within the next few hours. Their Luftwaffe controls the skies and is disrupting Allied communications and destroying their supply columns." He paused and looked at Valderano. Both men were grim and silent, each knowing that without a well coordinated British and French counterattack, the Germans would be in Antwerp in a matter of days.

"Well," said Roosevelt sadly, "will there be a demarcation point, a place where the Allies will hold firm?"

"I doubt it," Ruben volunteered.

"The next two or three days will be critical," said Marshall. "Unless the Germans can be thrown back, they will divide the Allies and control all of Belgium and Holland. The British will have to retreat."

"Cordell, anything new on the diplomatic front?" asked Roosevelt.

Hull shook his head and said the two sides were not talking.

"Mr. President," said Ruben, "I will leave for Germany in two days to serve as a neutral observer. I've already made arrangements with the Associated Press."

"How do you plan to get into Germany?" asked Hull.

"I'll fly into Lisbon, catch a flight to Zurich, and then take the train into Germany. I'll need diplomatic assistance to validate my credentials as an observer from a neutral country."

"Of course," said the president. "Cordell, see to it at once."

"You'd better hurry," said Quentin. "At the rate the Germans are moving, the fighting may be over by the time you get there."

There was nervous laughter in the room, but all of them realized that, unless the Allies stopped the German assaults, all might be lost.

After the meeting ended, Valderano, Marshall, and Quentin walked out together. Marshall spoke up first.

"Be careful over there, Ruben," warned Marshall. "Don't get in the middle of it."

"I promise to keep my head down," said Valderano. "France still has a large army and internal supply lines."

"Yes, I guess the French still have a chance to turn the tide," said the Cajun halfheartedly. Quentin knew that it was not the size of the French army or its equipment, but their tactics, morale, and will to fight that would be decisive.

* * *

A few days later, Nadine arrived in New York aboard the Amelie. Try as she might to appear happy and ready to celebrate her son's college graduation, Quentin quickly noted her weariness.

"What is it?" he asked when they were alone.

"Two days ago (15 May), one of Reynaud's (French Prime Minister Paul Reynaud) aides told me that France is facing defeat. He said they're burning their archives and preparing to evacuate Paris."

The news stunned Quentin. For a moment, he was sullen, unable to speak. Finally, he said, "It's too soon to talk about defeat."

But, the French woman smiled and shook her head. "No, Cherie, Luxembourg, Holland, and most of *La Belgique* are in the hands of the Boche."

"But, the British are still fighting in Belgium," he said, trying to add something positive to the conversation.

"Oh, Cherie, Etienne and Raoul informed me about the paralysis in the French high command and the disorganization at the front."

The Cajun pondered what she told him and was silent for a few minutes before speaking up. "I want you and your parents to leave France and come to New York."

"That is not possible," she told him, her eyes slowly filling with moisture.

"Why?" he asked insistently.

She told him about the many people who depended on her and the business and financial concerns that required her attention. There were other matters, she said, that conditioned her decision. Any indication of her departure from France in the face of the enemy would be interpreted as defeatism and cowardice. "There are different ways to fight the Boche," she said. "I can help people escape the Nazis and find ways to hurt their military."

They argued back and forth until Quentin realized she was adamant about remaining in France.

"It will be necessary for us to share your decision with Marlon. Best if we do so after his graduation ceremony."

She nodded, but did not speak. She could feel the disappointment and frustration in her lover. But, it was not possible for Nadine to veer from the mission she had set for herself, even if it meant danger, imprisonment, and perhaps death.

In spite of the escalating fighting in Europe, the MIT commencement ceremonies were very well attended. Quentin's parents, his brothers and sisters, and several cousins from Canada were at the graduation. Florence was sitting next to the Vandersteels with Kathleen and Camila just to her left. Marlon's valedictorian speech was brilliant and moving, and he received a standing ovation.

After the ceremony, Marlon was surrounded by family and friends. Quentin, Nadine, and most of the family, including three cousins from Canada, left for New York that afternoon. A reception was planned for the following night at the Vandersteel home. Marlon stayed behind in Cambridge to party with classmates and cousins. The following day, he cleared his apartment, sent his belongings home, and flew to New York City.

The reception at the Vandersteel home was lavish and well attended. A string quartet played chamber music. Nadine and Quentin were not surprised when Marlon asked Florence to join the quartet, but not before she played several of Marlon's favorites. During a lull in the music, Nadine took Quentin outside to a charming garden in the back of the Vandersteel home.

"Does Marlon have a girlfriend?" she asked the Cajun.

"He's never mentioned anyone special. Why do you ask?"

"He must know some young women," she said, looking directly at him.

"I know he's been dating. I've met three of his dates. They are attractive and very charming."

"I see," said Nadine, "but no one special."

He shook his head. They talked awhile until Bernice approached them.

"Marlon's been asked to say a few words," she told them. "Please come inside." The three of them locked arms and returned to the reception.

The following day, Nadine and Quentin asked Marlon to walk with them through Central Park.

"What are your plans?" asked Quentin, as they strolled through the lush, green park.

"I'm going to enlist in the French army."

Nadine studied him carefully, but waited for Quentin to say something.

"And how are you going to do that?" asked the Cajun.

"I don't know. I've thought about going to France and asking our cousins and friends to help me join the *Armeé de l'Air*."

"That may not be as easy as you might think," said Nadine.

The remark surprised Marlon, and he asked her to explain.

She said, depending on the outcome of the fighting and the priorities of the French army, earning a commission would be difficult and might require him to serve in an infantry unit.

Marlon shrugged his shoulders and said he wanted to fly.

"Before you do anything, let me make a few inquiries," said Nadine. "If you want to fly with the *Armeé de l'Air*, perhaps Raoul Mendeville and Etienne de Gavrelac can help. Both are serving in staff capacities," she said, looking directly at her son.

Marlon thought about what she said before speaking up. "How soon before you will know anything?"

"A few days," she replied. "I'll attend to it as soon as I return to Paris."

"Perhaps I should return with you."

"No," replied the Cajun emphatically.

"Why?" asked Marlon, surprised by his father's strong negative response.

"I want to train you to be a fighter pilot," said Quentin. "Give me three weeks so that I can teach you about fighting and surviving in combat."

"But I already know how to fly," said Marlon, "and I'm sure the French will instruct me in combat tactics and flying."

"Maybe, but I can teach you things about combat flying and how to defeat your adversaries."

"I don't know." *He's just stalling for time,* thought Marlon.

"Tell you what," said the Cajun. "Why don't we go up and do some mock combat flying. If after that you feel confident about your flying skills, I won't stand in your way."

"OK," said Marlon, convinced of his flying abilities and certain that he could easily parry any maneuvers by his father.

Nadine nodded in approval. She already knew what Quentin had in mind and doubted that Marlon knew what to expect. *He has the confidence of youth,* she thought, *but Quentin is experienced and far more aggressive in the air than Marlon suspects.*

The day before Nadine was to return to France, she, Florence, Marlon, and Quentin drove to the airport at Islip. Quentin had asked Brock Stopplemeier, the owner of the hangar and maintenance shops where he kept the Amelie, to rent two Stearman biplanes. The planes, one colored red and the other blue, were waiting when they arrived at the hangar. Brock and his son, Curtis, greeted them politely and quickly started up the Stearmans.

"All right," said a cocky Marlon as he put on his parachute and walked to the red Stearman. "You sure you can keep up with me?" he teased.

Quentin smiled.

Marlon thought he saw something cold and hard in his father's eyes. It disturbed him momentarily, but he quickly put it out of mind. It was time to show the old man what a good flyer he was.

The two planes lifted off together and climbed to about three thousand feet while Brock, Curtis, Nadine, and Florence watched from the ground. Marlon tested the controls of the Stearman and made a few maneuvers with his father. Abruptly, Quentin broke away and headed into the scud, disappearing for a moment. Marlon added power to the biplane and went after him. But, to the younger flyer's surprise, his father was nowhere in sight. A moment later, a blue blur swooped down on his tail. The Cajun was so close to Marlon's tail assembly that, for a moment, the younger pilot thought the other plane's propeller would shear it off. Marlon tried some evasive maneuvers, but the other plane was always above and behind him. A moment later, Quentin pulled even with Marlon and signaled that he was going to break off again. This time, Marlon did not wait, but went after his father. Much to the younger flyer's chagrin, the older pilot did a roll and a tight loop and was on his tail. When Marlon tried to dive away and do an evasive roll, just as he came out of it, the other Stearman passed over his wings. And so it went for the next twenty minutes with Marlon never able to prevent his father from getting height and excellent firing angles on him. After a final pass that completely surprised the younger pilot, Quentin pulled even and signaled that it was time to land. An annoyed and dejected Marlon followed his father to the field.

Marlon and Quentin taxied to the hangar, where Brock and Curtis approached the two planes. Brock helped Marlon out of the Stearman. As he alighted from the plane and was removing his parachute, the lanky old mechanic, now almost sixty years of age, smiled and said, "If you'd a' been using real bullets, yur old man would a' shot you down easy."

Marlon, annoyed and frustrated, walked toward his father and confronted him. "You did that on purpose to make me look bad," he said defensively. It irked him when his father just smiled in a cold and calculating way. "What's the point?" pressed the younger pilot.

Finally, Quentin put a hand on his son's shoulder and, making certain no one was within earshot, said, "Marlon, it takes more than just being a good flyer to survive in combat. You have much to learn. Let me teach you how to dogfight."

Marlon was surprised. At first, he thought the offer was nothing but a ruse to prevent him from enlisting. The way Quentin stared at him intently made him reconsider. There was a hard and menacing look in his father's eyes he'd never seen before.

"Marlon, you're a very good pilot. I know. I taught you how to fly. But, you're not a combat pilot yet," said Quentin. "I can teach you how to be a better pilot and how to survive in combat."

Before the two of them turned to join Nadine and Florence, Marlon dropped his head and, in a soft voice, said, "How long will it take?"

"Daddy, I didn't know you could fly like that," said an excited Florence.

Nadine just smiled at the Cajun in a knowing way. Her lover had just taught their son a valuable lesson. *If Marlon can put aside his pride,* she thought, *Quentin will teach him how to prevail in combat.*

After Florence, Nadine, Quentin, and Marlon arrived at the Norvell home, Nadine and Florence went into the kitchen.

Marlon said to his father, "You win, Dad. Teach me how to be a combat pilot."

The Cajun hugged his son without saying anything.

Early the next day, Florence, Marlon, and Quentin drove Nadine to Islip. At the airfield, Mark, Hardy, and Cliff were waiting by the Amelie.

"You're cleared all the way through to London," said Quentin. "Nadine will catch the train to the Channel and then cross on the packet," he said. "It's too risky for civilian planes to fly over the Channel or French air space." The three crew members nodded and said good-bye to Marlon and Florence. Mark took Nadine's bags onto the plane while Hardy and Cliff warmed the engines. Before

Nadine boarded the Amelie, she kissed her son on the lips and whispered something to him. She hugged and kissed Florence, who started to cry.

"No, no, Cherie," said a smiling Nadine, using her handkerchief to blot the young blonde's eyes. "I will be all right. I love you. Keep up with your music. You have a rare gift." She hugged and kissed Florence before stepping into the Amelie. A moment later, she waved through one of the windows.

They watched as the silver plane taxied to the end of the runway, turned, and quickly sped away, lifting into the sky and turning eastward.

* * *

Nadine finally reached Paris late on the twentieth of May. Getting to France from England had been complicated, but not as difficult as trying to go the other way. Along the route to Paris, there were dramatic signs of military activity with large numbers of troops visible at strategic sites along the railroad leading to Paris from the coast. Once in Paris, the mood among the people revealed nervousness and despair. The war was not going well for the Allies, and many in Paris feared that the Germans might prevail.

Between May 21 and 27, the news from the front was not good. Nadine learned from Etienne and Raoul, both serving as staff officers in the French *Armeé de l'Air,* that the Germans had beaten back attacks by French general Charles De Gaulle at Amiens and by the BEF near Abbeville. Almost 350,000 British, French, and Belgium soldiers were encircled near a coastal town called Dunkerque (Dunkirk).

On May 26, the English launched a rescue effort called *Dynamo* to evacuate the troops trapped at Dunkirk. Miraculously, the British evacuated 218,226 of their soldiers and 120,000 Frenchmen. The Allies were forced to leave behind their heavy guns, tanks, and other equipment.

"I'm afraid *La Hollande, La Belgique*, and Luxembourg are now fully controlled by the Boche," said a tired Raoul Mendeville at Nadine's home. He wore the uniform of a full colonel in the *Armeé de l'Air* and sat next to Etienne de Gavrelac, also in uniform, with the rank of lieutenant colonel. They were having a late dinner.

"What will happen now?" asked Nadine in a controlled voice. She was prepared for the worst.

"The British have promised us more squadrons," said Etienne, "and additional troops."

"It is up to our army to engage and defeat the Boche," said Raoul wearily.

From the tone of his voice, Nadine surmised that he was hoping for the best, but prepared for defeat. "Bon," she said, "let us trust in our military and say no more."

The following day, May 28, King Leopold III of Belgium surrendered to the Germans. The Dutch were already out of the war, and Queen Wilhelmina of the Netherlands moved her government to England. France was surrounded, fighting alone against the hated Boche.

* * *

In America, Quentin and Marlon went into the skies in the Stearmans to practice dogfighting five days a week. Quentin was a relentless taskmaster. He insisted that Marlon master basic evasive maneuvers until he was able to perform them flawlessly. Each day after their time in the air, Quentin went over in great detail what had transpired, the things Marlon had done wrong, and less so what he did right. By the end of the second week, Marlon had mastered almost all of the aerial tactics. He was surprised by how much his father knew about flying and what a patient teacher he was. During the debriefings, Quentin provided valuable insights and tips about flying and how to use the full potential of an aircraft. There were also warnings that Marlon now listened to carefully.

"The Germans have developed a new aerial tactic for their fighter pilots. They're flying in groups of twos. The second plane is a wingman and follows slightly behind the leader. If you attack the leader," said the Cajun, using toy airplanes to demonstrate the strategy, "the wingman will fall in behind you. When you encounter this formation, go for the wingman."

"How do you know this, Dad?" asked a puzzled Marlon.

"I got information from flyers during the Spanish Civil War about German fighter tactics," said Quentin. Marlon looked at him in disbelief.

"How'd you do that, Dad?" In the next ten minutes, Marlon learned how methodical his father was about flying and discerning new aerial combat tactics. He was impressed by his father's knowledge and flying abilities.

During the final week of their practice, Marlon's flying had improved dramatically. His father was unrelenting in teaching him about combat flying. On their last day of practice, Marlon was able to complete a tricky maneuver and briefly get on Quentin's tail. However, the Cajun feigned a right turn, rolled quickly, and went into a tight turn to the left. Had he not slowed slightly to follow his father, Marlon would have overshot him. Instead, the Cajun continued to tighten the turn, adding power to the Stearman until it seemed he would spin out. But, it was Marlon who spun out, unable to stay with his father in the turn. A moment later, when Marlon righted his plane, he saw his father flying next to him. Quentin smiled and motioned for Marlon to follow him down. The training was over.

"How'd you manage to keep that turn so tight?" asked Marlon when they were on the ground.

Quentin shared some things with his son that the young flyer never forgot.

"Marlon, good pilots know their plane's limits and fly at that level of performance. The best pilots also know how to exceed that point. It's what separates a good pilot from a great one. That's why I was able to push the Stearman beyond its limit and tighten the turn so you couldn't keep up with me. Two other things," he added. "Excellent physical coordination is crucial and essential in a dogfight. You've got that coordination, son. Don't waste it by getting overtired or drinking booze the night before a mission."

"And the other?" asked Marlon.

"Not being afraid to die," said the Cajun, looking off into the distance, remembering how he had almost been killed during the Great War.

"What do you mean, Dad?" asked a curious Marlon.

Quentin explained that the moment a pilot paid more attention to surviving than to defeating an enemy, he lost his "competitive edge."

"Sometimes fear is good," said Quentin. "But, if you're not afraid to die, you'll be OK."

Marlon marveled at what his father said. In the three weeks they had been flying together, he learned so much about him. At forty-two, his dad was lean and muscular and his reflexes razor sharp. Quentin looked like he was in his early thirties, but there was more. His dad had something dark and mysterious in him. Marlon came to realize and appreciate Quentin's competitive and focused drive to excel as a relentless hunter in the air. Coupled with his skill as a pilot, his father was up to date on new airplanes and fighter tactics. *I've got to follow Dad's examples, practice everything he's taught me, and do my homework about new flying techniques,* thought Marlon.

Before they drove back to New York, Quentin handed Marlon a sandwich and a beer. "You're ready," he told Marlon. "I wish we had more time together."

"Shall I call Mother and ask her about enlisting in the French air force?"

"No," said Quentin, taking a bite from his sandwich.

"I don't understand," said a confused Marlon.

"Go to Canada and join the Royal Canadian Air Force (RCAF)."

Marlon's surprised expression made the older pilot smile. Quentin explained that their cousins in Canada were influential and could help Marlon enlist in the RCAF.

"But why the Canadian air force?" asked Marlon, curious about his father's suggestion.

"It doesn't look good for the French. The Boche have forced the BEF to abandon all of the Low Countries and most of Northern France. They have air superiority, and their Panzers are pushing west and south and will threaten Paris in a matter of days." He paused a moment to read the expression on the face of his son, who remained silent. Marlon kept current with the news about the fighting in France. However, he realized that his father had more reliable sources of information than what he read in the newspapers or heard on the radio.

"So you think France will be defeated."

"Two, maybe three weeks," replied the Cajun. "I doubt whether there will be any army or air force in France for you to join by the time you get there."

Marlon thought for a moment before asking why he should enlist in the RCAF if the end in France was near.

"The British will continue the war. They won't give in to the Boche," Quentin told him. "If you want to make a difference in the war, train in Canada and then go to England. You'll find the war there."

Marlon didn't say anything. Instead, he looked directly into his father's eyes. He knew there was more and waited for the older pilot to speak up.

"If you go to Canada, you can earn a commission as a flight lieutenant. Then, you can volunteer to go to England. You'll fly a Spitfire. It's the best fighter in the world."

He's thought it all out, mused Marlon. *He's giving me a way to get into the war as a fighter pilot.* "Dad, you're special," said Marlon. "You've planned all of this, haven't you?"

The Cajun smiled and, rather than say anything, put his arm around Marlon's shoulders.

That evening, after dinner, held late because Quentin worked in his office from one in the afternoon until seven or eight at night, Marlon announced his decision. Florence was not with them, but Camila, Kathleen, and Fiona and Harold Vandersteel were.

"I have an announcement," said a serious Marlon. "I'm going to Canada and enlist in the Royal Canadian Air Force."

Camila and the Vandersteels were stunned. But Kathleen just looked at Quentin and deduced from his smile that he supported Marlon's decision.

"Marlon," said Harold, "you don't have to do this."

Fiona could not contain herself and asked Marlon to reconsider. Turning to Quentin, she said, "Quentin, tell him not to go."

The Cajun asked all of them to be calm. "My son has made an important decision, and I support it." Two days later, Quentin flew Marlon to Toronto where, with his cousins' help, he enlisted in the RCAF to train for a commission as a fighter pilot at Canadian Base Borden.

CHAPTER 7
THE FALL OF FRANCE

If I live, I will fight, wherever I must,
as long as I must,
until the enemy is defeated
and the national stain washed clean.
Charles Andre Joseph Marie de Gaulle,
Broadcast from London to the French people
after the fall of France [June 18, 1940]

Early in June 1940, Ruben Valderano and other military experts knew that France's fate was sealed. Valderano's communications to Quentin were detailed and underscored the key military movements and engagements the Wehrmacht and the Luftwaffe had performed. The German Panzers, especially those led by Heinz Guderian and Erwin Rommel, had broken through the opposition and were routing the Allies. In the air, by June 9, the Luftwaffe had air superiority and destroyed the Belgium, Dutch, and French air forces, and badly mauled the British squadrons sent to the Continent.

On June 10, the French government fled to Bordeaux and declared Paris an open city. Winston Churchill flew to Briare on June 11 to meet with the French War Council. He encouraged them to continue the fight. However, when the French asked that he supply them with more RAF fighter squadrons, Churchill declined. He had been warned against doing so by RAF Air Chief Marshal H.C.T. Dowding. When Churchill returned to London, he was certain the French would fall.

The fighting in France continued, but the German juggernaut was unstoppable. General Rommel captured General Fortune and his remaining British troops at St. Valery on June 12. The British managed to evacuate almost two hundred thousand Allied personnel before the Wehrmacht captured all of the French coastal towns. On June 14, 1940, the Germans captured Paris. The French sued for peace on June 17.

There was a sense of disbelief in America when news about the German victory over France was known. The strong isolationism in the country persuaded only the most sympathetic and progressive Americans that the United States should not be involved in the European conflict. Quentin understood what the defeat would mean for France. Hitler and his Nazis collaborators were cruel and vengeful people. France would be humiliated. But, the Germans would not stop. They would attack the British and carry the war to England. The Cajun worried about Nadine, who refused to leave France, and about Marlon, training at Base Borden in Ontario. He wondered what would become of them. At least he had convinced his son to go to Canada and train as a pilot instead of enlisting in the French air force. In Nadine's case, he had no effect on her decision to remain in France. He knew the lovely, headstrong woman would fight the Nazis in any way she could.

At home, Florence was beside herself the night before Marlon left for Canada. She said she loved him and begged him not to go. "You'll be killed." She was fearful and sobbing, but her brother was resolute. She tried to convince Quentin to intercede and "talk Marlon out of going to war." But, instead, he sided with Marlon. "He'll be killed," her voice filled with dread.

"No, he won't," said Quentin. "You mustn't think or say that."

Florence ran to her room crying and refused to talk with either Marlon or Quentin. The day Marlon left, she hugged him affectionately and kissed him on the lips. "Be careful and come back to me," she told him.

To Quentin, Florence said, "If anything happens to him, I'll never forgive you."

* * *

In Paris, the pain of a defeated nation was visible on the inconsolable faces of its dejected remaining denizens. For so many, the very soul of France had been violated. Those who could leave fled the once proud City of Lights, abandoning the less fortunate to the advancing Germans. Etienne and Argentina left France for Spain en transit to Portugal and then England. Christine, Nadine's daughter, and her husband Armand moved to Portugal where, with Nadine's assistance, he was employed in one of her enterprises. Desirée and Bertrand moved to Switzerland where Nadine provided work and sufficient resources for them to live well. Louis Bondurant wept when France surrendered and vowed not to return to Paris as long as the Nazis were there. Among those who stayed, even though he had the resources to leave France, was Raoul Mendeville. He and his family were joined by Nadine and her parents in Paris as they waited for the Germans to arrive. The lovely French woman knew their lives would change drastically, but she could not have imagined the extent of the change.

On June 18, Nadine, Moira, Noel, Millard, and all of the household servants sat quietly in the living room listening to the *Appeal* by General Charles de Gaulle carried by the BBC. He declared the war for France was not yet over, and rallied the country to support the "resistance" against the Boche. The appeal was emotional and his words inspired courage and action by the French and others to join a movement to continue the struggle against the Nazis. Nadine took to heart what de Gaulle said. She would do her part to fight the Boche, even if it meant danger and perhaps death.

The first few days following the Wehrmacht's entrance into Paris were solemn and quiet. There was little lawlessness and no overt signs of resistance to the invaders. However, Nadine noticed a collective pause among the Parisians as they prepared for the demands of their new masters. And it was not long in coming. By the middle of July, large numbers of German troops were in the city, and sweeping changes were under way. There were rumors about a curfew, the monitoring of all activities by the Nazis, and new regulations on what could be purchased and in what amounts. In August, the billeting of Wehrmacht soldiers and the dispossessions began. The elegant homes of wealthy Parisians were confiscated for the use of Wehrmacht senior officers and Nazi bureaucrats. Nadine's home was commandeered by a senior Luftwaffe general as was her parents'. She convinced Edmund and Arlene to leave Paris and move in with Louis Bondurant at his estate near Limoges, while she moved into a smaller home near the Bois de Boulogne. German troops, particularly specialized services personnel and support staff, were quartered in the homes of many Parisians. This, coupled with the displacement of Parisians from their homes and the new restrictions on their lives, created enormous resentment among the French. But, for Nadine, other requirements circumscribed her activities.

A few weeks later, Nadine's business and financial holdings in France were carefully scrutinized by the Germans. A cold-blooded Nazi official and his aide met with Nadine and demanded an accounting of her holdings and financial resources. They told Nadine not to try to hide any of her wealth. Otherwise, she would be punished and imprisoned. She shared with them all of her holdings in France, Belgium, Holland, and Luxembourg, and a few obvious ones in Switzerland. She did not tell them about the carefully disguised trusts and financial resources in Spain, Switzerland, Portugal, England, Canada, and the United States. Quentin had devised numbered accounts, blind trusts, and impenetrable corporations where Nadine's wealth outside of France was safely hidden. She had given him power of attorney to handle those extensive resources. Still, she was a millionaire with extensive holdings in firms and financial institutions in France, the Low Countries, and Switzerland.

"You will continue to perform your duties as a corporate officer," said an officious Nazi bureaucrat in August. "But, Herr Braustich will oversee all of your activities and make whatever financial decisions are deemed desirable for the Reich."

Kurt Braustich was a tall, older man with piercing gray eyes and had a habit of constantly licking his lower lip. He was a Munich banker almost wiped out by the Depression. However, the devious banker joined the Nazi Party. Because of his familiarity with investment strategies and his obsequiousness to Hitler and the Nazis, he was rewarded and given important roles in Nazi financial activities. Now, Braustich was assigned to manage Nadine's wealth and give the impression that the French woman still controlled her resources and made all financial decisions. In return for her cooperation, Nadine was given a very generous allowance on which to live and permitted "certain freedoms." She could draw money from some of her funds, but any request for large sums could not be done without Braustich's approval. She was allowed one motorcar and could retain access to her stables and some of her horses. Her summer home in Normandy was commandeered, as were apartments and other homes that she owned. The house she was allowed to keep near the Bois de Boulogne was ample and provided quarters for

Moira and three other servants. She could not travel anywhere outside of occupied or Vichy France without permission. She was restricted from traveling to any neutral countries. For all practical purposes, she was a prisoner in occupied France.

Moira, because of her Scottish background, had to be protected. The Scottish woman, loyal to Nadine and her family, refused to leave France. Nadine had documents prepared that indicated Moira was born Moira Tedoux near Poitiers and completed all of her schooling in France. Noel was allowed to continue employment with Nadine, but his activities were closely monitored by Helmut Ziegler, Braustich's assistant. Ziegler was an overtly pleasant person, yet something about him worried Nadine. She later learned that Ziegler was an informant for the Geheime Staatspolizie (Gestapo).

In spite of the Nazi repressive hand in Paris and elsewhere in France, Nadine was treated carefully by German officials because of her wealth, leadership, and as a patron of the arts. Moreover, she had a friend in the Boche military. At the end of August, Nicholas von Kleist called on her. She was not surprised by his visit. The generalmajor was Quentin's friend, and a strong bond existed between them. When they met, von Kleist apologized for some of the "unfortunate" treatment Nadine had endured at the hands of Nazi functionaries during the early phases of the occupation of Paris.

"Things will improve," said von Kleist, "once the new regulations and requirements are in place. If you have problems with any of our petty bureaucrats, let me know," he told her. When they could speak in private, he told her how to contact him secretly by using a priest in Paris to call Lorelei's priest in Germany. She nodded and thanked him.

"Will you be stationed in Paris?"

"No. My duties keep me in Berlin and at other sites. But, now and again I will be required to be here," he told her.

"Will you bring your wife?" she asked. He smiled and said Lorelei would be visiting Paris soon and asked if she could call on Nadine.

"Of course," said the lovely French woman with a charming smile. "I would be delighted to serve as her guide to Paris."

They talked for a while longer until Captain Stembeiler approached the general and whispered something to him.

"It's time for me to go," said von Kleist as he stood. "If you need to contact me, Hauptman (captain) Klaus Maria Stembeiler, my aide, will assist you," he said with firmness in his voice that was intended for the captain. In turn, Stembeiler bowed politely, clicked his heels, handed her his card, and told her he was delighted to be of any assistance.

The following day, von Kleist met with Braustich and Ziegler. As a highly regarded generalmajor in the Luftwaffe and the nephew of the generalleutnant Ewald von Kleist, Nicky had considerable influence within the Nazi apparatus. Moreover, von Kleist was part of the Old Prussian aristocracy and had distinguished himself in combat during the First World War, receiving Germany's highest medal for valor. He made his purpose in meeting with the two bureaucrats immediately known to them. In no uncertain terms, he demanded that Mrs. Desnoyers be treated with the utmost courtesy. The two men listened carefully to what the general told them. His strong words warned them that if the French woman was treated shabbily, they would answer to him. Both men said they understood and professed nothing but the best of intentions toward Mrs. Desnoyers. Braustich tried to remain composed and attentive during the meeting, but the nervous habit of licking his lip made it clear to the general that the bureaucrat was timorous and fearful. Ziegler gave the impression of being very solicitous of the general's demands and more than eager to be of any assistance. *The man's a toad,* thought von Kleist. *Still,* he thought, *he can be dangerous.*

* * *

Toward the end of August, Millard came to Nadine's house disguised as a contractor. She talked to him in front of Noel, with Ziegler listening intently to everything they said. Nadine had developed a code with Noel and Millard that was hidden in the house modification plans they discussed. She told Millard that Moira, her house manager, would occasionally meet with him to make certain that "Madame was aware of the work schedule and when workers would be in the house to do construction." Payment for services would be handled by Noel, her executive assistant. During their second meeting, Nadine, by the use of code words and carefully hidden instructions, put into operation the first phase of her plan to establish an escape route from France into Spain and on to Portugal. The second phase of the plan, the gathering of military intelligence, would have to wait. Nadine and her confreres were preparing to engage in a secret war against the Boche.

* * *

In Canada, the rigorous training schedule in the RCAF kept Marlon occupied from before dawn to dark. The physical training was demanding, but Marlon gradually adjusted to it and began to feel new strength in his body. The classroom activities and ground school, while demanding for many of the recruits, were easy for the

American. His academic training in science, mathematics, and engineering gave him important advantages that many of the others lacked. When it came to flying, Marlon's instructors quickly learned that he was an excellent pilot.

The fall of France at the end of June angered the recruits in Marlon's training class. The German conquest of Western Europe, in spite of the losses that they endured in Holland and Belgium, was overwhelming in its speed and precision. Marlon was angry and bitter when the Italians declared war on France on June 10. He and his fellow recruits listened intently to President Roosevelt's remarks on the radio.

Marlon took to heart the president's comment: "On this tenth day of June 1940, the hand that held the dagger has struck it into the back of its neighbor."

After the Wehrmacht took control of France, a lull in the fighting occurred. The Luftwaffe did not immediately challenge the Royal Air Force (RAF), but restricted its activities to attacking British convoys in the Channel. But it was only a matter of time before the war in the air would begin. When it did, Marlon wanted to be a part of that fight.

During his training in Canada, Marlon managed to telephone his father and Florence a few times. Florence wrote him once a week. He was popular among the trainees because of Florence's pictures on his desk, regularly admired by his colleagues.

Because of his flying abilities, the flight instructors accelerated Marlon's training in the air. By the end of July, they had him doing gunnery practice. He completed flight school at the beginning of August and was commissioned a lieutenant. There was no graduation ceremony for him. Instead, Marlon was given priority transportation to England to train in Spitfires. He arrived in England during the third week in August, just as the

Germans began their aerial campaign to attack the RAF airfields closest to the English Channel.

From London, Marlon took the train to Wales for training with Spitfires at Rednal, No. 61 OTU (Operational Training Unit). His introduction to Spitfires began on a damp day after a morning drizzle dissipated. He had completed ground school and textbook instruction on Spits and was ready for his first flight in the venerable fighter. The instructor walked him to a waiting Spitfire with the large letters TO-R painted on its side. He went through the preflight check and was helped into the cockpit by the flight crew. At over six feet in height, the cockpit was snug, and the seat had to be lowered to accommodate him. He glanced at the gauges before doing the preflight. Then, he adjusted his helmet, mask, and goggles and waited for the instructor.

"All right, you've got her for an hour," said the instructor. "Follow the railroad back here," he said with a smile.

Marlon manipulated the hand pumps and the starter buttons. The engine coughed and roared to life. He opened the radiator wide to avoid overheating the engine. After the engine was warmed properly, he taxied the plane to the runway and called the tower for clearance. He was given clearance, turned the Spitfire into the wind, and advanced the throttle. He remembered what his father had said about flying the speedy fighter. The Spitfire responded like a race car, and he was airborne quickly and raised the undercarriage. The marvelous fighter was everything his father had said it was. He set the propeller blades for cruising and climbed to ten thousand feet. Flying the fast and highly maneuverable plane was exhilarating. *No wonder Dad loves this plane,* he thought.

His training at Rednal was rapid; after fifteen hours of flying in Spitfires, he was posted for combat duty with

RAF Sixty-six Squadron at Gravesend. He arrived at the airbase just after the field had been bombed by the Luftwaffe. The place was in shambles.

The day after his arrival at Gravesend, Kenny Croyle-Marston, a flight leader, took Marlon up for a "familiarization" flight. Its purpose was to determine the new pilot's skill as a flyer. Quentin had warned Marlon about such an event.

"If a veteran pilot from the squadron takes you up for a routine maneuver, you can bet he's going to bounce you."

"Like test me?" the younger flyer surmised.

Quentin nodded and smiled.

Kenny was slight of build, stood about five feet eight inches tall, and had sandy-brown hair, blue-gray eyes, and a fair complexion. He was polite but reserved toward Marlon and was a close friend of Carlisle Napier, the squadron leader.

Once in the air, Kenny had Marlon go through some basic maneuvers in the Spitfire. When the English pilot was satisfied that the Canadian pilot was a good flyer, they climbed to five thousand feet. He radioed Marlon to follow him in a quick dive. But, as they began to turn and dive, Kenny broke off and disappeared into the scud. Marlon knew immediately what was coming. He added power to the Spitfire and climbed into the sun, turning and twisting through the clouds until he reached nine thousand feet and was certain Kenny was not on his tail. Using the clouds as cover and with the sun at his back, Marlon circled as Quentin had taught him, looking below and all around him for the other Spitfire. After a few minutes, he spotted two Spitfires beneath him, circling and hunting for him. He chuckled and lined himself up with the sun before diving on the trailing plane. He used height and speed to pounce on the second Spitfire and heard the pilot, a section leader, cry out on the radio,

"How the blazes did he do that?" When Kenny saw what was happening, he did an immediate roll and looped back to help the other Spitfire. But, Marlon was gone by the time Kenny completed his maneuver. As the flight leader scanned the skies for the new flyer, he heard "bang, bang, your dead" on the radio and saw Marlon come at him from out of the sun.

"Good show," said Kenny on the radio. "Let's go home."

When they landed at Gravesend, the ground crews were still working on the runways to repair the bomb damage done by the Germans. After taxing to the ready area, Kenny and the other Spitfire pilot turned off their engines and had the crew chief refuel them. Then, together, they walked toward Marlon.

"Jolly good, old boy. Where did you learn to fly like that?" asked Guy, the section leader.

"My father," replied Marlon.

"Well, he must be a bloody good pilot. Was he in the last war?" asked Kenny.

Marlon nodded.

"You'll do just fine," said Kenny. "I'll post you for duty with 'B' flight."

A few days later, because of the intensity of the German attacks on the RAF airfields, Sixty-six Squadron was moved to Kenly, another base to the east of London. In the days that followed, when weather permitted, Marlon and his flight were regularly scrambled to intercept German bombers and their fighter escorts. Sometimes his flight was sortied two and three times a day. The aerial combat was intensive. By September 3, 1940, Marlon had destroyed four German bombers and a Messerschmitt Bf 109. He had damaged several German planes, but only the confirmed kills mattered.

During the third week in September, Marlon's flight was scrambled around 10:00 a.m. There were broken clouds in the sky and a weather front was slowly moving in from the west. As Marlon's flight gained altitude and flew eastward over the Channel, they were told to climb to thirteen thousand feet. A few minutes later, he heard his flight leader on the radio.

"Bombers at two o'clock low. Have at them."

Marlon joined the five other Spitfires as they dove on the German Heinkels. In spite of the tracers that whizzed by him, Marlon pressed his attack on one of the German bombers and fired several bursts into the plane. After the fourth burst of bullets, he saw smoke emerge from the port engine, and the bomber rolled slowly to the left before diving down toward the Channel, flames engulfing its left wing.

Before Marlon could pull up, he heard Kenny say, "Me 109 on your tail." Immediately, Marlon banked sharply and started an Immelmann maneuver, but it was not executed fast enough—he felt the thud of bullets hit the Spitfire. The second burst from the German caused the Spitfire to shudder. *I've been hit bad,* thought Marlon, fighting to maintain control of the damaged plane and doing every maneuver he could to avoid the Messerschmitt's fusillade of machine gun and cannon fire. He barely had time to glance at his instruments and scanned the critical gauges that indicated the Rolls Royce Merlin engine was severely damaged and on the brink of quitting. Suddenly, smoke began to fill the cockpit. *No use,* thought Marlon, *time to get out.* He got his bearings and turned the dying Spitfire toward the coast of England. He was determined to bail out as close to the beach as possible; if only the Germans would not press their attack.

The last thing he remembered before throwing open the canopy and bailing out was hearing Patrick, a member of his flight, yell that Marlon's plane was on fire and he was diving on the pursuing Me 109. The rush of cold air hit Marlon like a slap in the face, and he tumbled through space. He pulled on his rip cord and felt the parachute begin to open. There was a sudden jerk as the canopy blossomed. He looked down and saw he was over land, but the wind was pushing him toward the Channel. Try as he might to manage the straps to the chute, he saw the water rush toward him. Then, he hit, and the impact of the cold water cut through him like a knife. He went underwater momentarily before coming to the surface. *Christ, it's freezing,* he thought. *Got to inflate my Mae West,* he thought, struggling to get out of the parachute harness. There was a moment of panic when he fumbled with the release mechanism to the chute and it would not actuate. He went under again and struggled to reach the surface. He felt the harness to his chute disengage and his inflated life vest buoy him in the frigid water.

Marlon bobbed in the cold water for a few minutes before getting his bearings. He struggled to move his arms and paddle toward the west and the shore. After what seemed like an eternity, he felt the waves push him toward the beach and saw people come into the water toward him. The next thing he knew, several men were dragging him toward the beach.

He remembered one of them saying, "We saw you come down, Laddie. Good thing we're here to help."

He began to tremble and tried to keep his teeth from chattering as the men helped him onto the beach and then to a horse-drawn cart. An older man was removing his life vest as another held out a cigarette for him. Marlon waved it off and was barely able to say how cold it was through his chattering teeth.

"You'll be all right, Laddie," said the same voice. "We'll take you some place dry and get you some hot tea."

It was then that Marlon finally relaxed. He had lost his plane, but was lucky to be alive. That same evening, Marlon was driven to Sixty-six Squadron. He was credited with destroying another German bomber and teased about going swimming in the Channel. But, the other members of his flight praised him for coming through the ordeal unscratched.

As the days wore on, several pilots in his flight and in the squadron never returned, especially among the younger and less-experienced flyers. Not a day went by without someone failing to return. Some were lucky and bailed out after getting shot up. They were greeted back at the base as survivors. However, Marlon noticed the increasing number of pilots who never returned. Losses were high and replacements were slow in filling the ranks of pilots ready for combat duty. There were times when the Spitfires could not be rearmed and refueled fast enough to get them into the air to intercept enemy planes.

After a full day of encounters with the enemy, Marlon was fatigued and exhausted, his body tired in ways that were physical and the result of psychological tension. He hardly had time to do little more than eat and sleep and try to be ready for the seemingly relentless "scramble" calls. By the beginning of October, Marlon had lost weight, was run down, and felt like an old man. His reflexes slowed because of the strain and fatigue. Over the Channel, three Bf 109s jumped him. The odds were too great, and he had to pull away and hide in the cloud cover. He lost the Germans, gained altitude, and emerged from the scud and searched the sky for enemy fighters. Finding none, he called control. He was informed that another flight of Germans was approaching at ten thousand feet. He checked his fuel before turning in their direction and climbing to fifteen thousand feet. When he spotted the flight of Heinkels, he used the sun to hide him and dove on the last plane. It took him two passes before smoke began to trail from the German's starboard engine. He was beginning a turn for home when tracers flashed by his left wing. He immediately did a roll and a loop and put the Spitfire into a steep dive to avoid his pursuer. As his plane rushed toward the earth, more tracers zipped by him, and he realized there must be more than one German on his tail. But it did not matter. The Germans broke off when several Spitfires fired on them. When Marlon returned to his squadron, he was teased about getting lost and then jumped by Jerries (Germans). He was never credited with downing the German bomber. All he could think about was getting back alive and living to fight another day.

The worsening weather provided time for Marlon to experience the formal and informal structures that governed the lives of the pilots at Sixty-six Squadron. He became aware of the subtle complexities that differentiated groups in his squadron. He could not help but notice the social structure and class distinction among the flyers of Sixty-six Squadron. Most of the senior British pilots were from aristocratic families and part of a strong brotherhood of nobles that through family ties and pedigree achieved rank and promotion in the RAF. Flyers like Marlon, from another country, were welcome in the RAF, but, unless they were exceptional—wealthy or from an old and highly regarded family—they were treated politely, but seldom included in the social activities of the titled pilots. Marlon did not reveal that he was an American, that he was born in France, or that his mother was from a long line of French aristocrats. Instead, among the pilots and leaders of Sixty-six Squadron he was regarded as a Canadian who came from a French-speaking part of Canada and had studied in the United States. But, there were characteristics and qualities about Marlon that impressed the senior pilots and leaders of Sixty-six Squadron.

As a present for graduating with distinction from MIT, Quentin and Nadine had established a large trust with a very generous annuity for Marlon. Each month, he received $1,500. In addition, he could draw on other resources with his father's permission. Marlon used his pay from the RAF mainly and barely touched the monthly income from the annuity. He asked his father to reinvest the unused monthly funds to increase the principal. Although he was very well off financially, he maintained a very modest lifestyle. There was little time because of his combat flying to spend but a small portion of what he earned. However, Marlon was always generous with his friends in Sixty-six Squadron. This did not go unnoticed among the senior flyers, and particularly among Carlisle Napier, the squadron leader, Kenny Croyle-Marston, and Foster Burleigh-Smyth, his section leader.

* * *

In America, early in July 1940, Quentin received an unexpected call from Kendall Valderano.

"Mr. Norvell, I need your help," said Kendall. When Quentin asked what he could do for him, the younger man said, "I want to join the RAF. My father says you have contacts in the British Air Ministry. Can you help me?"

"Are you certain about this, Kendall?" asked the Cajun.

Kendall replied affirmatively, saying he wanted to be a fighter pilot.

"Have you spoken to your father about this?"

"Yes, but he tried to talk me out of it," replied the young man. "I know he doesn't want me to go to England and be a pilot, but I was born there, and my mother and her family are there. I want to help. You must know what I mean," he told the Cajun in a serious voice.

"I understand," said Quentin, remembering how he too had left the United States in 1916 to join the French *Aeronautic Militaire.* "Let me talk with your father first. After all, you're only nineteen," he told the younger man.

Kendall answered immediately that he was old enough and that he was already a good pilot.

For a moment, Quentin mulled over Kendall's request. Yes, the boy was a good pilot. He had taught Kendall to fly. However, being a good flyer and a combat pilot were two different things. "Tell you what," said the Cajun. "Let me talk with your father first. I promise to get back to you as soon as he and I have talked."

"Please, Mr. Norvell, I need your help. If you won't help me, I'll find another way to get to England and join the RAF."

"I understand," said Quentin, convinced of the younger man's determination. "Sit tight until I talk with your father. Where can I reach you?"

Kendall gave Quentin a telephone number in California and promised he would be there until he heard from the Cajun.

The next evening, Quentin called Ruben, and they talked about Kendall's request.

"What did he tell you?" asked the Mexican.

The Cajun said, "He wants to go to England and join the RAF. He asked for my help."

"To do what?"

"To use my contacts in the air ministry and get him into the RAF."

"What did you tell him?" asked the Mexican, in a barely controlled voice.

"I told him I needed to talk with you first."

There was a pause before Ruben said, "I don't think it's a good idea for him to go to England. He's too young. From what I hear, the RAF is not doing well against the Luftwaffe."

"Yes, I know," said the Cajun, thinking about the brief letters that he received from Marlon about their losses and the strain of combat. "If Kendall wants to go to England and join the RAF, there's not much we can do to stop him. He was born in England and for all practical purposes has dual citizenship. Besides, the Brits need good pilots."

Ruben was silent on the other end of the line. Finally, he spoke up, his voice filled with unease. "As much as I want him to stay here, I can't stop him."

"Tell you what," said the Cajun, "if he's determined to join the RAF, perhaps we can convince him to let me improve his flying and prepare for combat. I did that for Marlon," he added. "Do you think Kendall will agree to this?"

The Mexican thought for a moment before responding. He knew his son would join the RAF. Quentin's offer was a much-needed gift. *Quentin's training might just help Kendall survive,* thought the Mexican before saying, "Thank you for offering to do this. Much as I dislike his determination to join the RAF, your offer to train him is critical. I'll speak to him."

By the beginning of August, Kendall had trained for three intensive weeks with Quentin. They flew every morning when the weather permitted, and the Cajun insisted that Kendall read everything that was available on fighter tactics and the characteristics of the Messerschmitt Bf 109.

"You need to know the performance capabilities of the Messerschmitt Bf 109," said the Cajun, "and how to deal with it in the air. But, remember," he warned, "determine the enemy pilot's skills and turn them against him."

Quentin contacted Air Marshal Dowding and told him about Kendall Valderano and his strong desire to join the RAF. Dowding asked about Kendall and his flying abilities. When Quentin mentioned that he taught Kendall to fly and was teaching him aerial combat tactics, the air marshal gave a barely perceptible chuckle and said they could use the boy.

"Keith Price and I will handle things from this end," said Dowding. "When can he be here?"

Quentin replied that Kendall could be in England in less than a week.

"Splendid," said Dowding. "Have him report directly to Keith. Do you have that address?"

Quentin replied no, and Dowding gave it to him.

"We wish more of your chaps could join us," said Dowding. "We could use them."

They talked a while longer before Dowding asked when Quentin would visit England.

"I'll try to get there in mid-October," said the American. "Any news about my son?"

"Keith tells me he's shot down another bomber. I believe that brings his total to six enemy aircraft destroyed. He's a fine pilot. We could use more like him," said Dowding wistfully. The two men talked briefly before hanging up.

As he replaced the telephone on its cradle, the Cajun could only imagine how desperate the situation was for the British. All that stood between England and a German invasion was the RAF. *They must win,* he said as a prayer.

Kendall left for England aboard the Amelie four days later. In less than a week, he was training to become a pilot in the RAF.

* * *

Quentin received a telephone call from Ruben Valderano just before he was ready to leave the office on September 27, 1940.

"What is it?" he asked the Mexican.

"Bad news," said Ruben. "The Germans have signed a pact with Italy and Japan."

"What!" exclaimed an incredulous Quentin. "So what does this mean?"

"It means the Japanese, allied with Germany and Italy, will push forward with their territorial expansion in the Far East. The defeat of the Dutch and the French and their alliance with the Germans gives Japan a free hand to take over European colonies and territories in the Pacific. It's not good."

"Have you spoken with the president about this?" asked the Cajun.

Ruben said no.

"Do you want me to call him?"

The Mexican said yes and encouraged Quentin to call General Marshall also.

A week later, Quentin and Ruben met with President Roosevelt, Cordell Hull, Harry Hopkins, and General Marshall to discuss the Tripartite Pact between Japan, Germany, and Italy.

"This is a worrisome development," said Hull. "The Japanese will use this agreement to pursue their territorial expansion plans in Southeast Asia."

"Have the British said anything about this pact?" asked Ruben.

"Yes, they're quite displeased with the Japanese," said Hull.

"But do they plan to do anything about it?" asked the Cajun.

"There's not much they can do," said Hull, looking at Marshall.

"Well, the British are in no position to begin hostilities with the Japanese," said Marshall. "They're having a very difficult time with the Germans at the moment."

"The Japanese have a first-rate navy and a large, modern army," said a somber Ruben. "They could sweep down the Malayan Peninsula, attack Burma, and threaten India."

Hopkins looked at Ruben and said, "We are talking with the Japanese to share our concerns regarding their treaty with the Germans."

"Yes, parts of that pact need to be tempered," said Hull. "I don't care for the language in it."

They talked for about twenty minutes before Roosevelt said he had another appointment.

"Gentlemen, I'm worried about our English friends," said the president. "They cannot afford a war with Japan. We must find a way to persuade the Japanese to check their territorial ambitions." He turned to Hull and said, "Cordell, express our concerns to Nomura (Japanese Ambassador to the United States) about the pact and their plans for expansion in the Far East. Then, ask Stony to contact the German ambassador in Berlin and arrange a meeting with Hitler's people. Maybe we can persuade the Germans to reign in the Japanese."

Ruben, Quentin, and Marshall made eye contact, a nonverbal signal that they should speak in private. After the meeting, the three of them walked out of the White House together.

Ruben spoke up. "I don't think your boss realizes how determined the Japanese are about expanding their sphere of influence in Southeast Asia. They want Burma, Hong Kong, and the British possessions in New Guinea and Malaysia. This pact may open the door for them to attack the British in the Pacific."

"You really think it will come to that?" asked the Cajun.

Ruben nodded and looked at Marshall. The general remained silent, but his body language and eye contact with Valderano indicated to Quentin that the two were of a mind.

War in Europe and now perhaps war in the Pacific, thought Quentin. *The Brits can't handle Germany and Japan alone. Meanwhile, we sit on our hands.*

* * *

The weather in eastern England at the beginning of October 1940 turned sloppy, with a steady decline in the hours of daylight, and frequent periods of clouds and rain. Dense fogs were frequent. When the weather permitted, Marlon's flight was scrambled often. The RAF's primary target was the German bombers. Getting at them, however, was difficult because of their fighter escorts. In desperation, the RAF was sending out flights to engage the German fighters so that other groups could attack the slower and vulnerable bombers. The practice was working, but losses among the British pilots were very high. The RAF was reaching a point when there were more fighter planes available than men to fly them. To Marlon, it seemed that, without some kind of miracle, the Nazis would force the RAF fighter groups to move out of range of German bombers and perhaps open England to invasion.

* * *

At the end of the first full week of October, Quentin received a long letter from Marlon. In it, he asked Quentin to share it with Florence. The Cajun read the letter that evening. When Florence came home, he asked if she would mind reading it aloud.

She fingered the letter gently before saying, "Please read it," her eyes suddenly clouding over with tears.
The Cajun began slowly reading what Marlon had written:

> *I can't begin to tell you how cold and damp it is here. The chill gets in your bones. And it rains often. But I've come to welcome fog or rainy days, like today, because it gives us time to catch up on sleep and relax...*

The Germans keep coming and coming. We're losing two and three pilots a day in my squadron, sometimes more. We're tired and badly in need of more pilots. It's tough to come back and see empty beds.

I've noticed something about the social structure here. The pilots from titled families stick together. They're friendly, but seldom include me in their social activities or plans. However, they all show a keen interest in Florence's picture. Tell her that I can't for the life of me imagine why!

Quentin paused a moment to look up at the face of his lovely daughter. She smiled at her brother's teasing, but she was visibly tense. She hunched her shoulders and shivered as if given an electrical shock. Quentin asked if he should continue reading the letter. She smiled bravely and nodded. Even with her eyes swollen and tears ready to flow, he noticed how beautiful Florence was. It pained him to see his lovely daughter so worried and distraught.

Our losses are high, especially among the pilots from aristocratic families. They're brave enough, but they may have achieved their rank and place in the RAF because of their family name and ties. It takes more than a family crest and bravery to be a good fighter pilot. Too many of our new pilots have little more than ten hours in a Spitfire. Some never have time to unpack before they're in the air and go missing. It's so sad.

Tell Funny Face I miss her. She would do well here. The Brits, especially the single young pilots, ask me about her often. They visit my room just to see and handle her picture. There are times when I can hear her playing the piano, especially on my way home after mixing it up with the Boche...

The Cajun looked up at his daughter, hesitating to read the final lines of Marlon's letter.

"What is it, Daddy?" she asked, a worried expression on her face. "Something's wrong, isn't it?" she said tremulously.

"No, honey, there's nothing wrong. It's just that what Marlon writes is very special for me," he told her.

"Please read it, Daddy," she pleaded, her hands wringing a small delicate handkerchief.

He nodded and continued.

I never did thank you for the lessons you gave me in dogfighting. If it were not for those lessons, I'd be dead or floating around the English Channel. Remind me to tell you about a few maneuvers I've learned from some of the older pilots.

I miss you and Flo more than I can say. Every day that we go up I know that some of us will not return. You must have felt the same thing when you fought in WW I. When I get back, we'll need to talk.

Quentin stopped reading and handed the letter to Florence. He looked away for a moment to clear his eyes of moisture. Memories of the time he had served as a combat pilot in France during the Great War flooded his thoughts. He remembered his tenuous existence living from day to day, not knowing if he would return from a patrol over enemy lines. He had steeled himself to the demands and his existential choice. He became hardened in a way that was complicated and difficult to describe. Something dark and ruthless replaced fear and turned him into a cold, determined, and methodical killer in the air. He closed his eyes and said a prayer that Marlon not become such a dark and callous person.

The autumn days of October passed quickly, and before he knew it, Quentin was flying the Amelie across the Atlantic to England. He, Hardy, and Mark arrived at an airfield west of London, well beyond the range of the German bombers that were pounding the large city day and night. When the three of them approached the center of London, they were unprepared for the fires and devastation. Where once buildings had stood now there were jagged fragments of houses and the skeletons of offices and homes shattered and charred by bombs. Although they had seen newsreels in movie houses about the "London Blitz," the actual sight of the destruction and loss of life was overwhelming.

"God damn the Germans," said Mark as they witnessed the suffering of the resolute English people, struggling to tear away debris to find loved ones in the rubble, or crying next to the bodies of family or friends killed in an attack.

I wish Americans at home could see this up close, thought Quentin. *Maybe then they would understand what this war is about and why we should help the Allies defeat the Nazis.* Deep in his heart, he knew that complacent American leaders in business, the media, and politics would scorn any pleas for involvement in the war. *What will it take for us to fight?* he wondered, as they moved slowly past the devastation that overpowered their senses by filling their nostrils with the acrid smell of smoke from burning buildings, their eyes unable to shut out the misery of lives and homes horribly destroyed, and their ears assaulted by the harsh bells and screaming sirens of fire trucks and ambulances plying through the rubble of the city.

"Jesus, this is awful," said Hardy in a low voice, as he stared inconsolably at the ruins and rendered life of a once tranquil part of London.

They slowly motored west until they approached their hotel in a part of London that had miraculously escaped bombing by the Luftwaffe. When they checked in, Quentin mentioned to Hardy and Mark that he would move them to another hotel on the west side of London and away from the bombing. But, neither man would have it so.

"No, boss," said Mark. "If you stay here, so do we!"

The Cajun admired them and said they had courage.

"It's not about being brave, boss," said Hardy. "It's about showing the Brits we're with them."

"That's very commendable," said Quentin, proud of his two friends and fellow flyers. "You're great guys, and I don't want anything to happen to you."

"Don't worry, boss, we'll be OK," said Mark, looking to Hardy for confirmation and support.

The other man nodded in approval.

* * *

The next day, Quentin met with Geoff at the air ministry. He inquired about Marlon and was told his son was well and had destroyed several enemy planes.

"Quite a pilot," commented the English general with a smile. "He's done quite well. Six enemy planes destroyed so far."

"What about Kendall Valderano?" asked the Cajun.

"Another of your protégés," said Geoff with a chuckle. "He's a sergeant-pilot and completed his flight training at Aston Down. He checked out on Spits at Rednal and was posted for flight duty two weeks ago. The RAF would like to hire you as a combat instructor," quipped the Englishman, grinning at the American.

They chatted on their way to Air Vice Marshal Park's office located at RAF Bentley Priory, in the London Borough of Harrow near Stanmore.

Geoff mentioned that Etienne de Gavrelac had inquired about him.

"Etienne's here?" asked the American.

"Yes, he and other French pilots and officers have come over," said Geoff. "They're forming a Free French Squadron. Etienne went through our intelligence screening at the Royal Patriotic School (Wandsworth). His charming wife is with him, you know."

"How can I reach him?"

"He's rather busy at the moment, but I'll let him know you're here and where he can call you."

Just as they arrived at the RAF Bentley Priory, they heard an alarm.

"Another raid?" asked the Cajun.

Geoff nodded nonchalantly as if the aerial assault was routine.

"They're late," said a caustic Keith Park about the German assault, as he greeted the two men.

"How's it going?" asked the Cajun, curious to learn the mood and determination of his friends in the RAF.

"Well, since Jerry stopped bombing our airfields and turned on London, we're holding our own," Park replied nonchalantly.

"I'd say we're doing better," commented Geoff, as they walked to a secure part of the building.

Price asked Quentin if he cared to visit the RAF headquarters command center, a hub for processing information about enemy planes advancing on British targets. Input was provided by radar facilities, ground observers, and, less frequently, direct observation from RAF planes in the air. The enemy advance was monitored in this center, and, once the course and altitude of the German planes was plotted, RAF fighters from different squadrons were "scrambled" to intercept the Germans. Keith Price stood behind one of the senior officers watching a flight of advancing German planes.

"London again," said Price in a dispassionate voice.

"I'm afraid so," said the senior officer, a pained expression on his face as he picked up a telephone and ordered two flights of fighters to intercept the Germans.

"So this is how you do it," said the Cajun, impressed by the RAF's system and precision. Quentin continued to observe how the women working on a lower portion of the large room moved pieces of wood with numbers on them.

"What are those?" asked the American, pointing to the blocks the women were moving with wooden rods on the large table. Price said they represented German aircraft such as bombers and fighters. He told the American that the RAF had fairly reliable intelligence about Luftwaffe airfields in France close to the English Channel.

"The moment their planes gain altitude, our radar begins to pick them up. We triangulate reports from different sites, and sometimes ground observers, to plot their direction and height. We're mainly interested in their bombers," said Price, as he noticed lights on a board illuminate to indicate RAF fighter squadrons that had been placed on alert.

"All right," said Price in a serious voice, "send them up."

Quentin realized that Marlon could be among the RAF pilots scrambled to intercept the Germans. *If he is,* thought the Cajun, *good hunting.*

As they were leaving the command center, Quentin asked Price if it would be possible to see Marlon.

"Why, yes, of course," said Price. "Let me make a call."

The daylight slowly faded to an overcast sky that promised dense clouds and perhaps rain. Geoff, Keith Price, and Quentin were sitting in the air vice marshal's office when an aide knocked on the door and said Lieutenant Norvell had arrived.

"Show him in," said Keith Price.

Marlon, puzzled by the summons to be at Air Vice Marshal Price's office, entered the room and stared in disbelief at his father standing next to Price and Geoff. "Dad," he blurted out, before coming to attention and saluting the two senior RAF officers.

"Close the door, Lieutenant," said an expressionless Price, turning to look at the Cajun and winking.

"Marlon, you know Geoff and Air Vice Marshal Keith Price," said Quentin, as he looked carefully at his son.

Marlon was dressed in a blue RAF uniform with the insignia of a flight lieutenant. He looked gaunt and tired, his hair disheveled, and there were dark circles under his eyes.

He's aged, thought the Cajun. Quentin embraced Marlon and then asked how he was.

The four men sat to talk, but not before Price had some tea, coffee, and biscuits brought into his office.

"Marlon's done quite well by us," said Geoff.

"Yes," Price commented while reading a message. "I see you've knocked down another bomber. Let's see now, that brings your total to seven enemy planes destroyed." He looked directly at the young fighter pilot to express in a nonverbal way his regard and satisfaction in Marlon's combat skills.

Quentin beamed at his son, proud of Marlon's accomplishments.

"How's Kendall doing?" asked Marlon.

"He's posted to Debden," said Geoff.

"Yes," added Price, "and he's already damaged a couple of Heinkel 111s."

"Good for him," said Marlon with an appreciative smile.

"Geoff, I'd like a word with you outside," said Price.

"Of course," Geoff replied, realizing the air vice marshal wanted to give Quentin and Marlon some time alone.

"We won't be long," said Price, as he nodded at Quentin.

When they were alone, Marlon and Quentin talked about Florence, their family, American attitudes toward the war, and about Nadine.

"Have you heard from Mom?"

"Yes, I've gotten messages from her. She's well, but kept on a short leash by the Nazis," he told the younger pilot. "I plan to visit her in December."

"How will you do that?" asked a troubled Marlon. "She's in occupied France."

"Remember, son, America is still a neutral country, and I'm one of your mother's attorneys. So far, the Boche don't know that we and your mother are related. But they soon will. When that happens, their attitude toward your mother and me will change."

"Dad, isn't there some way you can get her out of France?"

"I'm not able to tell you what your mother is doing, but she has good reasons to stay in France," he told his son. "In her own way, Marlon, your mother is fighting the Boche."

"But isn't that dangerous for her?"

The Cajun noticed exasperation in Marlon. "Your mother has fortitude and courage." The Cajun tried hard to check his emotions and not register any fear for Nadine that Marlon might detect.

"Dad, if the Nazis ever find out she's working against them, they'll…"

Before he could finish the sentence, Quentin took his son by the shoulders and said, "I hope it doesn't come to that, but, if her life is threatened, I'll find a way to get into France and bring her out."

Marlon saw a cold and determined look in his father's eyes that reminded him of something he'd seen before. *There's something hard and dangerous in Dad. If anyone can get Mother out of France, it's him,* he thought.

Quentin decided to change the subject and asked Marlon about the new fighter tactics he mentioned in a recent letter. They talked for a while about flight characteristics, formations, and weaknesses in the Bf 109. A few minutes later, Geoff poked his head into the office and asked how they were doing. When Quentin replied that they were almost done, the two senior RAF officers entered the office and chatted with Marlon and Quentin.

"I guess I'd better get back to my squadron," said Marlon looking at his father, a strong nonverbal expression of affection passing between them. Quentin stood and hugged his son.

"Your mother and our families are proud of you, as am I. Is there anything you need?" asked Quentin.

Marlon smiled and said, "Yes, Dad, some cannon for my Spitfire!"

At this comment, Keith Park and Geoff laughed and said newer models of Spitfires would be armed with cannons.

"Just a matter of a few more months," said Geoff with a smile.

After Marlon left to return to Sixty-six Squadron at Kenly, Price told Quentin how much the air ministry appreciated the "resources" the organization the American established in Switzerland had provided.

"We're using the funds to improve the armor and firepower of the Spits," Price told the American. "We also appreciate that you've sent us two well-trained fighter pilots. I wish you could send us more."

"What are your plans?" asked Geoff.

Quentin mentioned meeting with people in the U.S. Embassy and then with senior personnel in the prime minister's office.

"We do hope your business arrangements with Churchill's staff are successful," said Price. "By the way, a few of us had dinner with Glinda Pennington. We have you to thank for that splendid engagement. She's a lovely woman."

"And beautiful," added Geoff.

"Yes, I look forward to seeing her again," said the Cajun, careful not to mention Glinda's invitation for him to dine with her after a matinee the following day. "It's getting late, and I've taken up too much of your time already," said the American. The three men talked for a few more minutes before Quentin prepared to leave.

"Any plans for this evening?" asked Geoff, looking directly at the Cajun.

"Not really," said the American, visibly curious about Geoff's question.

"Splendid, I have a surprise for you," said the English officer. "We'll call for you around seven."

We, thought the Cajun. *I wonder what he has in mind.*

Quentin was waiting when Geoff's aide walked into the lobby of the hotel and paged him. When he approached the waiting car, the Cajun was surprised to see Geoff seated in the back of the sedan with two lovely women.

"Let me introduce you," said Geoff, as he identified Quentin to Margaret and Linne. That evening, the four of them had a light dinner at an exclusive club and then went to a musical performance. Quentin learned that Margaret was actually Lady Margaret Gibbon of Stockenchurch and the wife of an Earl. Her husband was the executive officer on a British destroyer in the South Pacific. She was Geoff's cousin. Linne Kidsgrove was the widow of a wealthy baron, Lord Conlon, killed while racing a motorcar in Italy. He was almost fifteen years her senior when they married. If she missed her husband, it was not apparent. In her late thirties, Linne was a very attractive woman with silky smooth auburn hair, large blue eyes, generous lips, and the kind of figure that turns men's heads. She was well educated too.

That evening, Linne continually asked Quentin questions and probed to learn more about the mysterious American. Geoff had mentioned to her that Norvell was a widower, and she was intrigued when Geoff mentioned that Quentin was a Cajun from Louisiana.

"What is a Cajun?" she asked.

Quentin recounted the story of the Acadians forced to leave eastern Canada by the English in 1755 and 1758. Many of them moved to the United States and settled in the Mississippi Delta. She was enthralled and pressed Quentin to tell her about his parents and particularly the women in his ancestral line.

When he mentioned Wenona and her ascribed witchy ways and presumed abilities to cast spells, the perky Englishwoman looked straight at him and said, "You mean you're descended from a witch?"

They all laughed, but Linne, smitten by the Cajun, asked in a teasing manner if he was capable of casting spells and using magic.

The American smiled and looked into her large blue eyes and said, "Yes, it's how I befuddle my adversaries and win over the hearts of young women!"

"You're awful!" exclaimed Linne, enchanted by the American. *He's so different from the men I know,* she thought. She knew mainly aristocratic Englishmen and had married into an old landed family with wealth and an extensive pedigree. Too many of the men she knew were self-absorbed and reflected aristocratic class values that were steeped in tradition. The role for women, a baroness in her case, was prescribed and confining by the rigid traditions of the landed nobility. Linne hated it when her mother and mother-in-law told her to behave in a "proper" manner. But, the Cajun's winning smile and friendly manner took her at face value. *How refreshing,* she thought.

When they stopped in front of Quentin's hotel, Linne stepped out of the sedan and asked him how long he would be in London. When he replied just a few days, she looked disappointed.

"Do you come to London often?" she asked, hoping for a positive answer.

"More now that I have business and other obligations here," he replied.

Wonderful, she thought. "Will you call on me when you return?" she asked with a lovely smile that revealed perfect teeth.

"Are you sure?" he asked. She nodded and handed him a card with her name and address in London.

"My number is on the back," she told him.

"You wouldn't have a younger sister?" he asked, the question surprising Linne and causing a frown.

"I ask because my son is a pilot in the RAF and needs to meet someone young and charming like you."

She gave a barely perceptible sigh of relief, and, after a minute of contemplation, mentioned she might be able to introduce his son to some charming young women from good families. She asked for and he gave her Marlon's name and address at Sixty-six Squadron.

"Remember to call me when you're in London," said Linne, as she stepped into the sedan, a mischievous smile on her face.

The following day, Linne called Geoff and thanked him for introducing her to Quentin Norvell. She pressed the Englishman for more information about the American. Geoff chuckled and mentioned meeting him during the Great War and relayed some of Quentin's exploits in the air. When he mentioned that the American was a solicitor (attorney) and a financial backer for the movie industry in Hollywood, she was awed by Quentin's background and professional life. He also mentioned that Etienne de Gavrelac, a lieutenant colonel with the Free French, was Quentin's friend. She inquired about Etienne, and Geoff told her about Argentina, Etienne's lovely wife of Mexican origin. The more Linne learned about Quentin, the more she wanted to see him again. *I should meet the Gavrelacs,* she mused. *But, why, Quentin Norvell, are you still single?*

* * *

The next day, Quentin met Glinda for dinner. As they sat and talked, sirens announced the advance of German bombers.

"I don't care to hide in a shelter," she told the American.

He wondered if it was bravery or a way to hide fear.

"Are you comfortable staying here?" she asked, to test the Cajun.

Quentin smiled and said, "I admire your courage," and remained seated. They sat and listened attentively to the explosions before the sounds faded and the all clear sounded. As they were enjoying their main course, Quentin asked casually if Glinda had seen Kendall. The elegant woman stopped eating, dabbed at her lips with a linen napkin, and smiled at him.

"Yes, I saw him before he started his RAF training and again when he finished," she said, before adding, "I'm in your debt."

"Oh!" exclaimed the American, wondering about the lovely woman's praise.

"Kendall told me you trained him for several weeks. He claims it gave him advantages that others in his training class didn't have."

The Cajun studied the features of the charming woman, realizing that, at almost forty, she was still a beauty. He thanked her for the praise and said that Kendall was already an excellent pilot and the added maneuvers merely fine-tuned his flying abilities.

"You're quite modest," said Glinda, smiling at the American. "I believe that my son's safety was your concern."

"And Ruben's," he added. She stiffened momentarily at the mention of Ruben's name but quickly regained her composure.

"Yes, Ruben and I talked before Kendall enlisted. I told him he was too young. He's only nineteen, after all," she said, pausing to sip her wine.

The Cajun sat quietly, watching the attractive Englishwoman across from him, waiting for her to continue. There was something in the way he looked at her that intrigued Glinda. He was an attractive man who possessed an inner strength. She felt comfortable trusting him with sensitive matters in her life.

"I learned from Ruben that you were an ace during the Great War. I had no idea you were such a decorated hero."

Quentin raised a hand to stop Glinda. "Let's not talk about me. I'd prefer to know how Kendall is doing."

The way the American tactfully changed the subject and his manner convinced Glinda of his sincerity and made her feel comfortable sharing her feelings. "Kendall admires you and especially Marlon," she said with a smile. "He keeps up with Marlon's record of planes destroyed. There is some hero worship there."

He asked her about the "Blitz."

"We're dealing with the 'Blitz' as best we can. We've been tested before and prevailed," she said proudly.

"But you're paying quite a price to stand up to the Germans," said Quentin, with a look of concern.

"Whatever do you mean?" asked Glinda, surprised by the American's remark.

"I mean that the defeat of the BEF on the Continent, the military losses, and the civilian deaths from the

German bombings are taking a toll on your country. I just wish America would do more to help England."

She was about to become defensive, but his last comments changed her mind. She realized that Quentin supported the British and wanted America to be an ally.

"Thank you for saying that," she told the Cajun. "I wish Americans could see how hard this war has been on us. Oh, when will it ever end?" she said, as tears flooded her eyes.

Quentin rose and handed her his handkerchief, which she used to dab her eyes. He looked down at the lovely woman and could not contain himself.

"What happened between you and Ruben?"

"What has Ruben told you?" she asked while drying her eyes.

"He praises you and says that he was young and impetuous."

"I was at fault," she volunteered. "I was young and foolish," she added with regret.

For the next fifteen minutes Glinda told Quentin about her relationship with Ruben, their marriage, and what led to their divorce.

"I owe Ruben so much," she told him, tears flowing down her cheeks. "He could have kept Kendall from me. But, instead, he made certain Kendall and I could be together often."

"Do you ever regret divorcing Ruben?" asked the American. His question did not seem to surprise Glinda.

"That's all in the past. I've so much to think about, especially now that Kendall's in the RAF," she replied. "I'm just thankful that things turned out as they did."

That evening, after Quentin returned to his hotel, he knew that Glinda had strong affection for Ruben. She had admitted to making a mistake causing them to divorce. The way she talked about Ruben made it clear to the Cajun that she still loved the Mexican.

In Paris, Nadine slowly gathered information about the precise location of Luftwaffe bases near the English Channel. Once the information was validated, it was sent to London through a carefully developed secret communication conduit that passed through southern France into Spain, then on to Portugal, where it landed in American operatives' hands. She knew the Americans would forward the information to the British. After several secret messages sent by Nadine's network were forwarded to British Intelligence by American operatives, the English attempted to find and contact the source of the information in France, but the clever French woman had told her operatives in France, Spain, and Portugal to work only with the Americans. She told Millard that the less their operatives involved in the intelligence network knew, the better it would be for all of them.

Nadine had recruited and placed reliable operatives at key locations in southwest France and northwest Spain. Through persons in Spain, mainly those who had fought against the Fascists and were antagonistic toward the Nazis, a network led to Lisbon. It began to carry valuable military information to the Americans. Nadine made certain that operatives in the chain knew little or nothing about others in the network. Arrangements were made for each operative to have a secret drop spot, and these were changed regularly to avoid detection. Moreover, only Nadine, Millard, Noel, and two others knew the people who formed the entire network.

As soon as she could, Nadine arranged for some of the operatives in southern France to receive and learn to use wireless equipment. However, she insisted that the communications be limited and only directed at safe and reliable operators in northern Spain. When Millard asked why they could not establish direct contact with the British, she smiled and said the risks were too great.

"Besides," she told Millard, "the Boche can easily track and trace wireless signals, especially those directed at England. If they catch any of our operators, they will torture them. It is better not to take that risk," she told him.

He nodded and said it was a wise precaution.

In time, resistance groups called Maquis developed in France. Nadine, without identifying herself, became known and respected by local Maquis and earned the code name "Eglantine." Millard and Noel carefully developed contacts with the heads of nascent resistance groups along the secret network that passed through southern France, into Spain, and beyond. This cultivation would pay off later as the network adopted a new role besides the transmittal of vital military information to the Allies, a safe conduit through France for downed Allied flyers, Jews, engineers and scientists, and political dissidents fleeing the Nazis.

In late October 1940, Nadine received a coded message from Quentin, delivered by a visiting Spanish nun. The message appeared to be a simple prayer but imbedded in it was information about Marlon and his success in the RAF, especially his victories in the air.

"Thank God he's alive and well," Nadine told her parents and Louis when she met with them at La Croisiere.

"Will Quentin visit France?" asked Louis, while Arlene and Edmund waited for her reply.

"Yes, Uncle, he will be here at the beginning of December," she told them in a tender voice that demonstrated her deep affection for the Cajun. "He will tell us about Marlon and his confreres across la Manche (English Channel)." She kept secret the plans to pass vital information about German military activities to her lover.

As the days passed into weeks and December 1940 approached, Nadine could hardly wait for her lover's arrival. His trip to France was justified as a legitimate business trip where he, as Nadine's attorney of record in the United States, brought documents and statements for her to review, as well as important papers to sign for the transfer of funds.

Nadine informed Kurt Braustich about Quentin's business trip to Paris and explained that he was the attorney responsible for her investments in the United States, Switzerland, and elsewhere. The German smiled and said it would be a pleasure to meet Herr Norvell. By the way Braustich said Quentin's name, Nadine knew the Germans must have a healthy dossier on her lover. She would have to be very careful with Braustich and Helmut Zeigler and not compromise Quentin's safety.

* * *

The Luftwaffe's daylight aerial campaigns against the RAF ceased at the end of October. However, the Germans continued to bomb London and its outskirts at night. Nadine was told by a reliable informer that Luftwaffe bomber losses were so high that it was prohibitive for them to continue the daylight raids. Nadine learned that the Germans were calling off their invasion of the British Isles and planned to turn their attention elsewhere.

"We must validate this," she told Noel, "and find out what the Boche plan to do next." Noel nodded and said he would make inquiries.

The next day, Moira passed along the information to Millard when he and another man came to work on Nadine's bathroom floor. A few days later, the Americans in Lisbon received the secret communiqué about the German's decision to abandon their invasion of the British Isles. British Intelligence validated the information as accurate. In London, key people responsible for espionage on the Continent were impressed with the reliable information provided by the secret intelligence network in France led by Eglantine.

After conferring with a top aide to the prime minister, a senior officer in British Military Intelligence met with two of his key personnel in London and underscored the need to make direct contact with Eglantine in France.

"The information we're receiving from this source is accurate and valuable. Do press our people in France to locate this Eglantine," he stressed. "We don't want to be dependent on the Americans."

CHAPTER 8
RESIGNED TO WAR

For all we have and are,
For all our children's fate,
Stand up and take the war.
Rudyard Kipling, *For All We have and Are*

For Marlon and Kendall, the beginning of November 1940 was a time of dramatic change. There were no more daylight raids by the Luftwaffe. Instead, Fighter Command now sent flights of Spitfires and Hurricanes to patrol the skies above the British Channel during the day and a few weeks later to attack German bases on the Continent. The intense aerial combat between the RAF and the Luftwaffe changed as clashes between the two moved to a new venue. Within the Eleventh Group of the RAF some major changes in personnel occurred. Air Marshal Hugh Dowding was replaced by Air Chief Marshal Charles Portal in November 1940. Air Vice Marshal Leigh-Mallory, allied with Portal, replaced Air Vice Marshal Keith Price.

Air Vice Marshal Leigh-Mallory ordered RAF bombers and fighters to attack German installations on the coast of France as well as patrol the English Channel. Patrol duty over the Channel was considered routine by RAF pilots and resulted in sporadic encounters with German fighters. However, for any careless English pilots who strayed too far over the Channel, German patrols waited, ready to pounce on them. Young RAF fliers, eager to engage the Germans, who tested the boundaries in the skies over the Channel, seldom returned. Marlon had known several young fliers from Sixty-six Squadron lost because of venturing too far over the Channel. There were rampant rumors within the RAF that a new strategy was in the mix, one that would prove dangerous for pilots assigned to fly the new missions.

During the first full week of November, Marlon received a call from Geoff. The brigadier mentioned that weekend passes to London would be available to pilots in Sixty-six Squadron. Marlon asked about the departure of Hugh Dowding and was stonewalled by the brigadier.

"When you get leave," Geoff told the young pilot, "do call before departing for London. I'll have a pleasant surprise for you."

Marlon was intrigued and wondered what Geoff had in mind. *Maybe he wants me to have lunch with him, or meet some of his friends,* thought Marlon. He soon put these thoughts out of his mind. Passes were issued on the following weekend to British pilots that formed the brotherhood of English aristocrats. It was another example of the class system that operated within the RAF.

During the second full week of November, Squadron Leader Napier informed Marlon and some of the other pilots not from the British peerage that weekend passes to London were available.

It's about time, thought Marlon. The evening before he was to depart for London, he called Kendall and asked if he was getting a pass. Kendall said no, but he indicated that perhaps they could coordinate their leaves in the future.

"I'll speak to my CO," said an excited Kendall, "and find out if he'll call yours and arrange for us to get leave together."

When Marlon arrived in London, he was greeted at the crowded train station by one of Geoff's aides, Captain MacNair.

"The brigadier has made reservations for you," said MacNair, as he walked with Marlon to a waiting car. A sergeant took his bag and put it into the "boot" (trunk). A few minutes later, they arrived at a comfortable and well-maintained hotel just to the west of central London.

"The brigadier would like you to call him at this number after you're settled." MacNair saluted before leaving.

Once in his room and unpacked, Marlon called Geoff.

"Lieutenant," said Geoff, "welcome to London. I trust you had a pleasant trip?"

Marlon replied affirmatively, and the two made small talk for a few minutes before Geoff asked about Marlon's plans for the weekend. When the young pilot mentioned his only obligation was to call on Glinda Pennington, the brigadier laughed.

"There is someone who'd like to meet you."

He thought he heard the Englishman chuckle.

"Who?" asked a puzzled Marlon.

"A friend of your father's," was the teasing reply. Geoff made arrangements for them to have lunch the following day.

Marlon rose early and visited a museum before arriving at the address Geoff had given him. When he entered the dining room, he saw the brigadier seated with two attractive women.

"Ladies, this is Lieutenant Marlon Norvell from America by way of Canada," said Geoff with a smile. He introduced the older of the two women as Lady Linne Kidsgrove and the younger one as Erleen Coxwythe. Both women were very attractive, but it was Erleen, the younger one, who caught his attention.

"Your father," said a grinning Linne, "asked that I introduce you to English society."

"I gather you've met my father."

"Yes, he's a fascinating man," she told him with a discernible grin on her face. "And I've met his charming friends, Etienne and Argentina de Gavrelac."

Marlon grinned and remained silent. He had heard that Etienne was in England with the Free French.

When they sat down, Linne said, "Geoff tells me that you know Glinda Pennington and her son Kendall."

Marlon nodded. Out of the corner of his eye, he noticed that Erleen was watching him carefully. All through the meal, as they talked about different subjects, Marlon noticed different things about Erleen. He estimated that she was about five foot six with a slight figure. She had lovely facial features, blue eyes, a straight nose, and cute lips—the lower one appeared soft and was a dark shade of pink. Her hair was a chestnut color and stylishly cut. He noticed her long, slender fingers as she played with a water glass. She had a melodic voice and spoke with a charming English accent he thought was the result of private schooling.

Their time together passed quickly. Before he knew it, Geoff looked at his watch and said he had to be off. It was 2:30 in the afternoon.

"Stay if you wish," said Geoff, as he stood and prepared to leave.

"Geoff, I need transport. Would you mind?" asked Linne. Geoff smiled and said he would be delighted to take Linne wherever she needed to go.

"You two don't mind if we leave you alone?" said Linne to Erleen and Marlon. They looked at each other, smiled, and shook their heads.

"Erleen," said Linne with a sly smile, "do call me later."

When they were alone, Erleen looked at Marlon and said, "That was rather obvious, right?"

He smiled, nodded, and said he would enjoy having her show him some of the sights in London, if she had time to do so.

She smiled and said, "Of course!"

For the rest of the day they visited parts of London that had escaped the bombing. It was impossible to avoid signs of the war. The sky was filled with balloons, and there were men and women in military uniforms everywhere. After visiting Buckingham Palace, the Tower of London, and a gallery along the way, Marlon commented about the lack of children.

"We've sent as many of the children to the country as possible," said Erleen softly. "It's the only way we can protect them."

"It must be awful for the parents," he said in a low voice.

Erleen smiled and gazed at the sky as if lost in thought before saying, "We owe the RAF so much. Churchill says you've stopped the Germans and prevented an invasion." She looked up at him with admiration. They were standing quietly facing each other, their eyes locked before she stood on her tiptoes and kissed him softly on the lips. "Thank you for risking your life for us," she told him.

He touched her cheek tenderly and kissed her. Then, they walked toward the Thames, neither saying a word. War and the risk of death intensify life for those caught up in it. Conventions are frequently disregarded, and what would normally take weeks or months is shared and experienced in moments. They walked holding hands, and it was as if they had known each other for years.

Marlon returned to his hotel that evening and thought about Erleen. He wanted to be with her that evening but had promised to meet Glinda Pennington for dinner. So, he asked Erleen to be with him the following day before he returned to Sixty-six Squadron. She smiled and told him yes.

When Marlon met with Glinda, she introduced him to Edith, a tall shapely blonde, and Gwen, a slender brunette. They were both very attractive and looked young, perhaps in their early twenties. The four of them were driven to an elegant restaurant. During the meal, the air raid sirens sounded and soon explosions were heard nearby. He noticed the expressions of resignation by the women to the bombing and the damage being done. There was a mixture of fear and anger in their faces. Yet, their spirits were high, and Marlon could see and feel their resolve to endure the German attacks. *These are brave women,* he thought with admiration.

It was just past midnight when Marlon arrived at his hotel. He had shared a wonderful evening with Kendall's mother and her female friends and learned how resilient the English were. The young women praised him for joining the RAF and fighting the Germans and wished him good luck and good hunting. Glinda was the first to be dropped off in front of her home. Before Glinda got out of the sedan, she kissed Marlon on the cheek and told him to be careful. The two stepped out of the car, and Marlon politely walked the Englishwoman to her front door.

"The next time you come to London, call Edith or Gwen," said Glinda. "I know they would enjoy seeing you again."

Marlon smiled and said he looked forward to his next visit to London.

The following day, Marlon and Erleen met for lunch. Afterward, they visited her parents' home where he was introduced to Jocelyn, her mother, and Sylvia, a younger sister. Her younger brother Thaddeus was at boarding school. Erleen's father, Sir Harry, was the captain of a cruiser somewhere in the South Atlantic. Sylvia mentioned that "Father was knighted by the crown, but we're not landed gentry." When he asked what Sir Harry had done before the war, Jocelyn said their family owned several large ship building and repair sites in Plymouth, Wales, and Scotland.

"We're part of the lesser nobility," Erleen teased.

Sylvia laughed while Jocelyn tried hard to repress a giggle.

Marlon was quickly learning about the rankings within the British aristocracy. The older, landed families with a long pedigree considered themselves the elites. The recently knighted were, except for those with extensive wealth, relegated to a lesser status. Marlon was intrigued by how the sons of landed barons, dukes, and earls in England vied with each other for recognition by members of the royal family and their immediate friends. *I'll have to ask Erleen about being a part of the lesser nobility,* he mused.

It was almost five in the afternoon when Erleen and Marlon arrived at the train station.

"I'd like to see you again," he told Erleen as they stood apart from the sea of men and women in uniforms crowding the platforms leading to and from the trains.

"I'd like that too," she told him, waiting for Marlon to do something. He removed his hat, took the young woman in his arms, and kissed her on the lips. They seemed to blend together, and time was suspended momentarily.

When she finally opened her eyes, Erleen looked at him fondly and said, "Do be careful and come see me again."

In the following weeks, Marlon visited London while on leave and was often joined by Kendall. On one occasion, he managed to meet with Etienne and Argentina de Gavrelac. They had dinner, and Etienne explained his role as a staff officer with a Free French squadron.

Marlon dated Erleen often during his trips to London and enjoyed her company. She taught him about English history, social structure, and customs. There were significant differences between English, French, and American societies. England had a long-lived class structure that separated the commoners from the nobility. While there remained vestiges of an aristocracy in France, the intermarriage between the wealthy and some of the older aristocratic families was insufficient to propagate a strong nobility and class system like England's. In America, there was no nobility. But Marlon worried less about class than caste in American society. Blacks and American Indians were still considered inferior by so many Americans. He had often raised these matters with his father and recently discussed class and caste issues with Erleen, but other pressing changes preoccupied Marlon's thoughts.

The shift in Luftwaffe raids from daylight to nights significantly altered RAF schedules and flights. RAF planes were not equipped to engage German bombers at night. Instead, English squadrons regularly patrolled the skies over the Channel during daylight. But, after November 1940, British bombers began to fly daylight missions to attack German-occupied ports on the French coast. Marlon's squadron flew fighter cover for the bombers on several raids. The clash between the RAF and the Luftwaffe over the coastal areas of France was devastating for the British. Losses among the RAF bombers and fighters were high. After some of the raids, photographic reconnaissance over the coastal areas of France was necessary, and RAF fighters were assigned to escort the planes specially equipped with cameras. The Germans made it a point to challenge these planes and were able to shoot down and damage numerous RAF planes. Marlon went on several of these missions; on two of them, he shot down a Bf 109 and damaged another. However, Leigh-Mallory's sorties over the French coast, often referred to as "rodeos," were taking a toll on the RAF. Pilot losses were mounting during the rodeos, and morale among the squadrons assigned to such missions declined. Flying routine patrols over the Channel where there were few encounters with German planes was preferable. Meanwhile, the nighttime bombardment of London by the Luftwaffe continued with mounting civilian injuries and deaths. Large parts of the city were badly damaged and in ruins. For Marlon and Squadron Sixty-six, most days were free from enemy attacks, and, except for escorting RAF bombers targeting German installations on the French coast, it felt as if the war had moved on to another place.

On one of his trips to London, Marlon and Erleen took the underground to East London. Erleen and Linne were part of a group of British women working to care for children displaced by the bombings. When they exited the underground, the devastation they witnessed was heart rendering. The smell of cordite, smoke from burning houses reduced to burned-out cinders, and the sight of the dead carefully laid out waiting to be taken away was heart wrenching.

"I can't tell you how awful this is for everyone," said Erleen, her eyes filled with tears. "It's the children I worry about the most," she told him, her voice on the verge of cracking.

Now Marlon understood how important what Linne, Erleen, and others were doing to help relocate children to the English countryside was. *How brave of these women to expose themselves to such tragedy,* he thought. *And how magnificent they are to do all they can to save these children.* He would never forget the destruction, the smell of the bombed areas, and the grudging determination of the British people to carry on. It motivated him to do all he could to help win the war.

* * *

November 1940 came and went quickly for Quentin. He saw Florence often, now seventeen and very much a young woman. When a letter from Marlon arrived, they tried to read it together. Her schedule at Juilliard was full, and the Cajun noted the long hours she practiced the piano. She always asked about any news from sources other than letters from Marlon. One evening, Quentin asked Florence how often she wrote to her brother.

"Once, sometimes twice, a week," she replied. "Why do you ask?"

"Just curious," he told her. "Now that the Germans have shifted their bombing to night raids, there's less fighting between the RAF and the Luftwaffe."

"What does that mean, Daddy?"

He looked into his daughter's large blue eyes, her face eager for any news that might signal less risk for her brother.

"It means the Germans have turned their attention elsewhere. Marlon will spend less time flying combat missions than he did a few months ago."

"Will that be better for him?"

He said yes and watched her face glow with the realization that perhaps the worst part of the fighting for Marlon was over.

"Can we see him?" she asked.

He nodded and said it might be possible for them to go to London after he returned from France. Her mood changed quickly at what he said.

"Daddy, why must you go to France? Won't it be dangerous for you?"

He nodded and said,

"It's important for me to visit Nadine, her parents, and Louis. "I'm still her attorney, and we need to discuss and resolve business matters."

"Can't she come here?"

"Honey, the Germans won't let her leave France. As I'm from a neutral country and representing investors still doing business with her firms, and with some German companies, I'm still welcome."

"But what about Marlon fighting with the RAF against them?" she said, her face skewed in anticipation of his answer.

"So far, the Germans don't know that Marlon and I are related. As far as anyone knows, he's a Royal Canadian Air Force pilot flying with the RAF."

"But don't they know he's Nadine's son?" She looked visibly nervous.

"Not yet," he said, trying to assuage her. He worried that if the Germans ever discovered that Marlon was his and Nadine's son, there would be the devil to pay. *I need to get her out of France,* he thought. *But how?*

During the second week in December, Quentin flew the Amelie to Ireland and left the plane and his crew there. He boarded a commercial flight from Dublin to Lisbon where he met with members of the U.S. Embassy staff and received instructions and the necessary paperwork to travel through Spain and into occupied France. He took the train to Spain and at Saragossa met with Ruben Valderano's cousins from Barcelona to go over business matters before continuing to the French border. He was questioned carefully by French border guards, and all of his belongings examined thoroughly while uniformed German officers watched. Once his credentials and purpose in France were validated, he was allowed to cross into France and catch the train to Paris that went through Toulouse, Limoges, and Orleans. He did not stop at Limoges on his way to Paris. He would do that on the return trip. Quentin easily spotted the German security men, probably Gestapo, following him. He had notified the German authorities through the U.S. Embassy several weeks before about his planned trip. By now, the Gestapo had his photograph and a hefty dossier on him.

The sight of the Paris *gare* crowded with German military personnel surprised the American. It was so different from the times during the Great War when he had visited Paris and been part of a sea of British, French, and then American uniforms. Now, the *gare* was awash in Boche with their distinctive gray uniforms and dark helmets.

The few French civilians traveling were like strangers in their own country. Many of them avoided eye contact with the Boche conquerors, while others were barely able to mask their resentment toward the invaders. It depressed Quentin to see the hatred and bitterness that the French defeat had caused.

Waiting for him at the main *sortie* (exit) was Nadine, tastefully dressed in a long leather coat, a silk scarf, and a chic hat. She was wearing high leather boots and soft leather gloves. The lovely French woman hugged and kissed him politely on each cheek, an acceptable form of public recognition intended for the Gestapo's prying eyes. But, once in her sedan, she caressed and kissed his hands tenderly.

"I've missed you so," she said, looking fondly at the Cajun with enchanting green eyes.

"I've missed you too," he replied, carefully studying his lover's face.

"There's so much I want to tell you," he told her while gently squeezing her hand. "But, I want to hold you in my arms and feel you close."

"Soon," she uttered softly, managing a brave smile to hide the sadness in her heart. "And Marlon?"

"He's well and sends his love." She turned away momentarily to hide the tears that formed in her eyes, and she quickly regained her composure. She wanted badly to learn about their son. Quentin told her how Marlon was doing, his exploits in the air, and getting shot down.

She closed her eyes, and a chill ran through her when he said Marlon was shot down.

"Don't worry," he reassured her. "He got soaked in the Channel, but he came out of it with nothing more than a little embarrassment at losing his plane." She released a sigh of relief. He kissed the beautiful French woman. Quentin was puzzled when they arrived at a building that he recognized as the site of Nadine's business office. "What are we doing here?"

"Appearances," she told him as the driver opened the door for them and whispered, "Be patient."

The elegant woman told the driver to leave Monsieur Norvell's bags, with the exception of his briefcase, in the back of the sedan. She gave the Cajun a nonverbal signal to bring his satchel with him.

"Appearance," said the American softly.

She nodded and smiled.

When they arrived at Nadine's office on the third floor of the building, two men Quentin did not recognize were waiting, along with Noel, her executive assistant.

"You must be Herr Norvell," said Kurt Braustich stiffly as he bowed his head politely.

Next to him was the smarmy Helmut Ziegler, trying to appear important and friendly. Quentin took the measure of both men quickly. He had met and dealt with financiers like Braustich before. They were careful and capable men steeped in financial traditions and assigned circumscribed roles in the business enterprises that employed them. The Cajun knew that the Nazis had ways to control men like Braustich that included punishments and rewards. Ziegler, however, was a different breed of cat, thought the Cajun. His kind was duplicitous, dangerous, and served one master only. Men such as Ziegler, thought the American, were informants eager to spy on the unsuspecting and unconcerned about the veracity of what they reported.

Braustich spoke up and asked Quentin if he cared for tea or coffee before they discussed business matters.

The American smiled and said, "Coffee, with cream and sugar."

Braustich looked at Ziegler, and the other man smirked and left the room. The German motioned with his hand for Nadine, Noel, and Quentin to follow him into a small conference room.

"*Bitte*," (please) said Braustich, motioning with his hand for Quentin and the others to be seated. "I've taken the liberty," said Braustich in a directive manner to indicate he had set the agenda for their meeting. In the next thirty minutes, the German financier carefully studied the information Quentin provided about income from Nadine's investments in the United States. He also inquired about Nadine's holdings in Spain and Portugal, but did not ask about those in Canada or other parts of the Americas. The American produced documents that required Nadine's signature and handed the originals to Nadine and copies to Braustich.

"I assume you will review these documents carefully," Quentin said nonchalantly.

The German nodded, asked Nadine for the originals, and handed her the copies. Then, he made a note of the number of documents and checked to see which ones needed signatures.

"You will find tabs to indicate where Madame Desnoyers must sign to either approve a contractual matter or agree to the earnings and determine their transfer and distribution," Quentin said while looking directly at the German. "I've also noted my firm's percentage for services rendered and share of the profits," he added.

"There are two fees?" asked Braustich with a frown on his face.

Quentin replied dryly that Barston, Marwick, Fowler, and Peterson charged a ten percent fee for handling Nadine's accounts in the United States and elsewhere. They also commingled their own and other financial resources to maximize earnings, which they shared based on the percentage of respective funds in the portfolio.

"Look on the last page where the budget is broken down and the earnings and charges are listed," Quentin told the German.

Braustich was about to hesitate when he noticed the American's hard look. For a moment, there was a battle of wills between them, but the German yielded and examined the budget and summary statement of profits, earnings, fees, and distributions.

"Hmm, impressive," said the German. He smiled and collected the documents and put them into a leather portfolio. "Madame Desnoyers and I will review these matters." Braustich started to rise.

"Sit down," Quentin told him in a firm voice, "we're not done yet."

Braustich was taken aback by the American's comment and his tone, and he hesitated for a moment.

"As Madame Desnoyers' attorney and legal representative in the United States, I require a document that stipulates your position and role in Madame's organization. My firm requests formalized authorization of your responsibilities and what decision-making powers you might have within the Desnoyers enterprises. Madame Desnoyers must cosign that document."

The German stiffened at what the American said. He was about to say something to challenge the Cajun, but he thought the better or it. He needed to consider the ramifications of Norvell's request and then confer with his contact in the Nazi apparatus. Also, his quick read of the income from the United States, which was in the hundreds of thousands of dollars, made him realize that it was best not to compromise such a lucrative arrangement.

"Very well," said the German.

"I'll need to see that document soon," said the Cajun.

Braustich was about to say something when the American spoke up. "My firm's reputation is based on thoroughness and dedication to our clients. It is how we do business and provide the high profit margins that we do. If you and Madame Desnoyers are not comfortable with our policies and service, then inform me of such and the relationship will be terminated."

The nonplussed German was surprised. Braustich cleared his throat and swallowed hard. He thought quickly and realized that if the American decided to terminate dealings with Desnoyers enterprises because of anything he might have said or done, it would not go well for him. The Nazis would surely blame him, and he did not want to be branded a failure. He knew how harshly the Nazis dealt with people who disappointed them.   "Very well," said Braustich. "I'll study the documents tonight and confer with Mrs. Desnoyers early tomorrow. When do you plan to leave Paris?"

"In a few days," replied Quentin, looking first at the German, then Nadine and Noel.

"I think we can attend to all of the matters discussed before you depart," said the German, as he waited for the American to say something.

"I'd like that document in two days."

The German forced a smile and said, "Of course."

Quentin stood and extended his hand to the surprised German, and, with a cold smile, said, "I know you will not disappoint me, Herr Braustich."

Nadine watched the interaction between Quentin and Braustich carefully and tried not to reveal her fascination with the exchange, especially her lover's manner. She had never seen Quentin so forceful with someone before. But, she knew the strength and determination within her lover, and also something else, something dangerous.

After Braustich left the room, Nadine spoke to Noel about her calendar. She told him to allow time in her schedule to meet with the German the next day. Then, she turned to Quentin and smiled. "Monsieur Norvell, will you be my guest for dinner tonight?"

"I'd be delighted," said Quentin with a smirk. "By the way, you mentioned making reservations for my stay."

"Yes," said a poker-faced Nadine, "Noel has arranged for you to stay at a comfortable residence near the Bois de Boulogne." The Cajun smiled and thanked the lovely French woman and winked at her.

Quentin was driven to a well-maintained home near the Bois de Boulogne. He was greeted by a housekeeper who called a man to take his bags to a quiet, tastefully furnished suite of rooms on the second floor. When he had unpacked, he heard a knock on the door and was surprised to see Noel.

"Please follow me," said the courteous Frenchman.

Together they walked down the stairs and then into a cellar. Noel greeted a man he introduced as Rouge, holding two torches. They slid open a part of the cellar wall and motioned for the American to follow them. They walked through a narrow passageway that was cool and damp for what seemed like the length of a city block. They emerged at another cellar, climbed a flight of stairs, and entered a corridor that led to a greenhouse with lush, green plants. Nadine was waiting at the other end of the greenhouse.

"Fascinating," said the Cajun, as he embraced the gorgeous French woman and kissed her passionately.

"Cherie, you're so impetuous," said a smiling Nadine. She took his hand and led him into the house and up the stairs to her bedroom. There she locked the door, turned, and began removing Quentin's light jacket, shirt, and undershirt. When he was bare-chested, she marveled at his muscular upper torso, the large, firm pectoral muscles and his hard biceps. Slowly, she ran a long slender finger over a scar on his left side caused by a German bullet in 1916. Then, she licked and kissed a barely visible scar under his left chin. Both wounds, and another high on his left shoulder, were received by Quentin when two German planes attacked him during World War I. They injured him badly, but the American survived and vowed to repay the Boche for what they had done to him.

As Nadine was caressing her lover, he kissed the enchanting woman hungrily, his passion stirring strong emotions and lust. He began to remove her clothing as they kissed. When her breasts were exposed, he took them in his hands tenderly and licked and caressed her nipples with the tip of his tongue. She shuddered and responded immediately to his caressing, something deep within her surfacing, and overwhelming her. The next thing she knew, they were on her bed and shedding their remaining garments. When both were naked, the American feasted lustily on her body, touching, fondling, and using his lips and tongue to excite Nadine. The foreplay seemed to last for hours, but it was only a few minutes before she took his member and stroked it. When they coupled, they gave themselves over to the sensuality of their sexual passion. After almost half an hour and three orgasms for Nadine, Quentin finally exploded, shuddered and squeezed his lover. After that, the two lay together in a loving embrace and drifted into a temporary sleep.

Nadine was the first to awaken. She looked at her lover and realized how lucky she was. Quentin at just over six feet in height was remarkably youthful for a man in his early forties. He looked much younger, perhaps as if in his midthirties. His trim figure, skin that tanned beautifully, handsome features, and a full head of hair made him appear youthful. When he smiled, his large, white teeth appeared almost perfect. *He is such a beautiful man,* she thought, *and does not realize it, or care.* As she was admiring her lover, he stirred, opened his right eye and then the other, searching for her face. They kissed and played with each other until Nadine said it was time for him to return to his residence.

"I will drive to your house, and, together, we will go to dinner at a small restaurant."

He smiled and asked the name of the place.

"It's a surprise."

That evening and the next two days that Quentin was in Paris, he saw the deep resentment by the French toward their Nazi oppressors. The Germans seemed overtly indifferent about the attitudes of their conquered subjects. But, Quentin knew better. The Boche military reacted swiftly and harshly to any perceived sign of a French person challenging a German soldier or official. In two different situations he observed quite by accident, French civilians accused of insulting a German official and military officer were immediately seized and beaten before being dragged away. *It's going to get worse*, thought the American. *God help these people.*

* * *

Braustich reported to the Gestapo about his meeting with the American, the French woman, and her executive assistant. His contact, a stern and emotionless Major Sigwald Eisenhardt, skimmed the dossier on the American and said nothing to Braustich. Then, he looked at the file on Nadine Desnoyers. The financier talked nervously, but the major and Hauptman Wolfgang Berthold, a tall blond man with piercing blue eyes, wearing the gray uniform of the Gestapo, paid him scant attention. Finally, Eisenhardt looked up at Braustich and told him to be quiet.

"We have Herr Norvell and the Desnoyers woman under surveillance. We will decide how to proceed with these two. They do not pose a problem for us at the moment. Provide the American with whatever he requires," ordered the Gestapo officer. The German major concealed his interest in the large sums of money the American was able to deliver. "Continue to keep us informed about Frau Desnoyers' financial activities and leave these matters to us."

After Braustich left the two Gestapo officers alone, Berthold asked if any steps should be taken toward the American and the French woman.

"Not yet," said Eisenhardt. "He is from a neutral country engaged in commerce with the Reich. And the Reich welcomes American dollars. We will watch him carefully. The woman, however, is a different matter," he said coldly.

The captain looked at the major, his interest piqued by Eisenhardt's comment.

"She is an asset we must control carefully. If she cooperates with us," he said while lighting a cigarette, "it will be a profitable relationship."

"But what if she does not?" asked the younger officer.

"We can be very persuasive when we want, Wolfgang," said the major with a smile. "I'm certain you would enjoy persuading Frau Desnoyers to cooperate with us, eh?"

The major's remark caused a crooked smile to cross the Gestapo captain's face.

* * *

Quentin and Nadine left Paris by train three days after his arrival, heading south toward Limoges. Once there, a car was waiting that drove them to Louis Bondurant's estate. The American spotted the surveillance at the railroad station. At La Croisiere, the greeting Quentin received at the doorway by Louis Bondurant was polite and formal. But, once inside the manor house, the old general embraced and kissed the younger man on the cheeks and then took his hands in his. The Cajun was saddened by the general's appearance. He had lost weight and seemed uncomfortable. Also waiting for them were Arlene and Edmund.

Quentin stayed at La Croisiere for a full day and two nights, leaving Nadine and the others early the second day aboard a southbound train. His stay at the general's estate was pleasant, but the Boche occupation was a bitter pill for Nadine's parents and Louis. They talked about the war, and when they were certain it was safe, the American shared information about Marlon. They were overjoyed by the news of his victories and relaxed when Quentin said that, even though Marlon had been shot down, he was safe and healthy.

During dinner the first evening at Louis's estate, Quentin tactfully asked about some of his friends and relatives in France. Nadine provided as much information as she had. The Cajun then asked if Arlene and Edmund were interested in leaving France.

"No," said a resolute Edmund. "This is our country, and we will not give in to the Boche."

"Very commendable," said the Cajun, his comment intended to praise the spirit and resolve of Nadine's father. But, he knew that if Nadine was linked with the French resistance, the older couple would be arrested by the Germans unless they went into hiding. *What a hardship that will pose on Arlene and Edmund,* he thought.

The last evening Quentin was with Nadine at La Croisiere, they exchanged identical books of poems. But, within the binding and covers of the book she handed the Cajun were microfilm and data on the location of German airfields close to the Channel, the types of aircraft and units located at each base, and approximate strength for each group. Also included were data on coastal sites in France where the Germans were building submarine docking facilities. She told him the microfilm contained research the Germans were doing on metals able to withstand high temperatures. Then, she shared two other things.

"Cherie, I've received reports of a new fighter the Boche are testing."

"Do you have any information about it?"

She produced a grainy photograph taken with a telephoto lens and then enlarged. He studied the image carefully and noted its sleek shape, the radial engine, and what looked like a bubble canopy. It reminded him of a plane he had seen before. But where? And then it came to him: Howard Hughes's racing plane, the H-1. He had flown it several years before. It was radical and super fast. Quentin recalled Kurt Tank, the German aircraft designer, asking about Hughes's plane. He had arranged for a few Germans to meet with Hughes to discuss the American financier's aircraft.

"Can you get more specific information about this plane?" he asked.

She nodded and said it would take awhile.

"Do what you can to get it, but please be careful," he implored.

"There's more," she said. "The English are bombing Boche military installations on the coast. They are losing many aircraft and air crews."

"How do you know this?"

"The resistance has managed to locate and hide some of the English flyers, but most of the English crews shot down are captured and sent to concentration camps in Allemagne," she said sadly. "We [resistance] are trying to help English flyers escape through France into Spain and then to Portugal."

A worried expression crossed the American's face, and he told Nadine that her activities were very risky and dangerous.

The lovely French woman smiled, kissed him, and said she would be careful.

When Quentin reached the Spanish border, his bags were searched carefully and his possessions examined thoroughly. He was asked to declare and account for each item he was taking out of France. He noticed that the border guards had a checklist of things he had brought when entering France. *These bastards are really watching me closely,* he thought. The book of poems was looked at and checked off the list. When the officials completed the inventory of his goods, they asked about the French cologne and scarves. He told them the items were for his daughter and other females in his family. It took almost an hour for Quentin to cross the border from France to Spain. As he boarded the train in Spain bound for Portugal, he noticed the surveillance. *Gestapo,* he thought. *I wonder how far they'll follow me.*

* * *

Quentin met with security personnel in the American Embassy in Lisbon for debriefing. He handed over the secret documents and information Nadine had provided. It was analyzed carefully by trained intelligence personnel, classified, and some of it forwarded to the British Embassy by courier. The following day, he boarded a plane for Ireland. On his arrival in Dublin, he called Hardy and Mark and told them to meet him at the airfield at six o'clock the next morning. Then, he called the appropriate Irish officials to file a preliminary flight plan for New York. The next morning, the Amelie, with Quentin, Hardy, and Mark on board, lifted off for the Canadian Maritime Provinces. As the plane gained altitude, the Cajun chuckled. Anyone trying to follow him would have a tough time doing it.

* * *

CHAPTER 9
STORM WARNINGS

Whare sits our sulky, sullen dame,
Gathering her brows like gathering storm,
Nursing her wrath to keep it warm
Robert Burns, *Tam o'Shanter [1791]*

It was the third week of December 1940 when Quentin returned to New York City from his trip to France. He suspected that German operatives in the United States might be watching him and sent the intelligence information Nadine provided by secret courier to General Marshall. After Marshall's people had examined the strategic information on Luftwaffe airbases near the Channel and the construction of submarine docks on the French coast, the Cajun received a call from the general.

"Quentin, I have good news for you. Ruben Valderano is coming to Washington in a few days. Care to join us? We can have dinner and go riding together."

It was part of a code they had agreed to use in case anyone was listening to their conversation.

"Of course," replied the Cajun. "Let me know when Ruben will arrive, and I'll join you."

Two days later, Quentin flew to Washington in the Amelie, and landed at National Airport. He arranged rooms for Hardy and Mark at a comfortable hotel off Dupont Circle while he stayed at the Mayflower Hotel. When he arrived at the Mayflower, there was a message from Healy Rohwer inviting him to dinner. Quentin smiled as he read the note. *I wonder what that wild woman is up to,* he mused. He called the number Healy left and learned it was for a hotel not too far away used by members of the press.

"Quentin, thanks for calling," he heard the journalist say. "Can you join me and some friends for dinner tonight?"

"Of course," he replied, curious about their meeting. "Where shall we meet?"

She told him to be the lobby of the Mayflower at 7:30 p.m. He inquired about the attire.

"Wear a suit and tie. And, remember, you owe me a drink." He laughed and said it would be fun to have dinner with her.

The Cajun was surprised and pleased when Healy approached him in the lobby of the Mayflower. Ruben Valderano and Brook Hamilton Stoner were with the exuberant curly haired strawberry blonde. They got into a taxi, and Stoner gave the driver the name of the restaurant. In a few minutes they arrived at a plush restaurant known for its seafood.

"Quentin, sit here, next to me," said Healy. "I need to be next to a single man, not these old married guys," she teased.

They all laughed.

"How about some champagne to start off?" said the Cajun. They all agreed. Quentin ordered the wine. A few minutes later, the waiter brought out a chilled bottle of excellent French champagne. Quentin said the champagne would be difficult to get later.

During dinner, they shared information about their recent travels. Ruben had been to southeast Asia while Healy had traveled through North Africa, Italy, Germany, and Sweden, with a quick visit to Norway. Stoner mentioned being in England, France, and Portugal. But, Quentin suspected the diplomat had also been elsewhere in Europe, and probably in Germany. He shot a quick glance at Ruben, and the Mexican winked and gave him a quick smile. When Quentin mentioned his recent trip to occupied France, the others could not contain their curiosity. Healy started by asking the Cajun about France.

"What was it like?"

"Depressing."

Stoner lifted an eyebrow and asked Quentin to explain.

The Cajun told them about the attitudes and sentiments among the French he had observed.

"They hate the Boche," said Quentin, "and also the collaborators."

"Well, there are plenty of them," said Stoner, referring to French people siding with the Germans and receiving positions of responsibility and considerable pay for their services.

"Yeah!" exclaimed Healy, "but I wouldn't be in their shoes for anything."

"You mean they may be in some peril," said Stoner cynically.

"You bet," she replied. "Sooner or later, those jerks collaborating with the Krauts will get theirs."

Ruben smiled and nodded.

The Cajun could almost read Ruben's thoughts. He most certainly would not want to be a German collaborator anywhere.

"What do you think the Germans are up to now?" asked the sly diplomat.

"I think they'll push into Yugoslavia and farther south," said Healy.

Stoner was intrigued and asked her to elaborate.

"Well, I'm no military expert, but the Krauts need raw materials, like the oil in Ploesti (oil fields north of Bucharest). I wouldn't put it past Hitler to attack the Greeks," she added. Looking directly at Ruben, she asked, "What do you think?"

The Mexican grinned and shook his head before wiping his lips, taking a sip of wine, and clearing his throat. "You may be right, Healy. It's logical for the Germans to control the Balkans. Attacking the Greeks may be tricky. But, then," he continued, "the Germans may have to honor some commitments."

"What are you referring to?" asked Stoner.

"Mussolini has sent troops to Greece and is trying to control parts of North Africa. I doubt the Italians will be able to defeat the Greeks or the British in North Africa without German assistance. And there's talk that Hitler might want to attack the Soviets."

Quentin remained silent, absorbing the last thing the Mexican said.

"Do you really think the Krauts will attack the Russians?" asked Healy. The Mexican nodded. Quentin realized that the war in Europe might soon be overshadowed by new fighting in the Balkans, Greece, North Africa, and Russia.

"What about Spain?" asked Quentin.

"Well," said Healy, sipping on some red wine, "Hitler met with Franco and nothing came of it."

"What do you mean?" asked a curious Stoner.

"Heard that after their meeting at Hendaye (southwest corner of France near Biarritz) in October, Hitler came away furious with Franco because he wouldn't cooperate with him."

Stoner nodded without saying anything.

"Yes," added Ruben, "Franco's not about to join Hitler. And he didn't let Hitler bully him."

Quick to understand what the Mexican implied, the Cajun nodded in agreement. But he decided to change the subject. Looking directly at Healy, he asked, "What's your take on Hitler's U-boat campaign against the Brits?"

They looked at the journalist. She thought for a moment before replying. "Well, the Krauts have really done some damage to English shipping. Last I heard they had sunk over 750,000 tons and 142 English ships. I hear they're building sub pens at four different French ports."

The men looked solemnly at the reporter before Quentin spoke up. "Is that information accurate?"

"Yup," she replied.

"Won't the Brits bomb these sub bases?" asked Quentin.

"I dunno," said Healy, motioning for Stoner to fill her wine glass. "The Brits are closemouthed about the sub pens and where they're located. And they won't say anything about bombing raids. But I do know they've lost a bunch of planes and pilots on daylight raids along the French coast."

Healy's remark confirmed what Nadine had told him. But, rather than speak up about Nadine's information, he decided to keep it confidential.

Meanwhile, Stoner sat quietly, his smile reminding Quentin of the Cheshire cat. *Healy's only corroborating what Stoner already knows. Maybe it's time to tweak him a bit.*

"Stony," said the Cajun, "you know more than you're telling us. Don't hold out on us. Sharing information is a two-way street."

Stoner feigned innocence, but the others stared at him.

"Come, come, Stony," said Ruben, "it's your turn to share." The Mexican's tone of voice made it clear to Stoner that if he withheld information, they would stop sharing what they knew with him.

"Stony?" asked Healy insistently.

"OK, the English have lost quite a few ships, and Churchill's very worried about more U-boats attacking their shipping. We've learned the Germans are building sub pens that the RAF can't knock out. Churchill has asked Roosevelt for help."

"What kind of help?" asked the Cajun.

Stoner nodded and said, "There's a deal in the works for us to lend the Royal Navy some old destroyers and minesweepers, and also sell them some long-range Lockheed bombers."

"The Krauts aren't going to like that!" exclaimed Healy.

"Probably," said the diplomat, "but there's not much they can do about it."

"Some firms in the U.S. are still doing business with the Nazis," said Quentin. "Will that change?"

"I don't think so," said the diplomat. "After all, we're a neutral country and can sell goods and services to any nation."

"Unless the Germans decide to sink any ships they think are carrying military equipment or supplies to England," said Ruben.

Stoner nodded and said that was possible.

While Stoner and Ruben talked, Healy nudged Quentin and asked if he would be in New York for the holidays.

Quentin nodded and whispered, "Why?"

"I'll be in New York for Christmas to see my folks. Can we get together?"

He grinned and nodded, his signal evoking a big smile on Healy's face.

The four of them talked for a while longer until Stoner said he needed to leave and reminded Quentin and Ruben that they had an early meeting. As he stood to leave, the diplomat kissed Healy on the cheek and whispered something to her that the others could not hear. Whatever his comment to the strawberry blonde was, she beamed and her eyes sparkled. A few minutes later, Healy, Ruben, and Quentin left after the Cajun had covered the bill.

When their cab stopped in front of Healy's hotel, Healy kissed the Mexican and the Cajun on the cheek and told them how lucky she was to have such handsome friends. "I'll see you guys later."

"*Es mucha mujer* [she's quite a woman]," said the Mexican.

"Yes," said Quentin, "she is indeed."

* * *

The next morning, Quentin and Ruben walked to the White House for their meeting with President Roosevelt. It was just after seven fifteen in the morning when they were ushered into one of the president's rooms. Roosevelt, Cordell Hull, Harry Hopkins, Brook Hamilton Stoner, and George C. Marshall were there. The president motioned for them to serve themselves food from the elegant service on a sideboard. When they were seated, Roosevelt placed a cigarette in his favorite holder, lit it, and said, "Quentin, that information you brought back from France is very valuable. I won't ask how you got it. We sent it to the English." Roosevelt looked at Marshall and said, "George, why don't you carry the ball."

"Quentin, the information about the air bases is accurate. The British were pleased to get it. As for the sub pens, that information is also accurate. The research on metals can only mean one thing," he said. "The Germans are working on jet engines, perhaps for use on airplanes."

"Possibly a fighter," said the Cajun. "What about the new fighter I mentioned, George?"

"The English think the Germans may be testing a Japanese fighter."

"I don't think so." Harry Hopkins spoke up and asked Quentin to explain.

As the Cajun was responding to Hopkins, the intercom buzzed. Roosevelt picked up the phone and listened before saying, "Send them in."

When the door opened, J. Edgar Hoover, the head of the FBI, and an aide entered the room.

"Care for some coffee?" asked the president.

"No thank you, Mr. President," said Hoover dryly. He was short and stocky, with dark hair combed straight back and wearing a dark blue suit. Hoover's piercing eyes examined the room carefully, and Quentin suspected he knew everyone without having to be introduced.

"J. Edgar," said the president, "this is Ruben Valderano, Quentin Norvell, and Brook Hamilton Stoner from the State Department. You know the others."

Hoover nodded at Ruben, Quentin, and Stoner, then sat across from them while his aide sat slightly behind and to his right.

"What've you got for us?" asked the president.

Without looking at his aide, Hoover extended his right arm backward and was handed a file.

"Mr. President, you were right," he began in a gruff voice. "General Valderano and Mr. Norvell have been followed by men we believe are Nazi operatives." He produced photos taken of men in doorways, street corners, sitting on benches, and others in cars. Some were pretending to read newspapers while others were preoccupied staring at someone or something.

"These and other photos," said Hoover, "were taken in New York, here in Washington, and in Los Angeles."

"How do you know they're Nazis?" asked the Cajun, examining the photos with Ruben.

Hoover replied that three of the men were associated with the German American Bund, and three others were followed and made contact with German nationals working in the United States with ties to the Nazi Party in Germany.

"We have extensive files on people we suspect are working for the Nazis."

"Are you going to arrest these people?" asked Cordell Hull.

Hoover shook his head.

"Actually," said the FBI head, "we're indebted to General Valderano and Mr. Norvell. We've followed these fellows, and they've led us to other people, people we're interested in."

"So, you don't propose we do anything about these Nazis?" asked the president.

"I didn't say that, Mr. President," Hoover replied curtly. "We want to keep an eye on them and see where they lead us."

"But won't they know someone's following them?" asked Hopkins.

"The Germans believe the bureau is busy rounding up thugs like Dillinger. They don't think we're much of an intelligence agency. I'd like to keep it that way," said Hoover with a smirk.

"I think you're doing the right thing," said Quentin. "Anything we can do to help?"

Hoover nodded before saying, "Don't let on that you know you're being followed. Be careful what you leave in your office or house," he warned. "I know you've been to Europe several times and brought out sensitive material. The Germans suspect you're up to something and they've gained access to your office but so far not to your home."

"You mean they've broken into my office in New York?" asked an annoyed Quentin.

"They've used a substitute janitor with the firm that cleans your law offices in New York. So far, they haven't done anything other than look through your things," said Hoover smugly. "But the next time you or General Valderano," he cautioned, "decide to go on a trip and gather sensitive information, let us know ahead of time."

"So how do we do that, Mr. Hoover?" asked the Mexican.

"I'll give you telephone numbers to call for dry cleaning services," said Hoover, again reaching back with his right arm so that his aide could hand him cards with telephone numbers.

Hoover slid the cards across the tabletop for Ruben and Quentin. "The name and address for the laundry service is on the front." He gave each of them code words for service they needed to request when they called to alert FBI agents. "In case of an emergency, call the number on the back of your card. Give your name to the agent and tell him the nature of the emergency. They'll handle it from there."

"Is there any danger for General Valderano or Mr. Norvell?" asked Harry Hopkins.

Hoover shook his head before saying, "Not at the moment, and we want to keep it that way. But, the Germans aren't dumb. They know the British have people in Europe spying on them. And, they're suspicious about people like you," he said, nodding in the direction of Quentin and Ruben. "They don't believe in coincidences and probably have extensive files on each of you. General Valderano, they know about your former wife in London and that your son is flying with the RAF."

Ruben was taken aback by Hoover's news and asked, "How do you know that?"

"We have our ways," said Hoover nonchalantly. "And, Mr. Norvell, so far they don't know your son is in the RAF. But, sooner or later, they're going to find out and trace him back to Mrs. Desnoyers, his mother."

Quentin was surprised and perplexed by what Hoover shared and the arrogant way he did it, but, most of all, he realized that if the FBI knew about Marlon and Nadine, it was only a matter of time before the Nazis would find out. There was a pregnant silence in the room as Ruben and Quentin digested the FBI chief's revelations. Roosevelt finally spoke up,

"Good work, J. Edgar. Anything else?"

Hoover shook his head.

"Keep me informed," said Roosevelt, intimating the FBI chief and his aide should leave. Hoover glanced at everyone in the room one final time before nodding to the president and leaving with his aide.

After Hoover left, the topic of RAF raids on French ports and their mounting losses was discussed.

"Not much we can do about this," said General Marshall. Instead, they turned their attention to possible German military activities elsewhere.

As they talked, the Cajun was preoccupied with Nadine's safety in France. *How soon,* he worried, *before the Nazis find out about Nadine and Marlon? And what if they already suspect her of spying?*

Before the meeting ended, Roosevelt thanked them and wished all of them a Merry Christmas and a Happy New Year. As they were leaving, the president told Quentin to stay behind for a few minutes. Ruben and Marshall said they would wait in the corridor. Hull, Hopkins, and Stoner shook hands with Quentin, wished him happy holidays, and left.

"Quentin, I know about your relationship with Mrs. Desnoyers and that your son is flying with the RAF. I suspect you want to get her out of France, but I want to persuade you not to do anything immediately."

"Why?" asked an incredulous Quentin.

"Well, Mrs. Desnoyers is a valuable source of information. She's sharing intelligence with you. We share some of it with the British, but don't mention the source. The British desperately need reliable contacts and sources of intelligence in France," said the president. "Unless you tell me otherwise, I think we should have her work mainly with us."

Quentin nodded, a frown on his forehead indicating growing concern for Nadine's safety.

"The Nazis are relentless and ruthless," said Roosevelt, taking a long drag through his cigarette holder. "They may find out about Mrs. Desnoyers. Then, it will be up to you to decide what to do," he said while looking directly into Quentin's eyes. "When the time comes and you need to bring her out of France, let me know and I'll do everything possible to help."

The Cajun exhaled slowly through his nose and barely shook his head, visible signs he was preoccupied with Nadine's safety. "Thank you, Mr. President. I'll need to talk with Madame Desnoyers about this."

"When do you plan to do that?" asked Roosevelt.

"I should visit France on business in late March or April," he replied. "If the Nazis suspect her and find out that our son is with the RAF, then she'll have to leave Paris."

"I leave it up to you to do what you think is best," said a serious Roosevelt, his eyes locked on Quentin's. "Remember, I'm here to help. Call me if you need my help."

The two men talked for a couple of minutes before Quentin stood and shook the extended hand the president offered. "Mr. President, I couldn't ask for a better friend."

Roosevelt chuckled and threw his head back. Then, he said, "Let's hope for the best."

* * *

In Paris, Nadine cleared her calendar and asked for and received permission from Braustich to spend the holidays with her parents and Louis Bondurant at La Croisiere.

She took Moira with her. Noel remained in Paris to handle Nadine's business affairs during her absence, with Ziegler monitoring carefully everything the Frenchman did.

Once at La Croisiere, Nadine noticed how uncomfortable Louis was. When she was alone with her father, she asked about the old general.

"He's hurt inside," said Edmund, tapping his heart. "These are dark times for him and for us too. But, in Louis's case, he loathes the Boche and the way they commandeered his business and estate." Edmund looked away to hide the sadness he felt. "We cannot go anywhere without being followed," he grumbled. "Even the doctor is interrogated by the Boche after every visit."

"But is Louis that sick?" she asked.

"Yes, he's losing weight and has trouble walking more than a few hundred meters."

"What does the doctor say?" asked the lovely Frenchwoman, her face showing signs of deep concern.

"His heart," said Edmund, again tapping his chest.

The next morning, Moira drove to a local market where she purchased staples and oranges. She secretly passed information about German aircraft experiments and new U-boats on the drawing board and under construction to one of Nadine's operatives. The following day, the information crossed the border into Spain on its way to the Americans in Lisbon.

The holidays passed quickly at La Croisiere for Nadine and her family. Just before the New Year, Louis caught a bad cold and was confined to his bed, something that angered him.

"You are a terrible patient," said the doctor with a shrug when he finished examining the old soldier. "It's fortunate for you that Madame Desnoyers is here. Listen to her and do as she says," scolded the doctor, as he closed his satchel and motioned for Nadine to join him. Once in the hallway, his mood turned solemn.

"He's very ill. He has suffered a mild heart attack. It's not his first. He was able to hide the others from me. But, now," he said, shaking his head and looking down the long corridor, "there are complications."

"What do you mean?" asked Nadine, almost afraid to hear what the doctor might say.

"There's fluid in his lungs, and he has a low fever. I'll prescribe some medication, but you may have to go to Limoges to get it, if they have it there," he said, frustration evident in his voice. "Try to keep him warm, and make sure he gets plenty of liquids. If his fever rises, call me immediately."

"How serious is his condition?" pressed Nadine, her long, slender fingers nervously twirling a pencil.

"Very bad," said the doctor. "If he gets pneumonia, he could die." At this, Nadine turned away and tried to suppress the urge to cry. But her lovely green eyes filled with moisture, and she could not prevent the salty tears that cascaded down her cheeks.

Sensing her anguish, the doctor put his arm around her shoulder and consoled her in a soft voice.

In the days that followed, Nadine hired a nurse to visit daily and make certain the old general was following the doctor's recommendations. Louis was grumpy and uncooperative, but, gradually, with Nadine's insistence, he did as the doctor ordered. Nadine returned to Paris at the beginning of January 1941. Louis improved, and, by the middle of January, he was walking easily. Only the cold winter weather prevented him from taking long walks with Arlene and Edmund.

The winter of 1941 seemed filled with long, cold nights, frequent sleet and snowfalls, and a depressing emotional chill in the City of Lights. While France had been humiliated, the German conquerors demanded that the arts continue to be celebrated. On occasion, Nadine attended opera and ballet performances, especially when students she had previously encouraged and supported were performing. Nadine attended the ballet or the opera with Moira or a close female friend. She was ever mindful of senior German officers who showed an interest in her. When they approached and expressed their desire to meet her, she politely refused their advances. Nadine knew that single or widowed attractive and cultured French women in their thirties and forties were actively pursued by senior German officers. The Germans wanted female companionship, and the more aggressive ones desired an attractive and sophisticated French mistress. While most cultured mature French women found ways to tactfully resist the advances of Boche men, some, for whatever reason, succumbed. These women were branded collaborators by the French and were especially disliked by the resistance. But, in some cases, unscrupulous German officers used intimidation and coercion to recruit a French mistress.

At the opera, a newly promoted German general noticed Nadine and decided to contact her. He was not the first senior German officer to approach her. She politely refused their advances. However, this particular general was insistent. The following day, he sent flowers. He continued to call Nadine, but she would not return his calls. He did not call for almost a week until Braustich approached her.

"Madame," he said coolly, as if talking to a subordinate, "General Meino von Harter has inquired about you." Nadine did not respond to him, but, instead, looked at the German as if to say *so what*. "He is quite taken with you."

Nadine looked dispassionately at Braustich and thanked him for his concern but said she was not interested in the general.

"Madame should be," added Braustich coolly.

"Why?" she asked.

"He is a rising star in the Wehrmacht, a brilliant thinker in *Heer* (army) tactics and military organization."

"I don't understand," said Nadine.

Braustich explained that von Harter had been a very successful teacher at the prestigious Prussian military academy and trained numerous officers for leadership roles in the Wehrmacht. "He has made inquiries about you and would like to meet you. I would not disappoint him," said the German contumely.

Nadine resisted the urge to rebuff Braustich. Instead, she asked if she was being forced to meet von Harter.

Braustich gave a low chuckle and said, "A word of advice. A polite request from von Harter should be handled carefully. He does not take rejection well."

"I see," said the lovely French woman, understanding the warning the German was sharing about General Meino von Harter. Not since the occupation of Paris and the takeover of her business and assets had Nadine faced such a threat. She had to devise a strategy to meet von Harter and keep him at arm's length if she could. If not, perhaps the resistance could help.

* * *

The days passed quickly for Quentin as he busied himself with new business opportunities provided by the war. England was looking for new sources of raw materials and also interested in finding capital to fund their war industry. Quentin's contacts in Canada and England were steadily bringing new revenue streams to Barston, Marwick, Fowler, and Peterson. Moreover, his work with the movie industry provided lucrative returns for clients on successful films. Another income source for the law firm was financing the construction of important projects like dams, bridges, new or upgraded airports, and roads. He even managed to direct engineering consulting and design work for a few large projects to his father's firm.

The Cajun's work schedule was demanding because he had to fly to different cities to oversee the uninterrupted flow of raw materials for shipment to England. Maintaining a strong working relationship with these suppliers was an important part of his portfolio. He became very knowledgeable about the construction of dams, bridges, and especially all-weather landing strips for commercial and military aircraft. His trips to Hollywood were frequent and provided the opportunity to meet with Ruben and Healy, whenever she was near the West Coast. In order to be with Florence as much as possible, Quentin would take her on as many of his business trips as possible. He made certain that she always had a tutor and would not fall behind in her studies. Wherever they went, he always managed a rental piano for her

The more Quentin and Florence were together on business trips, the more the Cajun learned about his daughter. She would be eighteen soon and was a woman of substance and beauty. She could fly the Amelie as well as Hardy, Mark, or Cliff Lachlan. At some of the construction sites they visited, the bosses and the workers looked with admiration and other interests at Florence. She was blonde and beautiful, friendly and self-assured, and extremely talented. Everywhere they went, Florence turned men's heads and was envied by many women.

While in California at the beginning of March, Quentin took her shopping for a swimsuit at an upscale boutique. When she emerged from the dressing room in a one-piece suit, Quentin smiled at her lovely figure and how stunningly attractive she was.

"Honey," he told her when they were leaving the expensive shop, "you have a terrific figure. Most women would give anything to look like you.

"You think so!" she said in a teasing way. "Then why haven't you introduced me to some of your movie mogul friends?"

"Because," he replied quickly, "I don't want them to try to make you a movie star!"

"Why not?" she shot back with a pert smile on her face.

"Because you're better than that," he said, giving her a quick peck on the cheek.

"Thank you, kind sir." She smiled and took his arm.

* * *

When they returned to New York, Quentin found a message from Nadine asking him to come to Paris as soon as possible. He checked his calendar and arranged to visit France during the third week of April 1941. Before confirming the date with Nadine, he called Roosevelt to inform him about his trip to Paris. The president's secretary called and asked if he could come to Washington for a meeting. He said yes.

"How are you?" asked a smiling Roosevelt when Quentin entered his office. With the president were Cordell Hull and Harry Hopkins. "Coffee?" asked the president, motioning to a coffee setting on his right. Quentin suspected the president knew he liked strong coffee, and had some made for their meetings. He poured himself a cup and asked if Hull or Hopkins wanted some. Hull motioned for the Cajun to add more coffee to his cup. Roosevelt, his teeth tightly clenched on his cigarette holder motioned for Quentin to take a seat.

"When are you leaving for France?" asked Hull.

The Cajun replied in a week.

"Going to Paris?" teased the president.

Quentin nodded as he sipped his coffee.

"Call the embassy when you arrive and arrange to meet with Stony," Roosevelt told him.

"What's up?" asked the Cajun.

"The Germans have invaded Yugoslavia and are pushing south toward Greece," said Hopkins. Quentin knew that the Italians had invaded Greece but were unable to defeat the Greek army and that their attacks had stalled. The Wehrmacht, however, was a much better military machine.

"The Italians haven't been able to subdue the Greeks," said the Cajun. "The same's true in North Africa. Mussolini has asked his Nazi friends for help. I doubt the Greeks will be able to halt the Germans," said Quentin. Roosevelt nodded while Hull and Hopkins remained silent.

"The British have an expeditionary force in Greece, but they aren't strong enough to stop the Germans," said Hull.

"What does George Marshall say about this?" asked Quentin.

"He thinks the fighting in Greece will be over before the end of the month and that the British will have to evacuate their troops," said Hopkins, while Roosevelt looked on pensively.

"Once the Germans secure Greece, they'll move south," said Quentin.

"Yes, but where?" asked the president.

"Crete, probably," said the Cajun, finishing his coffee.

The president shook his head and glanced at Hull and Hopkins with a look of frustration. "That's what Marshall thinks," said Roosevelt. "Quentin, the British are not doing well against the Germans. If they lose Crete and the Nazis begin to sweep across North Africa toward Cairo, well, it's not a pleasant scenario."

"I understand, Mr. President," said Quentin. "I take it you want me to do something during my visit to France."

"Yes," said a solemn Roosevelt. "We've received information that the Germans are planning something on their eastern front. The information indicates they're marshalling troops and equipment in Poland and Hungary. Our information comes from a French source with the code name Eglantine. The British have tried to make contact with Eglantine but have come up empty. Eglantine prefers to work through us."

"So we're in the middle of this intelligence game," said the Cajun.

Roosevelt nodded and said, "When you get to Paris, we'd like you to speak to Mrs. Desnoyers and find out if she can contact Eglantine directly."

"That could be dangerous for her," said a hesitant Quentin. "She's under surveillance now, and doing something like this would be very risky."

"Yes, I realize that," said Roosevelt, removing his glasses and massaging the bridge of his nose. "However, we need to know if the Germans plan to attack the Russians. Our British friends are barely hanging on. Churchill told me that if the Germans attack the Russians, he'll ask Stalin to join him as an ally. Churchill needs reliable intelligence on German plans."

The Cajun sat quietly as the other men stared at him, waiting for his answer.

Finally, Quentin gave a deep sigh and said he would ask Nadine if she could contact Eglantine. Quentin noticed the president relax and lean back in his chair, almost as if a heavy burden had been lifted from his shoulders.

"Quentin, I can't tell you how much I appreciate this," said Roosevelt.

"All I can do is ask Nadine Desnoyers if she'll help us," said the Cajun. "It's up to her. If she turns us down,

I wouldn't blame her." A week later, Quentin left for France.

* * *

When Marlon and Kendall met in London during the first week of April, the younger pilot shared news about a new assignment for his squadron.

"I've heard that some RAF squadrons, perhaps mine, will go to the Mediterranean."

Marlon nodded and waited for Kendall to continue, even though he had heard similar rumors about the deployment of squadrons to Cairo and North Africa.

"I won't know for sure until next week," said Kendall in a cheery voice. "I do hope I get to go."

Marlon asked him why.

"Well, it's warm and dry there, and I'll get a chance to do more than just fly patrols and reconnaissance flights."

"Don't be in such a hurry to get shot at," said Marlon. "Besides, I heard that groups redeployed to Cairo are flying Hurricanes."

"Yes, I've heard that too," said Kendall, trying to sound upbeat.

"The Bf 109 is superior to the Hurricane," said Marlon. "It won't be a picnic going up against Jerry in a Hurricane. Tough enough with a Spit."

"I know," said Kendall. "But, they also promised to make me an officer if I go to North Africa."

"Well, that is good news," said Marlon. "We should celebrate."

That weekend they visited with Glinda before joining their dates for dinner and dancing. Kendall was meeting Dorothy Skiffington, a charming young Englishwoman in the RAF serving as a photographic reconnaissance analyst. Dorothy was from a well to do family and had attended excellent schools. She was almost nineteen.

Marlon continued to be with Erleen often, but not exclusively. He dated other girls, ones Glinda had introduced him to, and others he met at parties in London. It was difficult for Marlon to be with Erleen exclusively. Something prevented him from becoming intimate with her. But with Hayley, a young woman he'd met at a party, they went to bed on their second date. Marlon knew the vivacious young woman was intimate with other men. It didn't matter. He didn't want to become entangled in a serious relationship with Erleen or any other woman. *Besides*, he told himself, *I don't know if I'll be here tomorrow.*

Every week, Marlon received a letter from Florence. He looked forward to getting them. The cold and damp English weather, with frequent overcast and rainy days, made him yearn for America and his sister. As he read what she wrote, he relished the things Florence shared, especially news about her music and places she had been with "Father." Marlon chuckled about the way Florence referred to Quentin as Father. He remembered that when they were together, she called him "Daddy," especially when the little minx wanted something. He found himself engrossed with news from his sister and missed the times they were together.

Although Marlon had been at war less than nine months, it seemed like an eternity. By word of mouth and then through formal channels, the news came of changes in the British Air Ministry. Air Marshal Dowding and Air Vice Marshal Keith Price were removed by Air Chief Marshal Charles Portal. When slightly tipsy, some pilots in Sixty-six Squadron, mainly from noble families, shared that Dowding and Price were removed because they were unable to stem the Luftwaffe nighttime raids on London. Marlon had learned during his tenure in the RAF that personal friendships often counted for more than talent.

Two of Portal's "allies" in the RAF were soon promoted. Shalto Douglas became air marshal and Trafford Leigh-Mallory became air vice marshal, replacing his rival Keith Park. It irked Marlon that Leigh-Mallory was promoted. Rumor had it that Leigh-Mallory's promotion was based on favoritism.

In the weeks that followed, Marlon's squadron was assigned new missions. The RAF began to send bombers and fighters across the Channel to attack German targets along the coast of France. After several weeks of sorties against German installations on the French coast, losses began to mount. Reconnaissance flights revealed that the bombings by the RAF were marginally effective, at best. While damage to Nazi installations was slight, the British lost increasing numbers of planes and men. The RAF replaced most of the planes shot down, but pilots and air crews were harder and costlier to replace.

Marlon noticed visible disheartened behavior by pilots assigned to escort duty for RAF bombers over France. The daylight raids were brutal and costly. The Boche scrambled large numbers of fighters to intercept the bombers and often overwhelm the RAF fighter escorts. The limited range of the Spitfires forced many pilots to break off or run out of petrol. Pilots not paying attention to low fuel level warnings often failed to escape German fighters or ended up in the Channel. German antiaircraft guns took their toll on British bombers. Marlon watched in horror one day as the lead group of bombers they were escorting flew directly into a German antiaircraft box. Once the Germans had their altitude, the flak was devastating and crippled three planes in the first wave, four in the second wave, and destroyed two in the final flight. *Christ,* thought Marlon observing the devastation, *these kinds of losses can't be sustained.*

By the end of April 1941, fatigue was evident in the faces of numerous pilots in Sixty-six Squadron. For the first time since he joined the RAF, Marlon noticed the stress on the faces of pilots in his squadron assigned to escort duty for daylight bomb raids. To the credit of the young pilots, they managed to control their fear and went on the missions. Sadly, a growing number of them never returned.

* * *

Quentin's trip to Paris was delayed first by the slow processing of his request to visit occupied France and then bad weather over the North Atlantic. By the time he cleared his calendar and filed a flight plan to Ireland, it was the beginning of May 1941. He was surprised when Florence lobbied hard to join him to Ireland so she could go on to England and visit Marlon. His daughter had contacted Marlon and Glinda Pennington and arranged to stay with the Englishwoman and see Marlon while he was on leave.

"Oh, Daddy, you can't refuse. I've worked everything out. I'll take a flight from Dublin to London and stay with Glinda. Marlon has arranged to get a pass for a long weekend. It's perfect, Daddy!" she exclaimed with delight. Try as he might to persuade her that the trip might be dangerous, there was determination in his lovely daughter's face, and he realized it was fruitless to argue with her. She would be eighteen in a few weeks and was every bit a grown woman. Besides, taking her to Ireland might be beneficial and confuse Nazi operatives that might be following him.

"OK," he finally relented, "but I want Hardy and Mark to go with you to London," he insisted. She agreed, saying it would be fun to travel with them. Quentin called Hardy and Mark and told them about his plans and that Florence would join them. He asked if they would accompany her to London. Hardy and Mark were booked at a small hotel close to where Glinda lived.

"I want you, Mark, and Hardy back in Dublin when I return from France," he insisted.

Florence smiled and kissed him on the cheek, and, in a teasing way, said his wish was her command.

"Really?" Quentin teased. "Don't make me come looking for you," he warned politely.

But there was something hard in her father's eyes that sent a slight shiver down Florence's back. She sensed danger and a steely resolve in him. The way he chased Marlon in the sky to show who was the better pilot revealed her father's dangerous side. And, from Bernice, she learned the kinds of dangers he had faced and overcome while growing up in the Louisiana bayous. She felt instinctively that he was not someone to provoke or disappoint.

The flight to Ireland was routine. The weather over the North Atlantic was clear. When they arrived in Dublin, large, puffy, white clouds drifted lazily across the Irish sky.

Quentin made arrangements for the Amelie to be kept in a hangar until Florence, Hardy, and Mark returned from London. Then, the four of them went to their respective terminals to catch their flights. Quentin watched as Florence, Hardy, and Mark boarded their flight to London. He'd consented to Florence's trip to London because Hardy and Mark would be her chaperones; she'd see Marlon and stay with Glinda. He was still uneasy and worried about her. On the flight to Lisbon, he continued to fret about Florence in London. However, fatigue overcame him. Before he knew it, his plane landed at Lisbon. A new concern visited him, the thought of entering occupied France and what he might find there.

The moment Quentin left the U.S. Embassy in Lisbon, he spotted the surveillance. They were German operatives. He was followed as he changed trains at the Spanish border. He felt a tightening in his stomach as they approached France. He put aside the worries about being in a country controlled by the Nazis and looked forward to joining his lover in Paris. Deep inside, however, Quentin knew that if the Gestapo found out that Nadine was helping the French resistance, she would be apprehended, tortured for information, and killed. He knew the Gestapo could be ruthless and barbaric.

CHAPTER 10
AN EXPANDING CONFLICT

War involves in its progress such a train of
unforeseen and unsupposed circumstances . . .
that no human wisdom can calculate the end.
Thomas Paine, *Prospects on the Rubicon [1787]*

Nadine was waiting for Quentin at the Paris *gare*. She was dressed in a dark blue suit with a sky blue blouse. She was radiant and greeted her lover with chaste kisses on both cheeks. She had a short, older man carry one of his bags to the exit, and once they were outside to a waiting sedan. As Quentin's large bag was put into the trunk of the sedan, he gave the older man a tip and noticed the surveillance. The tall, slender man watching them was a Gestapo agent assigned to follow the lovely Frenchwoman wherever she went. Across the street sat two men in a dark sedan. At a signal from the tall Gestapo agent, they followed Quentin and Nadine.

"First to my office for business," said Nadine, her eyes revealing the love she had for the Cajun. "How was your trip?"

"Fine until I reached the French border," he replied. "They don't miss a thing. Everything I have is examined and all of my belongings cataloged."

"It's that way for all visitors, especially those the Boche are watching carefully. But, you are here, and that is all that matters." She touched him in a reassuring way.

At her place of business, they were greeted by Noel and Zeigler. The German sycophant was like a bug that Quentin wanted to squash. But, instead, he tried to be civil to the Nazi lackey and made small talk with him until they reached Nadine's suite of offices where Braustich was waiting.

"How good to see you again, Herr Norvell," Braustich said stiffly. "I trust your trip was comfortable and uneventful."

Quentin forced a smile and said things had gone smoothly. Then, he handed over various documents and contracts for the German's perusal.

"I have statements of earnings and fund transfers that Madame Desnoyers and you should examine," he said to tantalize Braustich. "I believe you will find the earnings report of interest."

"Of course," said a smiling Braustich as he fingered the documents.

After business matters were concluded, Braustich handed Quentin a sealed envelope.

"This arrived by courier just before you arrived."

Quentin noticed a Luftwaffe seal and bold letters that ordered that the letter be delivered personally to Herr Quentin Norvell. Inside were a note and an invitation from von Kleist. Nicky said he would be in Paris the day after Quentin's arrival and invited him and Nadine to be his guests at a chamber music recital and then dinner. He left a number where he could be reached in Paris. The American smiled as he read the letter, carefully penned in Nicky's bold Gothic writing style. He handed the letter to Nadine and said they had been invited to a musical recital and dinner with General Nicholas von Kleist. He watched Braustich give a weak smile. Obviously, von Kleist's name carried considerable weight. Braustich realized that Norvell was on good terms with von Kleist, a general in the Luftwaffe.

It will not hurt to adopt a friendly and helpful attitude, thought the German, wary of the American's friendship with the general.

After conducting their business affairs, Quentin noticed how pleased Braustich was by the large sums of money earned by Nadine's investments in America and elsewhere. What the German did not realize was the careful way substantial sources of income were not listed. They were shielded by Quentin's clever tactics. He secretly and adroitly sheltered some of the earnings and lodged them in U.S. corporations where the funds were invested at high rates of return. It was his way of ensuring that the Nazis did not control all of Nadine's wealth.

When Quentin arrived at the residence used during his previous stay, Rouge was waiting and carried his bag to the second floor. In hushed tones, he asked the American to meet him in the cellar in fifteen minutes. Quentin unpacked quickly and went to the cellar where Rouge was waiting to escort him through the long tunnel and then into the greenhouse beyond. At the opposite end of the greenhouse, Nadine waited, a lovely smile on her face. She kissed the American firmly on the lips, took his hand, and together they walked to her bedroom.

It was almost five thirty in the afternoon when Quentin felt Nadine nudge him gently.

"Cherie, it's time for you to return to your room. We're going to the ballet tonight," she cooed to him.

He smiled and recalled their passionate lovemaking. They must have engaged in foreplay and then sex that lasted for almost an hour. He was exhausted, but satisfied. He rose slowly and pulled Nadine close to him.

"Come away with me to England," he whispered.

She turned her head and looked at him fondly.

"I cannot, Cherie. Not just yet."

"I worry about you. The Boche are devious and dangerous. Even in America they follow me."

Her eyes widened in near disbelief. "Don't worry. I have friends who watch the Nazi operatives and will intercede if necessary."

It was while they were dressing that Nadine told him how the workers doing repairs and modifications to the house had discovered listening devices installed by the Boche. She said the devices had been relocated in rooms that were seldom used. Nadine chuckled when she told Quentin that every week her home was swept to locate any new surveillance devices the Gestapo might have installed.

"I need to speak with you somewhere safe," he whispered. She nodded, and they walked to a part of the greenhouse next to a fountain with running water.

"It is safe here." Quentin told her about the request made by the American president.

"There is an important French operative called Eglantine that has provided secret information about Boche military activities to the American Embassy in Lisbon. I'm instructed to ask if you can contact Eglantine."

Nadine was quiet for a moment. She thought about telling Quentin that she was Eglantine, but she decided against it. She thought it best not to involve Quentin in her network.

"Is it that important?"

He nodded.

She took awhile to answer, lost in thought. Finally, she said, "If you want me to do so, I will, Cherie, but I do it only for you."

He embraced Nadine and kissed her, his hands gently caressing her lovely face. He loved her so much; yet, he was putting this gorgeous woman, the mother of his son, in jeopardy. "Please be careful," he implored. She kissed him on the lips, stepped back, and said they both needed to bathe and get dressed for the evening's entertainment.

"My driver and I will pick you up at seven tonight."

The ballet was very well attended, and Quentin noticed the many German officers escorting well-dressed women. From their box, his eyes filled with the mixed colors of German military uniforms that depicted various branches of the Wehrmacht: Heer (army), Kriegsmarine (navy), Luftwaffe, and Waffen-SS. Waffen Shultzstaffel (SS) were volunteers for military service selected because of their political and racial qualities by the Nazis. They often wore black uniforms, some with a death head logo on their lapels and caps.

Just before the ballet started, an usher knocked politely and entered Nadine's box. He carried a silver salver on which was a card. Nadine thanked the usher, picked up the card, and read it in the dimming light. It was from General Harter. He was somewhere in the audience, perhaps watching her at this very moment. She thought for a moment before putting his card into her program and setting it on the ledge in front of her. Quentin watched her carefully and waited until the intermission to ask about the card.

"From an admirer?" he said softly, while tapping the card with his left index finger.

She smiled, but didn't say anything. But her eyes sent him a silent message, one filled with love and passion.

They walked to an area where spirits and refreshments were served. Nadine had reserved a table for them, and a waiter approached and took their order. They sat and discussed the dancing. A few minutes later, a German officer in the dress uniform of the Heer approached, stood in front of Nadine, clicked his heels, and bowed politely. He spoke in very good French.

"Madame, allow me to introduce myself. I am General Meino von Harter."

Nadine looked up at the German and smiled, taking a moment to collect her thoughts before saying, "General, may I introduce Monsieur Quentin Norvell from the United States."

Quentin stood and faced the German, who did not recognize or show any interest in him, something that caused the Cajun to smile while his eyes hardened.

"Herr Norvell is a close friend and my attorney in America," said Nadine, again calling attention to the American.

Von Harter ignored Quentin, focusing his attention on the lovely Frenchwoman and with a polite smile said, "Madame Desnoyers, you are a difficult person to meet."

Nadine adopted a polite but cool manner with the German and tried to deflect his insistence. "If it is a business matter," she said, smiling coolly, "please contact my assistant, Monsieur Noel DeCloux."

The German, unaccustomed to a woman refusing him, raised an eyebrow and waved aside her response. Looking directly at Nadine, von Harter said sternly that he preferred to discuss matters with her in private.

"I see," said the lovely French woman. Again she tried to parry the German's pressured approach. "Then perhaps you should call my social secretary, Mademoiselle Moira Tedoux and arrange an appointment."

The German, not about to be put off so easily, moved a step closer to Nadine and said that it would be a simple matter for the two of them to talk here and now. While von Harter's focus was on Nadine, he did not notice the Cajun gradually move close to the French woman's side until the American leaned over and whispered something to her.

Without taking her eyes off General Harter, Nadine put down her champagne flute and said, "Yes, I believe it's time for us to return to our seats."

Von Harter, now visibly annoyed, stared venomously at the American. The two men locked eyes on each other. When the general looked into the Cajun's eyes, he thought he saw something menacing. The German was used to subordinates and lackeys, like the cowed French bureaucrats he bullied, yielding to his will. This tall and strange man, however, showed no sign of yielding. The American standing before him was perhaps a few inches taller than he, trim and broad shouldered, and his hands clinched into fists.

"Come," said Nadine, taking Quentin's arm to end the impasse between the two men. It took a moment for Quentin to heed his lover's call. All he wanted to do was smash in the German's face and kick the hell out of him. As she touched the Cajun's arm, Nadine felt rock-like muscle. Gradually, Quentin's fists opened, and he turned to look at his lover's face, smiled, and walked away with her, leaving behind the furious German.

"Cherie," whispered Nadine as they entered the box, "you must be careful with men like that. He's an important Boche officer and can be a dangerous enemy."

"Yes, forgive my behavior." He knew that agitating the German might cause Nadine trouble, but he wanted so badly to beat von Harter to a bloody pulp. "I hope I have not caused you any trouble," he said softly and apologetically to the lovely woman. Before they took their seats, she moved Quentin to the back of the box where it was dark and kissed him passionately.

During the final intermission, while Nadine went to the ladies room, Quentin searched for and found von Harter. The German was standing with two Heer officers, one a major and the other a colonel. He approached the general directly and stood in front of him, deliberately interrupting the conversation among the three men. The Cajun raised his left arm and opened his hand revealing von Harter's card torn in two. Slowly, Quentin turned his hand over and allowed the torn card to fall to von Harter's feet. The American waited for a response from von Harter, but none was forthcoming. Aware the German was not about to act on his challenge, the Cajun turned and walked away.

I'll kill you, thought a furious von Harter, his ego wounded by the American's behavior and challenge. He decided to call someone in the Gestapo and arrange to teach this meddler a lesson. He wanted the American imprisoned and tortured for insulting him.

That evening, when Quentin was driven to his residence, he changed his clothing and went through the underground passage leading to the greenhouse. Nadine was waiting on the other side; that night, they enjoyed each other's bodies.

The next morning before it was light, Nadine walked with Quentin to the greenhouse.

"I know you love me, Cherie, and would do anything to defend me, but we are not free. And the Boche are vindictive. Von Harter will try to find a way to hurt you. Please be careful."

He nodded and said he would see her and Braustich at her office later that day to finalize their business affairs.

On the other side of the tunnel, Quentin looked for Rouge. He found the heavyset man sitting in the kitchen reading the paper and drinking coffee.

"Rouge," said Quentin as he approached the Frenchman. "I need to speak with you and Noel as soon as possible. Can you arrange it?"

The Frenchman nodded.

"It's urgent."

Rouge nodded and said, "*Bon.*"

Elsewhere in Paris, von Harter met with Manfred Kohlmeier, a colonel in the Gestapo. He shared the American's name with the colonel and was surprised to learn that Norvell was under surveillance.

"Did the man insult or strike you?" asked Kohlmeier.

"He interfered and challenged me," said the general.

"What was this in regard to?" asked Kohlmeier methodically.

Von Harter mentioned the incident, but he did not mention Nadine's name.

"I see," said the colonel. "Leave the matter to me."

"You will see to it that this impudent—"

The Gestapo colonel raised his hand to cut him off. "General," said Kohlmeier dispassionately, "I will handle this matter."

Even though von Harter outranked the colonel, the Gestapo's reputation for being heavy handed and accountable to but a handful of leaders close to the Fuhrer gave them a hegemony that was seldom challenged.

"Very well," said von Harter, "I leave it up to you, but this American should be taught a lesson and never again insult a senior officer of the Reich."

"Agreed," said the Gestapo colonel as he walked von Harter to the door of his office.

When Kohlmeier was alone, he opened Quentin Norvell's file. The American was an intriguing person. He was bringing large sums of money from America to the Reich and was known by several senior and influential generals in the Wehrmacht. Among his friends were General Nicholas von Kleist in the Luftwaffe and his uncle Field Marshal Ewald von Kleist in the Heer. He noticed that Norvell had met with Goebbels and had made arrangements for the distribution of German films in America.

No, he thought, *it would not be in the Reich's best interest to intimidate the American, especially over some French tart.*

Instead, Kohlmeier picked up the telephone and called General Nicholas von Kleist. It took awhile for the two German officers to connect. When they did talk, Kohlmeier mentioned the incident with von Harter.

"So," said von Kleist.

The Gestapo colonel took a drag on his cigarette and suggested something to the Luftwaffe general. A few minutes later, Kohlmeier hung up the phone, closed Quentin's file, and thought, *Well, the American has been warned.*

Von Kleist, on the other hand, put down the telephone and swore to himself. As he did so, a smile crossed his face and he said to himself, *You should have shaken up that little troll, my friend.*

* * *

After meeting with Nadine, Braustich, and Noel to finalize contractual matters and have all the forms necessary for the transfers of funds to accounts in France signed, Quentin left the building and went shopping for Florence, Kathleen, and Camila. It was almost six when he arrived at the residence and found Rouge and Noel waiting for him.

"Is there some place we can talk without being overheard?" asked the Cajun.

Noel nodded, and they walked down to the cellar.

"You may speak freely here," said the Frenchman as they stood in a corner of the dank basement.

"Madame Desnoyers is in danger. She needs your help."

Noel wrinkled his brow and asked the American to explain. Quentin told him about the incident with von Harter.

"After I leave," said Quentin, "the Nazi pig will try to force himself on Madame."

Noel looked at Rouge and then at the American.

"You have something in mind?" asked Rouge.

Quentin nodded. "General von Harter must have a serious accident."

The two Frenchmen looked at each other before Rouge spoke. "I will enjoy cutting the swine's neck."

"No," said Quentin adamantly. "It must appear to be an accident. Otherwise, there will be reprisals. The Boche have no regard for French lives. We must not allow innocent people to suffer."

"D'accord," said Noel, a smile on his face. "Leave it to us. We will find a way." He was pensive while Rouge looked on, a wicked smile on his face.

* * *

Florence nervously paced back and forth in Glinda's parlor, worried because Marlon was late. Just as she was about to call Geoff, she heard the musical chime for the front door. She wanted to run to the entryway and see if it was Marlon, but, instead, she waited and heard Deanna, Glinda's maid, welcome some visitors.

"Flo, where are you?" she heard Marlon call.

She appeared in the doorway, facing the foyer where Marlon stood with two RAF officers. But, she had eyes only for her brother.

"Marlon," she said, embracing her brother and kissing him on both cheeks. "You're late. I thought something might have happened to you."

"Thanks for worrying about me, Funny Face," said Marlon, his eyes drinking in the sight of his lovely sister. She looked mature, beautiful, and desirable. Instead of his kid sister from America, in front of him stood a radiant and gorgeous young woman.

The exchange between Marlon and Florence was interrupted when the two RAF officers cleared their throats and approached Florence.

"I'm sorry," said a smiling Marlon, "Flo, say hello to Lieutenants Carter and Gibson."

The two RAF officers did not waste any time taking Florence's hand and kissing the back of it gallantly. Both began to ask Florence questions before Marlon put his hands on his hips and said, "Fellas, she's my sis, and I haven't seen her in a long time. Put a lid on it."

Florence, meanwhile, asked Deanna if she could bring out the spirits and hors d'oeuvres. "Why don't we go into the parlor," said Florence, smiling politely at Carter and Gibson, but giving her brother a wicked look.

The four of them sat to chat in the parlor, the two Englishmen enchanted with the beautiful blonde American girl. Marlon could not get a word in edgewise as his friends monopolized the conversation, asking Florence question after question, smiling and laughing after each of her responses. He noticed how enthralled they were with his sister. Her silky golden hair was cut to shoulder length and parted to one side, a lock of it combed across her forehead and held in place with a small silver and malachite barrette. Around her long and graceful neck was a matching malachite necklace. Florence had on a white silk blouse open at the neck and a formfitting dark tan skirt that came to just below her knees, revealing long, tanned, and shapely legs. She wore a wide, shiny leather belt with a large silver clasp inlaid with a turquoise stone that appeared to be from the American Southwest. On her right wrist was a silver bracelet with matching turquoise stones.

While Florence made small talk with Carter and Gibson, she glanced furtively at Marlon, searching for signals from her brother. After a few minutes, her heart missed a beat when she realized Marlon was staring at her; his eyes scrutinizing her. It tantalized Florence. The door chime sounded, and Florence's attention shifted. *Who can that be?* she wondered.

Marlon stood and walked to the front door, leaving Florence with the two Englishmen. She smiled politely at them but was curious to know who was at the door. She heard the sound of women's voices and was surprised when Marlon entered the parlor with two young women.

"Ladies," said Marlon to Erleen and Cora, "let me introduce you to my sister Florence and to Lieutenants Lyman Carter and Perry Gibson." Immediately, Carter and Gibson jumped to their feet to greet the newcomers.

Florence smiled politely and noticed the way Marlon was holding Erleen's arm. She was curious about the two women, but especially Erleen. They sat to chat while Deanna brought wine glasses for Erleen and Cora. It was almost eight when Marlon said they needed to leave.

"We have dinner reservations at nine," he told them and mentioned the name of the restaurant. "We'll have to go in two cabs. Lyman, why don't you and Perry take Cora and Florence? Erleen and I will lead the way."

Marlon's suggestion annoyed Florence. She was about to say something when he looked at her and said, "That OK with you, Sis?"

She hesitated for a moment before nodding.

During dinner, Florence watched Marlon talk with Erleen. The way the Englishwoman looked at her brother and held his arm annoyed the young blonde.

Lyman said something to Erleen that surprised Florence. Carter mentioned that his father, a baron, was present when Erleen's father had been knighted.

Was Erleen a member of the English aristocracy? she wondered.

After dinner, they drove to a private club that Perry belonged to where a small band was playing popular tunes and couples were dancing.

"Come on, let's dance," said Lyman, extending his hand to Florence. She shot a quick look at Marlon, who nodded before joining the suave RAF pilot on to the dance floor. He was a good dancer, but Florence surprised him by how well she moved on the dance floor.

Before the night was over, Marlon had danced with Erleen most of the time, a few times with Cora, and just twice with Florence. When they left the club at just past midnight, Florence, Erleen, and Marlon drove to Glinda's home. Once there, Marlon told the driver to wait while he walked Florence to the front door.

"Aren't you coming in?" she asked, trying to hide her irritation.

"Have to take Erleen home," he said, kissing Florence on the cheek. "I'll be back tomorrow morning early. Then we'll spend the whole day together."

"Sure," said Florence curtly before turning on her heel and walking inside. Marlon was surprised by her behavior but let it pass. He returned to the cab and took Erleen home.

The following day, Marlon arrived early at Glinda's home and rang the bell. Deanna opened the door and he asked for Florence. The maid motioned for him to come in and said "Miss Florence" was in the sitting room. He knocked before entering and was greeted with a plastic smile that he felt was insincere.

"Well," said Florence, "you don't look the worse for wear after being out all night. Did you and your 'friend' have a good time?"

Marlon noticed his sister's sarcastic manner, but rather than become defensive, he chuckled and brushed aside her remark.

"Hello, Funny Face. Have you had breakfast yet?" Florence looked casually at the magazine she was holding without responding. "Something bothering you?"

"It's nothing," she said tersely, standing and tossing her head back.

"There's a place we can go for breakfast not far from here," he said, watching his sister carefully, wondering why she was upset.

"Just the two of us, or will your girlfriend join us?" said Florence icily.

Now Marlon knew what was bothering her. "No, Sis, just the two of us. I haven't seen you in a while, and we need to catch up." He stood before her and reached out to embrace her. She stiffened in his arms, but he squeezed her; in a moment, the suspicion and tensions within Florence melted away. "I've missed you," he whispered as he ran his fingers through her silky blonde hair.

She wanted to say something, but the words would not form. Instead, she just buried her head into his shoulder. They stood together without speaking before Marlon gently lifted her chin with his hand so their eyes could meet and said, "Let's go get something to eat."

She gave him a big smile and said OK.

They spent the entire day and the next together, visiting historical places in London and walking along the Thames near Parliament and Big Ben. When Marlon mentioned the damage and devastation caused by the bombings to parts of London, Florence said she had heard about it but had not really seen signs of damage.

"You can't believe what these people have endured," he told her.

She shrugged her shoulders and didn't say anything.

Marlon made a snap decision to show his sister the effects of the war and its toll on the British. They took the underground, and, upon exiting the car, she saw people literally living on the platform. When they reached the surface, Florence was shocked by the ruins of buildings and the crews of men digging through the rubble searching for survivors. The sight of the devastation took away Florence's breath, and she coughed to clear her throat of the heavy atmosphere pregnant with particles of dust and soot, the offensive smell of exploded ordinance and smoke from smoldering fires. *This is hell,* she thought.

"OK, Sis, let's go," said Marlon, leading her back to the underground. They rode the train in silence.

Florence was stunned by the damage she'd witnessed, her mind trying to cope with the images of the destruction. It was horrible.

"I'm sorry to have to show you that," Marlon told her softly when they arrived at his hotel. "Let's have some tea before I take you to the British Museum." She swallowed hard and nodded before resting her head on his shoulder.

* * *

The evening before Marlon returned to Sixty-six Squadron, he and Florence sat together in Glinda's parlor. The only light in the room came from a tiffany lamp in a corner. In the semidarkness, the two talked quietly while suppressed emotional undercurrents strained to be released and shared.

"Flo," said Marlon after a long silence, "I've learned something about myself and about Dad."

"What?" asked Florence, intrigued by her brother's comment.

"I think I know what it was like for him during the last war."

She looked at him in the dim light, silent and expectant. "Now that I've been in combat, I'm glad Dad trained me to fly the way he did. If he hadn't done it, I'd probably be dead."

"Oh, Marlon, don't say that," she said nervously.

"It's true, Sis. He knew what it would be like and helped me. I owe him my life."

Marlon's words touched Florence's heart, interjecting a new appreciation for her father along with her love for Marlon.

"But, I'm not like Dad. There's something wild in him. I guess it's from growing up in the bayous."

His comments surprised her.

"I don't understand," she said hesitantly.

"Sometimes, Dad can be, well, scary. There's something hard and menacing deep inside of him."

She thought for a while and remembered two incidents when Quentin had acted quickly, forcefully, and violently.

"What are you thinking?"

Florence replied slowly and alluded to two scenarios. The first occurred one evening after she had stayed late at her prep school to practice the piano and Quentin came to walk her home. Two muggers accosted them. She told Marlon how Quentin had disarmed one man and kicked the other in the groin. "He moved like a cat," she said, her voice filled with awe. "He was choking the other man until I screamed. I thought Daddy was going to kill him!"

"And the other incident?" asked Marlon, the shadows hiding his eyes as he leaned forward anticipating her response.

"We were walking in the Village, when a couple of young guys came on to me. Daddy saw them and didn't do anything at first. But, when one of them took me by the arm and tried to get close, Daddy told him to let go."

"Did he?" asked Marlon, looking directly at his sister.

"No, he and the other guy dared Daddy to do something."

"What happened?"

She said that Quentin moved quickly and grabbed the arm of the young man holding her and twisted it behind his back. When the other young man came at him, she said "Daddy" knocked him down and kicked him senseless.

"There was a cold fury in Daddy that scared me," she said apprehensively.

"Flo, Dad will do anything, including risk his life, to protect us. I don't think he's afraid of anything when it comes to making sure we and my mom are safe."

"But you're risking your life flying with the RAF."

"Yes, but I'm not like Dad. I don't go looking for trouble," said Marlon, turning away to look into the shadows. "I hesitate before doing some things. I know Dad doesn't. That's why he was able to fly rings around me that day on Long Island."

"But you would have protected me from the muggers, right?"

"Sure," he said slowly, "but probably not as well or as violently as Dad."

Florence was silent for a few moments, digesting what Marlon had said about their father. She understood what Marlon meant about his being different from Quentin. The thought of her father being hard and dangerous was something she wanted to put out of her mind.

"Marlon, let's not talk about Daddy anymore. Let's talk about something else."

"Sure," he said, sitting back in the comfortable chair and crossing his legs.

"Marlon, do you like me?"

"That's a funny question, Sis."

"Do you?" she insisted.

"Of course I do, Funny Face," he said jokingly.

"What do you like about me?" The shadows were playing tricks with her face so that Marlon was unable to determine if she was serious or teasing him.

He began by telling her how talented and charming she was, and stressed her musical gift. Then, he mentioned she was outgoing, adventuresome, and a "darn good athlete."

"But what about me, inside?"

Marlon realized that Florence expected a different kind of analysis, something more personal than what he had shared. He was silent, lost in thought before responding. "Well," he finally said, "I think you're beautiful, and it's not just your looks. There's something unique and wonderful inside of you," he said, tapping his breast with his right index finger. "You're special, Flo." As he spoke, Marlon realized how much he cared for and admired his sister. She had so many appealing qualities. As he thought about them, they were the standards by which he measured other women. Nadine, his mother, was the epitome of the perfect woman. But, Flo was enticing and sensual, and though he knew her as a sister, there was another unmistakable attraction. After examining his feelings, Marlon felt uneasy and decided not to say anymore.

At first, Florence was puzzled by his silence. Intellectually, she understood and could feel her brother's love and regard. She was emotionally attracted to him and wanted desperately for some kind of reciprocation from Marlon. She stood, hesitated for a moment, walked to Marlon and kissed him gently on the lips.

Florence's lovely face and soft lips momentarily overwhelmed Marlon's senses. He wanted to pull her into his arms in a close embrace. Maybe it was her delicate perfume and personal civet that enthralled him. Before he allowed himself to yield to a desire that was a taboo, he spoke.

"Thank you, Sis."

Florence savored the kiss, still feeling his soft lips on hers. It was like no other sensation she had ever experienced. She wanted badly to have him hold her and to feel engulfed by his arms. She stood wavering in front of him expectantly, wanting what she knew was incestuous and forbidden. Finally, Marlon stood and said his throat was dry and that he needed something to drink.

"Would you like some water, Sis?"

The loving mood she so desired evaporated and reluctantly she said water would be fine.

"Wait here." He gently brushed her shoulder as he went to the kitchen.

What Florence did not recognize was the terrible struggle under way in Marlon's heart and mind. Her kiss had disturbed and confused him. He craved her and tried to resist the carnal urge. But he wanted her. What was this dangerous attraction between them? He had to get up and leave Florence for fear that he would do something rash and regrettable.

The following day, Glinda and Florence were joined by Argentina de Gavrelac. The three of them went to the train station with Marlon. Glinda and Florence cried while Argentina's eyes misted. He kissed all of them on the cheek and said he would be fine. Glinda told him to be careful and Argentina encouraged him to shoot down more Germans. Florence stood silently, her eyes focused intently on Marlon, a double meaning in her stare. She too wanted him to be careful...she also wanted him.

* * *

On their last night together in Paris, Nadine and Quentin attended a chamber music program followed by an elegant dinner hosted by Nicky von Kleist. The residence occupied by von Kleist was palatial. Lorelei was present and radiant in a long, black, formal gown cut short along the shoulders with an open back. She was stunning. Nadine wore a designer gown in white that was formfitting and accentuated her lithe figure. Her hair was combed up, with curly ringlets cascading along her temples. She was gorgeous and the envy of most women at von Kleist's soiree.

The German general was quick to mention how fortunate the American was to be with such a radiant creature.

"Nicky, you never say those things to me," said Lorelei teasingly.

"Perhaps, Lorelei, it's because he guards carefully his good fortune to be with you," said a smiling Quentin.

Lorelei kissed him on the cheek and said, "You are gallant and verbalize your thoughts well. Nicky, he knows how to praise a woman!"

"Yes, his kind is free with praise," scoffed the German, a twinkle in his eye. "Come, it's time we introduced them to our guests."

After the chamber music, von Kleist took the American aside and told him about his conversation with a Gestapo colonel. "It seems, my impetuous friend, that you agitated Meino von Harter."

Quentin smiled at von Kleist but remained silent.

"I was told to warn you about behaving badly toward a senior German officer in the Heer." Von Kleist said it in a matter-of-fact way. "You should have taught him a lesson."

"I tried to provoke him into a duel, but he wouldn't do it."

"Better this way," said the German, flicking some ash off of his cigar. "You might have killed him in a duel and caused yourself considerable grief."

Quentin nodded. He thought about smashing in von Harter's face.

"When do you leave?"

Quentin replied the following morning.

Looking around to make certain they could not be overheard, he told the American that the war would take a different turn for Germany.

"What do you mean?"

"The Fuhrer has an ambitious undertaking for us, one I hope will not cause us great harm."

"Does this have anything to do with the treaty of alliance with the Japanese?"

The German smiled and said, "Nein, but there are many well-informed officers in the Wehrmacht who consider the alliance a bad one."

"Then there is something else, perhaps a new front?" said the Cajun, trying to tease information out of von Kleist.

Nicky did not answer; instead, he focused his attention on his cigar.

"I hope this thing you are referring to will not place you in any danger," Quentin told von Kleist.

"My dear friend, we in the Wehrmacht are at the mercy of an unpredictable despot. But, let us talk no more of this. Will you return to Paris soon?"

Quentin mentioned that he would return at the beginning of November. "When you return I may not be here," Nicky told him, with sadness in his voice. "Things will change, and I fear perhaps for the worst."

Quentin did not bother to press Nicky. Germany was going to attack the Soviet Union. Something in Nicky's face and voice assured him of that.

The next morning Nadine woke and noticed that she was alone. She heard Quentin in the bathroom. He was leaving today. *Two days and two nights with stolen moments together,* she thought. When he emerged from the bathroom wearing only a towel, she motioned for him to come to her. She removed the towel and pressed herself against him, encouraging his arousal. They engaged in foreplay and then a feverish sexual encounter.

As they dressed, Nadine asked when he would return. He replied early in November.

"Bon, I have a few things for you." She reached for the duplicate book of poetry and handed it to him while whispering something in his ear. They walked into the bathroom, and she ran water in the sink and gave him critical military information.

"The Boche have three major army groups ready to strike at the Soviets. The Northern group in East Prussia is under the command of General Ritter von Leeb. The Center group in Poland is commanded by Field Marshal Fedor von Bock. And the Southern group in Hungary is led by General von Rundstedt. The Boche have three million troops and more than three thousand tanks ready to invade Russia. They will attack soon, perhaps in a few weeks."

Quentin hugged the beautiful French woman and kissed her. Two hours later, he was en route to Spain with information on German military plans. At the Spanish border, there was a thorough examination of his things by French guards, their German masters observing the activities scrupulously. The border guards checked to ensure he was departing with everything he'd brought into occupied France and nothing more. Quentin declared the small gifts he'd purchased for Florence, Kathleen, and Camila. In Spain, the Cajun detected the surveillance. *The Gestapo is so predictable,* he thought.

Quentin went to the American Embassy in Lisbon and from there contacted Florence, Hardy, and Mark about his arrival time in Ireland. Two days later, they met in Dublin. A few hours later, all of them were aboard the Amelie heading west. The Cajun noticed Florence's quiet and introspective demeanor. When he asked about her stay in London, she said Glinda sent her love, Marlon was well and wanted to know about Nadine, and when Quentin would visit England.

Sensing something was troubling Florence, Quentin asked if anything was wrong.

"Marlon and I went to a part of London that had been bombed. It was awful." She used this to deflect his question and avoid conversation about the emotional turmoil that her affection for Marlon was causing.

"It's not a pretty sight," he told her. "I'm just sorry that the bombings will continue."

She looked away and started to cry.

To assuage her, he said, "Don't worry, honey; Marlon will be all right."

The weather over the North Atlantic was clear, but with strong, turbulent headwinds. Florence asked to fly the Amelie. Once in the pilot's seat, Quentin noticed her determination and tension as she fought the buffeting to stabilize their flight.

She's fighting more than the headwinds, thought the Cajun.

As they flew westward fighting headwinds, Quentin recalled his recent meeting with von Kleist in Paris. Among the guests were General Ernst Udet and Lieutenant Colonel Adolf Galland, a celebrated German ace with over fifty-eight victories to his credit. Udet drank excessively and talked longingly about Inge Bleyle, the love of his life. Galland was eager to chat with Quentin, and they conversed at length about new aircraft and fighter tactics. Galland was a bright, fascinating, and outspoken officer. *He must be a great flyer,* thought Quentin. *No wonder Nicky likes him,* he mused. He sat back. A few minutes later, he fell into a fitful sleep.

CHAPTER 11
THE WAR EXPANDS

And blood in torrents pour
In vain—always in vain,
For war breeds war again.
John Davidson, *War Song*

The papers in New York City had banner headlines about the Germans attacking the Soviet Union on June 21, 1941, and the radio carried regular commentary about it. For Quentin, the news was innervating, releasing a hidden avidity within him for an enemy's misfortune. *Hitler might have taken on more than he can handle,* he mused. The information Nadine provided about the three major German army groups proved accurate. She even indicated that the Boche would attack on the twenty-first or the twenty-second. U.S. Military Intelligence told Roosevelt that Eglantine's information was reliable and that the source needed to be cultivated. When the Cajun spoke with Roosevelt about Eglantine, he said their first priority should be to protect and not compromise the French contact. By extension, Quentin wanted Nadine's part in intelligence gathering treated with the utmost secrecy and contacts with her kept to a minimum. He was determined to avoid exposing his lover to additional risks.

In July, Roosevelt asked Quentin to visit with him in Washington. When the Cajun inquired who else would be present, the president mentioned Cordell Hull, Secretary of War Henry L. Stimson, Secretary of the Navy William

F. Knox, Harry Hopkins, General Marshall, and Ruben Valderano.

"What's up, Mr. President?"

"We need your advice on a sensitive matter."

Quentin sensed that Roosevelt had something critical in mind. The Cajun recalled Stony saying that some matters should not be discussed on the phone, even with the president. He was told the date and time for the meeting. After hanging up the phone, he thought, *OK, it'll be interesting to find out what Roosevelt and his people are up to.*

The escalating war in Europe was affecting America more than most people had thought. President Roosevelt was supporting Britain and Canada. The Cajun knew the United States was helping the Allies by lending the British and Canadians destroyers and long-range reconnaissance planes. Now that the Soviets and the Germans were at war, Quentin's thoughts vacillated between optimism that the Soviet Union partnered with the British would be advantageous for the Allies, but he was uncertain about the Red Army and its capabilities. *The Russians did poorly against the Finns,* he worried. Would the Russians be able to withstand the German blitzkrieg? Perhaps in Washington he would find answers to his questions.

It was a hot, sweltering late afternoon in mid-July when Quentin arrived in Washington. He flew the Amelie to avoid the long train trip and crowded passenger cars filled with tourists and visitors. The heat and humidity in Washington could cause enormous discomfort for those dressed in suits and ties. A message was waiting for him at the Mayflower from Healy. When he called, she said to meet her at the Willard Hotel. When he arrived in the lobby, Healy and two others he recognized as syndicated columnists were waiting.

"Hi, Tiger," said Healy, greeting the Cajun with a kiss, and introduced the two journalists. Then, she took the Cajun's arm and walked into the bar. As he walked next to the blonde writer, the hint of scented talcum filled his nostrils and reminded him of the times they had been together, particularly their intimate moments. But, that had been long ago.

"What's up?" he asked.

Healy parried his question by asking about Florence. Quentin mentioned their recent trip to England. She raised an eyebrow and wanted to know why he had allowed her favorite "niece" to be out of his sight in "that dangerous city (London)." He laughed and mentioned Florence had stayed at Glinda Pennington's home.

"Hardy and Mark were her chaperones."

"More like accomplices," she quipped. "You better keep an eye on that girl," added Healy, "she's a real schemer."

The Cajun grinned and nodded, aware of the reporter's fondness for Florence.

"So what are you doing in DC?"

"Well, rumor has it that we're (the U.S. government) sending a delegation to Russia. State Department tight asses give us the usual 'no comment' bullshit," she said before ordering a drink.

He remained silent to avoid mentioning his purpose for being in the capital.

"We'll find out what's going on," she said with a wicked smile on her face.

I bet you will, thought the Cajun, well aware of Healy's resourcefulness.

"So what brings you to Washington?" asked Ernie, one of the columnists.

"A meeting with people in Treasury about my recent trip to France and some fund transfers."

"I should think that the State Department boys would be involved," said Travis, the other writer.

"They're involved at the front end," replied the Cajun. "I needed their permission to visit France and account for my activities. Tell me, what's this about a delegation to the Soviet Union?"

In the next fifteen minutes, they told Quentin that several influential people in the Roosevelt administration, and a few others outside of the government, were meeting with the "big boys" in the State Department. And, the president was holding private meetings with people they suspected would go on a mission to Russia.

Intrigued by what he was hearing, Quentin asked, "How do you know all of this?"

"We have our sources," said a smiling Healy, finishing her drink and ordering another.

"Look, Tiger, I wouldn't be surprised if you were asked to join the group going to Russia." She was testing him.

"Not likely. I just got back from France," he replied, "and need to go back there again. The Germans won't let me return to France if I'm part of an official delegation to the Soviet Union."

Healy looked at Ernie and Travis, their eye contact registering agreement. "Well, there's something you could do for me," said a smiling Healy.

Quentin remained silent, waiting for the blonde writer to continue.

"I'm pretty sure Ruben Valderano is in Washington."

"What makes you think that?" asked Quentin, trying to deflect attention away from his meeting with the president.

"I know he's here. I've tried to get in touch with him," she said.

Again, the Cajun played possum and waited for her to continue.

"But he's incognito."

"Hmmm, I see. So you want me to find out if Ruben is in D.C. *And, by extension, if he will be part of any diplomatic mission to Russia,* he speculated.

"Yeah," she said, looking directly at Quentin and giving him her best smile. "That's all, Tiger."

"Ruben's my friend," said Quentin, stalling to sort out what was going on. "Healy, this wouldn't have anything to do with confirming a possible diplomatic mission to Russia and trying to get on that junket?"

She glanced silently at Ernie and Travis, a nonverbal message passing between them.

"OK, so you figured it out. Yeah, we'd like to get into Russia. The Soviets are real hard-asses. They won't let in reporters from 'capitalist' countries."

"So," said a smiling Quentin, "if I find out Ruben's in Washington, you'll get to him and squeeze him for information. Not likely," he said flatly. "Ruben's my friend."

"We'll find out sooner or later," said Travis.

"But it won't be from me," said the Cajun, as he stood to leave. Healy motioned for the other reporters to remain seated and took Quentin's arm and walked him out of the bar.

"OK, bad strategy," said Healy. "But, if you do see Ruben, will you ask him to call me?"

He smiled and said he couldn't promise anything. She kissed him on the lips and whispered, "I owe you big time for what you've done for me, but I'm not asking you to betray Ruben. Just give him my message. Let him make the choice," she said, squeezing his hand before turning and walking back to the bar.

Healy, I've got to admire your chutzpa, he thought as she walked away.

* * *

"Mr. Norvell," said Horace, the hotel desk attendant at the Mayflower, "you have a message marked urgent."

The Cajun thanked Horace and handed him a dollar in exchange for the note. Ruben wanted Quentin to call him at the listed number. He stepped into a public telephone booth and dialed the number. After the third ring, he heard Ruben's familiar voice. They exchanged greetings before Quentin asked where the Mexican was.

"Can we meet for dinner?" asked Valderano.

"Sure. Where and when?" Ruben gave him the name of small restaurant in Adams Morgan and told him to be there at 7:30 p.m.

"What's going on?" asked the Cajun.

"I'll tell you when we get together." They chatted for a few minutes about Marlon and Kendall before ending the call.

When Quentin arrived at the restaurant, he was greeted by a stocky man with a pronounced accent that sounded like he was a Spanish speaker. Quentin mentioned he was meeting a friend.

"Your name? And your friend's name?" asked the man as he checked the reservation log. The moment Ruben's name was mentioned, the stocky man motioned for Quentin to follow him. They went up a flight of stairs where a heavyset man was seated. As they approached, the man stood. He was easily two or three inches taller than Quentin, broad shouldered, with his coat unbuttoned.

"It's OK," said the stocky man, motioning in Quentin's direction.

"He alone?" asked the tall man.

The other man nodded and turned to leave.

"Let me see some ID," the man told Quentin. He showed his driver's license and his pilot's license. The big man studied the IDs carefully before returning them.

"OK, in here," said the tall man, knocking on a door to his right before opening it and motioning for Quentin to enter.

Inside the well-lit room was Ruben Valderano, Harry Hopkins, Brook Hamilton Stoner, and two other men the Cajun did not recognize. Ruben gave Quentin an *abrazo*, a hug that Mexican men reserve for family or very close friends only.

"Come, sit down. Let me introduce you," said the Mexican. "You know Harry and Stony. This is Andy Kondretiov and Aaron Renzi."

When the Cajun shook hands with both men he noticed that Kondretiov wore a West Point ring and Aaron a Yale graduation ring on his left hand.

"Andy is with Army Intelligence, and Aaron is with the FBI," said Stoner, as he shook hands with Quentin.

Hopkins remained seated, smiled, and nodded his head at the Cajun.

"Forgive the cloak-and-dagger stuff," said Stoner, "but it's best to keep things close to the vest." The puzzled expression on Quentin's face caused Ruben to snicker.

"It's OK, hombre," said the Mexican. "You hungry?"

In the next half hour, while they ate, Quentin asked about the need for secrecy and was told Nazi operatives were still watching them.

"Nazi operatives monitor people going in and out of the White House, especially military personnel," said Aaron.

"Tomorrow, we'll meet at Treasury," said Stoner. "The chief (President Roosevelt) won't join us. Anyone following you," he said nodding in the Cajun's direction, "will think you're doing routine business with Treasury."

"Who's 'we'?" asked the Cajun.

Stoner mentioned the men in the room plus Cordell Hull, George Marshall, people from the navy, Military Intelligence, and J. Edgar Hoover.

"We're sending a diplomatic mission to Moscow," said Stoner. "The boss wanted you to know the score and do a few things for us."

"Such as?" said Quentin warily.

"Fill us in on rumors about a new German fighter," said Kondretiov.

"You mean the new fighter they're experimenting with, the one with the radial engine?"

Kondretiov nodded his head.

"Well, it's fast, maneuverable, and will probably become operational soon. From what I've learned, the Germans think it will shoot down anything the Brits have," he told them. "But let's talk about this diplomatic mission to Russia. Care to fill me in on what's involved?"

Stony looked hesitant to answer until Ruben spoke up. "The British have called the president and asked for help. We need to know if the Red Army can stop the Germans. If they can't, the president wants to know what to do."

The Cajun thought for a moment before proffering a suggestion. "Have the Brits sent the Reds any people to help them with air support?"

The other men in the room glanced at each other, uncertain about the Cajun's question and what he had in mind. Their silence answered the Cajun's question.

"Look," he told them, "there's a critical link between air support, tanks, and infantry. It's essential in blitzkrieg. It's tough to disrupt the relationship between tanks and infantry. But, if German air cover can be diminished, then the Soviets might stand a chance."

Ruben was the first to speak. "You're right. German armor is well led and equipped, and their infantry is strong and experienced. The weak link for the Germans might be air support. So, what do you have in mind, hombre?"

"The British managed to check the Luftwaffe and know their weaknesses. Perhaps the Brits could send a few of their best RAF pilots as advisors and trainers to help the Russians."

"I think you've got something," said Valderano, smiling at the Cajun. "Do you have anyone in mind?"

"Not really," replied Quentin. "This needs to be a British show. We can sell the Russians guns, bullets, and planes, and maybe offer them credit, but all of that will take time."

"Advisors, however, can be on their way in a matter of weeks," said a thoughtful Kondretiov.

Hopkins nodded in approval.

Quentin decided to change the subject. "Stony," he said, looking directly at the diplomat, "Healy knows about the diplomatic mission to Russia."

Stoner gave a weak smile before saying sarcastically, "Why am I not surprised."

"Maybe she's just fishing," said Hopkins.

"I don't think so," said the Cajun. "She knows Ruben is in town and will be part of a group meeting with the president tomorrow."

"Damn!" exclaimed Renzi.

"What does she want?" asked Hopkins.

"She wants to go on the trip," Quentin replied.

The room erupted in the annoyed chatter of men frustrated because a secret is compromised. Ruben, along with Quentin, remained silent before saying, "Gentlemen, perhaps we can turn this to our advantage."

"How?" asked Hopkins.

In the next few minutes, Ruben discussed including two or three journalists on the mission to Russia. His logic was simple but clever. As news about the diplomatic mission had leaked, rather than try to contradict rumors, inviting Healy and two more reporters as participants might help to disguise the visit as a simple fact-finding trip

"Of course," said Stoner, "we're neutrals and want the American public to know how the war is affecting the Soviets."

Hopkins smirked and asked how the reporters could be prevented from participating in the military and diplomatic discussions.

"Easy," said Stoner, "we'll have the Russian propaganda people keep them busy." The men in the room smiled and soon started to laugh.

The next day, Quentin met at the U.S. Treasury with the group Stoner had mentioned. They discussed the fighting between the Germans and the Russians and the rapid advances the Germans were making into the Soviet Union. General Marshall and Colonel Roper from Military Intelligence briefed them on German gains and possible strategy. When Quentin asked about air clashes, Marshall said the Luftwaffe had scored impressive victories against the Soviets.

"Do you happen to know the types of planes the Russians are using?" asked the Cajun.

Colonel Roper consulted a file and mentioned three kinds of Soviet airplanes. "Those are obsolete models," said Quentin. "They'll need better planes to stop the Germans."

In the next hour, the group discussed the planned visit to Russia and its purpose. After Quentin and Ruben shared their opinions, Hopkins called for a break.

Quentin took Ruben aside and asked if he was going on the diplomatic mission to Russia.

Ruben nodded.

"How long will you be gone?"

Ruben replied six weeks, possibly longer.

"Why so long?"

Ruben replied that getting into Russia was tricky and Stalin would decide their agenda and length of stay in the Soviet Union.

"Will you visit the front lines?" asked Quentin.

Ruben nodded.

The Cajun said it could be dangerous.

The Mexican smiled and said he had been shot at before.

Quentin just shook his head and told his friend to be careful.

"*Siempre* (always)," said Ruben with a big grin.

They returned to the meeting, Quentin concerned about his friend's safety, and Ruben thinking about the forthcoming trip to the Soviet Union. Before the meeting ended, Hopkins said that the mission to Russia would probably depart in September. When someone asked why they could not leave sooner, Cordell Hull motioned for Stony to speak up.

"Stalin is calling the shots. When he gives us the go ahead, we'll leave."

The meeting ended when Hull reminded them to keep what they had discussed in strict confidence.

As Quentin and Ruben walked out of the meeting, a secret service agent was waiting. He told them the president wanted to speak with them on a secure line.

"Ruben, Quentin, good you're here," said Roosevelt. He got to the point quickly. "Quentin, I like your suggestion about asking the British to send experienced pilots to help the Soviets. I've talked to Churchill this morning, and he liked it too. He'll contact Stalin directly and propose it. Then, it'll be up to Stalin. Quentin, I wish you were going on this mission," said Roosevelt. "But, I know the Germans will find out about it and who will be going. Frankly, I need you to continue with your activities in France."

The Cajun remained silent. *Yes,* he thought, *I do want to see Nadine again.*

"Mr. President," said Ruben, speaking into the speaker box. "I'm concerned about Japanese expansionism in the Pacific."

"Oh," said Roosevelt, "tell me what's on your mind, General?"

"Mr. President," continued Ruben, "I'm worried about Japanese intrusion into Indochina and their interest in Burma and the Malayan Peninsula."

"Ruben, I appreciate what you're saying. Cordell and I are imposing economic sanctions and an oil embargo on

Japan. We're not taking their acts of military aggression lightly. However, the greater danger is with the Germans, and we must do everything possible to help the British and the Russians."

"Is that wise, Mr. President?" asked the Mexican. "Their alliance with the Nazis has opened the door for them to expand into Indochina and perhaps elsewhere in the Pacific."

"I'm aware of their activities in China and Indochina. We've hinted at economic sanctions, and even an embargo on oil and scrap metal. Perhaps that will bring them around."

Ruben remained silent, but his concerns about Japan were not lessened by what the president said.

As Ruben and Quentin were leaving the U.S. Treasury building, the Mexican turned to the Cajun and, in a soft, but firm voice, said, "I don't think the president understands the danger we face from Japan."

Quentin appreciated what Valderano meant and worried that additional economic sanctions against the Japanese would probably not check their territorial ambitions.

"It's dangerous to underestimate the Japanese. The Russians learned that lesson the hard way," said Valderano.

Quentin glanced at him before saying, "I doubt the president and his advisors will take anything we tell them about Japan to heart."

"Yes, and that's precisely what's bothering me," said a frowning Valderano.

The two of them talked for a few minutes before Quentin wished Ruben well on the trip to Russia.

"Take care of yourself, *amigo*. When you return, let's get together for Christmas."

"Christmas in New York! Julia and I would like that," said a smiling Valderano as they parted.

In Paris, Nadine was preparing to leave the city and the summer heat of 1941 and visit with her parents and Louis Bondurant at La Croisiere. Normally, she would escape the heat of July and August by visiting her home at Normandy near the beach, but the Boche had commandeered the house. Moreover, the Frenchwoman required permission to leave Paris and provide a detailed account of her destination, purpose, and duration of the trip from Braustich and his superiors. Before departing in mid-July, she met with Braustich to discuss any last-minute details that required her attention. The smarmy Zeigler accompanied Braustich. She disliked the German sycophant but hid her feelings behind a polite smile. As she was signing the documents Braustich had brought, Zeigler, in an unctuous voice, said how unfortunate it was about General von Harter.

Without looking up as she continued to sign documents, Nadine asked what he meant.

"I thought you might have heard," Zeigler told her. "General von Harter died in an accident."

"How tragic," said Nadine, feigning sympathy.

"Yes," said Braustich with little emotion in his manner. "It seems the general fell down a flight of stairs and broke his neck."

"How awful," said Nadine solemnly, curious about the German's death.

That evening, before Nadine departed for La Croisiere, she spoke with Noel about General von Harter. The Frenchman raised an eyebrow when she mentioned his death.

"Most unfortunate," said Noel. "It seems the man had been drinking and fell. Too bad; he was scheduled to oversee logistical supply programs for the Boche invasion of Russia."

Nadine looked at Noel and the two of them smiled and nodded.

At La Croisiere, Nadine met secretly with Blue and Tan, the code names for two of her operatives. Blue provided information about increasing U-boat losses. He said the new Allied practice of sending large convoys of ships guarded by long-range aircraft and destroyers was gradually decreasing the tonnage lost to the U-boats.

"The Americans are 'lending' the British and Canadians older destroyers and long-range reconnaissance airplanes to help protect the convoys," said Blue. "Hitler has decided not to replace capital ships like the *Graf Spee* and *Bismarck*. Instead, they (Boche) will concentrate on the use of U-boats and surface raiders."

She thanked Blue for the information before hearing Tan's report.

"The Afrika Corps is making some progress," said Tan. "However, the Boche are not sending replacement tanks and aircraft to North Africa."

"What about fuel?"

"Fuel supplies for the Afrika Corps are not a priority. "Petrol and tanks are being sent to support their eastern campaign against the Soviets," replied Tan. "They are short on supplies and equipment and are giving priority to the Russian front."

She smiled at this and thought, *If the Allies can find a way to help the Russians and strengthen their forces in North Africa, it will go badly for the Boche.*

The next day under the pretext of shopping for fresh vegetables and cheese in the local village, Nadine met one of her operatives at an open-air market. She informed Nadine that a downed English pilot had been badly injured before being rescued by the resistance. He would remain in hiding until his injuries healed. She also learned that two engineers and a technician from Germany were being moved to southern France.

"No more than two people at a time will be sent along the escape route," she whispered, as she studied two beets.

The woman nodded.

Nadine knew that whenever groups of three or more people traveled south it alerted French officials and the Boche.

The next day when Nadine, Louis, and her parents visited a quaint restaurant in Limoges for lunch, the waiter, an older man, whispered that the Gestapo was following them.

Nadine smiled and thanked the waiter before inquiring about the soup du jour.

When it came time to settle the bill, Louis paid, but with paper money specially treated to hide information for the resistance.

That evening, Nadine received secret information about a jet engine the Germans were developing that ran on regular petrol. She knew this was a critical piece of information and had it sent immediately to Quentin.

An escaping technician provided intelligence on German tank development that included better armor, 88mm cannon, and improved communication systems.

The technician providing the information on the new German tank was using the escape route from Germany through France and into Spain. Most of the civilians fleeing were people persecuted by the Nazis, many of them Jews.

Nadine kept hearing rumors about the persecution of Jews in all areas controlled by the Nazis. There were also rumors about Jews arrested and sent to death camps, and the wholesale slaughter of Jewish communities. She told Noel to verify the rumors.

"*Oui, Madame,*" he told Nadine. "But it will take time."

She nodded and said, "Do it. I want to know what is happening to Jews arrested by the Boche."

However, the number of engineers, scientists, and technicians eager to escape from Germany and occupied France was increasing. Nadine was always cautious about people trying to use the underground route. First priority was given to British pilots and air crews. They needed the most help and their identities could be verified. But, among the civilians, Nadine knew Boche infiltrators would learn about the resistance and their system for helping people escape from France into Spain and beyond. She had established an elaborate method for learning about the escapees and whether they were, in fact, fugitives and not Boche agents. Several times, the resistance, at Nadine's insistence, had delayed the transfer of people until their credentials were verified. In three cases, Nadine's operatives discovered Germans posing as fugitives. Two were turned away by the resistance, saying they knew of no way to escape, while a third Nazi infiltrator was killed and made to appear accidental.

In mid-August, Nadine was summoned to Paris by Braustich. She was under constant surveillance. After all, she was a very wealthy woman with extensive assets in neutral countries that brought in thousands of American dollars and Swiss currency yearly.

A senior Nazi official commented, "She is a valuable source of income for the Reich. We must show our appreciation while handling her money."

In the next few months, Nadine continued to give the impression of resigned cooperation with the Germans. But, at diplomatic and cultural activities, she took pride in showing her patriotism. She was often accompanied to the opera or the ballet by Spanish or American diplomats. And, whenever Bishop Luis Valderano, the younger brother of Ruben, was in Paris on a diplomatic mission for the Vatican, they would dine together and attend the ballet, the opera, and the symphony. The Germans knew Luis and Ruben were related, but they did not know that Bishop Valderano was secretly helping Nadine send secret information to her lover and helping people escape from the Gestapo. Now and then, Nadine would write a letter to Marlon that either a trusted priest or a nun would carry into Spain and then, by secret means, to the U.S. Embassy in Lisbon. It was her way of communicating with Marlon. In turn, Marlon shared things with Quentin that were sent in secret code to Nadine. When Quentin visited Paris, he verbally shared news about Marlon's activities and whereabouts, always where they could not be overheard.

Marlon and Quentin regularly pleaded with Nadine to leave France, but she refused, saying, "I have a job to do." During one of Quentin's visits to Paris, she told him, "The Boche may have defeated our army, but many of us still resist. We will do whatever it takes to drive the Boche from France."

He knew it was useless to argue with her. However, he emphatically said that if the Germans discovered her role with the resistance, he would do everything possible to bring her safely out of France. She loved the American all the more for worrying about her. *If I ever need help, Quentin will be there.*

Nadine waited patiently as the months of August, September, and October of 1941 passed. Quentin had promised to return in November, and she could hardly wait for his arrival. She had important news about Boche military setbacks in Russia. And, from reliable informants, she had learned more about Field Marshal Rommel's supply problems in North Africa. She wanted to believe that these and other bits of news offered hope that the Boche military was overextended and their blitzkrieg faltering. She was overjoyed when Quentin's message arrived informing her that he would visit Paris during the second full week of November. *Come quickly, my darling,* she thought.

* * *

In England, Marlon continued to fly routine patrols and occasional missions escorting RAF bombers on daylight raids against German military targets on the French coast. The mounting losses of planes and air crews, and the limited damage done to German installations, compelled RAF leaders to scale back the daylight sorties. The main RAF bombardment of German military installations on the Continent was at night, and only infrequently required fighter escorts. Because Marlon could fly multi-engine aircraft, he was occasional assigned to cross the Atlantic and bring new bombers from Canada to England. It was a convenient way for him to see his father and sister in Canada and also visit with relatives in Quebec.

Kendall was transferred to a fighter base in North Africa in September 1941, and, in October, three senior pilots in Marlon's squadron were assigned to temporary duty on a secret mission. The previous year, not a single pilot could be spared during the ferocious air battles over London and the Channel. But, now, the RAF seemed to have sufficient fighter pilots. Marlon learned that the recruitment of air crews for Bomber Command was a priority.

Gradually, the dreary autumn weather diminished Marlon's time in the air. The increasing rains and periods of prolonged fog prevented routine patrols. The young pilot visited Canada once or twice a month to ferry bombers back to England. As compensation for this temporary duty, he was given leave from Sixty-six Squadron. During his leaves, he visited London and dated Erleen often, escorting her to different social functions. While accompanying Erleen to parties and musical events, he was treated politely but formally by members of the British peerage. Unless Erleen or Linne invited him to a social function or musical event planned by members of the nobility, no invitations were forthcoming.

Marlon observed the differences between landed and titled nobles and how they treated each other. The old landed aristocracy occupied the highest level of the social ladder and tended to look down on recently knighted persons, especially celebrities. Marlon considered some of the landed gentry he met the products of incestuous marriages and supercilious, especially to those they considered beneath them. Marriage among the landed nobility sometimes produced a person like Linne Kidsgrove. She came from a wealthy landed family, and her marriage to the head of an old and very wealthy aristocratic family made her a highly regarded baroness. Her former husband had attended the best schools in England and was a close friend of the Duke of Windsor. The baron's tragic death left Linne a wealthy widow. She was pursued by various suitors from the elites among the peerage eager to marry a woman of beauty, privilege, and wealth. However, from what Erleen had told him, Linne was bored by what she called "inbred and stuffy aristocrats." Instead, Linne was an avid reader, a talented sculptor, and devoted much of her time to help relocate children from London to secure areas in the English countryside. She was, in so many ways, a remarkable woman.

Whenever Erleen and Marlon met Linne at a social function, they sat together to chat. The baroness always asked about Marlon's father and seemed fascinated by every new detail she learned about Quentin. It amused Marlon that she was so keen on his father. He wondered if other women were attracted to his father. Like so many young men, he was amazed to learn the appeal some mature men had for women of all ages, particularly very attractive ones.

The days and weeks passed quickly for Marlon, and, before long, it was November. He was surprised by a new assignment for temporary duty in the Mediterranean. When he asked how long he would be away from Sixty-six Squadron, Carlisle Napier, his squadron leader, said, "Perhaps six to eight weeks. But not to worry…you'll train new recruits and get them familiar with aircraft the Yanks are providing. I think you'll enjoy the climate in the Mediterranean. It's charming there during the winter," added Napier with a sly smile.

"When do I leave?" asked Marlon.

"As soon as we can arrange transport for you," said Napier; "perhaps tomorrow or the day after."

Two days later, Marlon was on a ship headed for Gibraltar.

* * *

Quentin arrived at the French border during the second week in November 1941. The weather had turned cold, and the Pyrenees were mantled in snow. The crossing from Spain to France was delayed because of the extensive examination of his things by the French border guards. Once inside France, Quentin spotted the men following him. They were brazen and not the least bit concerned to hide their surveillance. It was a form of intimidation practiced by the Gestapo. *Ugly fellows,* he thought, as he boarded his coach.

When the train arrived at the southern *gare* in Paris, Nadine was there to meet him. She was dressed in a fashionable long tan leather coat that came to her knees, with high matching leather boots. She wore a pert hat that was fur lined and a lovely scarf with a leopard pattern. Her gloves were a tan color that matched her coat and appeared soft and fashionable. The lovely Frenchwoman looked like a model for a fashion designer and drew the attention of German officers and French civilians.

"Cherie," said Nadine politely as she kissed the American on both cheeks in a cordial manner. "Welcome to Paris," she said in heavily accented English. He praised her attractive attire. She thanked him and countered by inquiring about his trip, polite conversation deliberately designed to give the impression her meeting with the American was pro forma. Quentin recognized the short man with Nadine as one of her drivers. He took the Cajun's large valise, and the three of them moved through the crowd of mainly German military personnel to the nearest exit.

"General von Kleist will be in Paris tomorrow. I informed him that you would be arriving today," Nadine told her lover in the car while holding his hand in hers.

"Good," said the Cajun, "I look forward to seeing him."

That evening, when they were alone in her bedroom, she cried after they made love.

"What is it?" asked Quentin, confused by her tears. "Did I do something wrong?"

"No, no, Cherie," she replied, kissing him on the lips to reassure him. "It is just that I miss you so. The war, the Boche, and the tragedy that we experience in France are depressing things that press in on me. And now there are persistent stories about the slaughter of Jews by the Nazis. Oh, Cherie, when will this terrible war be over?"

He gently stroked her hair before asking, "Have you tried to verify these stories about what's happening to Jews?"

She nodded and said yes.

"Let me know what you find out," he told her before kissing her softly on the lips.

The following day, they met with Braustich to approve the transfer of funds and sign documents. Quentin brought new contracts for her and the German financier to examine and approve.

"These are new, lucrative opportunities in the United States and South America," said the Cajun, referring to clothing and porcelains that would be manufactured under patents and style lines controlled by Nadine's firms. Braustich was pleased by the prospects of added revenues, increases in capital for which he could take credit with his superiors. It disturbed Quentin immensely that so much of Nadine's wealth was controlled by the Nazis. He hated the idea of U.S. and South American money funneling its way into German coffers to support their military and territorial aggression. *When,* he wondered, *would America intervene and do its share to check the Nazi expansion?*

That evening, Nadine and Quentin met with von Kleist at an elegant restaurant frequented by senior German officers. The German was charming with Nadine and feigned sufferance for Quentin, his manner of teasing the American and demonstrating friendship.

"You realize, of course," said a smiling von Kleist as he looked at Nadine, "that he," nodding his head in the American's direction, "has the advantage."

"Whatever do you mean?" asked a smiling Nadine.

"The boorish fellow is over his depth with you. My dear, you are charming, cultured, and sophisticated, while he, well, I'm a gentleman and must hold my tongue."

"Tsk, tsk," said a smiling Quentin. "As usual, you've missed the essential elements. Nadine is all that you say and more. You forgot to mention that she is brilliant and beautiful."

The German smiled and said, "Commoners always discover the obvious."

"Touché," said a smiling Quentin. "But, a lovely woman appreciates being told she is smart and gorgeous. *N'est-ce pas?*"

Nadine laughed and told them to behave themselves.

"Tell me about your promotion," said Quentin to the German, noticing a change in his rank from *generalmajor* to *generalleutnant*.

Von Kleist deflected the question by saying it was just a small promotion and changed the subject.

But, Quentin would not be put off and asked, "How are things on the Eastern Front?"

"Fine," said von Kleist as he stiffened. He turned his attention to Nadine but tapped his fingers to alert the American to the Morse code he was using. While the German asked Nadine questions and listened to her responses, he tapped the words in French "problems in the east." Quentin nodded. Nadine quickly realized that von Kleist was communicating with Quentin by tapping his fingers.

After dinner, von Kleist drove them home. "When do you leave?" he asked Quentin.

"The day after tomorrow," answered the Cajun. "What do you have in mind?"

Von Kleist asked if they could get together for a walk the following morning.

"Whenever you like," replied the American.

"Shall we say 7:30 a.m. at my residence," Nicky told him. "I'll send my car for you."

When Nadine and Quentin were together in her bedroom, she ran the bath water and listened as he whispered information about Marlon. In return, she shared important military information. Then, they turned down the lights and removed their clothing. In her bed, Quentin feasted on her, touching and stimulating those parts of the beautiful French woman's body that aroused her passion. They engaged in a protracted form of lovemaking. He was a sensitive and passionate lover, considerate of a woman's needs, and always exploring ways to stimulate her. When he finally climaxed, they lay together in her bed, spent and satiated.

The next morning, Quentin and von Kleist walked through the Bois de Boulogne. When he was certain they could not be overheard, Nicky spoke softly so only the Cajun could hear him.

"Our offensives in Eastern Europe have stalled. The miserable Russian weather works against us. We must wait until the spring of next year to launch our new offensives."

"You're not pleased with the decision to attack the Soviets," Quentin told von Kleist.

The German nodded his head. "We have our differences with the Communists, but war with the Soviets was not a priority with the general staff."

"Hitler?" asked the American. Nicky nodded and snorted as a sign of disgust.

"I hear you have a new fighter, one with a radial engine," he said to change the subject.

"So you know about our Focke-Wulf 190. It will be a rude surprise for the Tommies," said the German with a smirk. "It was designed by a good friend, Kurt Tank. You've met him."

Quentin nodded, convinced that the new German plane would be a formidable fighter. He decided to change the subject and asked,

"How is Adolf Galland?"

The German smiled before responding. "Dolfo is a brilliant fighter pilot."

Quentin scowled as he looked at Nicky and said, "Dolfo."

"Ah, forgive me," said the German, "it's what his friends call him."

"A nickname," said the American as the German smirked and nodded.

"Dolfo, Günther Lützow, and Werner Mölder are our highest scoring aces. I have no doubts that each of them will destroy at least one hundred enemy machines," he said with pride.

"And Ernst Udet?" asked Quentin.

Nicky was silent and turned sober before responding. "Frankly, I worry about him."

"Why?" asked the Cajun.

"He is at odds with *Generalfeldmarschall* Erhard Milch," said von Kleist, annoyance in his voice. "You like Ernst?"

The American nodded.

"He's into his cups too often," said the German, referring to Udet's excessive drinking.

"The last I heard Milch was the head of the Air Ministry," said Quentin.

Nicky scowled and said contemptuously, "The Fuhrer's bootlickers achieve rank easily and without merit. But, I must not dwell on such matters. Tell me about your lovely daughter," said the German to change the subject.

They walked and talked about their respective families until Nicky stopped and looked at his watch and said, "We must go back. One thing," said von Kleist, as they retraced their steps through the Bois. "Will your country join the Allies and make war on us?" Quentin smiled and said America was neutral and determined to remain so.

"A civilized policy," quipped the German. "But, we do not live in civilized times."

The following day, Nadine joined Quentin on the train trip to Limoges where he stayed the evening at La Croisiere to be with Arlene, Edmund, and Louis Bondurant. The old general looked thin, but his posture was still strong and reflected his long years as a soldier and leader of men. When they could not be overheard, he shared news about Marlon. He also answered Louis's questions about the status of the war and the German offensives in North Africa and Russia.

"Will America join the Allies and help to defeat the Boche?" asked Louis.

Quentin shook his head and said he did not know. However, the question raised so many issues within the Cajun. He wanted America to join the war and defeat the Germans, but he also knew the strong isolationist sentiments in the United States augured against it.

Before Quentin left, he promised to return in late January or early February 1942. He kissed Nadine passionately at La Croisiere before they departed for the train station. At the train station, Nadine stood on the platform and watched her lover board his train and depart. She wanted so much to be with him.

PART III

❖

AMERICA AT WAR

Chapter 12
A War of Outrage

What American living in late 1941 could forget where
they were on that fateful day, the seventh of December?
Quentin was reading a brief in his study after returning
from a walk through Central Park. The night before,
he, Kathleen, and the Vandersteels had attended a recital where Florence played to a standing room crowd.
Her piano playing was superb. She surprised the audience by dedicating her performance to the valiant Allied
men and women fighting against the Germans and the
Italians. But, now, on a cool and crisp early December
Sunday afternoon, everything changed for America.

An excited Camila and Clara the cook rushed into
Quentin's study, tears in their eyes.

"What is it?" asked the surprised Cajun.

"Sir," said Clara, "the Japanese have attacked Pearl
Harbor."

Quentin could not believe what he'd heard. He sat
stupefied for a moment before leaping to his feet and
turning on the radio. It did not matter which station he
might have tried, all of them were reporting about the

Japanese air strikes against Pearl Harbor and the devastation. He remembered something that Ruben had told him. "We should not underestimate the Japanese. Our president does not consider them as much of a threat as the Germans," he warned. *Ruben was right,* thought Quentin. He realized that Roosevelt was bright but at times naïve. The Japanese had struck at America, and who knew the extent of the damage they had done and would do?

Twenty minutes after Camila and Clara burst into his study with news of the Japanese attack on Hawaii, Florence rushed into the living room where they were listening to the radio.

"Daddy, what's happening?" asked Florence, deep concern and anxiety evident in the beautiful young woman's face.

"The Japanese have attacked our military installations in Hawaii," he said solemnly. "I don't know the extent of the damage at Pearl Harbor, but I do know we'll soon be at war."

His beautiful daughter pressed her clenched hands to her face and began to cry. Immediately, Camila rushed to console her, while Quentin stood and put his arms around both women. *There are dark days ahead,* thought the Cajun as he held them, trying to convey a sense of strength and determination.

* * *

It was already dark on the island of Malta when an announcement blared out the message that the Japanese had attacked American forces in the Hawaiian Islands. Marlon, on temporary duty with an RAF squadron on Malta, was in a momentary state of disbelief at the news. He rushed to the radio room and found it crowded with young officers and enlisted men huddled around the wireless listening to accounts of the air raids launched by the Japanese against American naval and military installations at Pearl Harbor. Gradually, bits and pieces of information came over the radio with accounts of serious damage to American battleships and hundreds of planes destroyed on the ground. There were wild rumors and speculation about an invasion of the Hawaiian Islands and perhaps an attack on the U.S. West Coast. The lack of informed discussion on the radio angered Marlon and made him yearn for contact with his father and especially General Valderano.

Long into the night, the news of the strike at Pearl Harbor was heard on the wireless and on the radio, which carried the BBC news. Marlon was caught off guard by the attack and gradually recalled comments he had overheard General Valderano share with his father. The "sneak attack" by the Japanese angered and worried him. He wondered what the Japanese would do next. His thoughts turned to his father and sister in New York. What would happen to them? He grew sober as his mind conjured up different scenarios that might affect them. He put aside what he considered fruitless speculation. The only thing certain was that America would soon be at war, and it was all so unexpected.

The Japanese attack on Pearl Harbor raised new questions and concerns for British military personnel at Malta and elsewhere. Surely, the United States would declare war on Japan. How would a U.S. war with Japan affect England? What would it mean for the Allies? So much uncertainty and speculation caused by the lack of communication with key decision makers in the United States frustrated Marlon. He wanted badly to speak with his father, but given his location and assignment, that was impossible. All he could do was sit tight and wait.

* * *

Nadine recoiled in surprise when Moira called to her and announced the Japanese attack on Pearl Harbor. The radio in France was controlled by the Nazis. The German announcer's voice had been exuberant mentioning that "The Reich's ally in the Far East has struck a crippling blow against the Americans." A Nazi commentator came on the radio and said that the Imperial Japanese navy had destroyed most of the American naval squadron in the Pacific.

It took awhile for Nadine to calm down after hearing accounts on the German-controlled radio station about the Japanese attack on Hawaii. She wondered about the actual damage done and the U.S. reaction. Surely, they would declare war against the Japanese.

Nadine poured herself some brandy and sat to think about the attack on Pearl Harbor and its implications and ramifications. With the Americans occupied fighting the Japanese, what would happen in Europe? Her mind identified and analyzed different scenarios. She started to speculate about America's engagement in a war with the Japanese. Would this allow Hitler to concentrate on destroying the Soviet Union? Might the Japanese attack the Russians from the east? The lovely French woman stood up and paced back and forth in her study, slowly sipping brandy as she critically assessed different scenarios that war between the United States and Japan might cause and their effects on the situation in Europe. *Such speculation is useless,* she thought. Instead, she began to consider ways to expand her intelligence network. As she did so, her thoughts quickly gravitated to Marlon, and especially Quentin, who might soon be involved in American military activities against the Japanese. She could not know the turn of events that would take place in the following days.

* * *

After a moving address by President Roosevelt to the U.S. Congress on December 8, 1941, America declared war on Japan. President Roosevelt, in his stirring and memorable speech to the combined House and Senate, referred to December 7, 1941, as a "Day of Infamy." People in America, and elsewhere, were put on notice that the United States intended to defeat the Empire of Japan no matter the cost or the time required. If the American president's speech was intended to intimidate the Japanese, it did not. Following their strike at Pearl Harbor, Japanese forces immediately attacked the British Crown Colony of Hong Kong, the Dutch East Indies, and the Philippines. The next day, Japanese forces invaded Thailand and then Malaya. England too was at war with Japan. The British were unprepared for a series of attacks in the Far East. On December 10, Japanese planes sank the old battle cruiser HMS *Repulse* and the new battleship HMS *Prince of Wales*. The early days of December 1941 were dark ones for England and America.

Quentin tried to contact Ruben Valderano in Santa Barbara on several occasions. The Mexican had only recently returned from his trip to Russia. He was anxious to speak with him. There were so many questions he needed to ask. It was not until late on the eighth of December that he and Valderano spoke on the telephone.

"You were right about the Japanese," said Quentin. "How could we have been so unprepared?" Valderano, in a sober voice, said that it would take time to fully understand how the Japanese had managed to attack Pearl Harbor and the damage they caused. "Politicians in Washington will want to assess blame," said the Mexican.

"But, it's up to the administration to prepare for war against the Japanese. Things are going to be rather confused and hectic for our friends in Washington."

"Have you talked with George (Marshall)?"

Ruben said he had been unable to reach him on the telephone, but he'd left a message. "Should I go to Washington?" asked the Cajun.

"No," said the Mexican. "Better if you call the White House and leave a message for the president asking how you might be of service."

"I'll do it first thing tomorrow morning," said Quentin. They talked for a while longer until Quentin said it was late and there were things he had to do.

"*Amigo*," said the Mexican, "this war against the Japanese will be long and costly. We will become involved. I'm certain the president and General Marshall will call on us for help."

The next few days passed quickly as news of further Japanese aggression in the Pacific resonated on the radio and crowded the headlines and front pages of newspapers. Americans were stunned by Adolf Hitler's declaration of war against the United States on December 11. Germany, considered by many to be the strongest military power in the world, was perceived to be a greater threat to America than Japan. If Americans were worried about war with Japan, the thought of having to fight Germany was intensely disturbing.

"A two-front war," Quentin mumbled, as he heard the news on December 11 about Hitler's declaration of war against the United States. "Hitler will regret this," he said to himself. A profound sadness overcame him. Hostilities with Germany meant he could no longer visit Nadine. "Nadine, Nadine," whispered the Cajun as he stared longingly into space.

That evening, Florence, now eighteen, sat to talk with Quentin, her eyes betraying the uncertainty she harbored about the war with Germany and Japan and how this might affect her brother.

"Daddy, what's going to happen? Will Marlon come back to America now that we're at war with Germany?"

"It's too soon to tell what will happen," said Quentin. "Until such time as we're able to expand our army and navy, he'll probably remain in the RAF."

"But, Daddy, can't he just tell them he's an American and come home?"

"No, honey, it doesn't work that way," he said, thinking about the way he'd been summoned summarily by the U.S. Army in Paris that fateful day in 1917 shortly after America had declared war on Imperial Germany. He had been a captain and celebrated "ace" in the *Aeronautic Militaire Francaise* one day and the next, a captain in the U.S. Army Signal Corps. He remembered that abrupt and unsolicited transfer to the U.S. military. Now, he wondered about Marlon and how the American entrance into the war would affect his son.

"Honey, I'm certain things will change for Marlon and that he'll be given a choice to stay in the RAF or enlist in the U.S. Army. We'll just have to wait and see how things play out." He took her in his arms. She reminded him so much of Ione. Comforting the lovely young blonde, he said not to worry. "Marlon will be OK."

"Promise, Daddy?" she implored.

He nodded and looked away, thoughts about Marlon and Nadine flooding his consciousness.

Two days later, Quentin received a telephone call from George Marshall at his office.

"I was beginning to wonder if you'd ever call," said the Cajun.

"Sorry, Quentin, but we've been rather busy," said Marshall, fatigue evident in his voice.

"Things as bad as the newspapers make out?"

"We need to talk," said Marshall. "The chief (code word for President Roosevelt) wants to meet with you and the general next week."

Looking at his desk calendar, Quentin asked when Marshall had in mind. After Marshall mentioned two days, the Cajun said he would be in Washington, but finding a place to stay would be difficult.

"I'll have quarters for you and Ruben at a residence close to the White House," said Marshall. "Stony will be here and wants to have dinner with you the night before the meeting with the chief."

"OK," said Quentin. "Do you want me to send my plane for the general?"

Marshall said it would not be necessary. "I'll see you in a few days," said Marshall before hanging up.

That evening, Quentin spoke with Ruben, and they compared notes about the meeting with Marshall and Roosevelt.

"I'm too old for military duty," said Valderano and teased, "but you should be prepared to wear a uniform."

"Oh, you're not getting off that easy," said the Cajun. "I've a mind to tell Roosevelt that he needs senior officers with combat experience like you." They both laughed and talked a bit longer, using code words to identify Ruben's younger brother in the Vatican and some of his activities. Before the Cajun went to bed, he wrote a letter in code for Nadine. Bishop Luis Valderano would arrange for Quentin's letter to reach Nadine.

* * *

Nadine met with Noel presumably to go over her accounts and make new arrangements for funds going from North America to her accounts in three of the major Swiss banks. Using code, Nadine alerted her aide that she wanted to meet with Millard and a key member of the French resistance. Noel said he would schedule a meeting with Braustich, aware that their conversation was being monitored. Zeigler was listening to their conversation and told a Gestapo officer to contact Braustich. Later that afternoon, Noel told Nadine that Braustich had called and scheduled a meeting for late in the afternoon.

"Fine," said Nadine. "The war between the Americans and the Boche will change how we handle our affairs in North and South America." The clever Frenchwoman used a sign language that she, Noel, and Moira had developed for the exchange of short messages and instructions. "We will learn from Monsieur Braustich what the Boche want to do about my investments abroad."

Late that afternoon, Braustich and Ziegler met with Nadine and Noel. The German gave no hint of his purpose and new directives for handling the Frenchwoman's investments.

"Madame," said Braustich stiffly, "it is unfortunate that significant sources of revenues from the Western Hemisphere will be cut off. I have been informed that the Americans will impound all revenues from your investments in the United States, Canada, and elsewhere. Pity," he said.

"My superiors say that certain funds earned outside of Europe were sent to Switzerland. I assume Madame knows about this?"

Rather than deny the information, Nadine decided to give the impression of cooperating with the Nazis.

"Yes, the Swiss banks have registered transfers of funds from North America into my accounts," she said with a slight smile.

"Then, Madame will abide by our desires that these funds be recovered and sent here."

"I cannot do that," said Nadine, her response visibly annoying Braustich.

"And why not?" demanded the German.

"The accounts into which the funds have been deposited are numbered and can only be accessed by me in person," she replied, again smiling politely.

"And how is this so?" asked the German.

"It was the agreement Monsieur Norvell recommended when he established the accounts for me," replied a calm and composed Nadine, enjoying the financier's agitation.

"Well, we shall see about that!" said Braustich, coldly.

Nadine derived immense satisfaction at the sight of the thwarted officious German financier annoyed by his inability to access the numbered accounts in Switzerland.

After attending to some other matters with the Frenchwoman, Braustich left.

That evening, Braustich reported to his superiors about the financial arrangements Mrs. Desnoyers had with the Swiss bankers and the large sums involved.

"Several hundred thousand dollars and perhaps more," mused Herbert Klatt, the senior Nazi official to whom Braustich reported. Klatt was in his early fifties, of medium build, balding, with a fleshy face and deep set gray eyes. "We will look into this matter," he told the financier.

Seated in the corner of the room was Major Sigwald Eisenhardt from the Gestapo. *Interesting development,* thought the Gestapo major.

After Braustich left the room, Klatt turned to Eisenhardt and said, "Well, Major, what do you think?"

"First, let's find out if Madame Desnoyers is correct about the requirements for the numbered accounts in the Swiss banks," he said, lighting a cigarette. "If she is, then her American attorney is far cleverer than we suspected. But, no matter; we'll find a way to access these funds."

"I don't know," said Klatt, smoothing his small moustache while watching the Gestapo officer take a long drag on his cigarette. "Swiss bankers can be difficult. We need their cooperation," he said, writing a notation into Nadine Desnoyers' file. "I'll have our people in Switzerland look into Madame Desnoyers' arrangements with the Swiss banks."

"Very well," said Eisenhardt, rising from his chair. "But, under no circumstances will Madame Desnoyers be allowed to travel to Switzerland. We cannot afford to lose this woman."

Klatt nodded in agreement.

It did not take the Nazis long to make discreet inquiries in Switzerland and learn that what Nadine had said about the numbered accounts was correct. Only she, or her attorney in America, could access the accounts in the Swiss banks. Moreover, it could only be done in person, as stipulated by the contractual arrangement crafted by Quentin Norvell with the Swiss banks. It was discomfiting news for Klatt. Somehow, he had to find a way to recover the large sums of money in American dollars from the Swiss banks. It meant staying on good terms with Mrs. Desnoyers until the money could be seized.

Meanwhile, Nadine was using funds from other accounts in Switzerland to pay for valuable secrets that her operatives were collecting. Little by little, Eglantine's network was sending bits and pieces of critical German military information to the Americans in Lisbon. There were other challenges that preoccupied Nadine. The RAF raids over the Continent, especially those to bomb targets in Germany, were suffering high losses in aircraft and crews. Among the downed English airmen, only a few were saved by the resistance. The secret escape route Nadine had established continued to help RAF flyers and crew members escape to Spain and then on to Portugal. Her policy of transferring RAF personnel one or two at a time was slow but secure. However, British Intelligence wanted desperately to contact Eglantine and work with the person responsible for helping their airmen escape. They also knew that the Eglantine network provided small but critical and strategic information about German military activity. Nadine resisted British Intelligence overtures and, through Millard, informed the French Maquis that the Eglantine network would work only with the resistance. British Intelligence would not be put off. Their operatives in France were told to redouble their efforts to contact Eglantine.

* * *

The night before their meeting with Roosevelt, Ruben and Quentin met Stoner for dinner at a small restaurant in the District of Columbia.

"Good to see you," said Stoner, as they shook hands and walked to a private area set aside for them. Stoner told them that the fish at this restaurant was particularly good.

After ordering their meals, Stoner handed each of them a file.

"What's this?" asked Valderano.

"The chief wanted you to have this before the meeting," Stoner told them. "It's confidential material about the situation in the Pacific and some ideas people at the War Department have regarding Germany. You can study the documents here, but I need them back before we leave."

Quentin skimmed through the documents and noticed that someone had underlined critical passages in blue pencil. The information on the damage done by the Japanese at Pearl Harbor was sobering, but not as bad as he had thought. The American aircraft carriers had not been at Pearl Harbor and were ready to engage the Japanese. The fuel and dry dock facilities were spared, along with the crypto analytical facility. While Guam had fallen, the Marines at Wake Island repulsed the first Japanese attempt to take the island. However, the news was not positive about Wake. The Marines would not be able to repel another, better supported Japanese invasion. In the Philippines, General MacArthur was caught by surprise. The attacking Japanese naval air units damaged and destroyed most of the army aircraft on the ground. The few fighters able to get into the air, such as the Bell P-39D, were no match for the faster and more maneuverable Japanese Zero. A large Japanese invasion force supported by three Japanese fleets landed on Luzon on December 10, 1941. There was little possibility that American forces in the Philippines could be reinforced and supplied. At best, all MacArthur could do was wage a holding action.

Quentin read the passages in the document about the Dutch and the English positions in the Pacific. They had been overwhelmed by Japanese naval and land forces. Hong Kong and Taiwan were in Japanese hands, and the Philippines would fall soon. Japanese forces were moving south down the Malayan Peninsula, and had invaded Borneo and Sumatra and were poised to strike at Java and the Dutch East Indies. Australia was at risk of invasion too.

The Cajun was surprised that less than a page was devoted to the situation in Europe. A brief paragraph indicated the Germans would mount a spring offensive in 1942 against the Soviets and that the Afrika Corps under Rommel was engaged in a series of back and forth encounters with the British. There were three bold headers that caught his attention. The first was North Africa. The second underscored clearing the sea lanes in the Atlantic Ocean, and the third was England.

After he was certain that Ruben and Quentin had read the reports, Stoner asked if either of them wanted dessert or coffee before beginning their discussion.

"Just coffee," said Quentin, while Ruben nodded his head to indicate the same.

Ruben started the discussion by asking Stoner the purpose of the meeting with Roosevelt and who would be present.

Stoner sipped some tea before saying, "Aside from the chief, Secretary of War Stimson, General Marshall, Admiral King, Harry Hopkins, and I will be there. The chief is worried that we won't be able to hold on to the Philippines. Churchill has been calling regularly. He's worried the Japanese will invade Australia, Burma, and then move into India."

"Why the mention of Russia, North Africa, and England without any discussion?" asked the Cajun.

"Well," said Stoner, brushing some crumbs in front of him off the table, "that's what the chief wants to discuss with you. The material about the situation in the Pacific was provided as background."

"You mean that should not concern us?" asked a puzzled Ruben.

Stoner nodded and said, "No, it's important, but right now, the chief wants to focus on Europe, and that's where the two of you come in."

"So?" asked the Mexican. Stoner told them to give Europe their full attention and consider how the United States could best attack the Germans.

They talked until almost midnight before Quentin said it was time to get some sleep.

"Right," said Stoner. "Our meeting with the chief is at 7:30 tomorrow morning."

Quentin took Ruben aside and asked for a favor.

The Mexican said, "Si, hombre, what is it?"

Quentin mentioned wanting to develop a secret link with Nicholas von Kleist. He asked, "Is there a way your brother Luis can help?"

The Mexican smiled and said to leave the matter to him. Several months later, Ruben met with Quentin and shared the emergency information conduit that his brother, Bishop Valderano, put in place. "Luis will arrange everything. However, the system must be used only when it's of the utmost urgency." Quentin nodded and said he understood and thanked Ruben.

* * *

The next morning, Quentin woke early and went for a quick walk before returning to his room to shower and shave. He met Ruben in the foyer of the residence, and they walked to the White House. Quentin noted the added security at the gate and the Marine guards stationed around the building. Stoner greeted them and together they walked to the Oval Office.

"Welcome, gentlemen," said Roosevelt with a smile. "We're meeting in the conference room. George," said Roosevelt, turning toward his black valet, "is everything ready?"

George smiled and said it was.

"Good," said Roosevelt, "then let's go in."

At the meeting were Secretary of State Hull, Secretary of War Stimson, General George C. Marshall (chairman of the Joint Chiefs), Admiral Ernest J. King (Chief of Naval Operations), Harry Hopkins, Ruben, Quentin, and Stoner.

The president identified the men in the room and allowed them to greet each other before saying, "There's coffee." As they were drinking coffee, Roosevelt cleared his throat and said they should get started.

"I've called you here to talk about Europe and England. The Pacific will be a priority for the U.S. Navy. Douglas (MacArthur) will, I am sure, agree. Our response to Jap aggression will take time," said the president, looking at Admiral King. "Our British friends need help right away. George," said the president, motioning to General Marshall, "why don't you start."

Marshall stood and outlined some of the pressing concerns, finding a way to attack the Germans in Europe, helping the British to safeguard convoys in the Atlantic, and supporting the Soviets. He said sending war materiel to support the British was a priority. As soon as sufficient army troops could be outfitted, trained, and prepared for combat, they would be sent to England for an invasion of the Continent.

"How long before that happens?" Valderano asked.

"Not before October of next year," said Marshall.

Quentin frowned and asked, "What do the British say?" Marshall and the president made eye contact.

"Well," said the president, "we need to arrive at some agreement with our English friends. I'm sending George and Stony to meet with Churchill and his people."

Quentin asked when that would happen.

The president fit a cigarette in his long holder and said, "Oh, perhaps in late March."

"Ruben," said Marshall, "Henry (Stimson) and I would like to enlist your services as a liaison between the War Department, the president, and my office."

"What do you have in mind?" asked the Mexican, looking first at Marshall, then Stimson.

"You're an authority on warfare. We need you to join our team in the war room to plan our deployment of assets and advise us on which campaigns should be given priority. We'll also need your advice about new weapons," said Marshall. "You'll be based here in Washington and be given an office next to mine."

"Will it be necessary for me to do much traveling?" asked Ruben.

"I'm afraid so," said Marshall. "You'll accompany me to meetings with the British here and abroad and visit proving grounds where new vehicles and armaments are tested."

"Ruben, we're asking a lot of you," said the president, as he released a plume of smoke. "You'll work directly with Henry," he added, nodding in the direction of Henry Stimson who smiled politely but did not say anything.

Ruben asked if he would have to wear a uniform.

"Henry?" said Roosevelt, looking directly at Stimson.

"I don't think so," said Stimson, a thin smile crossing his face. Ruben asked when he would be expected to start.

"Next month?" said Roosevelt, glancing first at Marshall and then Stimson. Both men nodded. "Will you do it?"

The Mexican was silent for a moment, but his eyes read the facial expressions of the president and Marshall. He turned to look at Quentin, who winked. "Very well, Mr. President," Ruben replied, "I'll do it."

"Good," said the president. "We'll arrange temporary housing for you until we find something more suitable for you and your family."

The president removed the cigarette from his holder, snuffed it out, and turned toward the Cajun. "Quentin, George and I want to offer you a commission in the U.S. Army. I'd like you to work with Hap Arnold (head of the Air Corps) and his people."

"Doing what?" asked the Cajun, eager to learn what the president and George Marshall had in mind.

"We're not quite sure at the moment. Let me explain," said Roosevelt. "We need a senior-level liaison with the British, specifically with the air ministry and the RAF. I spoke with Churchill about this." The president paused a moment, watching the Cajun carefully through his glasses.

Quentin appeared composed, but a thin smile on his face encouraged Roosevelt to continue.

He said, "Churchill says your name came up when he talked with people in the air ministry. Any idea why?" Roosevelt paused as he and the others in the room looked at Quentin.

"I've met with senior people in the air ministry and have provided financial support for some of their research," replied the Cajun.

A bit more than that, Roosevelt thought, determined not to reveal the extent of Quentin's support for British Air Ministry activities. J. Edgar Hoover had briefed him on the large sums of money Quentin and several of his associates had loaned to the British Air Ministry through sheltered accounts in Swiss banks.

The president cleared his throat and said, "You have friends in London, and they've mentioned you to Churchill. He'd like to meet you."

Quentin was mildly surprised by what Roosevelt said, but he adopted a nonchalant posture and waited for him to continue.

"I'd like you and George to meet with Hap Arnold and let me know what the air force should do. Army Regulation 95-5 stipulates Arnold as head of the Army Air Forces."

"Yes, I heard about that. Happened in June of this year," said the Cajun. Roosevelt glanced at Marshall, who smiled. It was obvious to them that Quentin was monitoring closely developments in the air force.

"General Arnold has reorganized the air force and had his air staff develop a war plan for fighting both Germany and Japan. I've seen it and want you to look it over carefully," said the president. "George and I believe there's much to be done to get our air force up to speed and ready to take on the Germans and the Japanese. We need to start a strategic air offensive against the Germans. I think you can help Hap do that," said Roosevelt. "I'd like you and George to get together with Hap. Your job will be to help the air force start a campaign against the Germans as quickly as possible. I'd like you to go to London and meet with Churchill."

"All of this is rather sudden and still vague," said Quentin.

"Yes, I know," said the president, "but your knowledge about aviation, military service in the Great War, airfield construction, and organizational abilities are valuable. I'm counting on you to help Hap Arnold get the air force ready to take the offensive."

Quentin sat quietly listening to Roosevelt. He was being given the chance to fashion a job for himself in the army. However, there were several things that he wanted before considering such an opportunity.

"Well, what do you say, Quentin?" asked the president.

After a moment of silence to reflect on his choices, he spoke up. "Mr. President, if you have a commission in mind for me, it better be at the rank of brigadier general."

A smiling Roosevelt threw back his head and laughed out loud. "I thought you were going to ask for two stars."

"Not yet, Mr. President," replied the Cajun.

"Actually, George and I want you to be a brigadier. But, appointment and promotion to the rank of general must be approved by the Senate, and given their busy schedule, it may be a month or two before they approve my recommendation," Roosevelt told him, while glancing momentarily at Marshall who nodded.

"So what do I do in the interim?" asked the Cajun.

"George," said the president, motioning to General Marshall.

"We'll commission you as a full colonel. You had that rank when you left the army in 1919, and it's a simple matter to reinstate it. When the Senate votes to approve your appointment as a brigadier, that will be your permanent rank," said Marshall.

Quentin didn't respond immediately. He sat back in his chair and drummed his fingers on the edge of the conference table, thinking before asking, "Who will I report to?"

"To George," said the president, nodding his head in the direction of Marshall, who looked at the Cajun and nodded his head. "I want to be kept in the loop. If we locate you abroad," added the president, "you, George, and I will go over your assignment and work out your staff responsibilities."

"Will I be traveling often?"

"I'm afraid so," said Marshall. "Our British friends want us to name a liaison to their air ministry. We'd like you to take on that assignment and fly to London as soon as possible."

"OK," said the Cajun. "I'll need a long-range plane, especially if I'm going to do distance flying. I'll want something fast and reliable. And I'll pay for it."

Roosevelt glanced at Marshall and laughed.

"You'll pay for it!" said Marshall, as he chuckled. The others in the room started to laugh also.

"If I had that kind of cooperation from our business leaders," said Roosevelt, "this would be an easy war to fight. All right, you pick the plane. Anything else?"

"Yes, when do I start?"

"Yesterday," said the president.

At this, Ruben and the others in the room laughed.

"I have an eighteen-year-old daughter enrolled at Juilliard. I'll need to speak with her. Her brother is in the RAF and stationed in Malta. Entering the army will be disturbing for Florence," said the Cajun, looking out the window and contemplating how Florence would react to his joining the army.

"Yes," said the president, "I've met your lovely daughter. I didn't realize Florence was eighteen. Your in-laws are in New York," said Roosevelt, remembering the Vandersteels. "Anything else?" asked the president.

Quentin thought for a moment before responding. "Just a question for George. When should we get together with General Arnold?"

"We can have dinner tonight," said Marshall.

Quentin nodded.

"Good," said Roosevelt. "Now, I have some other things to discuss." He handed documents to all of them, and they began to discuss developments in the Pacific and then plans to mobilize the country on a war footing.

After Roosevelt called an end to the meeting, he asked the Cajun to stay behind for a few minutes. Ruben and George Marshall said they would wait for him.

"Quentin," said Roosevelt, fitting a cigarette to his holder when they were alone, "I need you on board as soon as possible. I'm asking you to make an enormous sacrifice. You could have said no to me, and I would have understood," he said, looking directly at the Cajun who remained silent. "Hap and his people will be suspicious of you at first. They'll think you're a spy for George (Marshall) or me. But, we need someone from outside the air force to critique their new structure and air staff's combat plan. That will be your job. It won't be easy. Then, there's the British. They'll try to get us to do things their way. George and I will need your advice on how to deal with them. You've worked with the British before. I'm counting on you to establish a good working relationship with them." The pilot's eyes never wavered from the president's. "This separation from your family will be painful," said the president, "and difficult for them to understand. If you like, I'll call Florence and the Vandersteels."

"That won't be necessary," said Quentin.

The president nodded as if to agree, but he decided to call Florence and the Vandersteels anyway. *It's the least I can do for him,* thought Roosevelt. "How soon can you leave the law firm and be here?"

"Ten days," said a pensive Quentin. He began to mentally consider the different things to be done before relocating to Washington.

"Good," said Roosevelt, "but if you can be here sooner, I would appreciate it."

"I'll try," said the Cajun, aware of the demands that would be placed on him.

"I'd like you to go to London and meet with Churchill and his people next month," said Roosevelt. "Stony will go with you. If you need anything, call me." He extended his hand.

"I will," said Quentin, shaking Roosevelt's hand.

Ruben and George Marshall were waiting in the hall outside the conference room.

"I know the president is asking a lot of you," Marshall told them as they walked to the exit. "I wish you were on the job right now. I could certainly use you. I realize you have family and obligations that require attention. Quentin, I'll leave a message at the residence about our meeting with Hap Arnold tonight. I'll send a car for you. Ruben, why don't you and I go to my office? I'll have you flown back to California tomorrow morning." They talked for a few more minutes before Marshall and Valderano left for the Pentagon. Quentin walked along the Mall before returning to the residence and making a few telephone calls.

That evening, Quentin, George C. Marshall, and chief of the Air Force Henry "Hap" Arnold had dinner in a private room at Fort Myer. Arnold wasted little time asking the purpose for the meeting. He wanted to know about Quentin, his role, and to whom he would report. The answers, because of the vague nature of the Cajun's assignment, did not sit well with Arnold.

"I'll be direct," said Arnold, looking at the Cajun. "Your role will cause concern among my people. You're not military."

"Hap, Quentin fought in the First World War and was promoted to full colonel," said Marshall calmly. "He was a combat ace, organized, commanded a squadron, and became one of (General) Mason Patrick's top staff. And, he flew fighter cover for Billy Mitchell back then."

Arnold was momentarily surprised by Marshall's remarks. However, he remained skeptical. Realizing that Arnold still had reservations about Quentin, Marshall continued. "Besides being a great flyer, Quentin has supported military aviation since the early 1920s. He's flown almost every type of plane there is, including Hurricanes and Spitfires. The RAF and the air ministry think highly of him."

Before Arnold could say anything, Quentin spoke up. "General Arnold, we have close mutual friends, and we have the same approach to air power. I want to serve my country, and the best way for me to do that is in the U.S. Air Force. All I ask is that you give me a chance. If I don't work out, just let General Marshall know, and I'm certain he and the president will find something else for me to do," said the Cajun, looking directly at Arnold, his intense stare finally forcing the general to look at Marshall.

"I hear you're friends with Benjamin Foulois," said Hap Arnold.

"Yes," replied the Cajun, "Benny was my superior officer during the Great War, and I've kept in touch with him over the years. He has a large collection of documents on air power and military tactics. Whenever I visit England, France, or Germany, I share with Benny what I've learned." Quentin knew that Arnold was a friend of Billy Mitchell. Mitchell and Foulois had been at odds with each other since before World War I. He wondered if Hap Arnold would hold his friendship with Foulois against him.

"Well," said Marshall, "more coffee?" Hap Arnold sat quietly for a moment before speaking up.

"OK, Norvell, I'll give you a chance. And yes, George, I'll have some more coffee."

In the days that followed, Quentin and Hap Arnold met regularly. At one of their meetings in late December 1941, Arnold asked Quentin about jet propulsion.

"It's the future of aviation," said the Cajun, taking Arnold completely by surprise.

"Care to explain?" asked Arnold intrigued by the younger man's comment.

Quentin mentioned his support for Whittle's jet engine and told Arnold about the Germans flying a jet plane and their intent to develop a jet fighter. The more Arnold heard, the more he was impressed by the Cajun. Although the general did not comment or mention how impressed he was by Quentin's knowledge of aviation and his forward thinking, he began to change his opinion about the younger man. But, it was Carl Spaatz, a senior member of General Arnold's top echelon staff, who befriended the Cajun. He and two others soon convinced Hap Arnold that Quentin was a valuable addition to the air force staff office.

* * *

It was cold and blustery in New York with Christmas two days away. The attack on Pearl Harbor, Hitler's declaration of war against the United States, and the swift and stunning Japanese victories in the Pacific added a sense of forbearance, and dampened what would otherwise have been a festive holiday season. Thousands of young Americans were joining the army, navy, and marines. The shock of being at war was still rippling through American society, causing uncertainty, anger, and an elevated sense of patriotism. Many older Americans remembered the First World War with its military sacrifices and how it disrupted an old way of life. So much had changed because of that war. Now, a new war, unprecedented because of its global implications, posed challenges for America and would change the nation dramatically. On this cold evening, Quentin met with Florence, and Fiona and Harold Vandersteel at their home. With them was Kathleen O'Meara, a nurse and close friend of the family.

"I wanted to speak with all of you before moving to Washington," said Quentin. He learned that President Roosevelt had called Florence and the Vandersteels and told them Quentin was needed in the air force. All three had strong reservations about Quentin going to war. The president had been persuasive and indicated in his inimical style how much he and the nation needed Quentin. Later, Fiona Vandersteel and Florence were surprised when Eleanor Roosevelt called. She told them the nation was facing a crisis of the greatest magnitude and sacrifices were necessary. Quentin was needed in the air force. She asked the two women to understand and accept the president's decision.

"I'll be in Washington from now on," he told them. "I might have to leave the country next year."

"Where will you go?" asked Harold.

"England, probably," said the Cajun. "After that, I don't know."

"Daddy, you're not going into combat, are you?" asked Florence, her voice on the verge of cracking.

He smiled at her, and, in a reassuring voice, said, "No, darling, I don't think so. I'm a little too long in the tooth for that."

"But you will be near the fighting," said Harold.

Quentin nodded and said maybe.

"What about Marlon?" asked Florence.

"When the time is right, I'll ask Marlon to leave the RAF and join the U.S. Army Air Force."

They talked for a while before the Cajun mentioned things he had to do and asked for their advice.

"Florence, you can continue to live in our apartment or move in with your grandparents."

After a moment of silence and looking down at her crossed hands, she replied, "Daddy, may I stay in the apartment?"

"If that's what you want, fine. I'll make arrangements for Camila and Clara to remain in the apartment with you. Clara is a wonderful cook, and Camila is like family," said the Cajun, noticing Kathleen smile and nod her head. "But, visit your grandparents often."

Florence nodded, stood, and hugged Fiona who started to sniffle.

Three days later, Quentin was on his way to Washington after settling his affairs with Barston, Marwick, Fowler, and Peterson. He arranged for Sarah, his secretary, to stay with the firm. A few months later, Sarah petitioned Quentin to find her a place in the U.S. military.

* * *

Meanwhile, Marlon's temporary duty in Malta was extended. The fighting in North Africa had intensified, and the Luftwaffe was expanding its forces in the Mediterranean. In addition to his role as an instructor, Marlon flew combat missions and scored another confirmed victory.

With America at war with Germany, Marlon considered his situation within the RAF. He wondered whether to continue flying for the British or transfer to the U.S. Army Air Force. *Wish I could talk to Dad about this*, he thought. *I wonder when I'll get to see him again.*

But, Marlon's fate was in his father's hands. Quentin would consult first with Marlon, but he was already designing a role for his son in the U.S. Air Force. Marlon had the educational background, training, and combat experience as a fighter pilot needed by the U.S. Air Force. It was just a matter of time when the opportunity would arise and Quentin could lobby people in the air force and convince Marlon to change his allegiance and uniform. *He's my son,* thought Quentin, *and I want him fighting alongside of me.*

CHAPTER 13
A DIFFERENT KIND OF WAR

There were noticeable changes in the German attitude toward the French as 1941 yielded to 1942. The German occupation required more French labor than before. Young and older men were pressed into service, mostly to build military facilities in France. But, for some, they left France to labor as slaves, many never to return to their homeland. Meanwhile, the German military was taking the best French agricultural products and food and providing little in the way of compensation. The French diet was suffering.

Because of the increasing number of attacks by the Maquis on German military personnel and installations, the Gestapo launched a brutal campaign of retribution. In concert with the puppet French authorities in occupied France, the Germans established a new and harsh policy to deal with anyone suspected of participation or complicity with the resistance. The French constabulary was pressured to identify and round up suspects. The people arrested were screened by French operatives closely monitored by their German overseers. Many of the prisoners were turned over to the Gestapo for interrogation. Gestapo and SS operatives cared little if prisoners were permanently maimed or died under torture. Gradually, informers emerged, eager to accuse others secretly in an attempt to escape imprisonment, torture, or death. Some did it to curry favor with the Boche. It was a shameful practice of collaboration with the invaders and providing false accusations against neighbors and friends. Innocent people were arrested and brutalized based on rumor and innuendo.

"We are like cannibals," said Millard to Nadine when he met with her and Noel and they were able to speak in private and away from Nazi surveillance. "It is hard to know whom to trust," he added bitterly.

"We must not relent in our efforts," said Nadine. "The Boche are beginning to feel the losses caused by the resistance."

"Yes, Madame, I understand," said the older man. "Just yesterday, my cousin's son was apprehended and imprisoned. The boy knows nothing. He's just thirteen."

"Has he been turned over to the Gestapo?" asked Nadine, deeply concerned, her forehead wrinkled.

"Not yet," replied Millard. "But, the swine (French police) are worse than the Gestapo."

"Is there anything we can do to help him?"

"Perhaps," said Millard.

"You should not be involved, Madame," cautioned Noel. "At least not directly."

"Is there a way to help him, Noel?"

He nodded and said money.

"A bribe? It will set a bad precedent."

The Frenchmen shook his head and said, "Madame, do you have funds to purchase expensive heirlooms?" She thought for a moment and said yes, intrigued by his question.

Turning to Millard and then Nadine, Noel said that if heirlooms were bought and given to those with family members detained by the French police, a few of them might be bribed.

"However," cautioned Noel, "the prisoners must not be involved with the resistance."

"D'accord," said a smiling Millard. "If Madame can underwrite the acquisition, secretly of course, of heirlooms to be used for barter…"

The three of them smiled, and Nadine said, "Do it. But, when the time comes, we should be prepared to expose and eliminate the French police collaborating with the Boche. I will make a list of those responsible for betraying us and later turn it over to the Maquis and the Free French."

Millard gave a wicked smile and said, "I can hardly wait."

* * *

Quentin worked several weeks in Washington to become familiar with the air force's new organizational structure. He was given access to top secret documents prepared by air staff and analyzed them carefully before meeting with Arnold and three of his top aides. He praised the work done, but critiqued some of the suggestions. While he agreed to give priority for a bombing campaign against the Germans, he stressed improving America's long-range bombers, particularly the B-17s. He mentioned that B-17s did not have enough defensive firepower. When Arnold asked him to explain, Quentin said bombing German targets on the Continent in daylight, especially beyond the range of available fighters, would require the bombers to defend themselves against Luftwaffe fighters.

"Many of our B-17s don't have tail guns," he told them. "I've read comments in the margins of the reports that recommend adding double fifty caliber machine guns here, and here," he said, pointing to places on a schematic of a B-17."

Arnold and the other officers glanced at each other before nodding in approval.

"See to it," said Arnold to one of his aides.

"What else, Quentin," said Hap, the use of his first name pleasing the Cajun.

He turned attention to fighter escorts and mentioned three planes: the British Spitfire, the American P-38, and the experimental P-47.

"I like the Spitfire, but it doesn't have enough range. Maybe we should do some tinkering to try to extend its range."

"What do you have in mind?" asked Carl Spaatz.

"An extra fuel tank," said the Cajun, "providing it's done with the IX version of the Spit the Brits are developing."

The other men in the room were impressed by Quentin's knowledge and information. Arnold made a mental note to ask Quentin how he managed to get information about new Spitfire models under development.

"Won't that slow down the Spits and make them less maneuverable?" asked Arnold.

"Yes, but if they have a quick release mechanism to drop the tanks if they're jumped by enemy fighters..." He did not finish the sentence because Hap Arnold said that someone should go to England and begin working on this. He said it while looking directly at the Cajun.

I think I know my next assignment, thought Quentin.

"What else?" asked Arnold, quietly impressed by Quentin's analysis and thinking.

"I don't think our P-38s are a good match for the German Messerschmitt Bf 109, especially their newer version. The new Bf 109 is more maneuverable and has improved firepower," he told them. "Also, the Germans have a new fighter, something they call the Focke-Wulf

190. RAF pilots have tangled with them recently, and they're not happy. The FW 190 is a fast, powerful plane, and has several advantages over the current Spitfires."

"Is that why you think we should be experimenting with the IX version of the Spitfire?" asked Spaatz. Quentin nodded.

Arnold told him to continue.

"Well, I haven't had a chance to see or learn about the new P-47 under development," said Quentin. "I know it flew for the first time last May (1941). But, I don't know the results of the testing,"

Arnold said he'd get him the information.

"Quentin, this is solid work on your part. I'd like you to go to England and talk to the designers at Supermarine Aircraft (division of Vickers-Armstrong, Ltd., responsible for manufacturing Spitfires) about auxiliary fuel tanks for Spitfires. Do you know any people there?"

Quentin smiled and nodded.

Why am I not surprised? thought Hap Arnold. "See if you can get them to work up an operational model. Also, there's going to be a high level confab next month in London about coordinating bombings against the Germans. I'll be there," said Arnold, "but I'd like you to be with me," he said, a thin smile crossing his face.

Quentin grinned, nodded, and said, "Yes, sir."

After the meeting with Hap Arnold and his aides, Quentin returned to his office and found a message from Lockheed Aircraft. He called the number and spoke with the vice president about a Lockheed with extended range. The plane was a modified version of their twin engine Lodestar. Its range was twenty-nine hundred miles and with a top speed of 280 miles per hour.

"I'd like to fly one," said Quentin.

"When can you be here?" asked the vice president.

Quentin said in three days.

"We'll have one ready for you."

Three days later, Quentin flew the new Lockheed. He was pleased by the plane's smooth ride and performance, and the twenty-nine-hundred-mile range convinced him. He asked, "Can it be fitted with extra fuel tanks?"

"Sure," said Gilchrest, the head of production. "We can boost the range to thirty-four hundred miles with auxiliary tanks."

"How soon can you have one for me?" Quentin asked Gilchrest.

"April," replied Gilchrest.

"Make it March and you've got a deal," said the Cajun. Gilchrest made a quick telephone call. After hanging up the phone, he smiled and said they could have a plane for him by the end of March. Quentin wrote out a check to Lockheed for several thousand dollars as a deposit and handed it to Gilchrest.

"Colonel," said a very pleased Gilchrest, "it's a pleasure doing business with you. We'll have it ready before the end of March."

"Remember, it has to have all the modifications and requirements for the air force."

"Yes, sir," said Gilchrest, "you can count on us."

The two men shook hands and Quentin filed a flight plan for his return trip to Washington.

* * *

Early in February 1942, Quentin was summoned to the White House. Roosevelt met with him, George Marshall, Cordell Hull, Harry Hopkins, and Brook Hamilton Stoner.

"How are you and Hap Arnold getting along?" asked Roosevelt.

Quentin said they were working well together. Roosevelt glanced at Marshall, who nodded. The Cajun noticed Stoner's grin. *Well,* he thought, *the president is keeping tabs on me.*

"Quentin," said Roosevelt, fixing a cigarette in his long holder, "I need you in London. How soon can you finish up what you're doing here?"

The Cajun replied a couple of weeks.

"Make it sooner," said the president, "I have an assignment for you. Stony will fill you in on the details. You'll be meeting with Churchill and some of his people."

Quentin shot a quick glance in Stoner's direction. The diplomat smiled and winked at him.

"Hap and George will follow a few days later," said the president.

Quentin asked, "If you don't mind, Mr. President, what's the purpose and the agenda for the meeting with Churchill?"

"George will fill you in on that too," said Roosevelt. "But, the follow-up meeting with their air ministry people and bomber command will be critical. We've got to reach an understanding with the British and coordinate our air offensives against the Nazis. It won't be easy," said the president. "George, why don't you tell him?"

"Churchill's been listening to Air Chief Marshal Charles Portal, Air Marshal Sholto Douglas, and Commander in Chief RAF Bomber Command Arthur Harris," said Marshall dryly. "They've convinced him to do large scale night bombings on the Continent. Do you know any of these fellows?"

Quentin nodded and waited for Marshall to continue.

"Portal and Harris want to do area bombing. Do you know what that means?"

Quentin nodded and said,

"It's bombing an area, like a city, rather that focus on a precise target. They've probably decided on area bombing because their accuracy may be off at night," said Quentin. "Their bomb sights aren't as good as our Norton (excellent U.S. bomb sight)."

"Also," said Marshall, "Harris and Trafford Leigh-Mallory favor this tactic as a way to demoralize German civilians." Quentin shook his head. Roosevelt immediately picked up the Cajun's negative reaction to the British strategy of area bombing.

"Quentin," said Roosevelt, "you don't seem to approve of area bombing."

"No, Mr. President, I don't. It kills civilians."

"Isn't that what the Germans are doing to London?" asked the president.

"Maybe, but that's not a reason for us to engage in area bombing," said Quentin. "Our bombers should strike targets with high military value. If we can cripple and destroy key parts of Germany's military industry, that will help us win the war."

"George?" asked the president, looking at Marshall.

The general nodded and said he agreed with the Cajun.

"Very well," said Roosevelt glancing at his clock. "That's what you'll tell our British friends when you meet with them in London. By the way, Quentin," said the president, changing the subject, "Hap Arnold is supporting your promotion to brigadier. George and I have sent the request for your promotion to the Senate."

"Thank you, Mr. President," said Quentin. After the meeting was over, Stoner walked with Quentin.

"Sport, there's infighting within the British Air Ministry. We don't want to get in the middle of it. I know you and Geoffrey Barries-Cole Hawkins are good friends. Find out what he has to say about things in the air ministry."

Quentin nodded. *Something else to keep me busy,* he thought glumly. Always in his mind, however, was Nadine's safety. If only he could get her out of France.

Quentin arrived in London on February 13, 1942. The weather was damp and miserable, and the long nights added to the feeling of cold and discomfort. He contacted Geoffrey immediately and asked about meeting with the design people at Supermarine about fitting a quickly detachable auxiliary fuel tank to a Spitfire. Geoff said he thought Supermarine was working on it. The next day, Geoff called to say a meeting was scheduled for the following Monday with the head of Supermarine and key production personnel. Geoff would accompany Quentin to the meeting.

Two days later, Quentin and Stoner, along with a military attaché from the U.S. Embassy in London, met with Churchill and his key people. At the meeting were Air Chief Marshal Charles Portal, Air Marshal Sholto Douglas (head of Fighter Command), and Sir Arthur Harris, recently appointed as commander in chief of Bomber Command.

Quentin knew that Churchill liked cigars and was either smoking one or had one close at hand. It surprised the British Prime Minister (PM) when the Cajun handed him a box of excellent Cuban cigars.

"Is this a bribe?" teased Churchill.

Quentin grinned and said it was a simple overture of friendship.

"Do you know each other?" asked the PM, encouraging one of his aides to make the introductions.

"Well, let's get down to business," said Churchill, peering over his glasses at the Americans. In the next twenty minutes, the discussion ranged from joint military ventures and how America could "best" help the British war effort.

Quentin observed that Churchill remained silent during the discussion, occasionally whispering something to one of his aides. *He's a sly old fox,* thought the Cajun.

Sir Charles Portal mentioned that it would be helpful if American troops and aircraft were used to "reinforce" RAF squadrons and personnel.

"Do you mean become part of British military units?" asked Charles Brinkman, the U.S. military attaché.

"Not a bad idea," said Sir Arthur Harris. "Of course, it would only be until your chaps get the proper training and have seen some combat."

"Are you referring to an arrangement like the Eagle Squadrons?" asked Quentin, "or did you have something else in mind?"

Harris gave a forced smile and said it could be something like the arrangement for the three Eagle Squadrons. Three RAF squadrons, no. 71, no. 121, and no. 133 were composed of American pilots commanded by British squadron and flight leaders.

The way Brinkman flushed told Quentin that he was against such an arrangement. Before he or Stoner could say anything, Brinkman said it was not possible.

"It has been a longstanding policy of my government," Brinkman told them emphatically, "that Americans will not fight under the flag of another country."

"Ah, yes," said one of Churchill's aides, "but the Eagle Squadrons and some of the American volunteers in British army units would appear to diminish that argument."

Stoner and the Cajun saw the approaching impasse.

"Perhaps," said a smiling Stoner, "we should set this matter aside for the moment. I'm certain that it will be dealt with properly at a later date." At this, Churchill chuckled and took a long drag on one of the Cuban cigars. As he let out a plume of aromatic smoke, he locked eyes momentarily with the Cajun and tapped the long cigar as a sign of appreciation.

"Put that on our agenda when we meet with General Marshall," said Churchill. "Now, shall we move along?"

After the meeting ended and the participants were shaking hands before departing, Churchill asked Quentin to remain for a moment.

"I'll not keep him long," said the PM to Stoner.

When they were alone, Churchill mentioned he'd heard very positive things about him.

"You must be careful not to put too much trust in what people say," said the smiling American, "especially when it involves old fighter pilots."

"Really!" exclaimed Churchill. "And why is that?"

"Well," said the Cajun, "fighter pilots are notorious for exaggerating."

Churchill chuckled and motioned for the American to be seated. "You've been making funds available for Whittle's research on jet propulsion," he said. "And, your son is in the RAF and stationed in Malta."

Quentin nodded.

"I appreciate your helping us," said Churchill. "But, tell me about this meeting with the people at Supermarine?"

In the next few minutes, Quentin explained his interest in working with the engineers at Supermarine to develop auxiliary fuel tanks for the Spitfire that could be quickly jettisoned.

"Hmmm," said Churchill, "you realize that will cost Supermarine and take some personnel away from their duties."

"Understood," said the Cajun with a thin smile, "but I'm prepared to underwrite the cost of the project if the people at Supermarine agree to do it."

"So you'll cover the cost for the entire project?" said the sly PM.

The American nodded and thought, *Churchill doesn't miss a thing. He'll probably add on some overhead.*

"In that case," said the PM, "I think your meeting at Supermarine will be productive."

"Thank you," said the Cajun. "I knew we could do business."

At this, Churchill laughed, said he enjoyed talking with Quentin and wished him "good luck."

* * *

Marlon was working with a gun crew on a Hurricane in February 1942. The weather was cloudy but comfortable at Malta as they adjusted the guns on the plane.

"Leftenant," said a corporal in a strong cockney accent working with Marlon, "any truth to the rumor we're 'bout to get some Spitfires?"

"I've heard that too," said Marlon, as he finished adjusting the machine guns. "But, it's risky getting them here with Jerry attacking our convoys. We'll just have to wait and see."

A sergeant approached and called out to Marlon, "Sir, you're wanted in operations."

Marlon nodded and told the sergeant he would be along as soon as he cleaned the oil off his hands. A few minutes later, he entered the operations shack.

"Ah, Norvell," said Captain Danverford, "be a good chap and pull up a chair." Danverford, the son of the first baron of Litchfield, was his squadron leader. "We have a rather interesting job for you." Marlon sat and listened as the squadron leader mentioned he and two new pilots would fly escort for a reconnaissance mission. The next morning, Marlon and two RAF pilots lifted off Malta to escort a reconnaissance plane for a fly over Gazala, just to the west of Tobruk in Libya. British Military Intelligence wanted to confirm that Rommel's offensive started in January 1942 was to capture Tobruk and then move east into Egypt.

As they flew over the blue Mediterranean, the expanse of water and the nearly unimpeded view of the horizon gave Marlon a sense of floating in the atmosphere. Their flight path was just north of the arid North African coastline. At Tobruk, they turned inland and proceeded toward Bir Hacheim. The reconnaissance plane, a de Havilland Mosquito Mk1, dropped down to begin photographing the area.

"Enemy fighters," called Pilot Officer Talley over the radio, "three o'clock." Marlon looked north and immediately spotted the dark specks drawing close.

Marlon's flight was high and with the sun at their backs. *They may not see us,* he speculated. He watched carefully as the German fighters approached intent on closing with the reconnaissance plane. He used hand signals and motioned for the others to follow him. He motioned to drop their auxiliary fuel tanks. Then he gained height before diving on the formation of German fighters. *If we're lucky, we can knock out one or two of the Jerry planes in the first pass,* he thought. Marlon focused on the lead enemy fighter and attacked it. His eight machine guns found their target, killing the pilot and sending the Messerschmitt spiraling to earth trailing smoke. Talley and Manston each scored hits, but the other enemy fighters scattered and used their maneuverability to turn on their adversaries. Marlon went after a Bf 109 that was on Talley's tail and managed to hit it, causing the German to break off. However, one of the German pilots got behind Manston and disabled his aircraft, forcing the Englishman to call for help over the radio. By the time Marlon arrived, he could see Manston's plane trailing smoke and losing altitude.

Marlon called out, "Head for Tobruk." He wondered if the damaged Hurricane could make it.

Meanwhile, the Mosquito finished its reconnaissance and was climbing with a Bf 109 on its tail. Marlon immediately went after the German fighter. Just as he positioned himself to fire on the German, tracers zipped by, and he felt the impact of bullets hitting his plane. He juked the Hurricane to avoid his pursuer's fire and sent a stream of bullets at the Bf 109 ahead of him. Then, he began an Immelmann roll to escape the pursuing German. However, his adversary was an experienced pilot and easily countered the move. By now, the Hurricane was performing sluggishly, and Marlon decided on a desperate tactic to shake the pursuing German. He did a quick roll and lowered his flaps to reduce his airspeed, causing the German fighter to zoom by him. All Marlon could do was send off a stream of bullets at the German fighter as it sped by. But, it was enough to cause the German to break off. And then it was over.

When Marlon scanned the sky, he could see the Mosquito well ahead of him speeding back to Malta. Neither Talley nor Manston were anywhere in sight. He tried to close with the Mosquito, but the Hurricane could not make speed, and he was having trouble trimming it. He called the reconnaissance plane and asked it they were all right.

The pilot responded and said they had taken a few hits, but they were OK and heading home.

"You're trailing smoke from underneath," said the Mosquito pilot.

"How bad is it?" asked Marlon.

"Just a thin line of gray," said the other pilot. "Can you make it back?"

"I'll try," said Marlon. "Have you seen the others?"

"I think they both bought it."

Marlon settled down for the flight back to Malta, but he began to fall behind the Mosquito. Finally, the Mosquito pilot called and asked if he should slow down.

"No," replied Marlon, "get back to base. I'll probably have to ditch."

"We'll notify our chaps," said the other pilot.

Fifteen minutes later, Marlon's plane could no longer maintain altitude. His oil pressure was dropping, and the engine temperature rising rapidly. He checked his watch and compass heading and calculated he was about twenty minutes from Malta. He managed to send off an SOS with his approximate position. Then, he felt the plane shudder badly, and his gauges signaled the engine had died, along with his radio.

He put the Hurricane into a glide, made certain he had the survival kit with the life raft secured, opened the canopy, and bailed out. When the parachute opened, he watched the Hurricane crash into the Mediterranean and break apart. It sank immediately. He drifted slowly toward the east before splashing down into the blue Mediterranean. The water felt cool, but not like the biting cold of the English Channel months ago when he was shot down.

Marlon released his parachute harness, inflated the life raft, and clambered aboard. He tried to save the parachute, but he only managed to cut part of it loose from the rigging before it sank. He was wet, exhausted, and depressed. He covered his eyes from the sun and dozed off.

* * *

"Madame," said a sardonic, recently promoted Gestapo *Oberstleutnant* (lieutenant colonel) Sigwald Eisenhardt, "your assistance is required." The Gestapo colonel and his aide, Hauptman Wolfgang Berthold were in Nadine's conference room with Braustich, Zeigler, and Noel DeCloux. Nadine was silent and calm, waiting for the German to continue.

"French citizens must cooperate fully with us," he said with an ingenuous smile.

"I don't understand," Nadine replied, giving the impression that the French were doing what the Boche wanted. She sat calmly, waiting for the German to continue. Eisenhardt removed a cigarette from an expensive silver case, tapped the slender cigarette on the lid, and waited for Zeigler to strike a match so he could light it.

After taking a drag from the cigarette, Eisenhardt said, "You see, there's talk about the resistance. We do not consider the gnat bites of a few misguided criminals of much concern. In time, we will attend to these malcontents."

Nadine feigned listening attentively to the Gestapo colonel. But, beneath the veil of tranquility was a seething anger and resentment. *If the resistance is not important,* she mused, *then why try to downplay their efforts.*

"We seek the assistance of influential leaders, like you," said Eisenhardt.

"For what purpose?" asked the handsome Frenchwoman.

"It would be helpful for you to communicate the advantages of good relations and cooperation with the Reich."

She asked how, feigning interest.

"There are times and places where a few comments to encourage cooperation with the Reich can be helpful," said Eisenhardt, as he studied the slowly dissipating smoke from his cigarette.

"I'm already working with the German authorities," replied Nadine.

"Yes, that's true, but there is more that you can do," said the colonel coolly.

"I'm not a political leader," she replied.

"Nevertheless, you are a person of influence, and your name is well known in France and elsewhere," pressed the colonel.

"I can speak only for the arts," she told him.

"Yes, yes, we know you are a dedicated and generous supporter of the arts. Your name as a person of wealth and culture draws attention. But it is precisely that recognition that makes you a valuable ally for the Reich."

"So, you want me to speak in favor of the occupation?" said Nadine, suppressing her anger and the desire to spit in the German's face.

"Precisely," said Eisenhardt, a smug look on his face.

"I will have to think about this," said Nadine slowly.

"Your hesitation, does it involve reservations about speaking in favor of cooperation with the Reich?" he asked, the question designed to trap Nadine.

"No," she replied calmly. "I would not know what to say."

"We are prepared to assist you by providing certain phrases and examples."

"I see," she said, looking down at her hands. "I may not be persuasive."

"And why not?" asked Eisenhardt.

"Oh," said Nadine carefully considering how to respond. "I will be sharing perspectives that may require time for people to accept."

"You mean that some of your confreres may have reservations about ties with the Reich," he said, a thin smile on his face. She noticed Hauptman Berthold listening to the conversation intently while staring at her.

"No," she replied, "it's just that it will take time for them to accept me in a new light, as someone speaking with a political voice."

"Of course," said Eisenhardt, his eyes narrowing. "We realize this will take time and that some of your friends and associates may want additional information. After all, it is best if these things are done slowly." He stood and turned to Berthold who handed him a folder.

"Here are the names of influential French citizens we expect you to cultivate," he said, handing her a typewritten page with ten names. "They are prominent people needed to help develop stronger ties with the Reich. We are prepared to reward them for their cooperation," he said flatly. "Some, however, may be slow to see the advantage of cooperation with the Reich. You have but to let me know who they are and we will 'assist' you to gain their cooperation."

Nadine knew, then, exactly what the Gestapo colonel wanted. By refusing to cooperate with him, she would be accused of working against the occupation and the Boche. If she talked with the people on the list and shared what the Nazis wanted, they would know who could be co-opted, and who might be against them.

"I have a very full schedule, and my activities are controlled by your personnel, Colonel," said Nadine, holding the typescript page in her hands without looking at it.

"I understand," said the German, a plastic smile forming on his face. "But, we are prepared to make 'adjustments' in your schedule to accommodate these new requirements."

The word 'requirements' was a message not lost on Nadine. She realized that no matter what she said, this new task was an order and not a request. Nadine decided that her best strategy was to give the impression of cooperating and then delay the assignment.

"Very well," said Nadine, taking the typescript in both hands and folding it. "I'll see what can be done."

"Excellent," said Eisenhardt. "Hauptman Berthold and Herr Zeigler will assist. They will contact you. Let me express the gratitude of the Reich for your cooperation in this matter. Your efforts will not go unrewarded," said the Gestapo colonel, as he closed his portfolio and stood.

Nadine watched in silence as Braustich and Ziegler followed Eisenhardt. Berthold stood and smiled at Nadine; his piercing blue eyes had a hard and menacing look. She returned his smile, and the captain clicked his heels before leaving the conference room.

"Well, Noel," said Nadine after the Germans had left, "let us get to work." She signaled to her assistant with her hand that they should speak privately and away from the prying eyes and ears of the Gestapo.

Later, while Noel was walking Nadine to her car and they could not be overheard, she whispered to set-up a meeting with Millard as soon as possible. Noel nodded.

Two days later Nadine, Moira, Noel, and Millard met in the cellar where they could not be seen or overheard. Nadine patiently explained to Millard what the Boche colonel wanted.

"It's a trap," said Millard.

Nadine nodded and said the Boche were devious and dangerous.

"Perhaps we can turn this 'assignment' in our favor. This is what we will do." Nadine outlined her plan.

After the lovely Frenchwoman mentioned her strategy, Noel said, "It may delay the Gestapo, but not check them. They are certain to demand other things from Madame that will most certainly compromise your loyalty to France."

"That may be their plan, but I will not betray my country," said Nadine with a firm timbre in her voice. "When the time comes, we will leave Paris and join the resistance elsewhere."

They all nodded in agreement. Millard gently took Nadine's hand and kissed it.

"You can always count on my friendship and assistance," he told her.

She smiled and kissed the burly Frenchman on both cheeks.

She is a magnificent woman and an exceptional patriot, thought Noel. He too would do everything in his power to protect Nadine.

Marlon passed the remainder of the afternoon checking his meager stores from the survival kit. As he floated on the gentle swells of the Mediterranean, he used his compass and a trailing line to determine the drift. The soft zephyrs were pushing him east, southeast. *That's good,* he thought. *That's in the direction of Malta.*

He began to play over in his mind critical things to do. *I've got to make my water last,* he thought. *I'm not hungry. Besides,* he said to himself, *none of this stuff looks appetizing.* He used part of the parachute canopy to fashion a turban to protect his head and neck from the sun. The strong Mediterranean sun was hot, and the glare from the water was intense.

It was almost four in the afternoon with the sun low in the western sky when Marlon thought he heard a plane. He searched the sky in all directions until spotted a speck well off in the distance. *Wrong direction,* he said to himself. *Probably a Boche patrol plane.* The plane turned and passed south of him. He was not able to make out the markings on the airplane and worried that it was a German. *They must have spotted me,* he thought, a wave of uncertainty overcoming him momentarily.

When the sun disappeared over the western horizon, the air cooled, and he felt chilly. He wrapped himself in the remaining part of the parachute canopy and lay back in the rubber dingy. Alone and adrift on a vast sea, he waited for the crescent moon to rise. The inky sky above was filled with pin pricks of light from distant stars. To entertain himself, he tried to make out the constellations. He had studied astronomy as a boy and tried hard to remember the location of the major constellations and find the North Star. To pass the time, he thought about ancient mariners and what it must have been like to sail at night under a cloudless sky, the stars above the only guides for their passage. "I don't have a sail," he said aloud, "so I've got to trust the winds and currents will move me toward Malta."

Marlon hummed to himself and then drank some water. It was late when the moon rose, and he watched the large crescent shape rise slowly over the horizon. At first it seemed enormous, but gradually its proportions changed. He began to whistle tunes with the word "moon" in them. Then, he sang softly to himself, a ploy to avoid the pressing feeling of loneliness and abandonment. He hummed some melodies before dropping off to sleep.

He woke with a start and realized he had turned and bumped his head on the inflated side of the rubber dingy. Marlon cursed in French. He needed to urinate. *Careful,* he told himself, *not in the direction you're drifting.* "And, for Christ sakes, don't fall into the water," he spoke aloud as if talking to someone. Slowly he drifted back to sleep. But he woke several times before there was a faint orange glow on the eastern horizon.

It was almost 11:00 in the morning when he heard the sound of the engines off to the southeast. At first, he thought it was an airplane, but the sky was clear in all directions. Then, he saw the tip of a boat's mast on the horizon. Was it a German E-Boat? He reached for his revolver. *Stupid,* he berated himself, realizing resisting a patrol boat armed with machine guns was futile. As the boat approached and engine noise intensified, he saw the British Union Jack. He waved at the approaching torpedo boat. *It's going to be all right,* he told himself.

CHAPTER 14
A WHIRLWIND OF WAR

And, pleas'd the Almighty's orders to perform,
Rides in the whirlwind and directs the storm.
Joseph Addison, *The Campaign* [1704]

The days in England passed slowly for Quentin, working with engineers and technicians at Supermarine from early in the morning until well past seven in the evening. When the weather permitted, he logged hours in a new version of the Spitfire. It was more powerful and faster than the one he'd flown several years before. He even managed to get in some gunnery practice to test the plane's cannons. *Yes, Marlon would love flying this plane,* he thought. He wondered how his son was doing on Malta.

The work at Supermarine on the auxiliary fuel tank for the Spitfire frustrated Quentin. A single auxiliary tank was rejected because of the Spitfire's undercarriage and air scoop. Adding two auxiliary tanks, like those used on Hurricanes, complicated the project. The double tanks, plumbing, and electrical devices required for the extra tanks to function properly added weight and seriously impeded the operational qualities of the speedy fighter. Getting the things to fit properly and eject quickly preoccupied the Cajun. Work on the project proceeded slowly with numerous problems that needed to be solved.

The weather turned sour on the tenth day at Supermarine when a deep low pressure system arrived and brought an intense rain to the area. It provided a good excuse for the Cajun to take a long weekend and visit London for a few days. When he arrived at his hotel on Friday, there was a message from Geoff. Quentin unpacked, relaxed, then sorted his mail. He put the items that required attention in a small pile and discarded the others. "I'll call Florence this evening," he whispered to himself. After washing his face and sipping on some brandy, he called Geoff.

"Well, Colonel," said the ebullient Englishman, "what brings you back to London?"

"Bad weather," said the Cajun, "plus the need for a break."

"Any plans for this evening?"

"Maybe a musical," said Quentin, kicking off one of his shoes.

"Do you mind company tonight?" asked Geoff. "I know a good show that's playing to rave reviews, plenty of good songs, and some lovely creatures dancing in the chorus."

"Can we get tickets?" The brigadier chuckled and said to leave everything to him.

"I'll come by to collect you around sevenish," said Geoff.

It was just after seven when Geoff's car pulled in front of the hotel and the driver came around to open the back door for Quentin. Seated in the back were Geoff and Lady Margaret Gibbon of Stockenchurch. The American remembered Lady Margaret and smiled politely at her and took the hand she extended in friendship. She was Geoff's cousin and her husband was an officer in the Royal Navy. When he inquired about her husband, she said his destroyer had been sunk by the Japanese.

"Is he all right?" asked Quentin.

She smiled and replied that her husband had been rescued and transferred to serve as the executive officer on a cruiser in the Indian Ocean.

The show they attended was gay and filled with catchy tunes sung by very attractive young women. And, as Geoff had mentioned, the chorines were attractive and leggy, and their synchronized dancing was impressive. Geoff would often elbow Quentin gently in the ribs and nod his head at a particularly attractive young singer or dancer.

After the show, they went to Geoff's private club and listened to soft piano music that was soon interrupted by air raid sirens and then the sound of bombing off in the distance.

"You look tired, Quentin," said Lady Margaret, gently patting his left forearm.

"Yes, I am," he replied. "Sorry to be such a drag on the two of you, I need to find my bed and recharge my batteries."

"We'll take you to your hotel," said Geoff, about to call for the check. Quentin shook his head and said he'd catch a cab. He kissed Lady Margaret on the cheek, shook the brigadier's hand, and said good night to them and left.

Before going to bed, Quentin wrote to Nadine. His letter would go via Portugal to Spain, where a Catholic priest and two nuns would see that it was secretly delivered to Nadine in France. The letter was in code, and no names were mentioned in case it fell into the wrong hands. He turned off the lights and opened a window before getting into bed. A few minutes later, the sirens signaling the all clear blared in the distance.

Quentin woke early the next day and went for a walk, but a biting sleet, whipped along by a sharp wind that cut right through his clothing, curtailed his walk. He returned to the hotel, picked up a paper, and ordered some coffee.

It was well after ten on Saturday morning when Geoff's telephone rang. He heard Linne Kidsgrove's voice on the other end. They exchanged greetings and chatted for a few minutes before Linne said she spoke with Margaret earlier and learned that Quentin Norvell was in London.

She asked, "Geoff, do you know how long he'll be in London?"

He replied until Sunday.

"Do you happen to know his plans?"

The brigadier replied, "He mentioned something about having lunch with Glinda Pennington."

She asked where he was staying, and Geoff told her the hotel and its telephone number.

"If you call right away," he said, "you might catch him."

Linne thanked Geoff and said she'd ring him later about a recital the following week. After ending the call with the brigadier, she telephoned the Cajun's hotel.

Quentin was in the lobby sitting next to the fireplace and reading *The Times* when he heard his name paged. He inquired at the desk and was told he had a telephone call.

"You can take it in booth two," said the older man behind the desk.

When Quentin answered the telephone he heard Linne's voice.

"Quentin Norvell, I'm rather disappointed in you," she told him.

He asked why.

"You promised to ring me when you were in London. I learned from a friend you were in London having a grand time. I feel slighted."

He chuckled and asked her to forgive him. "Well," she said in a charming manner, "you could redeem yourself by asking to see me."

He thought for a moment before saying, "I've an engagement with a friend in a little while, but perhaps we could have dinner tonight."

"If you're trying to bribe me for being in London without calling, I will consider this as partial penance," she said, her voice sparkling.

They chatted about dinner and Quentin mentioned he was not fond of traditional English cooking. He asked if she knew a restaurant that served spicy food. Linne thought for a while before giving a laugh and saying, "Yes, I know an Indian restaurant that serves spicy food."

"Bon," he told her. "Let me have the address and I'll meet you there."

"You'll do no such thing. I'll provide transport. Can you be ready around seven o'clock?" Quentin replied affirmatively and was about to restate his willingness to meet at the restaurant when she said, "I shan't hear it. I'll collect you at seven."

* * *

Quentin and Glinda had a pleasant lunch while outside the weather continued cloudy with occasional snow flurries. Quentin asked about the weather.

"Is it always like this in the winter?"

She smiled and said pretty much so, but that there were days when they did see the sun. They both laughed. When he asked about Kendall, Glinda's expression grew serious.

"He's fine, but stressed by his assignments," she said, then mentioned some of what Kendall wrote in his letters. "He can't really tell me where he's stationed or his duties. All of that is censored," she said. "But, from what he writes, I can tell he's busy and tired."

"He'll be all right," said the Cajun to reassure her.

"How is Marlon?" asked Glinda. In the next few minutes, the Cajun shared news about his son and mentioned he was stationed at Malta.

"How do you know that?" asked a surprised Glinda.

The Cajun smiled and said he had sources in the RAF.

She laughed, and asked, "How long will you be in London?"

"Probably until tomorrow," he replied.

"Do you have plans for this evening?" she inquired.

He smiled at her and said, "I'm going to dinner with a friend."

She smiled and decided not to make any further inquiries and wished him well.

* * *

Linne's sedan arrived promptly at seven at Quentin's hotel. It had started to snow, and the American walked briskly to the Englishwoman's car and stepped into the backseat.

When Quentin settled next to Linne, she pointed to his military attire and said, "You're in uniform. Are the Yanks already here?"

He nodded and said he was part of a U.S. vanguard.

"Capital," said a smiling Linne, "then we'll see more of each other." She gave the driver the instructions, and the car moved forward slowly.

"The restaurant's on the east side," she told Quentin, "and the Jerries have hit that area pretty hard. We'll have to skirt some bombed-out places."

As they drove to the restaurant, Quentin asked Linne if she lived mainly in London. She gave a perky laugh and mentioned that her work required stays in London, in the countryside, and long trips to her country estate near Stoke-on-Trent. When he asked where Stoke-on-Trent was, she chuckled and said it was northwest of London, several hours by train.

"Is that where you were born?" he asked.

"Oh gracious, no," she replied. "I was born near Claydon, just north of Ipswich."

Quentin mentioned knowing of Ipswich.

"It's north of here and on the coast," she said. "I grew up not far from Cambridge."

"So how is it that you have a country estate near Stoke-on-Trent?" he asked.

She mentioned it was her former husband's manor house and grounds.

"As his wife and the mother of his two children, I've inherited the estate. His mother still lives there," she said casually. "But enough about me; I want to hear about you."

The restaurant was filled with a mix of Indian and English patrons, most of the men in uniforms. They were ushered to a corner table that provided some privacy.

When they sat down, Quentin asked about the restaurant. She said it was well regarded. By the way the maitre d' smiled at Linne and treated her like royalty, the Cajun surmised that she had been at the restaurant more than a few times.

During their meal, Linne asked Quentin about Louisiana and where he had grown up. "Is it true you grew up in the swamps with wild animals all about?"

He laughed and said the bayous were still raw and undeveloped parts of Louisiana.

"I've heard the bogs abound with alligators and serpents," she said, her face aglow with curiosity.

In the next hour, he told her about the bayous and then about his family and his mother's ancestors. Bernice's side of the family intrigued her. She was impressed that his mother had taught him to survive in the swamps.

"She must be a remarkable woman," said Linne, admiration evident in her voice.

"That she is, and more," said the Cajun.

"I've met your son," said Linne cautiously. "He's a very attractive young man. I've heard you have a lovely daughter, but nothing about a wife."

He mentioned Florence by name and said her mother had died shortly after childbirth.

"Oh, I'm very sorry," she told him, reaching across the table to touch his hand.

He decided to mention Nadine as Marlon's mother. When he did, she was surprised.

"Then your son and daughter are—" she began before Quentin politely cut her off.

"I guess honesty is the best policy," he said and told her about meeting Nadine during the Great War and their relationship. Her eyes grew wide. He mentioned meeting Ione in America, their marriage, her death, and then Henri Desnoyers' death and learning that Marlon was his son. She was quiet for a moment before asking him about Nadine and whether they were married, now that Henri Desnoyers had died. He told her no.

"I'm confused," she told him. "You say she's in France. Why?"

He sipped his wine and slowly mentioned Nadine's loyalty to France and her determination to stay and care for her parents and manage the family's business.

"But there's more," she said, beginning to speculate about Nadine. "Is she part of the resistance?" she asked in a hushed tone so no one could overhear.

He was solemn and said, "I really can't comment on that." It was his way of avoiding her question.

Linne was silent for the longest time until Quentin asked if he had said anything to upset her.

"Either you are somewhat cavalier about the mother of your son, or Nadine is a very special person," Linne said, looking directly into Quentin's eyes. He was quiet and swallowed hard. "Please forgive me for prying," Linne said solicitously. "You're just so different from the men I know. I'm a bit off balance and need time to sort out what you've told me."

"I didn't mean to upset you," he said, wondering how Linne was reacting to his commentary about Nadine.

"No, no, Quentin, please don't think I'm upset. Surprised, maybe," she said.

They talked until the waiter arrived and asked if they wanted anything else. Quentin said no and asked for the check.

"Please," said Linne, gently touching Quentin's sleeve, "let me."

"That's very kind of you," said the smiling Cajun, "but I want to support your economy. And what kind of cavalier would I be to allow a beautiful woman to pay for my meal."

She blushed and smiled at the American, her eyes never leaving his.

That evening, before Linne went to bed, she wrote in her diary about Quentin and what he had shared. He was so fascinating and attractive. The knowledge of his love for a French woman, the mother of his son, somewhere in occupied France was disturbing. Her approach toward him changed. She abandoned the idea of knowing the American in an intimate way. As she closed the diary and looked wistfully at the solitary flower in a slender vase, her heart made a decision that overcame reason. "Quentin Norvell," Linne whispered, "you are a unique man and I want to see you again."

* * *

The next morning, Geoff insisted on having lunch with Quentin before driving him to the railway station. During their meal, Geoff asked if Quentin was interested in flying as an observer during an RAF raid over the Continent. Quentin almost jumped out of his chair.

"Well, old man, it appears I've got your attention," Geoff teased.

"Of course I'd like to participate. Tell me what you have in mind," said an excited Quentin.

In the next few minutes, Geoff mentioned a diversionary mission by the RAF over a German aerodrome close to the French coast. When Quentin asked when the flight would take place, and its target, Geoff said Wednesday or Thursday of the following week, depending on the weather. He said he could not disclose the target.

"We'd prefer to keep your chaps out of the loop," said Geoff. "So, if you go, it will be on your own recognizance."

Quentin thought for a moment and considered what might happen if he tried to contact the military attaché in London or get permission from Washington. He knew that U.S. officials would prevent him from serving as an observer on a combat mission.

"OK," said the Cajun, "I'll do it incognito."

"That's the spirit," said Geoff. "I'll make all the arrangements from our end. We'll call you the day before the raid and have you fly to a designated air base. They'll be waiting for you and provide you with all the information about the diversionary flight. You lucky devil," said Geoff wistfully. "I wish I were going along with you."

Quentin received a telephone call shortly after the noon hour at Supermarine. He was informed that a courier would arrive shortly and have documents for him. An hour later, an RAF courier arrived and handed the American sealed orders. After signing for the documents, he read the letter and headed for the Supermarine office. He handed the person in charge a letter requesting that he fly a new model Spitfire to an RAF facility east of London.

"Yes, I've been expecting this," said Sir Reginald, the officer in charge of his project. "It's been cleared with us. We'll service the aircraft and see you back here in a few days. Good hunting," he told the American with a big smile.

Late that afternoon, Quentin left Supermarine in a new Spitfire. As he approached the RAF airfield close to the Channel, he called the field on the radio frequency mentioned in his orders and used a code word and identification number. The air controller told him to wait as he verified the information. A few minutes later, the controller was back and gave him landing instructions. He was told to follow a lorry when he landed. After touching down, he approached a small truck with a sign that read "follow me," and taxied to a hangar. There, he was met by several RAF officers.

"How was your flight, Colonel?" asked a slight, ruddy-faced Englishman wearing a dark leather jacket over a white turtleneck sweater. Quentin could not determine the man's rank. He replied that the flight had been uneventful.

"Splendid. I'm Lieutenant Colonel Bromley, and this is Major Hooper and Captain Cook-Allison. They exchanged greetings before walking in the direction of a pair of sedans waiting for them. "Don't worry about your plane," said Cook-Allison, "our ground crew will refuel and arm it." The Cajun learned that Bromley was a wing commander and Hooper a squadron leader. Cook-Allison was a flight leader.

They drove to a low building and entered a secure area where several enlisted men and women were busy checking radar monitors and plotting information on a large map.

"Through here," said Bromley as they walked down a narrow corridor to a conference room. "We're glad to have you on board," said Bromley, motioning for all of them to be seated. In the next twenty minutes, Quentin learned about the diversionary raid that would be performed by a flight of six Spitfires and four Mosquito fighter-bombers. The target was a German aerodrome close to the French coast.

"Our job is to attack Jerry's airfield near Montreuil before our chaps hit their target up here," said Bromley, as he pointed to a spot near Calais. "Jerry will think we're after his installations at Montreuil and a rail yard here," he said, again pointing to a spot on the map. "The Mosquitoes will hit the aerodrome first and then buzz the rail yard."

"What's the primary target?" asked Quentin.

"Best if you not know that," said Bromley. "In case you get shot down, the less you know the better."

The Cajun nodded and thought, *I'm not planning to get shot down.*

They talked about the mission and the logistics until almost six in the evening. Bromley said they should have supper and led them to a cramped dining area where they ate a less than inspiring meal. Quentin was shown to an adjacent building where he would sleep.

The following morning, Quentin met the other pilots in the mess area and together they attended the orientation session where they were given last-minute information on the weather and gun emplacements at the German aerodrome.

The briefing officer warned them that the Germans might have Focke-Wulf 190s at this particular aerodrome.

"Try to avoid them if you can," he said nonchalantly as several pilots chuckled nervously. "Takeoff is at 0830 hours," said the briefing officer. "Any questions?"

Once the flight was airborne, Quentin fell into his position slightly behind the six Spitfires flying in formation close to the four Mosquitoes. They flew low over the

Channel to avoid German radar and did not gain altitude even after crossing the French coast. They flew inland and directly toward their target. Then, something unpredictable happened.

The RAF flight gained altitude as it approached the German aerodrome. Quentin noticed two Focke-Wulf 190s were airborne and gaining altitude. Several German fighters were preparing to take off. *They've been alerted and scrambled,* thought Quentin. The Mosquitoes quickly dove to bomb the field while flight leader Cook-Allison ordered four of the Spitfires to catch and engage the airborne 190s while the remaining Spitfires flew cover. Quentin made a quick decision and added power to the Spitfire, banking the speedy fighter sharply and putting it into a shallow dive. He positioned himself behind one of the 190s as it was gaining speed on the runway and began firing at it. His marksmanship was excellent, and the German plane seemed to hang in the air for a moment before falling out of the sky. Quentin immediately did a tight loop and positioned himself behind another German plane that had just lifted off the runway. This time, his cannons shredded the nearly defenseless 190, and it burst into flames. By now, the two remaining Spitfires dove down to cover the American, but the Cajun was not done yet. Instead, he dove on a third German fighter and blasted away with his guns just as the enemy plane was gaining height and retracting its landing gear. Not satisfied with what he had done, Quentin, adrenalin pumping through his system, coolly strafed the planes on the ground and then fired on the enemy control tower. Quentin savored the attack, and his victories in the air. For a moment, he was back in France during the Great War shooting down German planes.

"Break off, Yank," he heard Cook-Allison yell on the radio. Quentin did one more pass over the enemy flight line and felt the Spitfire bounce slightly from an explosion beneath him. He'd hit a petrol truck and detonated it. When he looked back, he saw the orange fireball mushrooming and turning to black, greasy smoke. Only then did he gain altitude and advance the throttle on the Spitfire to catch up with the remaining flight of Spitfires. It was immensely satisfying for the Cajun to know the damage he'd caused the Boche.

"Good of you to join us," he heard Cook-Allison's cynical remark on the radio.

Once in the formation, Quentin noticed that none of the Mosquitoes were in sight. One of the Spitfires was missing and another was trailing gray smoke from its engine. As they approached the English coastline, the damaged Spitfire was unable to maintain speed and altitude. The flight leader ordered one of the Spitfires to follow the crippled craft to an auxiliary RAF field close to the Channel. A few minutes later, they sighted the airfield, and Cook-Allison called the controller for landing instructions. After taxing the Spitfire to the flight line, Quentin noticed Bromley and another officer waiting for Captain Cook-Allison to alight from his plane. He shut down his engine and closed all the switches before opening the canopy and dropping the side piece. The ground crew helped him out of his parachute and mentioned that his plane had a few holes in it, perhaps from shrapnel.

"Sir," said a red-faced sergeant who had just run over to his plane, "Colonel Bromley's compliments; he'd like you to join him." The Cajun took off his helmet and goggles and walked to where Bromley, Cook-Allison, and another officer were waiting.

"It was my impression that you were to be an observer on this mission," said Bromley to Quentin in a controlled tone. "Your little 'escapade' was unauthorized and dangerous. What the blazes did you think—"

Quentin hooked his thumb under the eagle on his lapel that denoted his rank as a full colonel, letting the

RAF wing commander know he was speaking to a superior officer.

Bromley paused momentarily before saying, "I know you outrank me, Colonel, but you're the RAF's responsibility. Had anything happened to you, all of us would have caught it from fighter command."

The Cajun nodded in approval, but he held his ground. Captain Cook-Allison said that Quentin's behavior was uncalled for and could have compromised the mission. Bromley was about to say something when Quentin extended his left hand with the palm up and said, "Gentlemen, my behavior was 'rash,' and I'm sorry if I in any way jeopardized the mission. I hope you will all accept my apology." The three RAF officers were silent and continued to stare at the American before Bromley spoke up.

"Apology accepted. You were lucky this time, Yank. I hope this is your first and last combat tryst. An older chap like you mixing it up with the Huns...well, it's just plain foolish." He turned to Cook-Allison and said, "Captain, be kind enough to escort our visitor to the debriefing area. After that, sir," said Bromley glancing at the Cajun, "your plane will be serviced and you should be on your way."

On his return trip to the Supermarine plant, Quentin was humming to himself as he played with the controls of the speedy and maneuverable British fighter. During the debriefing session, he had been credited with three FW 190s destroyed and two others damaged. He had asked that his "exploits" remain confidential and not shared with others. Bromley had just looked at him and shaken his head before saying, "Agreed." But, it would not end there.

That he might be shot down or killed did not enter Quentin's mind during the sortie over the German aerodrome. He was a trained fighter pilot, and felt his purpose was to attack and destroy the Germans. But there was something else, something deep within the Cajun that craved combat.

* * *

Nadine was occupied with business concerns and other matters. Braustich was demanding increased productivity from the mills producing military uniforms and boots for the Wehrmacht. She had no control of the synthetic oil and rubber plants and received no compensation for their operations and production. The other firms that she continued to oversee did provide regular income appropriated by the Nazis. She was given a generous monthly living allowance that was sufficient to pay her employees and cover the costs for her home and business office. She lived well, but she could make no decisions or travel outside of Paris without Braustich's approval. Increasingly, Hauptman Berthold would arrive unexpectedly at her offices and speak with Zeigler. The German captain always made it a point to see and greet Nadine during his visits. His manner, while polite, was cold and intense, most certainly designed to intimidate her. There were times when she felt Berthold was disrobing her. She disliked Berthold and considered him ruthless and dangerous. Nadine suspected the Boche captain enjoyed humiliating and hurting people.

While at the opera, accompanied by a visiting Catholic priest, Nadine received news about Allied activities. She was pleased to learn that the combined British, Canadian, and American navies were successful in fending off attacks to their convoys by German U-boats. The news from the East was mixed. The Boche armies penetrated deep into Russia but had been stopped short of Moscow. Moreover, their thrusts to the north and the south had failed to capture Leningrad and Stalingrad. She learned that the

Germans would begin a new offensive against the Soviets as soon as the weather improved. The news from North Africa was disturbing. Rommel's Afrika Corps was inflicting serious defeats on the British and gaining ground. His objective was to capture Tobruk and then press on into Egypt to cut the Suez Canal. However, she learned nothing about what the Americans were doing.

Nadine had several sources of information from different parts of Europe. Through her network of operatives in France and elsewhere, critical bits and pieces of intelligence reached her. She carefully prioritized the information and forwarded it through three channels. One was the network that passed through southern France into Spain and onto Portugal, destined for the Americans. The second was her contacts with Millard and the French Maquis. It was up to them how to deal with the knowledge provided. The third was a one way delivery by Noel to a British agent outside of Paris. The last channel Nadine used only for the most sensitive information that required immediate attention by British Military Intelligence. She was careful to limit Noel's direct contact with a British agent for critical matters only. There were other ways she got messages and information.

From time to time, Nadine hosted nuns traveling on church matters. There was always a sister who carried a message for her. This was how some of Quentin's letters arrived. She also received communiqués in the confessional at her parish church. When a message was being held for her, a young boy, usually one of the altar boys in the church, would come by her home to ask for spare clothing, food, or donations. By a predetermined hand signal, the lad would let her know she needed to go to confession the following day. Once in the confessional, the priest would secretly pass an unmarked envelope to her.

Nadine was followed constantly by the Gestapo. However, she was endangered by a different Boche source. There were German officers who admired and lusted after her. Two German officers, a major and a colonel, tried to force their intentions on Nadine. To counter this, Noel and Millard arranged for her protection. One or two members of the resistance shadowed the Boche surveillance, prepared to intercede immediately if she was accosted. Moreover, when the two German officers tried to intimidate and have their way with Nadine, they suffered "deadly accidents." Noel and Millard gave orders that if the Gestapo agents tried to apprehend the Frenchwoman they should be killed. So far, it had been necessary for the resistance to act against two Nazis only.

It was late February when Nadine received a message from Quentin. She took the letter home and read it carefully. It was in code and not addressed to anyone and was not signed. However, Nadine knew it was from Quentin and quickly deciphered it to learn he was well and that Marlon was well also. The Cajun professed his undying love and a strong desire to see her. She clutched the letter to her lips and said a prayer for him. She allowed herself the luxury of a second reading before burning it.

Nadine cried after burning Quentin's letter. She turned off the small desk lamp and sat quietly while the light from the blaze in the fireplace bathed the room in sepia tones. The lovely Frenchwoman stared into the flickering flames and imagined shootings, bombings, and killing. War was grotesque, and all she could think about was the pain, suffering, and loss of life caused by the fighting. She hated that Marlon was in danger and yearned for the comfort of Quentin's arms. She prayed for a rapid Allied victory. There was a knock on her door and she heard Moira's soft voice ask if there was anything she needed.

"Perhaps some tea," said Nadine, as she opened the door and greeted Moira.

"I'll make some right away," said the younger woman. "Will you take the tea here?"

"Join me for tea in the parlor," said Nadine, as she stood.

Moira smiled and said yes.

During the last week in February, Noel told Nadine about his meeting with a Dutch professor hunted by the Gestapo. In return for helping him escape to Spain and then Portugal, the Dutchman promised to share what he knew about German experiments with "heavy water." Noel had pressed the professor to share more information, but the Dutchman refused.

"The Gestapo want to apprehend this man badly," said Noel.

"How do you know this?" asked Nadine.

Noel mentioned that a spy working within the Gestapo headquarters in France had seen SS documents marked urgent, directing all field officers to find the Dutch professor. Intrigued by what the Dutchman might know, Nadine told Noel to hide the professor until she could make some inquiries about "heavy water."

Nadine contacted Hugh Jordan, a friend and former professor at a top polytechnic institution in France. The Nazis had forced Jordan out of a teaching and research position at a prestigious French polytechnic college when he refused to cooperate with them. Nadine found Jordan a job working as a chemist in a plant making synthetic products. She secretly asked him about "heavy water." Jordan was cautious and asked why she wanted to know. She mentioned hearing that the Germans were experimenting with heavy water. He grew sullen before saying that the process was important in making deuterium oxide. When she asked about deuterium, Jordan gave her a scientific explanation for its use.

"Please," she told Jordan, "I don't understand the technical things you just told me."

"Yes, it is complicated," said Jordan. "Let me try to suggest something that might help you to understand." In the next ten minutes, he told her about several aspects of heavy water research. "One possible reason the Boche may be doing research with heavy water involves nuclear fission.

"If the Boche are experimenting with heavy water and it's related to nuclear research, what would they expect to accomplish?" she asked Jordan.

He thought for a moment before saying, "Perhaps a weapon. But I cannot be certain."

She asked if there was any way for her to determine the possible direction of the Boche heavy water research.

He considered her request and after a few minutes smiled and said, "Can you find out if any members of the Boche *Uranverein* (Uranium Club) are involved in this research?"

She asked why he wanted to know.

"If Erich Schumann, Walther Gulach, Abraham Esau, or Kurt Diebner is involved, I will need to know."   She asked him about the men he'd mentioned. "First, find out if one or more of them is involved. If any one of these names is associated with heavy water experimentation, let me know immediately."

Several weeks later, Nadine again spoke with Jordan and shared that Schumann, Gulach, and Diebner were part of a group of German scientists either interested in or associated with research on heavy water and nuclear fission. Jordan grew serious and told her that Schumann, Gulach, Esau, and Diebner were part of an exclusive club of German physicists like the brilliant Werner Heisenberg working on nuclear energy research.

"They may be trying to develop some kind of explosive device," he told her. "This kind of research is outside of my areas of knowledge. I suggest you ask someone grounded in theoretical physics."

After leaving Jordan, Nadine made a decision to help the Dutch professor in exchange for additional information. When Noel spoke with the Dutchman and mentioned the names of Schumann and Gulach, the professor looked solemnly at the Frenchman and told him they were part of the research. Noel mentioned Uranverein, and the professor shook his head and told the Frenchman about the Germans experimenting with nuclear fission.

"Enough," said Noel. "We will help you escape to Lisbon, but you must share what you know with the Americans there. D'accord?"

The Dutchman nodded.

It was the middle of April 1942 when the Dutch professor was debriefed by U.S. Military Intelligence in Lisbon. He was immediately flown to London.

* * *

A British torpedo boat picked up Marlon and returned him to Malta. A lorry was waiting at the dock. The driver, a corporal, said he would drive him to the RAF airbase. When they arrived at the base, Squadron Leader Danverford greeted them.

"We'll have the doc look at you first," said Danverford. "Then, we'll hear your report."

After being checked out by the flight surgeon, Marlon cleaned up and got something to eat. Afterward, he went to the operations office and made his report. At debriefing he learned that the Mosquito pilot had given his course and approximate flight path to British air-sea rescue. Also, his SOS had been heard on Malta. The air-craft he had seen late the previous afternoon while in the water was an RAF search plane looking for him. They spotted him and verified his approximate position; the next morning, a boat was sent to "collect" him. Marlon learned that one of the Hurricanes had been lost. The pilot of the second plane had ditched close to Tobruk and had been rescued. Marlon was credited with destroying a German fighter.

"Jolly good show, Norvell," said Captain Danverford with a grin. "That's you ninth victory."

When Marlon asked about his next assignment, Danverford smiled and said, "We'll be sending you back to England in a few weeks." Marlon nodded and sat back in his chair to wonder what awaited him in England.

* * *

Quentin and the production people at Supermarine had worked out a system for auxiliary fuel tanks for the IX model of Spitfires, but a few problems remained. The added weight of the two tanks made the plane sluggish, and it buffeted when diving and turning. Moreover, the quick release mechanism was still not reliable. The release device would "stick" and not jettison one or both tanks. There were other problems that confronted the team at Supermarine. On one flight, a partially filled auxiliary tank was released and hit the ground close to a small town. The town's folk were frightened by the incident, thinking the Germans were bombing them. The production people at Supermarine were told that all further tests must be done over lakes. That too posed problems. Finally, when the team thought they had a workable model, it was decided to test the quick release system over the Channel by flying out of an RAF auxiliary field near Southampton.

Quentin and two other Spitfires would conduct the test by flying south along the British coastline. Because their flight might take them within range of enemy fighters, all three Spitfires were armed. There were two layers of broken clouds over the Channel south of Plymouth and a rapidly moving weather front approaching from the west. *It'll be all right,* thought Quentin. *We'll be back before it gets too bad.*

On March 2, 1942, the three planes took off and climbed to eighteen thousand feet. They proceeded south, encountering strong winds that pushed them eastward. When they had been out for almost thirty minutes and preparing to jettison the auxiliary tanks, Quentin spotted three planes flying southward, below them at eight o'clock. He immediately signaled the other two planes by wagging his wings and pointing in the direction of the planes. Quentin looked up and noticed that the sun was on his right and probably preventing the three unidentified planes from spotting his flight. As the two flights closed, Quentin saw that the planes were German. The twin engine plane looked like a Junkers Ju.88 with two Bf 109s flying cover.

Quentin did not hesitate, signaling the other pilots to release their tanks and follow him. Something within him compelled his behavior. He did not fear death. All he wanted was to attack and destroy the Germans. After pulling the release mechanism, he felt the speedy fighter bounce upward when both tanks fell away. He switched off the safety on his guns, rolled up and over to his left, and dove at the flight of German planes from out of the sun. Quentin focused his attention on the trailing Bf 109 and opened up with his guns as he closed the distance between them. By the time the German pilot spotted the diving Spitfires and the stream of tracers ahead of him, it was too late. The German plane flew directly into the bullets fired by the American. The cannon fire shredded the right wing and cockpit of the Messerschmitt, killing the pilot instantly. The lead Bf 109 immediately tried to go after Quentin, but the trailing Spitfires where on him in a flash. Meanwhile, the Ju.88 pilot banked his plane sharply and turned toward the east.

After destroying the trailing fighter and watching it drop in pieces, Quentin did a quick recovery move and gained altitude. He spotted the Ju.88 trying to escape, advanced the throttle on the Spitfire, and quickly closed the distance between them. He saw tracers from the German gunner's machine gun, located on the top and rear of the Ju.88, whiz by him. With little regard for his safety, the Cajun juked the speedy fighter from one side to the other and opened up with his own guns. He missed with the first burst of bullets, but the German pilot made the fatal mistake by trying to turn down and away from the Spitfire. He presented Quentin with an excellent firing angle. With the advantage of height and speed, the Cajun fired several more bursts, the second and third ones knocking away pieces of the starboard engine and wing, and the final burst smashing into the cockpit of the Ju.88. Quentin did a tight loop and rolled for another pass at the Ju.88. He fired one more long burst with his machine guns and cannon into the stricken bomber and saw its right wing erupt in flames and a portion of it fall away. He immediately broke off and searched for the other planes. To the west he saw a trail of smoke and flew toward it. Over the radio, he heard Lieutenant Franks say they had shot down the other German Bf 109.

"OK, let's go home," said Quentin.

On their arrival at the RAF airstrip near Southampton, Lieutenant Franks and Corcoran-Grieves were jubilant. They praised the American for his daring and for shooting down the trailing Bf 109 and then going after and downing the Ju.88.

"I think we should keep this to ourselves," said a modest Quentin, aware that he had been very lucky. Or was he? Something within had impelled him to turn on the Germans. Now in his early forties, he was too old to be a combat fighter pilot. Yet, the opportunity was there, and he never thought about the risk of getting shot down, or killed.

"Sir, I doubt that will be possible," said Franks. "We bloody well have to account for using our guns. Besides, shooting down three Jerries is something to celebrate."

Quentin relented, but worried what might happen if the American military command in England found out about this and his previous sortie over France. *Christ, if they* [U.S. Army] *find out, I'll be in hot water.*

Quentin was praised by the wing commander after both Franks and Corcoran-Grieves reported their encounter with the three German planes.

"Rather a bit along in years to be playing at dogfighting, Colonel," Lieutenant Colonel Sturbreey, the RAF wing commander at the base, said with a serious expression. "Your people will play hell with us when they learn about these activities?"

Quentin forced a smile and shook his head. "We'll have to send this information along to fighter command," said Sturbreey with a thin smile. The RAF colonel wanted the American's behavior known to appropriate personnel at fighter command. It was the only way the Yank might be prevented from doing this sort of thing again and losing his life.

Three days after his return to Supermarine, Quentin received a call from the U.S. Embassy in London. He was ordered to report to London the following day.

"What's up?" asked Quentin, afraid that news of the encounter with the three German planes had reached the army brass.

"I'm not privy to that information, sir," said Major Pranderholt on the other end of the line. Pranderholt inquired about the train Quentin might take and offered to have a car waiting for him. Quentin said he would take a cab.

When Quentin arrived at the U.S. Embassy, he was immediately driven to a small nondescript building guarded by U.S. Army personnel. After showing his AGO identification card, he was escorted to a small room and told to wait. Almost an hour later, a brigadier general and an aide entered the room. Quentin stood and saluted the general, a man he remembered seeing in Washington. The brigadier returned the salute and walked to a small desk and sat down. The Cajun remained standing. The sour expression on the general's face did not bode well.

The brigadier was a tall, thin-lipped man with eyes that did not miss a thing. The aide, a major, handed the general a file folder, which the senior officer opened and skimmed. Quentin remained standing at attention. Finally, the general addressed the Cajun. In a loud and stern voice he said, "Colonel, what the hell do you think you were doing going into combat?" Quentin remained silent. "Somehow, you managed to get yourself on a flight over enemy territory with the RAF and failed to report this to your superiors. In this army, that's a court martial offense," he barked. The Cajun looked straight ahead without saying a word, convinced that he would be court martialed. "And I see that a few days ago you attacked a flight of German planes while on some kind of training mission. Mister, these kinds of unauthorized activities will stop. You're too old to be a fighter pilot. You had your time as a fighter pilot twenty years ago."

Quentin stood at attention, convinced that his days in the U.S. Army were over. *I guess I screwed up,* he thought. *But, what the hell, it was worth it.*

The general continued to berate Quentin for the next few minutes, but the more the general ranted, the more a welling up of emotion and anger built in the Cajun. Finally, when he could no longer hold his tongue, Quentin interrupted the brigadier.

"General," said the Cajun firmly, "I am unaware of your name and the purpose of this meeting."

"What?" shouted the surprised brigadier, while the major tried to hide a smile. "Why you impudent—"

Quentin, still staring at him, spoke in a firm voice, "Military courtesy requires that you state your name, sir."

At this, the general turned red in the face and gave the Cajun a blistering stare. The two men locked eyes, and it was the brigadier who backed down, realizing there was no fear in the other man's eyes. "I'm General Eaker," he said, while returning Quentin's stare.

"General," Quentin spoke up before Eaker could say or do anything, "if you intend to charge me for my conduct, I request military counsel to advise me of my rights."

"Damn you, Norvell," said a blustering Eaker. The brigadier studied the Cajun's face and the hardness in his eyes, and he sensed he was unafraid. Moreover, Eaker realized that shouting at the colonel had not and would not intimidate him. "That won't be necessary," said Eaker. "You're going to Washington. I've orders to put you on the first available flight."

"Begging the general's pardon," said Quentin, "I have my own plane and can leave as soon as you order it."

"What?" exclaimed Eaker, thoroughly surprised by what the Cajun had said. "You've got your own plane?"

Quentin mentioned that the information about the Lockheed plane he had purchased should have been in the dossier in front of the general.

"Don't get smart with me, Colonel," said Eaker in a reprimanding voice. "What the hell did you do before the war?"

"I was an attorney in New York, sir."

"I might have known," said Eaker cynically. He turned to the major and motioned for him to hand the Cajun some documents. "Colonel, you will leave here tomorrow and return to Washington. Your orders are to report to General Smith at the Joint Chiefs of Staff. Is that understood?"

"Understood, General. I'll need a flight crew," said Quentin, continuing to stand at attention.

"Major," said Eaker to his assistant, "see to that."

"Is that all, sir?" said Quentin.

"You're going back to the States, Colonel. If by some miracle you manage to stay in the army, I hope you're put behind a desk." He glared at the Cajun and said, "Dismissed," and saluted. Quentin returned the salute, did a smart about face, and left the room.

After the Cajun left the room, Eaker produced a pipe and put tobacco into it. He turned to the major and said, "That man's absolutely fearless. He may be too old to be a fighter pilot, but he's got guts." Eaker sat back and lit his pipe. He admired Norvell.

When Quentin arrived at his hotel, there was a message from Geoff. After checking his other mail, the Cajun called the English brigadier. It was almost four in the afternoon when he reached Geoff. He was pleasant but eager to learn about the Cajun's exploits. The American mentioned being sent home for "acting without orders from his superiors."

"I see," said Geoff. "Listen, old boy, I'm frightfully sorry we got you into the soup."

"What do you mean?" asked Quentin.

The Englishman replied that he and others in the RAF had asked Quentin to go on the raid into France.

"Yes," replied the American, "but you didn't authorize me to attack the German planes at their aerodrome."

Geoff chuckled and said a good officer knows when to take the initiative. "From what I heard," he told the Cajun, "you did exactly what any other pilot would have done."

Quentin, in a soft voice, said that his superiors would not see it that way.

"Really," said a bemused Geoff. "I'd have thought your people would praise you for shooting down five enemy planes." Quentin thought quickly and realized Geoff knew about his recent encounter with the German planes over the Channel.

"I don't think that will fly with the army brass," said a dejected Quentin.

Geoff chuckled and asked the American about his plans for the evening.

The Cajun replied he had things to do before returning to Washington the next morning.

"Anything I can do to help?" asked a solicitous Geoff.

Quentin thanked him and said no. The two men chatted for a few minutes before they said good-bye.

Geoff called Air Chief Marshal Charles Portal after talking with Quentin. He told Portal about the Cajun and his predicament. Before they ended their conversation, Portal chuckled and said he would call the PM. When Geoff hung up the phone he smiled and whispered, "It's the least I can do for you, old boy."

CHAPTER 15
THE CONSEQUENCES OF WAR

*They were going to look at war, the red animal
—war, the blood-swollen god.*
Stephen Crane, *The Red Badge of Courage*

After training the new pilots, Marlon was given leave and flown to Cairo. As a boy he had visited Egypt with Nadine but looked forward to exploring the land of the Pharaohs on his own. He joined a group of British army officers billeted at a hotel taken over by the military for a tour of the famous pyramids and other antiquities nearby. Even during the winter, the Egyptian sun was bright and warm. Some of the British officers teased Marlon about his sunglasses. But, after a full day out in the bright sun, all of them bought aviator style sunglasses like Marlon's.

During his brief stay in Cairo, the buzz among British military personnel was almost exclusively about the Afrika Corps advances and their brilliant commander, Field Marshal Erwin Rommel. The German general was a master of desert warfare and had managed to play "fox and hounds" with his British adversaries. However, this time the "Desert Fox" (the name the British gave to Rommel) was intent on taking Tobruk and pressing across the North African desert toward Egypt. Marlon listened to the British officer discuss Rommel's strategies and how eventually the English army would defeat him. *Easier said than done,* he thought. What surprised Marlon was the limited commentary by the British about the U.S. role in the war. It was as if America's part was of secondary consequence.

After a few days of sightseeing, Marlon received orders to return to England as soon as transportation could be arranged. He waited for almost a week before told to report to a vessel that was part of a convoy that had recently come through the Suez Canal bound for Portsmouth, England. He boarded a cargo ship and the following day it got under way as part of a small convoy headed west toward the Straits of Gibraltar. He was told the passage would be slow because of possible enemy air attacks.

Three days out of Suez, the small convoy was attacked and Marlon's ship badly damaged by small arms fire and a bomb that seriously damaged the stern. Temporary repairs were made, but the stricken vessel had to stop at the British base at Gibraltar. There, Marlon and the other military passengers were told to wait until other transportation could be provided. Ten days later, Marlon finally boarded another ship headed for England.

* * *

Florence filled her days with coursework at Juilliard and constant practice on the piano. She was highly regarded by her instructors and encouraged to perform as a soloist. At a recital in Boston, Hugo Mandeville, a prominent impresario, noticed her and was impressed by her playing and beauty. He chatted with Florence briefly and learned about her schooling at Juilliard. A few days later, he approached her primary instructor at Juilliard and inquired about Florence. The dean and her academic program director agreed that it would be beneficial for Florence to consider doing a brief tour during the summer of 1942. Mandeville wanted Florence to join a group of classical musicians playing at select sites across the United States.

Most of the proceeds for the performances were given over to support the war effort.

When Mandeville met with Florence and offered his services and mentioned the tour he had in mind for her, she smiled politely and surprised him by making a counteroffer.

"Is there a possibility for me to play in England?"

He was intrigued and said he would have to look into that. Not to be put off, he asked Florence to consider playing at a few U.S. cities while he explored a booking or two in England.

"Hmm," said Mandeville, "it will be a bit expensive to cover your travel costs to England and places like Chicago, Denver, San Francisco, and Los Angeles."

"You needn't worry about my transportation costs," said Florence with a lovely smile. "I can handle my own travel and lodging."

"Really?" said Mandeville pleasantly surprised. "Does that include expenses for a trip to England?"

She gave a charming laugh and said of course. Hugo Mandeville was enthusiastic about signing Florence for a tour during the summer. His curiosity about the beautiful young musician prompted him to contact the dean at Juilliard.

"Don't you know," said the dean while they were having lunch, "she's a wealthy heiress. Her mother was Ione Vandersteel, a gifted cellist. Her family has great wealth." The dean informed Hugo about Ione's tragic death after childbirth and how Quentin Norvell, her father and a wealthy attorney, spared no expense educating Florence and supporting her musical development.

"Marvelous," said Hugo Mandeville. "I will find her a booking or two in England."

In addition to her class work and long hours of practicing the piano, Florence was physically active every day except Sunday. Quentin had hired a personal trainer for Florence; along with swimming and tennis playing, he insisted on muscle development to improve strength. Tall, shapely, and beautiful, Florence was the envy of so many young women and the center of attention by young men from the wealthiest families in New York and New England. With the war, most eligible young men with the highest pedigree were in the military, especially the navy or in staff positions in Washington. However, continuous publicity about Florence as a glamorous debutant, an heiress, and a gifted musician brought the attention and interest of men of all ages. An Ivy League graduate serving as an aide to a prominent U.S. senator said about Florence, "She has charm, talent, beauty, and above all else, a fortune."

But, if Florence was constantly mentioned in the society pages and roundly celebrated for her beauty and musical accomplishments, she was remarkably well grounded and sensible. Courteous and polite to would-be suitors, she kept her distance from men who tried to curry favor with her. She did allow two close friends to escort her to social functions, but there was no steady beau in her life because of her affection for Marlon.

Every week, Florence wrote to Marlon. His letters were infrequent; in them, he apologized, saying the war and his duties prevented him from writing regularly. He mentioned being shot down over the Channel. Her heart skipped a beat until she read that he was well and had not sustained any injuries other than to his pride. In his last letter, Marlon mentioned his tour of duty in the Mediterranean was almost over and a return to England was in the works.

Florence could hardly contain her enthusiasm over the opportunity presented by Hugo Mandeville to visit England and play at a couple of recitals. The prospect of visiting England during the summer and getting together with Marlon was innervating. Her father, now in London, gave her another reason to visit. She was determined to make her way there and be close to Marlon. Deep-seated, compelling emotions within Florence urged proximity with Marlon and the chance to explore the attraction that she believed was mutual. She did not care about conventions and proper conduct that considered an emotional and physical attachment taboo between siblings with different mothers. She knew only the compulsion of her love for Marlon and strengthening the bonds between them. *He must know how much I love him,* she told herself. *One way or another, I'm going to England this summer and be with Marlon.*

* * *

Quentin was delayed in Ireland because of a strong weather system over the North Atlantic. Once the disturbance passed, he flew to Halifax, refueled his plane, and then went directly to Washington and arrived early in the evening. He decided to call Florence the next day and see her after learning the army brass's reaction to his "unauthorized" activities.

A room was reserved for Quentin at the Bachelor Officers Quarters at Fort Myer in Virginia, where he spent a fitful night wondering what awaited him the following day. The best he could hope for was a desk job in Washington. His worst fear was to be forced to leave the army. *Oh, well,* he thought, *I can still do things as a civilian to help the war effort.*

Quentin reported promptly the following morning to General Bedell Smith's office at the Pentagon. He arrived a few minutes early for the 10:00 a.m. meeting and was told to wait. It was almost 10:30 when the secretary ushered the Cajun into Smith's office. Quentin stood at attention and saluted the general who just stared at him with cold annoyance.

Unknown to Quentin, Bedell Smith had received a call from the White House ten minutes before their meeting. After reading the stipulations in the Cajun's dossier and General Eaker's notes, he was prepared to severely reprimand and discipline the colonel. But, instead, he was told to send Norvell to the White House to meet with the president ASAP.

"Colonel," said an ireful Smith, "I don't know whether you're a grandstander or just plain crazy. If it were up to me, you'd be kicked out of the army." Quentin made eye contact with Smith, and his focus never wavered. Smith noticed the other man's cold stare. *God damn this guy,* Bedell Smith thought ruefully. "You're too old to be a fighter pilot," Smith spat hotly, "and you failed to follow orders and then refused to report your activities to your superiors in England. Either of those infractions warrants a court martial." As Smith berated Quentin, he used numerous expletives, but his verbal abuse and haranguing were ineffective on the colonel. Finally, in frustration, Smith bellowed, "Get your ass over to the White House right away, Colonel. The president wants to see you. I hope he kicks you out of the army."

Refusing to reveal any emotion, Quentin saluted General Smith before saying, "Will that be all, sir?"

"God damn it, Norvell," roared Smith as he returned the salute, "just get the hell out of my office." After Quentin left his office, Smith shook his head and thought, *I've seen that look in Norvell's eyes before. Guys like that are fearless and dangerous.*

When Quentin exited the Pentagon, a car was waiting to take him to the White House. He identified himself at the gate and entered the building. A navy lieutenant commander walked him to the Oval Office. Quentin was announced and told to wait. Ten minutes later, a group of men, some in uniform, exited the Oval Office. George

C. Marshall greeted Quentin and together they walked in to meet the president.

In the next twenty minutes, Quentin's world changed dramatically. Instead of being reprimanded, Roosevelt praised him. Churchill had called Roosevelt to speak on Quentin's behalf and asked that he return to England to serve as a liaison with the British Air Ministry.

"Quentin, your exploits in the air are extraordinary," said a smiling Roosevelt as he fitted a fresh cigarette into his holder. "Wouldn't you say so, George?" the president said to General Marshall, who suppressed a smile. Marshall made it a practice not to laugh at the president's attempts at humor. "But," a grinning Roosevelt said as he lit his cigarette, "I can't have one of my generals acting like a teenager."

General, thought Quentin. *What's he talking about?* The surprised look on the Cajun's face evoked a laugh from Roosevelt, who said, "You tell him, George." Marshall mentioned Quentin's promotion to brigadier general had been approved by the Senate. He would return to England as Marshall's aide and accompany him to a critical conference with Churchill and his top aides. The purpose of the conference was to hammer out an agreement over the type and extent of U.S. military operations in England.

"I've asked Stony to be part of the team," said Roosevelt. He went on to emphasize the meeting's importance. "If the outcome is favorable, I might want you to stay in England."

Just before Quentin left the president's office, Roosevelt teased him for being out of uniform and needed to add a star to denote his rank as a brigadier. Quentin grinned and said he would attend to it immediately. After the Cajun left, Roosevelt told Marshall to prepare a commendation for Quentin and recommend an appropriate medal to award. "I don't want to do this right away," said a sly Roosevelt. "Let's wait awhile for the grumblings about his combat 'exploits' to diminish." Roosevelt chuckled, and Marshall nodded but refused to smile.

* * *

Quentin called Florence in New York but learned from Camila that she was at Juilliard. He asked when she was expected home, and the charming Cuban American woman said around four or five in the afternoon.

"Can she be reached at Juilliard?" asked Quentin. Camila said yes and gave him the number at the music school. "When she gets home, let her know I'll be there to take her to dinner." He called Juilliard and left a message for her to expect him at home around five that afternoon. After calling New York, Quentin prepared a flight plan for La Guardia. He contacted the flight crew and met them at National Airport. They lifted off at 1:00 p.m.

At Quentin's Manhattan residence, Florence was surprised and excited to see her father. When she saw the shiny star on his lapel, she squealed in delight and called to Camila and the cook.

"Daddy's a general," said Florence. Quentin waved off the admiration and changed the subject by asking how Florence was doing. He motioned for all of them to go to the living room. He talked about Marlon and then asked about Camila and the cook. They chatted for a while before Quentin said he had a few things to do before taking Florence to dinner and then to see the Vandersteels.

On their way to dinner, Florence wanted to know what would happen to Marlon.

"Do you mean whether he will stay in the RAF or join the U.S. Army?" asked Quentin. Florence nodded. "Well," said Quentin, as they approached the restaurant, "I'll try to get him to join the U.S. Army."

"Good," she replied before inquiring about Nadine. He mentioned getting occasional messages from her. She noticed the pained expression on his face as he talked about Nadine.

Daddy loves her so very much, she thought.

During dinner, they talked about Florence's studies, her music, and other activities. She mentioned the possibility of the recitals in England during the summer. The Cajun was surprised and asked if her Juilliard advisor approved. She beamed and said yes. Quentin warned that the Germans were still bombing London and said he wanted her to be safe.

"I'll be all right, Daddy," she said, reaching across the table to put her hand on his forearm in an affectionate way. Then, she asked how long he would be staying in New York.

"Just long enough to see your grandparents and perhaps have lunch with Kathleen tomorrow. I'm going to drop by the law firm before returning to Washington."

"Will you be stationed in Washington?"

"I don't know yet," said Quentin with a smile. "The army will let me know what they have in mind for me."

The next day Quentin had lunch with Kathleen and learned she was preparing young women to become army nurses. He praised her and asked if there was anything he could do to help. She smiled and touched his face with her hand, the way a parent would caress a loving son.

"No, Quentin, I'm doing just fine. But, I do worry about the boys who will be injured and killed in this war." He noticed the sadness in her voice and the way her eyes misted. "I hope it's over soon," she said before wiping her eyes and blowing her nose.

Later in the day, Quentin visited the offices of Barston, Marwick, Fowler, and Peterson. He was greeted warmly by the staff and met with the senior partners. Quentin informed them about some opportunities that he would steer in the firm's direction and asked that someone follow up with him on these matters. A senior partner was identified to work with Quentin.

As he was preparing to leave the firm, he inquired about Sarah and was told about her reassignment to one of the junior partners. He walked to the office where she was working. The moment she saw him, she jumped to her feet and embraced him. He was momentarily surprised by her behavior, but he smiled as he held her hands and asked how she was. They chatted for a moment. He asked about her parents and relatives, especially the ones who had escaped from Poland. She told him they were all well. Just before Quentin was about to leave, she gently took hold of his sleeve.

"I know this is asking a lot," she said, "but is there a way I could work with you?"

"Do you mean working for the U.S. Army?" She nodded. "What about your job here?" She hunched her shoulders and remained silent, but her eyes betrayed her. Quentin knew immediately that she was not happy at the law firm.

"Tell you what," he said, holding her right hand with both of his in a friendly way, "I'll talk with people in Washington and see what I can do." He could tell she wanted to express her gratitude and embrace him again, so he smiled, stepped back, and reached for his satchel and coat.

Sarah's large brown eyes focused on the Cajun. In them, he saw admiration, friendship, and uncompromising loyalty. He'd try to find something for her in the army if at all possible.

* * *

"Moira," Nadine whispered to her companion, "I have a mission for you." They were working together in the greenhouse and away from the prying eyes and ears of the Gestapo.

"Yes," said the attractive Scottish woman. In the next few minutes, Nadine mentioned a message she had received from the resistance. It involved the construction of a new chemical plant to supply critical compounds for the manufacture of synthetic petroleum and rubber products in Germany. The information pinpointed the exact location of the plant adjacent to the town of Bielefeld on the North Rhine.

"This plant will become an important strategic target for the Allies," said Nadine in a hushed voice. "Contact Millard and set up a drop for one of our couriers. It's imperative that the British get this information as soon as possible."

Moira nodded and said she would arrange the drop and pickup.

"One more thing," said Nadine as she finished trimming an orchid, "we will have a visitor in a few days. Bishop Valderano will be in Paris for a meeting with the Boche."

Moira nodded. She knew that the bishop, a member of the Vatican diplomatic arm, often visited Spain, France, Portugal, and Belgium. Whenever he was in Paris, the bishop would stay a few days and meet with Madame Desnoyers.

Two days later, Bishop Valderano arrived and met with Nadine. They agreed to attend the opera. Nadine had a box at the opera, and the bishop enjoyed the standing invitation to accompany her. She also had a box at the ballet. However, the Boche officials in Paris had taken over the boxes for the use of senior Nazi officials and Wehrmacht officers. Nadine could petition to use one of them. When she mentioned needing the box so that Bishop Valderano from the Vatican could attend a performance, the Nazis were accommodating. She knew the Nazis wanted to maintain good relations with the Vatican.

When Nadine picked up the bishop at his residence in Paris, he greeted her with his usual warmth. Luis Valderano was a strikingly handsome man. He was taller and thinner than his older brother Ruben. A Jesuit, he had served in various capacities before the Vatican recruited him for its diplomatic arm. Ruben had donated considerable sums of money to the Vatican that helped Louis move up in the Catholic Church hierarchy. Luis Valderano had traveled extensively on important diplomatic missions and was highly regarded by his peers and superiors. He gave the impression of strict neutrality on political matters, but, secretly, he helped Ruben secure confidential information about the counterintelligence activities of the Germans and Italians. And, when possible, he brought Nadine messages from Quentin.

They enjoyed the opera that evening, even though they had to sit next to two Boche generals and their escorts. After the performance, Nadine drove the bishop to his residence.

"Will you come in for a moment?" asked the bishop. "They are doing some renovations to the chapel that you might find of interest."

She agreed and told the driver to wait.

Once inside the residence of the Catholic Church and away from prying eyes, Luis handed Nadine a letter from Quentin. "He's well," said Luis, "as is your son."

Nadine kissed the bishop's hand, and he could feel the moisture of her tears.

"There, there," he said in a gentle voice to comfort her, "we should trust in our lord. He will protect Quentin and Marlon."

Nadine thanked him profusely. He was kind and modest, and his manner always soothed her.

"I saw your daughter when I was in Lisbon recently," he told her. "She and Armand are well. They send their love."

"Have you seen Desirée?" she asked. He nodded and mentioned visiting Switzerland and having dinner with her younger sister and her husband. It was moments like these that sustained Nadine. Any bits of information about her family and her lover were precious.

"Will you see Quentin?" she asked expectantly.

"No, not now that he is in the army," said the bishop. "But, I'm certain he will find a way to send you messages." They talked for a few minutes before Nadine left with Quentin's letter safely in her purse.

That evening, Nadine read the coded, unaddressed, and unsigned letter from her lover. She thanked heaven for what he shared about Marlon and himself. Nadine destroyed it after a second reading. If the Gestapo found a coded communication in her possession she would be arrested and probably tortured.

In the days and weeks that passed, a trickle of downed RAF pilots and crew members slowly worked their way through the Eglantine escape route into Spain and then to Portugal. Most of the RAF personnel were shot down in Northern France or the Netherlands. Air crews shot down over Germany seldom made it into France. Occasionally, an Allied pilot might escape from Germany and manage to contact the Maquis, but it was rare. Nadine always worried about these situations. She told Millard and her contacts in the resistance to be very cautious about any Allied flyers who claimed to have made their way out of Allemagne.

"We risk a Boche infiltrator discovering our network," she told Millard. "A Boche spy disguised as an Allied flyer working his way through our network into Spain and then Portugal would be disastrous. We must protect our people along the escape route. The Gestapo are resourceful and relentless," she stressed. Nadine told Millard that if anyone within their network made a mistake, the person would most certainly be apprehended by the Gestapo. He knew Madame was correct and carried her warning back to his contacts in the resistance.

* * *

It was the beginning of the second week in March when Quentin joined General Marshall, Harry Hopkins, Cordell Hull, Brook Hamilton Stoner, and Ruben Valderano to plan for the conference with Winston Churchill and his aides in London. Marshall wanted American forces to use England as a staging ground for an invasion of France in 1943. And, he wanted American bombers to be based in England and begin an aerial campaign to destroy key German military targets and industrial sites on the Continent. Ruben mentioned that an invasion of France in 1943 might be premature. However, he agreed with Quentin and Marshall that American bombers be sent to England and begin bombing critical German targets. They discussed the war plans and recommendations submitted by the army and air force staff before Marshall asked Ruben to mention plans for the Pacific Theater of Operations.

Ruben outlined the role the navy and marines were assigned as the spearhead for activities in the South Pacific. Supply lines and communications from the United States to Australia had to be protected. Ruben mentioned that Admiral Nimitz was the choice of the Joint Chiefs of Staff as overall commander. He mentioned several strategic targets in the South Pacific, such as The Gilbert, Marshall and Solomon Islands, and New Guinea. One name Ruben emphasized was Guadalcanal.

Sounds like something big is going to happen there, thought the Cajun.

The group worked until almost noon. As they were leaving, General Marshall asked Quentin if he could leave for London the next day.

"I have some things for you to carry to our embassy personnel," he told the Cajun. "Stony, can you arrange your schedule to leave with Quentin?" asked Marshall. Stoner said he could. The next day, Quentin and Stoner departed for England.

* * *

The March 1942 meeting in London between General George C. Marshall and Winston Churchill was a test of wills between a seasoned military leader and a master politician. As he listened to the conflicting positions proposed by Churchill and Marshall, Quentin realized that any plans for an invasion of the Continent in 1942 were premature. Even one in 1943 appeared unrealistic. Marshall wanted to attack the Germans in a place that would provide the most direct route into Nazi Germany and victory for the Allies. However, Churchill eventually prevailed and got Marshall to commit American troops to help the British in North Africa. In return, Marshall demanded a key concession, the establishment of American air bases in England from which American bombers could attack targets on the Continent.

After the meeting, the American delegation met in the U.S. Embassy to consider strategic and logistical matters.

"Quentin, I want you to remain in London and develop a team to identify air bases for our bombers. I'll contact Hap Arnold and his people about this. You'll need to ask the RAF and the air ministry for assistance. I know you have friends in both places. Work out a plan I can present to the president."

"How soon will you need the plan?" asked the Cajun.

"The sooner the better," replied Marshall.

"Just two things," said Quentin. "My son is a fighter pilot in the RAF. I'd like him brought over to the Army Air Force and promoted to captain." When Marshall asked the Cajun to elaborate, Quentin mentioned that Marlon was an excellent fighter pilot with nine enemy planes destroyed and experience as a flying instructor. "He's also a graduate of MIT and a terrific engineer," he added. Marshall nodded and said he would speak to Hap Arnold and have Marlon transferred to the U.S. Air Force.

"Once he's part of our air force, what do you have in mind for him?" asked Marshall. They talked for a few minutes about Marlon before Marshall nodded and said he approved of Quentin's plans.

"You mentioned two things," said Marshall. "What's the other one?"

"I'd like to find a job for my former secretary in the army. Can you help with that?" Marshall asked about his secretary and was pleased by what Quentin told him.

"We may not be able to pay her what she's making now," said Marshall. "But, if she's as good as you say, we can certainly use her. Have her call me at this number," he said, writing a private number on the back of his card and handing it to the Cajun.

"Once you meet her, you won't be sorry," said Quentin.

* * *

Quentin's next few weeks in England were filled with long days and nights coordinating activities between the U.S. Army Air Force, the RAF, and the British Air Ministry. Sites for American bases in England were needed. Initial elements of the U.S. Air Force would be strategic heavy bombers (B-17 Flying Fortresses). Once suitable air base sites in England were selected, Quentin as part of the top echelon planning group would also oversee the construction of the required facilities. Heavy bombers with full tanks of fuel and large bomb loads required all weather landing strips made of concrete. Constructing secure and self-contained air bases would take time.

The VIII Bomber Command established on January 19, 1942, at Langley Field, Virginia, was reassigned to Savannah Army Airbase, Georgia, in February 1942. Major General Carl A. Spaatz was in command. The first U.S. bomber groups were delayed in departing for England. Quentin learned that serious logistical problems had to be overcome before any American heavy bombers were ready for combat. B-17 Flying Fortresses were in short supply, especially ones fitted with the modifications that Quentin had recommended. Moreover, air crew training needed to be improved. Quentin's duties in England prevented him from exercising any direct influence on pilot and crew training for heavy bombers. However, with Marlon's assistance, it might be possible to enhance and speed up the instructional process. Quentin also wanted Marlon, because of his combat experience, to critique the American fighter pilot training program. *I just hope Marlon sees how important working on these projects will be,* he worried. Early in April, a miffed Marlon met with Quentin at High Wycombe, England (RAF Bomber Command Headquarters), where advanced elements of the U.S. Air Force were temporarily housed. Marlon noticed that his father was a brigadier general.

"Well, I guess congratulations are in order," said the younger pilot dryly. Quentin, aware Marlon was upset, embraced his son, motioned for him to be seated, and asked, "Would you like something to drink?" Marlon shook his head.

"Before you start on me for the transfer to the U.S. Air Force, hear me out. If you don't like what I tell you, then you'll have a choice," said the Cajun. In the next few minutes, Quentin explained Marlon's responsibilities. After a long pause, the younger man spoke up irately.

"I'm a fighter pilot. I belong in the air, not behind a desk or flying between training bases in the States."

"You'll get to do your share of combat flying," said the Cajun, "and perhaps command your own fighter squadron if that's what you want. But, for the next few months, there's a critical job that needs to be done. Think of it as preparing the pilots who will fly with you to knock out the Luftwaffe."

Marlon was silent, digesting his father's comments.

"One other thing," said the Cajun. "I'll need you to help develop new fighters."

After considering what he had been told, Marlon asked, "Is there more?"

"Yes," said Quentin with a smile, "you'll be promoted to captain, and then to major by the end of this year."

"You can do that?" asked an incredulous Marlon. The Cajun nodded and smiled in a way that convinced Marlon his father had the confidence and support of top brass in the U.S. Army and perhaps beyond.

"All right, you win," said Marlon with a sense of resignation.

In the weeks and months that followed, Marlon operated out of Washington and visited every fighter pilot training base in the United States. Marlon, along with a handful of fighter pilots who had miraculously escaped from the Philippines, pilots from the Flying Tigers in China and the Eagle Squadrons, were a critical core of combat flyers. Their experience and knowledge about dogfighting needed to mesh with the training and preparation for new air force recruits. After visiting several training bases and talking with a few of the experienced combat pilots, Marlon realized the value of his father's planning. *I've got to give Dad credit,* thought Marlon grudgingly. *Without the things I've learned in combat about dogfighting, many of these recruits wouldn't survive their first encounter against an experienced German pilot.* Marlon's other responsibility involved monitoring the development of new U.S. fighters like the P-47. He had little time for leisure activities. Try as they might, Marlon and Florence saw each other only twice between February and July of 1942. Their encounters were brief. Florence had a full schedule as she prepared for the summer 1942 tour and possible visit to England in August of that year.

* * *

April, May, and June 1942 passed quickly. Quentin and other American military personnel in London were buoyed by the news of Lieutenant Colonel Doolittle's raid on Tokyo on April 19. Although the attack was considered reckless by many top military personnel, it was a daring strike at Japan and helped to bolster American morale. Even more significant was the American defeat of the Imperial Japanese navy invasion force near Midway on June 4, 1942. U.S. Navy cryptographers had broken the Japanese Naval Code and had advanced knowledge of the enemy strike on Midway. The Battle of Midway pitted three American carriers against four large Japanese carriers. Outnumbered in the air (272 Japanese bombers and fighters vs. 180 American planes), U.S. Navy pilots destroyed all four of the mainline Japanese carriers. Although the carrier Yorktown was lost, Royal Navy personnel in London said the American victory at Midway was a critical turning point in the war in the Pacific. Later, in Washington, when Quentin talked with Ruben and George C. Marshall about the Battle of Midway, they said the Japanese expansion in the Pacific had been stopped and in a few months the Allies would go on the offensive.

Events in Europe and North Africa, however, were still going in favor of the Germans. Tobruk surrendered to Rommel on June 21, 1942. Meanwhile, the Luftwaffe was pounding Malta with air strikes from Sicily and had sunk a Royal Navy aircraft carrier, two cruisers, and eleven merchant ships. To the Americans gaining advantage in the Pacific, it seemed the British now more than ever needed help.

When General Marshall, Admiral King, Quentin, and other U.S. military staff met with Churchill and his key people in London during the summer of 1942, the Cajun could see and feel the intransigence between Marshall and the Churchill. The general was like a stone statue, refusing to show any emotion or reaction to Churchill's comments. The stoic, leather faced Admiral King seemed impenetrable to Churchill. No matter what the charismatic PM tried, Marshall and King held fast to their perspectives. Only when Churchill explained emphatically the dangers posed by a German victory in North Africa did the Americans decide to caucus before continuing the meeting.

When the Americans met in private, Quentin spoke up. "The Brits are in a bad way in Malta and North Africa. They need help."

A somber Marshall nodded and said, "Yes, we might be able to send them some of our new Sherman tanks and additional supplies." He looked at Admiral King.

The admiral nodded and said, "Just get the tanks and supplies for the English to New York, and we'll put together a convoy."

They talked for a few more minutes before Quentin asked about plans for an invasion of France. Marshall, stressing an attack against the Germans in Europe was a top priority, said, "Stalin's calling the president regularly. He wants us to open a second front as soon as possible."

"Can we?" asked the Cajun.

King looked away as Marshall considered the question quietly before responding. "Well," an irritable Marshall finally replied, "that'll depend on how serious the situation in North Africa really is. Our British friends have to be honest with us."

They agreed that a change in American plans and timetables would depend on what Churchill told them.

After returning to the meeting and hearing from the British, the Americans nodded silently in agreement. The British desperately needed help in North Africa.

An invasion of Europe isn't in the cards until the Germans are kicked out of North Africa, thought Quentin.

After considerable wrangling, the meeting ended. An annoyed Marshall told Admiral King and Quentin that the United States would have to delay its invasion plans for Europe until the "mess in North Africa" was cleaned up.

"Quentin," said Marshall, before turning to leave, "let's have dinner tonight. I need to share a few things with you."

That evening, Quentin joined General Marshall and General Eaker for dinner. Eaker grudgingly congratulated the Cajun on his promotion. During dinner, Marshall shared the immediate key objectives for the air force in England. The completion of all weather airfields for American heavy bombers was critical. The president had promised Churchill that American bombers would begin arriving in England during the summer of 1942. He asked Quentin about the construction of the air bases.

"Two are operational and the rest are almost done," Quentin told him and Eaker. "We've located the Ninety-seventh Bombardment group at RAF Polebrook," he told them. U.S. Air Force ground personnel had arrived at Polebrook, England, on June 9, 1942. "We've located the Fifteenth Bombardment Squadron (Light) at RAF Molesworth. They're equipped with British Boston III twin engine bombers."

"How soon before they're ready to go?" asked Marshall.

Eaker replied that it would take a few weeks of familiarization training before they could go into combat and said that Hap Arnold wanted to bomb a German target on the Fourth of July. Marshall nodded and pursed his lips before saying, "Good. Quentin, do what's necessary to make that happen." Quentin nodded and smiled.

"When are our heavy bombers arriving?" asked the Cajun.

Eaker said the planes would be in England in a few weeks and ready for combat at the end of July. The three men talked about logistical matters including Quentin's recommendation that VIII Air Support Command and VIII Fighter Command move their headquarters to Bushy Park. Marshall looked at Eaker who nodded in agreement.

Turning toward Quentin, Marshall said, "Quentin, I know you've been working day and night seven days a week to get things done over here. I've also heard about your hedge hopping in a small plane all over the English countryside. Why can't you drive instead of fly?" he asked.

"It's faster to fly between construction sites. Besides," said the Cajun, "the RAF loaned me a Westland Lysander Mk. I. It's a safe and maneuverable little plane and can land almost anywhere."

"General," said Marshall, looking intently at the Cajun, "I don't want you taking any unnecessary risks."

Eaker, with a tight smile, watched the exchange between Marshall and Quentin. *Good luck,* he almost said aloud.

"I want you to take a week off," insisted Marshall. "That's an order, General."

The Cajun smiled and said he would comply as soon as construction on the critical heavy bomber airfields was completed. The Fifteenth Bomb Squadron joined six RAF crews from RAF Swanton Morley for a low-level attack on Luftwaffe airfields in the Netherlands on July 4, 1942. The next day, Quentin left for London. It was his first liberty since late February.

Before they parted, Marshall told the Cajun that he had interviewed Sarah and was very impressed by her.

"You didn't tell me how attractive she is," said Marshall, "and that she can read, write, and speak German. We'll find a place for her," he said with a tight smile. Sarah was recruited by U.S. Military Intelligence and worked for the Office of Strategic Services (OSS) in New York City, and later in London.

* * *

"Geoff," said a tired Quentin after recently arriving in London. "I've got five days of leave. I'd like to take in a show tomorrow. Can you recommend a good musical?"

"Back from the wars, are you?" teased Geoff before greeting Quentin and asking how he was. After chatting with the American for a few minutes, he mentioned two popular musicals. "You can always catch Glinda Pennington in her new show," added the Englishman. "I hear it's quite lively."

"I'll call her and maybe take in her show in a few days."

There was a slight pause before Geoff spoke up. "By the way, I'm going to a recital on Sunday. It's a benefit. Classical music; you interested?"

"Where is it?" asked Quentin.

"In Buckinghamshire, not far from High Wycombe," Geoff told him. "We could drive there together…maybe have a late breakfast. You up for that?" Quentin thought for a moment before agreeing.

"Jolly good," said the Englishman. "I'll collect you around ten-thirty on Sunday morning at your hotel."

When Geoff's car arrived, Quentin was surprised. Seated in the back of the large sedan was Major General Ambrose Middleton, an old friend and next to him an attractive woman.

"Quentin, how nice to see you again," said Middleton now in his late fifties. "This is my wife Ardys."

The Cajun smiled and nodded at her. She appeared to be in her fifties. They chatted as the large sedan made its way westward through the English countryside.

Almost an hour later, they arrived in front of a large hall next to an imposing church. "Well, we're here," said Geoff. They stepped out of the car and walked into the foyer of the building and were greeted by several women conservatively attired. Prominent among them was Linne. She beamed at the sight of Quentin and extended her hand to him.

"Welcome," said Linne. She greeted Ardys with a kiss on her cheek and then extended her hand to the two generals. "May we take your hats and coats?" she asked. The Cajun smiled, removed his trench coat and cap, and handed them to a young girl of perhaps fifteen or sixteen wearing a school uniform.

"I see you're a brigadier," commented Linne with a smile. "Congratulations." Quentin grinned but remained silent. "Claire, be a dear and show General Hawkins, General Middleton, and his wife to their seats," she told another teenager with large blue eyes and hair the color of corn silk. "You come with me," she told the American. Linne took Quentin to the front row and told him they would sit together. "First, I have a few things to do," she told him. "Be a dear and entertain yourself until I return."

After Linne left, he introduced himself to the people to his right and then to his left, older couples dressed fashionably but conservatively. Just before the program started, Linne returned. She whispered that the recital was a benefit to raise money for children evacuated from London to the country to avoid the bombings. During the intermission, Linne took Quentin to where refreshments were served. Again, she left him with Geoff and Middleton.

"Quite a woman," said Middleton, nodding his head in Linne's direction.

"Yes, she's extraordinary," added Geoff with a smile. "I daresay there are several men in this room eager to be in your shoes, Quentin."

The Cajun nodded as he sipped his punch.

After the recital, Linne invited Quentin, Geoff, Middleton, and Ardys to join her for tea in an adjacent parlor used for small receptions by the local bishop. There, she introduced Quentin to several people, most of them aristocrats, the bishop, and his assistant. Between conversations with various people, Linne found time to speak with the Cajun, and put two important questions to the American.

"How long will you be in England?"

"Through the end of the year, maybe longer," he replied.

"Will you continue to be a stranger and force me to call you?" she stressed while looking at him with her lovely blue eyes.

He took a sip of tea, and, over the rim of the delicate china, grinned before responding. "I'll be in London often. I still have your card and number and promise to call when my schedule is open," he replied.

"Promise!" she insisted. He nodded.

That evening, Quentin's thoughts moved between Nadine and Linne. There was no question about his love for the Frenchwoman. He was emotionally and passionately involved with Nadine and missed her terribly. Linne, on the other hand, provided a fresh and intriguing distraction. If he could not be with Nadine, perhaps getting to know Linne better would help combat loneliness in his life. It occurred to him that the young Englishwoman might want more than he was willing to give. He considered the challenge and resolved to keep Linne as a close friend and their relationship platonic.

CHAPTER 16
THE SHARPENING OF SWORDS

The sword is the axis of the world,
and grandeur is indivisible.
Charles André Joseph Marie de Gaulle,
Le Fil de l'Epée [1934]

In the weeks and months that followed, Quentin immersed himself in staff work to prepare for the arrival of bomber groups to the new air bases in England. General Marshall assigned him to strengthen ties between the U.S. Air force, the RAF and British Air Ministry. And, because of his friendship with Etienne de Gavrelac and other French air staff, Marshall appointed him a liaison officer to the Free French. When they met for lunch one day, Etienne teased the Cajun by saying that he was either a glorified intermediary or some kind of spy. Quentin laughed and said perhaps he was both.

During the summer of 1942, Marlon spent most of his time in the United States. However, at the beginning of August, Quentin recalled him to England.

"What's up?" asked the younger pilot when he met with his father.

"The Brits are going to attack a German port in Northern France. I can't tell you any more at the moment. The RAF wants to commit a large force of fighters to this battle. All three Eagle Squadrons will be involved. I want you to fly with them."

Marlon was surprised and speechless as he listened to his father. He wanted to get back into the war; now was his chance.

"I'll need to—"

"Hold your questions. I've already told you more than I should have. My main concern is to get you into a new Spitfire IX. Supermarine has improved its performance and firepower. I'll make arrangements for you to test fly the IX Spit in a few days and then do some gunnery practice with it," he told the younger pilot.

"What'll I do in the meantime?"

"You're going to read the flight manuals for the IX and do some ground school work. In six days, you're going to get cleaned up and join me at your sister's recital in London."

Marlon's jaw dropped open, and he looked genuinely surprised. "Funny Face, here in London, playing the piano?"

Quentin nodded and smiled. "She's doing two performances. We'll go to the first one. She's excited about playing here and wants to spend some time with us," said the Cajun.

"When's she coming?"

Quentin said in a few days. "Do you want to stay at my place?" asked Quentin, "or will you make other arrangements?"

"I'll manage," said a smiling Marlon. "Got time for dinner?" Quentin nodded and said he'd get them a reservation at a place he knew.

* * *

Florence visited England as part of the musical tour prepared by Hugo Mandeville. She was among the small group of musicians that had played at several places in the United States and Canada. The positive reviews about her playing and as a new talent on the piano spread quickly. Mandeville decided to feature Florence as a soloist during the London concert.

Florence arrived aboard Quentin's plane during the first full week of August. Quentin insisted that she stay at his London residence. He had leased a large and well-appointed flat in a fashionable part of London. It was near the underground. As a general, Quentin was assigned a staff car and driver, Lucinda Hollingsworth, a pert and charming uniformed Englishwoman. Lucinda quickly realized that Quentin was a special person and became very fond of him.

The night of her London recital, Florence dressed in a lovely black gown with sequins and gray accents that contrasted beautifully with her blonde hair and tanned skin. She was absolutely stunning. She had requested an Erard piano and began by playing Benjamin Dale's *Piano Sonata*. Her second selection was Chopin's *Nocturne #3*. For an encore, she did *The Millstream* by Sir William S. Bennett. Florence played flawlessly and with panache to an audience enthralled by her beauty and virtuosity on the piano. The British audience appreciated that the gorgeous American pianist played two selections written by English composers. She easily became the darling of the program.

Quentin had asked Linne to accompany him. She was impressed by Florence's playing and by her beauty.

"Your daughter is lovely and plays splendidly," she told him, squeezing his arm gently as an expression of appreciation. He smiled to acknowledge her compliment.

Marlon, meanwhile, escorted Erleen to the recital. After each piece that Florence played, Marlon stood, clapped enthusiastically, and shouted, "Bravo." His enthusiasm for his sister's playing encouraged others around him to join in praising the young pianist's artistry.

Linne scheduled a reception for Florence after the recital and invited several people and a few influential music critics. She introduced the lovely pianist and asked those gathered to join her in applauding "a fresh, new talent." Florence glowed at the attention and appreciation she received. But, when she saw Erleen on Marlon's arm, coolness overcame her. Quentin noticed the subtle change. Marlon continued to praise Florence and complimented her effusively. However, her smile seemed contrived and her rigid body language signaled displeasure. Quentin waited until he could speak privately to her and, in a soft voice, asked if anything was wrong. Florence forced a smile and said she was tired and needed to relax, but the Cajun noticed that she glanced constantly in her brother's direction. *Now what's this all about?* he puzzled. It was the first of several observations the Cajun mulled over about his son and daughter.

After the reception, Linne invited a few people to join her and Quentin for supper at a private club. Three of the critics joined them, along with Marlon, Erleen, General Hawkins and his escort, General Middleton and Ardys, and a few close friends. They stayed until almost eleven that evening.

As they were leaving, Marlon kissed Florence on the cheek and hugged her. He said he would see her the next day. Disappointed, she joined Quentin in Linne's car and sat back in the soft leather seat and closed her eyes. It seemed to Quentin that Florence drifted into a semiconscious state.

"Are you all right?" he asked, his voice revealing concern.

"I'm fine. I just thought Marlon would be with us," she replied softly.

"He'll be here tomorrow, and the two of you can spend the entire day together."

She looked at Quentin with a puzzled expression and asked if he was not going to be with them.

"Honey, I'm sorry, but I'll be at a meeting tomorrow that will probably go until the afternoon. Perhaps the three of us can have dinner tomorrow night," he offered "and get together with Glinda Pennington."

She nodded without saying anything.

The next day, Quentin left early for his meeting. It was almost nine in the morning when Marlon arrived. Thomas, Quentin's valet, greeted the young pilot and said that "Miss Florence" was in the living room. When he entered the room, she greeted him icily, and he realized immediately that she was upset. He smiled and asked, "What's up, Sis?"

"Nothing," the lovely blonde replied tersely while looking away from her brother.

"You sound annoyed," he probed.

"Well, how observant!" she replied, her voice sharp and cynical.

"What's upset you?" he pressed.

"How kind of you to ask," she shot back.

Wow, she's really angry, he thought. "All right," he said firmly. "If you don't tell me what's wrong, perhaps I should leave you alone."

She replied angrily, "Go ahead. I'm sure your English girlfriend will be glad to see you again!"

"Flo, what's the matter with you?" he asked, trying to understand her annoyance. "Did Erleen say something to annoy you?"

She crossed her arms, turned away from him, and stood silently, glaring into space.

He approached Florence to embrace her from behind. Once she felt his arms begin to wrap around her she stiffened and pushed away his arms angrily, the hostility of her move surprising him. *She's never been like this before,* he thought as he stepped back.

"This isn't getting us anywhere," he said, turning and walking toward the entryway. "Call me when you really want to see me," he told her as he walked away.

Florence stood quietly, her anger slowly draining away only to be replaced by the mounting realization that her brother, whom she loved, had left and would probably not return. A panic seized her, and she bolted for the door, but Marlon was nowhere in sight. She ran down the stairs and out of the flat in a desperate race to catch him. On exiting the building, she looked both ways on the street until she saw Marlon, a solitary figure walking dejectedly in the light mist.

"Marlon, Marlon," she cried out to him at the top of her lungs, running toward him unperturbed by the mist that was falling and beginning to dampen her light cardigan sweater. "Wait, please wait!" He turned and watched her approach at a run until she collided with him and buried her head into his shoulder. He gently lifted her face and saw tears in her eyes. "I'm sorry. I'm sorry. I love you so," she said between sobs.

Marlon kissed her softly on the lips, took off his trench coat, and put it around her shoulders. Together, they walked back to the flat.

They hardly spoke, even when Marlon brought a towel and dried her face and dabbed at the moisture on her sweater. She was so beautiful. His eyes drank in the lovely contours of her face, the radiance in her eyes, and the exquisite golden hair so full and silky.

"Sis, you're gorgeous." His voice was melodic, and the words emanating not from the mind but the heart.

Florence smiled, her lovely lips parting slightly to reveal perfect teeth. He returned the smile and touched her face affectionately. Gradually, she calmed down. Slowly, he teased out of her why she had been so angry. She confessed a jealousy for any woman who stood between them.

"Sis," he told her softly, "there's no one like you."

"But do you love me, Marlon?" she asked insistently, her eyes searching his.

"Of course I do," he replied. "You're my beautiful and talented Sis."

"No, do you love me in a romantic way?" The question did not surprise him. He rather expected it. Marlon took a moment to formulate a response that was so critical for them.

"Yes, Sis, I love you in a way that frightens me. I can't act on what I feel."

She was in a maelstrom of emotions and wild thoughts, a terrible yearning within her feeding a passionate turbulence threatening to erupt at any moment.

He held her tightly at arm's length, afraid that if they came closer he would lose control. "I'm afraid of my feelings toward you," he confessed, as she hung on his every word. "It's against everything we've been taught and told. I mustn't have these thoughts. It's...it's not right!" he confessed with resignation.

She immediately spoke up. "Marlon, I don't know how or why, but I love you and want to be with you."

"Flo, please don't say any more. This thing between us, it can't be," he said, turning away from her.

"How can I deny what's in my heart, Marlon?" she demanded emphatically. "I can't bear the thought of you being with anyone else."

"This is insane," he whispered.

"Marlon, don't you think I've thought about what this means for both of us? I've tried so hard to understand my feelings for you and to make sense of what it means. Don't ask me to try to wish them away."

He was silent for the longest time, looking intently at his beautiful sister with conflicting emotions and thoughts in his heart and mind. Finally, he said one of them had to be strong and resolve to do the "right thing."

"You mean put aside our feelings toward each other?" she asked. He nodded. She embraced him, and they stood that way for the longest time.

"Let's go for a walk," he told her. She nodded, and the two of them went out together and visited different places in London. They held hands and talked occasionally. It was almost six in the evening when they returned to the flat where Quentin was waiting.

"You two look so solemn," he said jokingly. "Are you hungry?" They both nodded.

During their meal and afterward, Quentin sensed the undercurrent of emotions in Florence and Marlon. Their behavior alerted him, and he decided to ask about it.

"Something bothering you two?"

Florence shook her head and remained silent.

Marlon, however, forced a smile and said the war and the uncertainty in their lives made it difficult to be upbeat and live a normal life.

The Cajun nodded, giving the impression that he accepted Marlon's explanation for their solemn behavior. However, he could not put aside his suspicion that something was going on between his two children.

After dinner, they drove Marlon to the train station. He had to be at a forward air base that evening. As he hugged Florence, she kissed him on the cheek and whispered something that Quentin could not hear. Marlon smiled and looked at her fondly. The interchange between his children kindled the memory of a special moment long ago. Quentin recalled a scene at the cemetery on Long Island where Ione was buried next to her sister. Marlon had just moved to New York from France after learning Quentin was his real father. It was the first time he had taken Florence and Marlon to the grave site together. He saw Florence as a little girl gently reach out and take hold of her older half brother's hand. From that moment on, a strong bond developed between his two children. Now, that bond was stronger and the behavior of his children puzzled him. *I'll talk to Florence tonight,* thought the Cajun. However, when they returned to his flat, Florence said she was exhausted and excused herself. The next morning, Quentin drove her to the train station where she met Mandeville and the other members of the American musical group touring in England.

Before Florence joined the others, Quentin took his daughter aside and said, "I know something's bothering you, honey. I can see if affecting you and Marlon. I hope the next time we're together we can talk about it."

She forced a smile, hugged him and looked up into his eyes. *Does he know,* she wondered?

He kissed her on the forehead and watched as she boarded the train. *Something's going on with her and Marlon,* he told himself, aware of the strong emotional attachment between his children.

* * *

At the beginning of August, Noel informed Nadine of a message he had received from the French Maquis in the Seine-Maritime Province. Noel informed her that Bouveilles, a man from Envermeu, a town close to Dieppe, had shared important information.

"What is it?" she asked when they met in the cellar, away from the Gestapo's prying ears.

"The Boche are conducting military exercises along the coast near Dieppe."

"What kind?" she asked. He mentioned mortar and artillery fire on targets on or near the beaches near Dieppe.

"What else?" she pressed.

"The Boche have alerted three of their airfields near Dieppe, and new FW-190 fighters have arrived."

"What do you think this means?' she asked Noel.

"The British may be planning an amphibious operation, perhaps a commando raid. Whatever it is, the Boche know something is coming and are preparing for it," he speculated.

"Should we contact the British about this?" He nodded, but his body language signaled something that alerted Nadine. She asked him what the matter was.

"Madame," he said in a reserved tone, "any alert we send to the British must be direct and will be picked up by the Boche. It is a considerable risk for us to take."

Nadine knew the Germans monitored all radio traffic between France and England and used tracking devices to locate wireless operators. Only under the most serious of circumstances did she approve contacting directly British Military Intelligence in London. But, the information she received was reliable and needed to reach the British as soon as possible, regardless of the risk.

"Send the information directly to the British," she told Noel. They exchanged eye contact briefly, both realizing the danger involved.

A few days later around midnight, a coded message was sent to the British by a French underground wireless operator. The Germans monitored the transmission and managed to pinpoint its source. Instead of apprehending the suspected wireless operator, the Gestapo waited and quietly identified the resistance operative, a woman. The Gestapo colonel in charge of that region was a former police officer and a clever man. His plan was to follow the woman unobtrusively and see if she led them to others in the resistance.

"One is not enough," said Oberst (colonel) Hagan Martzrek to his key subordinates. "We shall have the entire crowd. Follow the woman carefully and identify the people she meets. If necessary, we'll investigate everyone she talks to," he said coldly.

On August 20, Nadine heard about the British and Canadian attack on the Boche-occupied port of Dieppe. It had not gone well for the Allies. A few days later, she learned that over thirty-six hundred Allied soldiers were killed, wounded, or captured. The Germans claimed to have destroyed over 140 Allied planes. The French underground learned later that about 120 Allied planes had been lost. The outcome of the raid on Dieppe was nothing short of catastrophic.

"The Boche must have known," said a troubled Millard when he met with Noel, Moira, and Nadine.

"D'accord," Nadine told Millard pensively. She wondered about the warning they had sent the British. *If they received our warning about Boche preparations, why did they go ahead with their operation at Dieppe?* She was at a loss to understand the British behavior.

In the days and weeks that followed, the Maquis tried to locate and hide Allied soldiers and flyers who managed to escape capture by the Germans near Dieppe. Only a handful evaded capture. Colonel Martzrek and the Gestapo learned about two downed Allied flyers taken in by the Maquis. Rather than apprehend the flyers and their French helpers, Martzrek had them followed to record every contact they made. Gestapo operatives followed the Allied flyers and their escorts from the outskirts of Rouen and then south to Alencon. There, the Maquis discovered they were being followed and dispersed after killing a Gestapo agent.

When Nadine learned of the Gestapo undercover operative's death at the hands of the Maquis near Alencon, she immediately instructed Noel, Moira, and Millard to suspend all Eglantine operations in the area between Dieppe and Chartres.

"The Boche will retaliate," she said apprehensively. "The Gestapo will not admit publicly that they were following the Allied flyers and members of the resistance."

"So you think the Gestapo swine have been following our people," said Millard. Nadine nodded. "Then we must warn them," he said.

Nadine replied and warned, "Bon, but do it without direct contact between our people and the Maquis."

The next few months passed ever so slowly for Nadine. In late September, Hauptman Wolfgang Berthold began to visit Nadine weekly and ask about her progress in meeting with the French leaders on the list they had given her. She had met with a few and relayed information that was noncommittal to the Gestapo. However, Nadine learned from the resistance that two of the Frenchmen on the list were quietly collaborating with the Germans. She met with both of them and implied that she was contemplating improved financial ties with the Nazis. Both men indicated that it might be advantageous to cooperate with the Boche. When she reported this to Berthold and Zeigler they were pleased.

Nadine continued to meet with French leaders on the list and gradually learned who the patriotic ones were and their attitude toward the Germans. She also learned about others who could not easily be intimidated. There were, however, some on the list she suspected of being opportunists and profiteers. The latter, she told Noel and Millard, the resistance should monitor. She knew that if they were Nazi collaborators, the resistance would deal harshly with them.

In early November 1942, Nadine was visited unexpectedly by Oberstleutnant Sigwald Eisenhardt and Hauptman Wolfgang Berthold. Braustich and the smarmy Zeigler accompanied them.

"Madame," said Eisenhardt, as he lit a cigarette and looked coolly at her. "We appreciate your cooperation in meeting with some of the leaders on the list we shared with you. Since that time, a few have made an 'accommodation' with the Reich." He took a long drag on his cigarette and stared at the lovely Frenchwoman, his eyes cold and hard. He released the smoke through his nose and continued. "Although you were uncertain about the loyalties of two men you met, we have since learned that they are not fully cooperating with us. That will soon change," he said with a sinister smile, as he made eye contact with Berthold who grinned wickedly.

"You may be interested to know that one of your close friends, Monsieur Mendeville, is under surveillance. Nadine gasped, but quickly regained her composure. "Don't worry," said Eisenhardt, affecting a solicitous manner. "At the moment, we are only watching him closely. However, any activities or behavior on his part that reveals resistance to our occupation could be painful for him and his family. But, if Monsieur Mendeville should change his attitude toward the Reich, I'm certain that he will continue to enjoy his freedom." He waited for Nadine to respond, not bothering to look at her, instead paying attention to the half smoked cigarette he held.

"I don't understand," said Nadine, uncertain how to deal with the oberstleutnant.

"Come, come, Madame, it's really quite simple," he told her with a wink. "You are a clever woman."

"You want me to spy on Raoul?" she said slowly.

"No, Madame," said the grinning German, "advise is a better term. Don't you think?" Now his purpose became patent. Either Raoul cooperated with the Boche, or they would do whatever they wanted to him and his family. Her role in the matter was also clear. If she cooperated with the Nazi pigs and spoke to Raoul about changing his attitude toward them, she might be allowed to continue with her life as it was. If she refused, then the consequences would be harsh. She decided to stall for time.

"What is it that you want me to do?" she asked, feigning temerity.

"Good," said Eisenhardt. "Here is what we expect." In the next five minutes, the oberstleutnant outlined how she should approach Raoul. "He will listen to you," said the German slyly. "His response will, of course, involve his family. I'm certain you will convey that to him," his voice a cold warning.

"One thing I don't understand," said Nadine to test the Gestapo officer. "If Raoul is under suspicion, why do you want me to warn him?"

He smiled and shot Berthold a knowing glance before answering. "Madame, it is best if friends persuade Monsieur Mendeville to, ah, shall we say, take a new path, than to 'threaten him' with harsh treatment. Your assistance in this matter would be helpful to the Reich and to Monsieur Mendeville and his family." As Eisenhardt spoke to Nadine, she noticed the air of insouciance on Braustich's face and Zeigler's plastic smile. But, the evil grin on Berthold's face was scary.

After the meeting, Nadine waited until she could meet privately with Noel and Moira. She relayed the discussion about Raoul and the task Eisenhardt had forced on her. In a somber voice, Noel said the Nazis were "tightening a noose" around the necks of Nadine and Raoul.

"It is only a matter of time before the Nazi swine arrest Monsieur Mendeville and imprison his family," said Noel. "Then they will turn on you," he said dejectedly to Nadine.

She knew Noel was right and saw great concern for her safety in his and Moira's eyes.

"What will you do?" asked a solicitous Moira.

"I'll speak to Raoul. Perhaps we can find a way to keep these brutes at bay," she said, hoping for the best.

Noel and Moira nodded in agreement, but they knew the Gestapo was unscrupulous and capable of anything. If they ever suspected that Madame Desnoyers might be working with the Maquis or that she might be Eglantine, they would apprehend and interrogate her viciously. They knew that death would be merciful compared to torture by the Gestapo.

"Perhaps," said Noel, "Madame should consider plans to leave Paris before the Gestapo looks closer at our activities."

She nodded and knew time was running out for her.

* * *

After the Dieppe raid, Quentin met with an exhausted and frustrated Marlon. He had flown several sorties with the Eagle Squadrons and seen firsthand the way the Germans gained air superiority.

"Most of our Spitfires were no match for the new FW 190s," he told his father glumly. "And our bombers were unable to knock out their airfields and gun emplacements," he added. "Our fuel was critical, and we couldn't stay over the target for more than twenty minutes."

Quentin nodded to acknowledge Marlon's comments and observations but did not share the additional information he had about the raid. The attack on Dieppe had been devastating for the Allies. The British plan to lure the Luftwaffe into open battle and damage them severely failed. Instead, the Allies lost 119 planes, and the Royal Navy suffered 555 casualties.

"We've learned a great deal about where and how to mount an amphibious operation," said Quentin. "We managed to knock out some of their radar installations and figure out how well it works. We also learned the Germans are better prepared to repel an operation like the Dieppe raid than expected."

"So what happens now?" asked a dejected Marlon.

"We build up our bomber squadrons and start attacking enemy strong points on the Continent," said the Cajun. "The RAF will bomb at night, and we'll do it during the day."

Marlon sat soberly listening to his father before speaking out. "Dad, unless we provide cover for our bombers, they'll be exposed to German flak and fighters the moment they cross the Channel. Besides the P-38, none of our fighters, especially the Spitfires, has the range to stay with the bombers much beyond the coastline."

Quentin nodded and stood, turned slightly away from his son as if marshalling his thoughts before speaking. "You're right. You've also named your own assignment. Your job will be to help with a new fighter able to escort our bombers, even when they cross into Germany. The P-38 has the range, but it's no match for the new Bf 109s and especially the FW 190s. Marlon, we'll need a fighter superior to anything the Krauts have with the range to stay with our bombers no matter where they go!" he said emphatically.

Marlon sat quietly, digesting his father's words. His recent experience flying sorties over Dieppe encouraged him to speak up. "OK, Dad, I'll do whatever I can."

They looked at each other silently, each man aware of his obligation and determined to do whatever was necessary.

* * *

It seemed to Quentin that he hardly had any free time. His duties included monitoring the construction of additional U.S. Air Force bases, coordinating support elements for new bomber and fledgling fighter groups for combat duty in England, and liaison duties with the RAF and the Free French air squadrons. The Cajun flew to Washington two and sometimes three times a month to meet with Marshall and occasionally the president. During some of his visits to Washington, Ruben would attend the same meetings he did, and they tried, when possible, to meet in the evenings or on weekends to socialize. Julia, Ruben's wife, was gracious and solicitous to Quentin and always asked about Marlon and especially Florence. Julia was very close to Eleanor Roosevelt; through her, Quentin developed a strong friendship with Mrs. Roosevelt. There were times when the First Lady would see Quentin at the White House and ask him to sit with her for a few minutes to talk. He admired Eleanor Roosevelt and would never hesitate to do whatever she asked of him.

After a long and tedious meeting at the White House early in December 1942, Quentin was leaving the building when Eleanor Roosevelt called his name.

"Walk with me, Quentin," she said, locking her arm in his. There was something soothing in Eleanor's voice and manner that the Cajun appreciated.

"Quentin, you look tired. Are you taking care of yourself? I know from Julia and Ruben that you've been working very hard."

He nodded and said to her softly that the war and the many meetings, especially the contentious ones, often frustrated him.

"Yes, I know. There are times when Franklin is almost impossible," she said, looking directly at the Cajun. "And I know why—long, unproductive meetings. But, enough of that," she said with a warm smile. "I'm going to host a reception for the wives of distinguished scientists who left Europe. I'd like Florence to play for us. Do you think she'd mind?"

"I think she would enjoy doing that for you. If you like, I'll call her. Do you have a particular date in mind?" The first lady squeezed his hand affectionately and told him the date, time, and place. "I'll call her tonight and get back to you."

"Thank you, Quentin," she said graciously. "Now I'll let you in on a little secret." The puzzled Cajun looked at her expectantly. "You cannot tell a soul about this until it becomes official. You'll need to add another star to your lapel," Mrs. Roosevelt told him in a friendly way.

The next day, Quentin met with Marshall, Henry Stimson, Admiral King, Ruben, and the president. Marshall and Roosevelt assigned Quentin two new projects, one that involved going to North Africa, and told him he would accompany Marshall for a new round of talks with Churchill and his aides. Just before the meeting broke up, the president spoke up, "Quentin, we have something for you. George, tell him."

"Congratulations," Marshall told the Cajun as he handed him an envelope. "Go ahead, open it." Quentin opened the envelope and read about his promotion to major general.

"The Senate has confirmed my recommendation for the promotion," said Roosevelt. As Ruben and the others in the room congratulated the subdued Cajun, his thoughts were about Eleanor Roosevelt and what a grand person and friend she was.

"Quentin," said a tired Roosevelt, trying to sound upbeat, "George has told me what you've done to operationalize our new fighter squadrons in England. I know it's been demanding. Hap Arnold appreciates what you've done and wants you assigned to him." He paused for a moment before continuing. "George and I can't spare you. I know flying a desk is tough for an old fighter pilot. But we need you."

"I understand, Mr. President," said Quentin, fingering the letter promoting him to major general. "I'll do my best."

* * *

Try as he might to be with his children for Christmas, Quentin was delayed in North Africa. American troops had landed in Morocco on November 8, 1942. The French North African forces went over to the Allies a few days later. The U.S. Army's II Corps was headed by Major General Lloyd Fredendall and linked to the British First Army, which was commanded by Lieutenant General Kenneth Anderson. Quentin met first with General Fredendall, who did not impress him, and then with British General Anderson. He inquired of Anderson about air support for II Corps and was assured that the British Desert Air Force (DAF), a consolidation of squadrons composed of English, Polish, South African, and Australian units, would provide air cover. When Quentin asked to inspect the DAF air bases and squadrons, he was referred to Air Vice Marshal Arthur Coningham and through him met General Lewis H. Brereton, who was in charge of the U.S. Army Middle East Air Force (USAMEAF). U.S. Air Force personnel assigned to the Fifty-seventh Fighter Group composed of P-40s and the Twelfth Bombardment Group of B-25s were conducting sorties over enemy territory as "observers." All of this changed.

Quentin remained in North Africa ironing out the transition of the USAMEAF to the Ninth Air Force. Three days before the New Year, he left for Lisbon where he met with Brook Hamilton Stoner.

"Well, sport," said the polished diplomat, "you seem to have gotten a little sun," referring to Quentin's tanned face and arms.

"It may be winter," said the Cajun, "but the sun doesn't seem to know that in the desert." In the next twenty minutes, Quentin told Stoner about the transition of USAMEAF to become the Ninth Air Force. "It wasn't easy," said the Cajun, "and there are still some things that need to be worked out," he cautioned.

"You've done about as much as you can there," said Stoner. "Now, it's up to Ike (General Eisenhower) and

Bedell Smith," he added. "You're needed back in London ASAP."

"OK," said a tired Quentin. "Bring me up to date on what's happening in Russia and the Pacific?"

The diplomat smiled and said, "The Soviets have mauled the Hungarian, Italian, and Romanian troops supporting the German Sixth Army," he said. "The Red Army has stopped the Germans near Stalingrad and bottled up General Paulus and his army." Quentin smiled and asked about the Pacific. Clearing his throat, Stoner began. "We control Guadalcanal. In New Guinea, our troops and the Australians have pushed the Japanese back to Buna and Gona. Looks like the Japanese will lose their foothold in southern New Guinea."

"That's great," said Quentin, pleased by the news. The two men had dinner, and, early the next morning, Quentin departed for London and arrived there on December 30. He called Linne to inform her he was back in London. The perky Englishwoman called him immediately and invited him to a New Year's Eve party and celebration. He decided to accept her invitation.

During the New Year's Eve party, Linne introduced Quentin to several members of the landed gentry, including three prominent lords and their wives. They treated him politely, but with a reserve that reminded Quentin about the class differences that differentiated the English from the Americans.

Linne seemed to know everyone at the party and danced as often as she could with Quentin. Several men asked her to dance, trying to impress her; however, Linne had eyes only for the Cajun and would return to his side and take his hand in hers.

At the stroke of midnight, the band played "Auld Lang Syne," and Quentin remembered that the lyrics were from a Scottish poem written by Robert Burns in 1788 and had been set to the tune of a traditional folk song. Linne pressed up against Quentin and kissed him hard on the lips. A few minutes later, the band began to play "God Save the King," the British national anthem. As Linne and others in the room sang the lyrics, Quentin instead mouthed the words to "America," a song with the same melody he had learned as a boy. The words were indelibly impressed on his memory: *My country 'tis of thee, sweet land of liberty, of thee I sing.*

Linne looked at the Cajun and realized from the way his lips were forming words that they were different from the UK anthem. She pulled him close and asked, "What is it you're saying?"

"The lyrics to 'America the beautiful,'" he told her.

She looked confused and said she did not understand.

"In America, we have different lyrics to that tune," he replied.

She was momentarily taken aback but recovered quickly and kissed him again on the lips.

"Then you must tell me about things like this," she whispered sweetly.

CHAPTER 17
THE NOOSE TIGHTENS

Yield not thy neck to fortune's yoke,
But let thy dauntless mind
Still ride in triumph over all mischance.
William Shakespeare, *King Henry the Sixth,*
Part III

In Berlin, events were taking place that would lead German authorities to suspect Nadine of crimes against the Reich. Major Lutz Eldred was a Heer officer wounded in the Balkans while leading a Panzer attack. His left leg was badly damaged; even though the doctors were able to save it, he would always walk with a limp and require the use of a cane. Eldred had been a brilliant university student and excelled in history, philosophy, and mathematics. Above all, he was a highly organized person and gifted with a curious nature. Admiral Canaris recruited him for the Abwehr (a German Intelligence organization) and assigned him to Central Division. He was given the responsibility for gathering and organizing intelligence information. A scrupulous and tireless worker, Eldred expected his staff to be meticulous and sensitive to any links that might surface in the data that they gathered and analyzed. In January 1943, Hauptman Helmut Beronka von Teslar brought some files for Eldred to review.

"What is it?" asked Eldred, as he glanced at the documents handed to him.

"Sir, I've found some things that are curious?"

"*Ja*, what is it?" asked the major. In the next few minutes, the captain told Eldred about the birth certificate of Marlon Aleron Desnoyers, the child of Henri and Nadine Desnoyers in Paris, France. Henri had been a midlevel French diplomat and died in March 1929. Madame Desnoyers was an extremely wealthy widow with numerous lucrative enterprises in France, Belgium, Holland, Spain, and other parts of the world. She had several profitable investments in Canada and the United States. The income from these investments was located in American and Swiss banks and could not be accessed by German authorities. Her solicitor in the United States was Quentin Norvell, a senior partner in the New York law firm of Barston, Marwick, Fowler, and Peterson. Norvell was a celebrated ace and highly decorated hero during World War I. He had visited France and Germany often since 1928 and met with several senior members of the Nazi party and German Wehrmacht.

"Our dossier on Norvell is intriguing, Major," said von Teslar.

Eldred, his face emotionless, motioned for him to continue.

"Norvell is now a general in the American Army and meets regularly with General Marshall, the head of the Joint Chiefs of Staff. He appears to have direct access to Roosevelt, the American president."

At this, Eldred's countenance changed, and he leaned forward in his chair, focusing on the intersections of information von Teslar had provided.

"There is more," said von Teslar.

"Records from the French authorities indicate that Marlon Aleron Desnoyers left France in 1929 and moved into the household of Quentin Norvell. Some time later, Marlon Desnoyers assumed the surname of Norvell." At this, Eldred raised an eyebrow, his attention focused intently on the materials in front of him.

"There is more," continued von Teslar.

"Marlon Aleron Norvell graduated from the Massachusetts Institute of Technology in 1940. We have information about a Marlon Norvell enlisting in the Royal Canadian Air Force. Now a captain, Marlon Norvell surfaces in the American Air Force. Major, these are not coincidences."

"Clearly," said Eldred, thumbing through the documents in front of him, "drop whatever else you are doing and examine this matter carefully. Also, find out what the Gestapo may have on Madame Desnoyers and Quentin Norvell. Good work, captain," said Eldred.

In the next few days, Captain von Teslar gathered additional materials on Nadine Desnoyers and finally contacted the Gestapo to request any information they might have about Madame Desnoyers and Quentin Norvell. He did not hear back from the Gestapo immediately; however, a week later, he received a call from an officious major who asked about the nature of his request. When von Teslar mentioned what the Abwehr had uncovered, the major told him the Gestapo already had files on the Desnoyers woman and the American. Try as he might to persuade the Gestapo major to turn over all recent information they had on the two subjects, von Teslar was stymied. Frustrated, he reported his lack of progress to Major Eldred.

"Supercilious bureaucrat," said an irate Eldred. "They must have pertinent information about Desnoyers and Norvell. I'll see to this," he told von Teslar.

The next day, Eldred called the officious Gestapo major and was told to submit a request in writing for information about Desnoyers and Norvell. Furious, Eldred called his superior officer, Oberst Hans Pieckenbrock. A meeting with Pieckenbrock was scheduled for February 3, 1943.

* * *

The New Year had come and passed quietly for Nadine. But, late in January 1943, Noel told her about highly sensitive information offered by a German engineer anxious to escape to England. The German was employed by Messerschmitt and had worked on a new fighter, one that used jet propulsion rather than a conventional propeller engine. Curious, she asked, "What kind of airplane is that?"

"It's a jet fighter," said Noel, "because it uses jet propulsion engines. It is reputed to be faster than any propeller driven airplane."

"Have the Boche perfected it?" she asked.

Noel told her that the engineer speculated the German jet might become operational in a few months. "He claims to have detailed information about the plane and its capabilities," said Noel.

"Why did he leave Germany?" she asked. Noel told her that the German's wife was half Polish and that her parents were Jews. "Have we verified what he's told us?" she asked.

Noel nodded and said the engineer's story was genuine and that the Maquis had checked him out thoroughly. He also said the Boche were doing everything they could to apprehend the engineer. "The Allies will want to interview him," said Noel.

"Very well," replied Nadine. "Is he alone?"

"No, he is with his wife and daughter. But there is something we should consider carefully, Madame," said Noel. Nadine raised an eyebrow and motioned for him to continue.

"The Boche engineer insists that his family get to Portugal. He has firsthand information about what the Boche are doing to Jews. They are arrested and sent to camps where they are killed."

"No!" exclaimed a shocked Nadine. "Can this be true?"

Noel, his face registering sadness, continued, "I'm afraid it's true. We've heard from reliable sources in *Allemande* that Jews and Gypsies arrested and sent to places like Buchenwald and Dachau are systematically killed."

Nadine could not contain her emotions and tears welled up in her eyes. "They are beasts!" she exclaimed

"Madame, if we help the engineer, we must arrange for his wife and daughter to accompany him."

"Then it must be done," said Nadine. She realized the Germans were hunting the engineer not just because of his knowledge of the German jet fighter, but because his wife was Jewish. Smuggling one and possibly two persons out of France along the escape route to Spain and beyond was difficult. However, trying to move three people at the same time was risky and dangerous, especially with the Boche determined to arrest the German engineer and his Jewish wife.

"There is more," said Noel.

"Tell me," she told him.

"There is a Polish technician forced to work for the Luftwaffe at a place called Peenemünde on the Baltic Coast of *Allemande*. He's an expert on metallurgy and was assigned to a project the Boche call *Vergeltungswaffe*, or flying bomb. His group was tasked to develop a strong, but lightweight, metal for the jet engine that powers the bomb."

"A flying bomb!" whispered Nadine. "Do the Allies know about this weapon?" she pondered.

"Probably not. This weapon," said Noel, "does not require a pilot and can attain high speeds. The technician does not know the bomb's range or speed, but he believes it may be faster than any Allied fighter."

"My lord," exclaimed Nadine, "what a horrible weapon! Do we know how far along the Boche are in developing it?" Noel mentioned that the technician believed the Luftwaffe was completing the final tests on the flying bomb. "We must ensure that this man reaches Lisbon as soon as possible," she said, nervously biting her lower lip. "Is he alone?" she asked. Noel said the technician's wife had died in Poland just after he had been pressed into service by the Luftwaffe and sent to Peenemünde late in 1940.

A twinge of fear rippled through Nadine's thoughts. The engineer and the technician's information were extremely valuable. She knew the Germans would do anything to prevent either man from reaching the Allies. Try as she might, she could not rationalize delaying sending the engineer and his family, along with the technician through the Eglantine escape route. The military information they possessed was critical and must reach the Americans as soon as possible.

Noel watched Nadine's face as she made the decision to send the four people through the network.

"All four of them at the same time?" asked the worried Frenchman. She nodded reluctantly.

"Before we do so," she told him, "I want each man to write down everything he knows. I will keep the notes in case something happens."

Noel nodded, but he suspected that the German engineer and the technician might be reluctant to do so.

"Yes, I know it will be difficult to convince them," said Nadine, preoccupied with the actions she must take and the risk involved.

Noel looked at the beautiful Frenchwoman and resigned himself to the task. What she wanted was extremely dangerous. Yet, he would gladly give his life for this woman, a resourceful organizer and an uncompromising patriot. He said, "Best if we wait until the end of the month to move them. First, I have to convince them to write down their information."

Nadine looked at him with a quiet determination in her eyes before telling him to go ahead. A sense of foreboding engulfed the lovely woman and she mustered all of her strength to avoid showing her disquietude.

* * *

On February 5, 1943, Nadine's parents called and informed her that Louis Bondurant was critically ill. She made arrangements with Braustich and Zeigler to leave Paris to be with her uncle.

"You say his illness is critical," commented Braustich diffidently. She nodded. "Very well," he said reluctantly. "But if you are delayed returning to Paris, inform me immediately."

Before leaving for La Croisiere, Nadine met with Moira, Noel, and Millard. She told Noel to use their private code to keep her informed about the transit of the German engineer and his family, and the Polish technician. Moira and Millard would monitor any new intelligence the resistance might provide.

"Moira," said Nadine, "under no circumstances are you to meet with anyone claiming to be from the resistance. Work only through Millard. If Millard cannot meet with you directly, he will send Rouge. Be careful," she cautioned the Scottish woman and kissed her on the cheek. She extended her hand to Millard who took it and kissed it.

"I hope your uncle can survive this illness," said the older man sympathetically.

* * *

Nadine arrived late the evening of February 7 at Limoges and was driven directly to her uncle's estate at La Croisiere. As she alighted from the car and walked past the large, carved wooden doors, she saw her father standing in the foyer, his eyes filled with tears.

"Papa, what is it?" she asked nervously. He wiped his eyes with a handkerchief and said Louis had slipped into a coma. He coughed to clear his throat, but he was unable to speak again; instead, he turned his head to one side to muffle the sob that escaped from his throat.

"Where is he?" Nadine asked anxiously. Edmund motioned for her to follow him, and Nadine took his hand. When she touched her father's hand, she remembered the times as a girl that taking Edmund's hand was reassuring and a sign of support and protection. Now, his hand was moist and trembling. His despair infected her immediately.

When they entered Louis's room, Nadine saw Arlene, her mother, and Clovis, a close friend and neighbor, next to the bed. On the other side of the bed two of Louis's close friends, both retired generals from the French Air Service, sat solemnly. They acknowledged Nadine immediately and stood to welcome her. A nurse turned to watch Nadine greet everyone in the room. Her eyes met Nadine's as the lovely Frenchwoman moved to hug her mother. Nadine saw in the nurse's eyes resignation and lack of hope. *Louis is dying,* she thought, as a cold feeling overcame her. When she embraced Arlene, the older woman trembled and her sobbing came in almost rhythmic spasms as she struggled to gulp air. Nadine cupped Arlene's face in her hands to reassure her, but the older woman shook her head and continued to sob. From somewhere deep in her soul, Arlene was expressing in physical terms Louis's fading life. Nadine moved to the bed, stood next to Louis, and gently took the old soldier's hand. It was warm but devoid of any strength or movement. She loved this man not just as an uncle but as a surrogate father. They had shared so much and on many occasions his words of encouragement and support bolstered her and helped to overcome hardships she faced. Now, the once strong and resilient old soldier was thin and struggling for life.

Two hours later, the doctor arrived to examine Louis. He cleared the room except for the nurse. A few minutes later, he emerged and spoke with Edmund, who motioned for Nadine to join them. The doctor recognized Nadine and smiled politely at her.

"I think you should summon a priest," he told them.

His words caught Nadine like a blow to the body and she momentarily lost her breath.

Edmund looked away and tried to muster his strength, but the way his shoulder's slumped, it was apparent he was on the verge of losing the struggle to control his emotions.

"Doctor," said Nadine softly, "is there no hope?"

The doctor shook his head and said, "I'm afraid not. He has an advanced case of pneumonia, and his heart is very weak. I can do nothing to control his fever. He will not regain consciousness," said the physician in a tired voice.

"Perhaps if he was in a hospital?" asked Nadine. The doctor shook his head and said that when Louis went into a coma and his temperature began to rise, there was little that could be done to save him.

"If we had more warning and the proper drugs, something could have been done," said the doctor. "The Boche control everything now, especially medication. Everything is rationed, and access to medicinal drugs is cumbersome and time consuming. All I can do is make the general as comfortable as possible before he dies," he told them.

The Boche, the damned Boche, thought Nadine, her despair for Louis momentarily displaced by anger and hatred toward the Germans. She wanted to shout and rant against the invaders and what they had done to her country and now to Louis. She refused to reveal her anger at the Germans, checked her emotions, and internalized the grief she was feeling.

"I understand," she told the doctor.

"Summon a priest," he repeated solemnly.

Nadine turned to Edmund and assigned him that task. After thanking the doctor, she consoled her mother.

Louis Bondurant never regained consciousness. It was almost three in the morning the following day when Nadine felt a gentle nudge from the nurse, who whispered, "Madame, the general's breathing is erratic, and he is trying to say something."

Nadine woke immediately and rushed to his bed. Louis was delirious and his body burning with fever. He muttered a few incoherent words and then slowly began to drift away, one painful breath at a time, until it seemed he gasped and let out a slow, weak stream of air. Then he was gone.

* * *

In London, Quentin was swamped with work. He had been temporarily assigned to review and critique the logistics of supply and demand for the air force in England. He put together a small group of five staff officers and four enlisted personnel to help him. They reviewed the procedures and channels for requisitioning new aircraft, parts and ordinance and examined carefully the way these assets were apportioned to the various combat groups. After reviewing the dispersal of requested aircraft parts and ordinance, they surmised that supply depots for aircraft and spare parts needed to be enhanced. Quentin and his analysis team recommended a reassessment of priorities to fill requests from combat groups and squadrons and support units.

In addition to his responsibilities to examine the supply side of replacement parts and aircraft, Quentin reviewed the allocation of new personnel. Increasing numbers of U.S. Army Air Force personnel were arriving in England, particularly those assigned to bomber groups and squadrons. A steady stream of new pilots, navigators, bombardiers, flight crews, and support staff were arriving fresh from training in the United States, but he soon learned that personnel replacements were only loosely prioritized to maintain bomber groups at strength. Quentin and his analysis team learned that friendships and favoritism, along with influence that sometimes involved bribery and even coercion, bypassed established priorities for replacements.

When Quentin reported his analytical team's findings to the top U.S. brass in London, they were questioned by several generals. He realized immediately that people were being protected and that the favoritism his group had uncovered extended to senior level army staff. Rather than engage in a war of words and memos, the Cajun went directly to General Walter Bedell Smith, General Eisenhower's recently appointed chief of staff. Quentin had met Smith in Washington and knew he could be crass and prickly. However, the Cajun respected the general for his clear thinking and no nonsense manner.

It did not take Smith long to realize that the report from Quentin and his analytical team was valid. "All right," said Smith to the Cajun, "what do we need to do about this?" Quentin suggested two things immediately. "So, you want me to kick some ass," said Smith. The Cajun nodded. "All right, I'll do it, but you damn well better be right or I'll send you packing."

"One last thing," said Quentin before leaving Smith's office.

"Yeah, now what?" Smith said with annoyance. The Cajun mentioned the increasing losses among the combat bomber squadrons. "I've seen the numbers, General," Smith said testily.

"There's a direct correlation between limited fighter cover for the bombers and losses," said Quentin.
"So!" exclaimed Smith gruffly.

The Cajun held his ground and said," We need to accelerate the development of a new long-range fighter to escort our bombers deep into enemy territory."

"Have you talked with Hap Arnold about this?" Smith inquired. Quentin shook his head and remained silent. "Well, why not?" Smith asked brusquely.

"I haven't received any direct orders to do so," he replied.

"What the hell, a 'little' thing like orders hasn't seemed to stop you so far," Smith chided.

The Cajun shrugged off the remark and said, "I'd rather not have to go over people's heads here and cause a flap in Washington."

"The hell!" exclaimed Smith, "since when are you a stickler for protocol, Norvell?" The Cajun held his tongue and just stared at Smith. The older officer studied the Cajun carefully, aware the pilot would not back down or drop the subject. "All right, God dammit," Smith blustered. "I'll speak to Ike about it." Quentin saluted and left Smith's office. When he was alone, Walter Bedell Smith chuckled and thought, *Norvell, you've got balls!*

A few weeks later, Quentin was called to Washington and met with Generals Marshall and Arnold. He was given a new assignment: review progress in the development of a new, long-range fighter.

"Just one thing," said Quentin after accepting the new responsibilities. "I was promised that my son would be promoted to major and assigned to a combat fighter squadron." A thin smile appeared on Hap Arnold's face as Marshall glanced at him.

"It's already done. Orders assigning him to a fighter squadron in England were cut yesterday," said Arnold. "We thought you might ask," he said, grinning. Quentin thanked both men and shook their hands.

* * *

At his meeting with Oberst Pieckenbrock, Eldred shared the intelligence they had gathered on Nadine and Quentin and mentioned the lack of cooperation from the Gestapo. The oberst studied the information carefully before saying, "Our colleagues in the Gestapo believe they are the only ones able to uncover pertinent information about possible enemies of the Reich." He picked up the telephone and spoke with Admiral Canaris. After signing off with the admiral, he waited a while before calling the Gestapo.

The next day, Lutz and von Teslar were summoned to Gestapo headquarters in Berlin and given access to their dossiers on Nadine and Quentin.

The Gestapo files on Nadine Desnoyers and Quentin Norvell were extensive. A report from Oberst Hagan Martzrek of the Gestapo in France caught Eldred's attention. His agents had followed several persons considered to be members of the resistance. One of the suspected members of the resistance had met several times with a carpenter who had worked at Madame Desnoyers' home in Paris. There were also photographs of Madame Desnoyers' personal secretary, a woman identified as Moira Tedoux, meeting with a woman suspected of working with the resistance. The Gestapo was about to investigate the Tedoux woman. Eldred made a note to follow up with the Gestapo about this woman.

The file on Norvell was hefty and filled with photographs and monitored conversations in Germany and the United States. Norvell was assumed to be Madame Desnoyers' lover. However, what interested Eldred most was the American's friendship with General Nicholas von Kleist of the Luftwaffe. The two men had met often before the Reich declared war on the Americans. The information gathered by the Gestapo convinced Eldred that further investigation was needed. It was time to focus attention on the Desnoyers woman and her personal secretary. First, however, a meeting with General Nicholas von Kleist was in order.

Three days later, Eldred met with Nicholas von Kleist. Their conversation was formal and at times strained. Von Kleist answered all of Eldred's questions and was guarded about his relationship with Norvell. He admitted that the American had spared his life during the Great War. When asked about Nadine, he replied knowing her through Norvell but would reveal little more.

"Major," said von Kleist intemperately, "what is the purpose of these questions regarding Madame Desnoyers and Herr Norvell?"

When Eldred said the Frenchwoman was under investigation because of her son's service in the RAF and her association with Norvell now a general in the U.S. Army, von Kleist maintained a nonchalant air. "Is that all?" he asked. Eldred said that the Gestapo had extensive files on Desnoyers and Norvell and was prepared to "question" the Frenchwoman and one of her employees. Von Kleist remained composed, but, inside, he understood what the Abwehr major was doing. It was only a matter of time before the Gestapo apprehended Nadine Desnoyers and her employee for "questioning."

Trying to sound annoyed, von Kleist asked, "Major, is there more? I have important things to do."

"General," Eldred said coolly but cordially, "we serve the Reich as soldiers and have seen combat. And, we are fellow officers of the old school." He waited to see how the general would respond to his comments, but von Kleist remained impassive. "The Gestapo," he continued, "can be heavy handed. If there is anything else you would care to share with me…"

His last words carried a hidden message and made an impression on Nicky, but he remained impenetrable. Instead, he asked again if that was all. Eldred said yes for the time being, thanked von Kleist, saluted, and left.

That evening, Nicky spoke with Lorelei where they could not be overheard. He told Lorelei to meet with her priest and send an urgent message warning Madame Desnoyers that the Gestapo was preparing to apprehend her for questioning. Nicky and Quentin had earlier devised a way to communicate with each other. Bishop Valderano assigned a priest to the church Lorelei attended. In case of an extreme emergency, the priest would make contact with Madame Desnoyers' priest in Paris. Both priests were part of a secret communication system Bishop Luis Valderano had arranged at his brother Ruben and Quentin's request.

Lorelei met for confession with her priest in Berlin and said Madame Desnoyers in Paris should be warned that the Gestapo was about to arrest her. That evening, Lorelei's priest sent a coded message to Nadine's priest in Paris about the danger. The priest in Paris tried to reach her. Because Nadine was at La Croisiere, Moira took the message and quickly deciphered it. She called Noel immediately. When they met, she shared the news about the Gestapo's plans.

"I'll call Madame," said Noel, "and tell her you are bringing documents that she needs to sign and return as soon as possible. Do not return," he warned her.

"What can I do?" Moira volunteered. As he sorted some papers, Noel told her,

"I will warn Millard, Rouge and his contacts in the resistance about the Gestapo's plans to arrest Madame Desnoyers. They (Gestapo) will try to arrest all of us. Tell Madame that I will leave Paris and communicate with her through one of our people in B4C (a prearranged code for the town of Bergerac in southern France)."

He paused for a moment to organize his thoughts before saying, "When you reach Limoges, look for a taxi driven by a man called Quennel. He will ask where you want to go. Use these words." He gave Moira the code words and also some microfiche, which she hid in the lining of her umbrella.

"Madame must have the microfiche. If at any time it appears that you will be stopped and questioned, discard the umbrella." He gave her a hug and in a soft voice said, "Now go."

Moira caught the first train she could to Limoges and sent a message to Nadine indicating the number of the train and its expected time of arrival. However, because of military traffic that had priority on all rail lines in France, passenger trains were regularly sidetracked and delayed. All the way to the *gare* she sensed the surveillance, but she dared not give any indication to alert anyone following her. In fact, two Gestapo agents, a man and a woman, were shadowing her.

Nadine was completing arrangements for Louis's funeral when Noel called. Using a predetermined code, he alerted her to the danger. She paused momentarily to catch her breath before telling him in code that she was going into hiding immediately. Nadine thanked him for the call and said Moira would be expected. After ending the call, the lovely French woman realized her peril. *It was bound to happen*, she thought, while considering what needed to be done. First, she had to send her parents to safety. Next, Quennel had to be contacted and instructed to meet Moira at the train station in Limoges. Then, she would go into hiding.

On the pretext of purchasing fresh cheese and wine, Nadine visited a store in the nearby village run by a man and wife working with the resistance. After making some purchases, she pretended to examine the oranges and left a note written in code. The couple alerted the local Maquis that Madame Desnoyers needed help to avoid arrest by the Gestapo.

It was late in the afternoon when a small delivery truck arrived at the gates of La Croisiere and drove to the side entrance of the chateau. The driver, an older man, perhaps in his early fifties, rang the bell to the kitchen and said he had oranges for Madame Desnoyers.

"I am Jules," he told Nadine. In the next few minutes, Nadine was instructed to bring her parents to a place in the nearby woods at midnight. They packed a small bag and prepared to leave as soon as it was dark. Nadine told Jules to alert Quennel and be at the Limoges train station when Moira arrived. He showed Jules a picture of Moira before he left.

"We must leave tonight, before the Boche come to arrest us," she told her parents. Edmund and Arlene were aware that Nadine was working with the resistance, but not the extent of her efforts, or that she was Eglantine. However, they realized that if Nadine was arrested, they too would be apprehended.

"Where will we go?" asked Arlene nervously.

"To Spain and then Portugal," she told them. "I will let it be known through informers that you are headed for Switzerland to be with Desirée and Bertrand. That should divert the Gestapo. I will make certain that Christine and Armand in Lisbon expect you."

"If the Gestapo comes to arrest us before we leave, go to the cellar and use the hidden passageway to reach the stables. Stay there until Phillippe (the gardener) takes you to safety."

It was just past eleven when Nadine and her parents used the hidden passageway to reach the stables. They waited until Phillippe arrived and escorted them to a thicket and then to a stream where a small boat was waiting.

"This is Gerard," whispered Phillippe. "He will take you to the rendezvous. God be with you," he told them before disappearing into the darkness. They followed the wide stream for a few kilometers until Gerard pulled in his oars and let the row boat drift around a bend. He made a sound like an owl and waited. A moment later, a call, like that of an owl, came from the southern bank ahead. Gerard rowed until they landed at a place where two armed men were waiting. After leaving the boat, Nadine and her parents walked along a narrow path in the woods known to the men leading them. There was a partial moon hidden by clouds. Arlene, unaccustomed to this kind of activity and the darkness, stumbled often. After what seemed like an eternity but was in fact less than twenty minutes, they came to a small clearing.

Two men and a woman were waiting. They carried small arms and appeared young, perhaps in their late teens or early twenties. Nadine spoke to them and was asked certain questions by the young woman, which she responded to in code. After a few minutes, the tallest of the three told them to follow him. He said something to the two men who had led Edmond, Arlene, and Nadine to the clearing and shook each of their hands. The two men disappeared into the woods. Then, he motioned for his confreres to take Edmund and Arlene's small bags. They walked in silence for almost an hour until they reached a small farm. The tall man asked them to wait while he made certain no Germans were in the area. They made their way as quietly as possible to a small barn.

"Madame," said the tall young man softly to Nadine, "a small truck will arrive before dawn and take your parents south. They will be in Spain in about four or five days."

"You're not coming with us?" said a surprised Arlene. Nadine replied that she had to wait for Moira and then meet with Noel later.

"But, child, you are in danger here," Arlene said anxiously.

Edmund put his arm around Arlene's trembling shoulders and in a soothing voice said, "Nadine has 'obligations' here and will follow when the time is right."

Before her parents left for the trip south, Nadine hugged them and said, "Give my love to Christine and Armand in Lisbon. Tell Christine to visit the American embassy in Lisbon and meet with Brook Hamilton Stoner, an American diplomat and a friend." She described Stoner and said, "He must be informed that I've fled Paris and will try to contact him and Quentin when the time is right."

A small rickety truck arrived just before dawn. Arlene and Edmund were squeezed into a hidden compartment. Nadine watched the truck leave, bouncing over ruts in the dirt road. Sadness overcame her, and tears clouded her vision of the old truck as it turned into the woods and headed south. She felt alone, now a fugitive from the Gestapo. But, at least her parents were safe and would soon be united with their granddaughter in Lisbon. As the sun, barely penetrated the horizon, and began to illuminate the day, Natalie, the young woman with the resistance, asked if she was hungry.

* * *

"Idiots!" exclaimed Oberst Hagan Martzrek, as he read the file Major Lutz Eldred from the Abwehr had given him. It was the second full week of February, and they were in Martzrek's Paris office.

"I beg your pardon, Colonel," said Eldred, standing in front of Martzrek.

"I'm referring to Lt. Colonel Eisenhardt and Captain Berthold," he said in a desultory manner. "They should have brought Madame Desnoyers in for questioning."

"Are they the officers waiting in the next room?" asked Eldred.

"Ja," said a displeased Martzrek closing the file. "I commend you, Major, for your work on this matter. I will see to it that your superiors learn of your diligence."

"One more thing, Colonel," said Eldred. Martzrek motioned for the major to continue. "This Moira Tedoux may not be who she claims to be," he said. The colonel looked at Eldred with a frown and asked him to explain. "We have researched the documents of all Madame Desnoyers' immediate staff. Their records and certificates of birth are valid, except for the Tedoux woman. A French child, one Annie Tedoux was born in the same village and at the same time as listed by Moira Tedoux. However, that child died a month after birth. Here are the birth and death certificates," said Eldred, handing Martzrek two documents. "I took the liberty of researching the Tedoux woman's records of schools attended and completed. They have been falsified."

Martzrek raised and eyebrow before asking,
"What do you make of this?"

"It is just a supposition," said Eldred cautiously, "but Moira Tedoux may be a British agent. She may even be a person we have been hunting, Eglantine, or someone very close to that person."

"Excellent," said Martzrek, a thin smile crossing his face. "You are to be commended."

"Much of it was done by my aide, Hauptman Helmut Beronka von Teslar," said Eldred.

"You are an exemplary officer and a credit to the Reich," Martzrek told him. "But, enough of this; I must deal with those incompetents," he said, rolling his eyes in the direction of the outer office. "Major, you may leave by that door," he said, motioning with his head to a side entrance.

Eldred clicked his heels and said, "Heil Hitler," to which Martzrek replied with a perfunctory salute.

After Eldred left, Martzrek pressed the button on the intercom and had Eisenhardt, Berthold, and two other Gestapo officers ushered into his office.

"Stand at attention," barked Martzrek. "I want no excuses. You are to arrest Madame Desnoyers and her personal staff immediately, especially Moira Tedoux. I want them taken alive."

Less than an hour later, Martzrek learned that the Desnoyers woman was at a place called La Croisiere near Limoges making funeral arrangements for her uncle and that her personal secretary had left by train for Limoges. He also learned that Noel DeCloux her executive assistant was missing. *They must have been warned,* he thought. *But how?*

He ordered Madame Desnoyers apprehended at La Croisiere along with her personal secretary. As he made a notation in Nadine's file, the intercom buzzed.

"What is it?" asked Martzrek, slightly annoyed.

"A report of some interest," said his secretary.

"Bring it in," said the colonel. His secretary entered the room, saluted, and handed him a report. The message stated that a group of five people, among them two men wanted by the Gestapo for treason and flight, were intercepted near Agen. A gun battle ensued, and three men were killed and two German agents seriously wounded. Among the dead were a Frenchman presumed to be with the resistance, a German scientist, and a Polish technician.

"Excellent," said Martzrek, pleased with the death of the two men wanted by the Gestapo. He sent a message of congratulations to Hauptman Helmut Zollner, the Gestapo field officer in Agen. Zollner was known to Martzrek as resourceful and relentless.

Later than same day, Martzrek received a telephone call from Limoges. The Desnoyers woman and her parents had fled.

"Incompetents," said the colonel as he ran his finger over the names of Eisenhardt and Berthold. He barked orders to have Eisenhardt telephone him immediately. It took less than an hour for Eisenhardt to call Martzrek.

"The Tedoux woman is in that area and will probably meet with Madame Desnoyers. We have people following her. Do not arrest Tedoux. Follow her. She will lead you to the Desnoyers woman. Then arrest both and anyone with them," he ordered and hung up the telephone. He called Hauptman Zollner in Agen and spoke to him about Madame Desnoyers and Moira Tedoux. Martzrek instructed Zollner to get in touch with Eisenhardt and Berthold.

"I'm assigning you to this case. Apprehend the Desnoyers woman and her secretary, and anyone who helps her."

"What about Oberstleutnant Eisenhardt and Hauptman Berthold?" asked Zollner.

"You will handle this matter and they will assist you. If either of them causes you any trouble, send them back to Paris. That's an order," stressed Martzrek.

* * *

In America, a lonely Florence immersed herself in musical studies at Juilliard and practicing the piano at home until late in the evening. It was her way of coping with the absence of contact with Marlon. She wrote to him often, but he was slow in answering her letters. The days turned into weeks and she missed seeing her brother. She knew he was now assigned to a fighter squadron in England and was flying combat missions whenever the weather permitted. *When will I see you again?* she asked herself.

Frustrated by not being able to be with her brother, Florence searched for a way to visit England. She would soon be twenty and had an independence that people of wealth and privilege enjoy. She toyed with different strategies to visit London, but none of them allowed her to continue her studies at Juilliard. It was frustrating for the young pianist to love someone so much and want to be near him and not be able to fulfill her strongest desire.

During a clear and dry spell in mid-February, she went to the airport at Islip to fly one of the planes her father kept there. She called ahead. When she arrived, the plane was fueled and ready. She flew for almost an hour and reluctantly returned to the air strip. After landing and putting away her flight suit and goggles, she noticed a small poster on the bulletin board. It was a call for female pilots by the Women's Auxiliary Ferrying Squadron (WAFS). She noted the name and address for the program and decided to research it.

Florence called close friends whose fathers or older brothers were in the U.S. Army Air Force to learn more about the WAFS. Her persistence yielded results. Florence learned that the famous Jacqueline "Jackie" Cochran and test-pilot Nancy Harkness Love submitted proposals prior to America's entrance into World War II for female pilots to fly noncombat missions for the U.S. Army Air Force. Hap Arnold had turned down Love's proposals. But, after the attack on Pearl Harbor, the resourceful Love petitioned General William H. Tunner, head of the Air Transport Command (ATC), for a civilian position with ATC. Tunner agreed, and, soon, women pilots began ferrying planes from factory to military airfields as part of ATC.

Before Florence decided to contact Nancy Love, she did some research on the female test pilot. Nancy Love had graduated from Vassar and had been a flyer since age sixteen. The more Florence learned about Nancy Love, the more she wanted to meet this flyer. Finally, she decided to contact Love. Her first attempts to reach Love were unsuccessful because of the test pilot's busy schedule. However, a determined Florence turned to her father's cousin, U.S. House of Representative Forrest Marmion, for help. A telephone call from Forrest to General Tunner resulted in Love finally returning Florence's call. She was in Delaware and surprised when Florence identified herself and wanted to learn more about the WAFS program.

"You want to join?" asked Love.

"If you let me fly planes to England," said Florence.

"Are you a licensed pilot?" asked Love. When Florence said yes and told her the number of hours she had flown solo, that she could fly multiengine planes, and had flown across the Atlantic on several occasions in her father's plane, Love began taking notes.

"Your father wouldn't be General Quentin Norvell?" asked a curious Love.

"Yes, he's a major general in the army," Florence told him. "But, I don't want to involve him. I want to do this on my own."

Intrigued by what Florence shared, Love asked Florence to send a resume and background information to her. Florence took down Nancy Love's address and said she would send the resume and other materials in a few days. After ending their telephone call, Nancy Love decided to make a few inquiries about General Norvell *and* his daughter.

* * *

Marlon, now a major, arrived in England during the middle of February 1943 for service with the Fifty-sixth Fighter Group. He was assigned to a new squadron at Horsham St. Faith, England, as the executive officer. His orders were to help train new pilots for combat duties. New models of the P-47 Thunderbolt were arriving along with replacement parts. Marlon was assigned to overview ground support personnel and make certain they became efficient in servicing and maintaining the new aircraft. Because of Marlon's combat experience, the commanding officer (CO) relied on him to "whip the squadron" into shape.

The new squadron would not become operational and go into combat until Marlon and the squadron leader were convinced the pilots were ready. Formation flying, tactics, and gunnery practice were essential. But, the weather in February 1943 was uncooperative and sometimes deadly. On several training missions, some pilots were lost because of rapid changes in the weather. Unpredictable fast moving weather systems and storms swept across England, along with dense fogs that reduced visibility to just a few feet. Even though the squadron had yet to fly a single combat mission, seven pilots lost their planes because of fog and foul weather. Three of them had been killed.

"The weather is as bad a killer as the Krauts," said Lieutenant Colonel Tully Kilmer, the squadron leader. "Keep working the boys on instrument flying, and I'll get on the weather guys to give us better info than the crap they've sent," he told Marlon. Tully was from North Carolina and had seen action in the Pacific before being sent to North Africa as "liaison" with the British Desert Air Force (DAF). While in the Pacific, he had shot down four Japanese planes. With the DAF, he had flown numerous combat missions and shot down seven German planes. Marlon considered Tully a "top notch" fighter pilot and a strong leader.

The weather closed in on Horsham St. Faith often, and Tully told Marlon to give leave to the squadron's pilots and ground personnel. "Rotate 'em," said Tully. "Make sure we have enough pilots and personnel to get into the air if we're alerted." Marlon nodded.

"This weather stinks," Tully continued. "A bit of R&R in London will help our guys," he added. "You and I'll trade off time for being away. One of us has to be here all the time."

Late in February, Marlon got a long weekend pass. The weather was frigid, with sleet during the day turning to snow flurries at night. He traveled to London and arrived at his father's top-floor flat and learned that Quentin was "away." He called Erleen and told her he would be in London for a day or two. She asked if he could join her for dinner that evening. He said yes and asked what time for dinner.

"Dinner is at eight," she replied. "Where are you staying? I'll send Fowler (her chauffer) to fetch you." He gave his father's address and telephone. Erleen said her car would "collect" him at seven. He grinned at the sound of her voice and the vernacular she used. He looked forward to seeing her.

It was dark and bitterly cold when Fowler arrived. The English winters were brutal, and the damp cold, especially when it was windy, cut through Marlon's clothing like a knife. He greeted Fowler politely and made small talk with the older man as they drove through the darkness. Marlon was surprised when Fowler drove up to a large home in an exclusive part of London. He did not recognize the home and asked Fowler about it.

"This is Lady Linne's home," said Fowler. "Miss Coxwythe is expecting you."

When Marlon rang the bell, the ornate doors were opened by an older man dressed in formal attire. The pilot kicked the snow off his shoes and stepped into a large and well-appointed foyer.

"May I take your things?" asked the older man.

As Marlon was handing his cap, scarf, gloves, and overcoat to the servant, Linne approached him. She was lovely, dressed fashionably and wearing a sparkling dark blue stoned necklace with matching earrings. She greeted Marlon with a charming smile that revealed white teeth and kissed him on the cheek.

"Erleen is in with the guests," she told Marlon while taking his arm.

He inhaled her scent, a soft perfume that was pleasing to his sense of smell.

"Your father is away," she told him, "otherwise, he would be with us."

He smiled at her without saying anything. But, he was curious about her knowledge of Quentin's whereabouts and wondered about the two of them. He was quickly distracted from thoughts about Lady Linne and his father when they entered a large room filled with people, most of them in British uniforms. He scanned the room quickly and saw Erleen excuse herself from a group of British officers. She smiled affectionately at Marlon as she approached.

She's quite lovely, thought Marlon, as he took her hand to kiss the back of it.

"I've missed you," said Erleen. "Have you been hiding?"

He smiled and said his new duties were demanding and did not allow much time for him to be in London.

"Where are you stationed?" she asked.

"Near Horsham St. Faith," he said without being explicit.

She made a mental note of it. "Would you like some champagne?" she asked.

He smiled and said, "Absolutely."

That evening, Marlon realized several things. He was one of four American officers in the room. They were treated politely, but not fully integrated into the groups of British officers.

The U.S. officers (a captain, a major, and a lieutenant colonel) were staff personnel. Among the four, he was the only one with combat experience. Three of the British officers were Royal Navy and had seen action. Even though he shared combat experience with the three British officers, there was little other than a brief, polite exchange between them. There were several very attractive young women in the room, but Linne and Erleen were special to Marlon. The single English officers wasted little time surrounding both of them, something that amused him. While Erleen was young and vivacious, Marlon took time to reassess Linne. He watched her closely and discovered that she was clever and witty, and she easily parried the advances of the single men and one or two married ones.

During dinner, Linne asked Marlon to sit on her left. A British brigadier and his wife sat on her right. Erleen sat on Marlon's left, and, during the meal, she chatted with the American and with Linne.

They talked about different topics, but the conversations around the dinner table, for the most part, focused on the war. The British naval officers had the most positive news to share, saying they (Royal Navy) had destroyed several of the best German capital ships. The news about the British army was not as good. The English were holding their own in North Africa and, with the help of the Americans and the Australians, were starting to push back the Japanese in New Guinea. They all cheered and toasted the brave Allied sailors and soldiers.

Just after the main course was served, the brigadier asked Linne how she had managed to get the fresh vegetables and beef they were having. She smiled and said that General Norvell had introduced her to Lt. Colonel Tinker and that the American colonel provided the food. She recognized Tinker and praised his efforts and generosity in locating the beef and vegetables. Tinker smiled modestly and said nothing. However, the brigadier finished his second glass of wine and paid the Americans a backhanded compliment. Marlon was annoyed by the remark and wanted to say something, but he held his tongue. Perhaps the brigadier was angry at something and had had too much to drink. He nudged Linne and nodded in the English officer's direction. She put her left hand on his right forearm, acting as if she was going to talk past him to Erleen, and whispered that the brigadier had been passed over for command of a regiment that was going to North Africa. Marlon nodded. But he wondered what his father would have done and perhaps said to the brigadier.

The next day, late in the afternoon, Marlon met Quentin at his flat. The Cajun had recently returned from a trip. As they sat together in front of the large fireplace where a warming fire burned, Marlon shared some of what had taken place at Linne's home.

"I didn't appreciate what the brigadier said," Marlon told him. "I just don't understand."

"What do you mean?" asked Quentin, intrigued by his son's comment.

"Well, we're here to help the Brits, but they don't seem to appreciate us."

Quentin thought about Marlon's remarks. A few minutes of silenced passed between them before the Cajun spoke up. "Marlon, you need to consider a few things. Not all Brits resent us. I've met many English people glad we're here to help, but we do have our share of detractors."

Marlon looked intently at his father, waiting for him to continue.

"We're newcomers to the war, son," said the Cajun. "The English have been fighting since 1939 and have suffered considerably. The German U-boat campaign has deprived England of food and supplies. Some of the people here are barely making it. A few resent us for not entering the war sooner. Hard to disagree with them on that," he said softly. Marlon sat quietly, listening. "Every week, son, hundreds of GIs arrive in England. I see increasing numbers of them at new air bases and army compounds. However, not everyone cares for our troops."

"Why, Dad?" asked Marlon.

"Well, our GIs are better paid and better outfitted than the Tommies. Our troops are well fed, have an abundance of candy bars, cigarettes, and chewing gum. It's hard for some Brits to see that after all they've endured. Too many of our GIs don't realize or appreciate the English institutions, such as the monarchy. We may share a common language, but it stops there." He paused to give his son a chance to say something. Instead, Marlon was silent and waited for his father to continue.

"Parents of English girls are concerned that GIs are becoming too familiar with their daughters and changing their attitudes. Our music and culture are new and differ considerably from the English."

"Why do some of the Brits, like in the RAF, look down on us?" asked Marlon.

"It's the class system," said Quentin. "We have class differences back in the States, but no titled, landed gentry. The separation between aristocrats and commoners is what you've experienced," said the Cajun. "The privileged here have priority in the military. It's not always a good thing. We have our share of favoritism in the army and navy," he mentioned, "and it causes problems." Marlon nodded. They talked for a while longer before Quentin asked if Marlon could join him for dinner.

"Can't, Dad," said Marlon. "I have a date. You having dinner alone?" asked Marlon.

"No, I'm getting together with a few of our top brass and three visiting congressmen. I'm introducing them to Glinda Pennington." Marlon chuckled. "Tell me how you're doing with the new squadron?" asked the Cajun.

Marlon shared how pleased he was to serve under Lieutenant Colonel Tully Kilmer.

"What about the P-47s?" asked the Cajun.

"It's a tough plane and a good fighter, but its range is limited," said Marlon. His father smiled and mused about what an excellent fighter the Spitfire was.

The Cajun asked him about the XP-51 currently under development. Marlon said it was a good design, but it needed more power and other improvements. Quentin said he understood and told Marlon changes were coming. "It's just a matter time," added Quentin.

tunnel, and Jacques and Teodoro, two older men with the resistance.

"You need to change your clothes," said Alcina. In the next twenty minutes, Nadine and Moira changed their clothes and covered their heads with shawls to look like the local women. Moira removed the microfiche from the umbrella and handed it to Nadine.

They were eating when a knock on the kitchen door surprised them. Jacques cautiously asked who it was and heard the voice of a young boy reply. He opened the door, and a red faced boy stepped into the kitchen. In an excited voice the boy said, "Boche soldiers are in the village."

"How many and where?" asked Quennel. The boy said two truck loads—about twenty soldiers and several other men in dark leather coats.

"Gestapo!" exclaimed Alcina. "You must leave immediately," she warned. "Rene," she said to the boy, "take them to the old livery stable near the pond." Then, she gave Nadine and Moira shopping baskets to carry while Teodoro handed each of them a pistol.

Quennel left first and disappeared down the street heading south. A few minutes later, Rene, Nadine, and Moira left the house by the rear entrance and walked toward the south side of the village. Rene led them through some back yards until they approached a pond and what looked like an old barn. They entered the stable from the rear and saw Quennel talking with two men next to a delivery truck and an old Citröen.

"We must separate," said Quennel. "Madame," he told Nadine politely, "please go with Lawrence in the car. Mademoiselle," he said to Moira, "you will come with me in the truck." Nadine was about to say something when they heard shots.

"Go, go," Quennel shouted at Nadine and Lawrence. Then, he told Rene to leave immediately. Nadine got into the Citröen with Lawrence while Quennel opened the front doors to the stable so that the car could get out. Once it was gone, he and the other man helped Moira into the truck and prepared to leave. As luck would have it, the truck's engine would not start. Quennel jumped out and threw open one of the flaps over the engine.

"It's the carburetor," he told the other man. "I'll need a moment to fix it." It took Quennel less than three minutes to replace a spring on the carburetor. "Now try it," he said to the other man. The starter cranked several times before the engine coughed and came to life. Just as they left the stable and turned to the right, a large, dark convertible pulled up behind them and a soldier fired a machine gun at the truck, shooting out one of the rear tires.

"No good," said the driver. "Run to the woods on the other side of the pond," he told Quennel and Moira. "I'll try to hold them here." Quennel took Moira by the arm and led her in the direction of the woods, trying to use the truck to shield them. However, a tall German officer pointed at Quennel, and a marksman fired a Mauser with a telescopic sight, hitting the Frenchman square in the back and knocking him down.

"Go," pleaded the wounded Frenchman to Moira. "Don't let them catch you," he said, struggling to his knees and drawing his pistol to fire at the Germans. Moira cocked the pistol Teodoro had given her and shot at the advancing Germans. She managed to wound one of them, but the marksman hit her in the right shoulder, spinning her around and momentarily knocking her to the ground.

Moira felt an intense burning pain as the bullet hit her shoulder, and she let out a cry. She heard more shots. She turned in time to see Quennel fall backward, hit by a fusillade of bullets from a German MP 40 machine gun. She staggered and stood up, turning toward the pursuing

Germans and began shooting at them until one of them fired his submachine gun.

Moira shuddered from the impact of the bullets and wavered momentarily. The pistol dropped involuntarily from her hand. She no longer had any control over her body and fell to the ground. The last thing she saw was the tall German officer running toward her. He seemed strangely distressed. Then, her eyes closed forever.

Hauptman Helmut Zollner kneeled next to Moira and examined the lifeless woman. He searched for a pulse but could not find one.

"I told you I wanted her alive," he said angrily to the soldier with the submachine gun. The German soldier did not respond to the reproach; instead, he stood stiffly at attention. Zollner opened a portfolio with photographs and removed a photo of Moira and compared it with the dead woman. He wrote a note to himself and then began searching the body.

"Search the Frenchman too," he barked "and that truck. I want to know who owns it." After both bodies were searched, Zollner collected what Quennel and Moira had and what was found in the truck. He told the sergeant in charge of the squad of soldiers to drag the bodies to the side of the road and leave them there.

"Booby trap them," he told the sergeant. Then, he got into the large convertible and told the driver to go.

* * *

Lawrence sped along the road heading south, with Nadine looking back expecting to see the truck follow. But after five minutes she realized Quennel and Moira were not coming.

"Madame," said Lawrence, "we must leave this road and hide the car. The Boche will set up roadblocks ahead." He turned onto a dirt road and headed west until they reached a copse of trees. He drove the car off the road and stopped in front of some dense underbrush and asked Nadine to step out.

"Help me push it into the bushes," he told her. After the car was deep in the undergrowth, they covered it and wiped away any traces of where it had gone off the road.

"Come," he told her. "We walk from now on."

The weather was cold and bitter, and although her clothes were warm, Nadine's feet felt icy. Lawrence walked briskly and Nadine kept pace with him. He admired her. She was in good shape and resilient and did not complain. Twice they hid in the bushes as a single engine German observation plane flew over them.

The sun was low on the horizon, partially obscured by clouds, when Lawrence said they should rest for a while.

"The Boche want you very badly," he told Nadine. She smiled but remained silent. "We need to go several more kilometers," he said. "We'll stay at an abandoned farm tonight. Tomorrow, we'll go south until we reach a place where you will be safe."

They slept in an old barn that night and rose before dawn. The clouds were thickening, and Lawrence said it might rain and perhaps snow.

"We must reach a safe house before the weather worsens," he told Nadine. "We must hurry."

"I understand," she told him. "I'll keep up."

He looked at her and smiled. *She's lovely and courageous,* he thought, *the kind of woman every man wants.*

The rain began in the early afternoon, a few scattered showers at first, then a wind came up, and the showers increased. They hurried along footpaths that were narrow and muddy. It was almost three in the afternoon when Lawrence said they were close to the safe house. They reached a clearing and hid at the edge of the woods just as the rain began to intensify. In the clearing was a small house with smoke coming from a chimney.

"Do you have a pistol?" he asked. She nodded and showed it to him. "Do you know how to use it?" Again, she nodded. "Good," he told her. "I'm going to the house. If you hear shooting, hide in the woods."

Nadine watched Lawrence walk cautiously toward the old house, peer in through the windows, and then disappear around the side of the building. She stood in the woods holding the pistol in her right hand covered by part of her shawl to keep it dry. The cold rain penetrated her clothing causing her to shiver. She worried about Lawrence until she heard him say, "Madame, it's all right; come this way." He was holding a lantern and waving at her. They walked to the entrance of the old house and were greeted by an older couple and a young girl.

"You'll be safe here," said Lawrence.

It would take Nadine almost eight days to reach Bergerac. The railroads, all the main roads, and even some of the unpaved back roads were swarming with Gestapo and SS troops. The cold and rainy weather worked in the favor of the Maquis and Nadine, preventing German observation planes from flying over fields and paths they used to travel south. Maquis from different districts along the route south took responsibility for transporting Nadine from one area to the next. The lovely Frenchwoman was guarded carefully by members of the resistance, determined to prevent the Gestapo from apprehending her. Although her protectors did not know she was Eglantine, a few suspected it.

On the last day of February 1943, a thin, tired, and resolute Nadine arrived at a safe house on the outskirts of Bergerac. Under the cover or darkness, she was hidden in a wagon and taken to a farmhouse just to the west of Bergerac. As she was helped out of her hiding place in the wagon, she recognized a familiar voice. When she alighted, Nadine recognized Noel and hugged him.

"Madame," said Noel in a solicitous tone, "it's good to see you again. Come, we have food and fresh clothing. A bath can be arranged."

"Moira," she said, the name uttered with profound sadness.

Noel, his voice sad and soft said, "Yes, we heard. Please, come inside," he told her. "We have much to tell you."

* * *

Quentin was working late on March 2 when the duty officer knocked on his door and said he had an urgent telephone call. He thanked the lieutenant and picked up the telephone and heard a serious Brook Hamilton Stoner greet him.

"What's up?" asked Quentin, his interest piqued by the diplomat's call and manner.

"We need to talk," said Stoner, "now." When Quentin asked what it was about, the diplomat insisted they talk in private.

"All right," said the Cajun. "I've got some—"

"I'll pick you up in a few minutes."

Quentin realized something serious had happened.

Ten minutes later, Stoner arrived in a black sedan. He opened the back door and motioned for the Cajun to get in. Once Quentin was in the car, Stoner told the driver to go to the U.S. Embassy.

"What's going on?" asked an apprehensive Quentin.

"The Germans are after Nadine. She's fled Paris," said Stoner. The Cajun was silent and somber as Stoner shared the information he'd received from Christine in Lisbon. "I would have come sooner, but the weather kept me grounded," he said.

"Do we know where she is?" asked the Cajun.

"She's still in France, but we don't know where," he told Quentin. "She said she'd contact us when it was safe," he added.

"God damn it," said Quentin angrily as he squeezed the strap at the side of the door in the sedan. "I never should have left her in France."

When they reached the embassy, Stoner took Quentin to a small conference room. It was almost 7:30 p.m.

"You hungry, sport?" asked Stoner. Quentin said no, and instead asked for coffee. Stoner used the intercom to order coffee.

Stoner said that Nadine was not in Paris when the Gestapo ordered her arrest. She was at La Croisiere. From the French underground, they (American Military Intelligence) learned that Nadine, her executive assistant, Moira, and most of her personal help had fled. He said, "Her personal secretary, Moira Tedoux, was killed along with some members of the resistance in a small town called Trelissac."

"How do you know that?" asked Quentin.

Stoner said the French resistance had provided the information. He watched the Cajun's expression turn from apprehension to a controlled anger. They sat and talked for almost fifteen minutes before the diplomat asked Quentin what he was thinking.

"I'm going to France and bring her out," said Quentin sternly.

"I don't think that's possible," said Stoner, trying to be tactful.

"She won't leave France unless I bring her out," Quentin told him forcefully.

"The brass won't let you go," said Stoner, watching carefully the expression on the Cajun's face. He'd heard about a cold and determined streak in Quentin, but this was the first time he'd seen him so intense.

"Well, we'll see about that," said Quentin, standing up preparing to leave.

"What are you going to do?" asked Stoner, curious about the Cajun's plans.

"I'm going to talk with Eisenhower," he replied.

Stoner shook his head and wished him good luck, convinced Eisenhower would never consent to Quentin going to France.

In the next few days, Quentin met with his superior officer and then tried to meet with General Eisenhower. However, Ike was not available. Instead, he was referred to General Walter Bedell Smith. It took a few days for the Cajun to finally meet with General Smith.

"You want to do what?" screamed Smith. "You're out of your mind," he added.

"I need to go," said the Cajun, speaking up before a red-faced Smith could say anything.

"Let me make it simple for you," said an angry General Smith, "the answer is no. God dammit, Norvell, we're not letting you go to France and that's final. Now get the hell out of my office." Smith glowered at Quentin. But, once again, he saw something in the younger man's eyes that alerted him. *The son of a bitch is going to do something crazy,* thought Smith.

Quentin saluted Smith, turned, and walked out of the office. That afternoon, he called the embassy and asked to speak with Brook Hamilton Stoner. A few minutes later, Stoner was on the line.

"What's up, sport?" Quentin said he needed his help. "What do you need?" asked the diplomat. In the next few minutes, Quentin asked Stoner to contact Roosevelt and have the president approve a meeting with him in Washington to include Ruben Valderano and General Marshall.

"I don't know," said a cautious Stoner. "The president might not want to do this."

"When you speak to the president," said Quentin, "tell him it's a personal matter, and I'm calling in a promise he made to me."

"All right," Stoner told him, "but don't get your hopes up." The next day, the diplomat called the White House and said he wanted to speak with the president on an urgent matter. Two hours later, Roosevelt called Stoner and listened to the diplomat's petition from Quentin. Roosevelt asked a few questions before saying he would get back to him.

Twenty-four hours later, Quentin received an urgent message from Washington, summoning him to the White House. That same day, Quentin met with his superior officer in London and shared the orders calling him to Washington. The next morning, he was on a plane heading to the United States and the White House.

The weather in Washington was clear and cold, with an icy wind blowing across the nation's capital. A military car was waiting for Quentin at the airport and took him to Fort Myer in Virginia. A room was reserved for him on the post and a confidential message informed him about a meeting with the president early the following morning. There was also a note from Ruben Valderano and a telephone number where he could be reached.

Quentin called Ruben, and they agreed to meet at Valderano's home for dinner that evening. After dinner, Julia Valderano hugged Quentin and left the room. When they were alone, Ruben and Quentin talked about Nadine.

"You want to go and get her, don't you?" asked Ruben.

Quentin nodded.

"*Hombre*, do you realize what's involved?"

Quentin didn't respond.

After waiting a moment, Ruben continued. "Let's assume you get into France. How will you find Nadine?

Remember, the Gestapo is looking for her. If you do manage to find her, can you convince her to leave with you?"

Quentin remained silent, but his jaw was set and his eyes focused squarely on Ruben.

"*Amigo*," Ruben spoke up, trying to reason with the Cajun. "You're not trained in infiltration. If the Germans get you—"

"They won't," snapped Quentin, cutting off the Mexican.

"Think, *hombre*," Ruben said quickly, "what you want is extremely dangerous and nearly impossible." He watched Quentin carefully, waiting for his response. Much to his surprise, the Cajun sat back in his chair and calmly said he had a plan. It required the president's permission and assistance, and Ruben's brother, Bishop Valderano, must help.

After hearing what Quentin had in mind, Ruben frowned, but he did not say anything.

"Will your brother help?" asked the Cajun.

"I don't know," replied Ruben. "You're asking quite a bit of him."

They talked for over an hour before Quentin said it was late and he needed to go. As he stood to leave, the Cajun looked at his friend and said, "Ruben, I need you on this. I can't do it without you."

The Mexican sighed, stood, and embraced the Cajun.

"We're friends, but what you're asking, well, it's not easy," said Ruben. The two men stood looking at each other without saying anything. Finally, Ruben said he'd think about it.

* * *

It was early in the morning when Quentin arrived at the White House and was escorted to where Roosevelt,

Marshall and Ruben were waiting. He noticed that the president looked tired and had aged considerably since the last time he saw him. After exchanging greetings, the president began by asking Quentin what was on his mind.

"Mr. President," said the Cajun, "I'd like your help to get into southern France and bring out Nadine Desnoyers."

"Do you know where she is?" asked the president.

The Cajun replied no, but quickly followed up that he had two ways to locate her.

"Tell me," Roosevelt pressed.

Quentin replied that Ruben's brother, Bishop Valderano, could locate her.

"And if he refuses?" challenged the president.

The Cajun proposed going to Lisbon and meeting with Christine, Nadine's daughter, to make contact.

Roosevelt turned to look at the Mexican and asked, "Will your brother help?"

Without hesitation, Ruben told the president he was prepared to call his brother and ask for his assistance.

"Can he locate her?" asked Marshall.

"I think so," replied Ruben.

The president was silent for a long time, a pregnant pause that kept the other men in the room waiting. "Ruben, contact your brother immediately. Quentin, you must abide by what Bishop Valderano does. If he declines to help, I won't approve your plan to enter France. However, I will ask Colonel Donovan (head of the Office of Strategic Service) to see if his people can locate Madame Desnoyers and find a way to bring her out of France."

Quentin looked at the president intently before speaking up. "Thank you, Mr. President. I hope Bishop Valderano agrees to help. If he declines, I doubt anyone within the OSS can find and convince Nadine to leave France."

"What makes you think you can persuade her to leave France? Assuming, that is, you can find her?" asked Marshall.

"She's given me her word," replied the Cajun. "Besides, she's more valuable to us in London working with our intelligence people than hiding in France."

Ruben glanced at the impassive Marshall and then turned his attention to Roosevelt for his reaction. The president took off his glasses and massaged the bridge of his nose before saying anything. Quentin noticed how tired he looked. *I hate to put more things on his back,* thought the Cajun, *he's already carrying quite a load.*

"All right," Roosevelt finally pronounced. "Remember what I said, Quentin."

* * *

Quentin returned to London and waited to learn whether Bishop Valderano would agree to help locate Nadine. He decided not to mention Nadine's flight and pursuit by the Gestapo to Marlon. *Besides*, he thought, *he might want to come along, and I can't allow that!*

Five days later, Quentin was summoned to the U.S. Embassy in London. He was ushered into a small room where a man in civilian clothes identified himself as Richard Kraemer with the OSS.

"Colonel Donovan has assigned me to handle your operation," said Kraemer. "We've heard from a diplomatic officer in the Vatican that he'll help locate 'B' in France. 'B' is the codeword for Madame Desnoyers."

Quentin remained impassive as Kraemer outlined what would happen. The Cajun would be relieved of his duties in London with a cover story that he was on temporary duty at a secret base in the United States where a new fighter plane was being tested. An OSS operative had been assigned to work with him. The next day he would leave for commando training.

"We're going to give you an accelerated training program," said Kraemer. When the Cajun asked how long the training would last, the OSS officer said three weeks and maybe less if news about "B's" location reached them. They talked for a few minutes longer with Kraemer answering the few questions the Cajun put to him.

"All right," said Kraemer, "you need to get back to your office and clear your schedule. A car will pick you up at eight o'clock tonight in front of your residence. Pack your B-2 bag and bring it along.

That evening, a dark sedan was waiting for Quentin when he exited the building. A stocky man approached and asked if he was General Norvell. When Quentin said yes, he opened the back door to the sedan. A man seated in the back motioned for him to get in and asked to see his AGO card. He used a penlight to compare Quentin's face to a small photograph he had of the Cajun and then carefully examined his identification. When he was satisfied, he told the man waiting at the side of the car to put Quentin's B-2 bag in the trunk and get in the car.

"OK, let's go," said the man in the backseat.

The following day, Quentin arrived at a nondescript, isolated English farm. At the gate to the property, a man in civilian clothes examined his documents. A few minutes later, he was escorted to a large, charming old house. There, he was met by two men. The older of the two was gray haired, medium height, and perhaps in his late forties. The other man was younger, about five feet eleven and trim.

"Welcome," said the older man, "my name is Simpson. From now on, you will use the code name 'Crow.' You will not use your regular name. Is that clear?" Quentin nodded. "Good," said Simpson. "This is Lieutenant Romero. His code name is 'Robin.' Now, follow me."

Quentin was briefed thoroughly about the rules at the "facility" and what he could and could not do. He would have no contact with the outside until a decision was made regarding the "operation." After the orientation, Lieutenant Romero, Robin, showed him to his room and said he should change into fatigues. "We're going to do some target practice," he said.

In the next few days, Quentin rose early and did long runs with Robin. His language skills were improved by native Spanish and French speakers, and he was taught to use colloquialisms prevalent in Northern Spain and southern France. His language trainers were impressed with his ability to speak both tongues fluently and without any accent. At target practice, Robin was impressed with his marksmanship. At the beginning of the second week he was assigned to an instructor for hand to hand combat training. Even though Quentin was in his midforties, he had excellent balance and coordination and was physically fit from his daily fitness regimen. He took numerous falls, including some that bruised him. However, he did not complain. It did not take him long to master the different moves and techniques taught by his instructor, including the use of a knife for fighting in close quarters.

From the first day that Quentin began his training at the facility, he was given things to memorize. His cover listed him as born in Amedo, a small town in Spain in the province of Navarra. He was forty-two and a widower. His parents were killed during the Spanish Civil War, and he was taken in by a family in the Rioja wine area. There, he learned his trade: making, scouring, and repairing wine barrels. He completed eight years of schooling. He traveled to southern France each year since 1939 to work in wineries that relied on him and others from Spain to help with the harvests. Manpower in France was limited because of the forced labor required of Frenchmen by the Germans. Every day, his trainers tested him regularly about his background, schooling, and training as a cooper until he could respond flawlessly to any question.

At the beginning of the third week, Quentin was taken to parachute training. After the second day, he did two practice jumps. He landed hard at the end of each jump, but he rolled in the way his instructors had taught him. "Good job, Crow" his trainer said while patting him on the shoulder after the second jump. "That'll do it for you," he added.

By the middle of the third week of Quentin's training, Robin addressed him as Crow and complimented the Cajun and said he was doing very well. Quentin liked Robin and trusted his abilities and the confident way he did things. There was a toughness and determination in Robin that impressed the Cajun.

On Friday of the third week, Quentin was awakened at 1:30 a.m. and told to dress in clothes that Robin gave him. He was instructed to leave all of his things in the room. They were taken by small plane to an air strip in southern England. It was raining when they landed at the isolated airfield. The plane taxied to a hangar where they were greeted by two men and a woman. Quentin was taken to a small room where he was given a Spanish identity card and travel documents. Then, he was subjected to a two-hour intensive interrogation and cross examination, including several slaps in the face by the woman. He did not flinch at the blows and stuck to his story.

Elsewhere at the airfield, Lieutenant Romero met with a major in the OSS and was given special instructions.

"Lieutenant," said the major in a serious voice, "you must not let Crow fall into enemy hands. If you're in danger of being apprehended, terminate Crow. Is that understood?" Romero was silent, instead, looking at the major without blinking an eye. "Lieutenant," said the major, raising his voice. "Did you understand what I told you?" Romero answered affirmatively. "If you cannot do it, we scrub this operation," said the major, his blue eyes studying Romero carefully.

"I understand, sir," Romero replied forcefully. He had been on several missions into occupied France to deliver guns and ammunition to the Maquis and to help people, usually downed flyers, escape through southern France into Spain. But, this was the first time he was ordered to eliminate a fellow American if the person was in danger of being caught. He put the thought of killing Crow out of his mind. *But can I do it?* he wondered.

It was almost eleven in the morning when Quentin's interrogation and testing was finished.

"I'm sorry I had to strike you," said the woman with an English accent. "But, if the Jerries get you, they'll do far worse. Don't get caught," she warned.

"There's one last thing, Crow," said one of the men as he handed Quentin a small matchbox. Inside was a white pill. "It's a cyanide pill. If the Krauts catch you, take it. It works fast." Quentin pocketed the small matchbox without saying a word.

"It's almost lunchtime," said the woman. "We have sandwiches and coffee." She and the two men walked with Quentin to a small dining room. Waiting for them was Romero and a major that Quentin had never seen before. No names were exchanged, just handshakes.

Before the six of them sat to eat, the major, referring to them as Robin and Crow, mentioned that they would leave as soon as it was dark. As they ate, Quentin wondered about the people at this air strip. They were OSS personnel, and he surmised it was an operational area where last-minute briefings were given to operatives headed for the Continent. He wondered if other operatives were given cyanide pills in case they were caught.

The OSS personnel made small talk and shared information about Allied military activities in North Africa. When they finished eating, the major told Quentin and Romero about a small room where they could relax or sleep until it was time to go.

At first, Quentin thought he could not sleep because of his anticipation. He stared at the metal ceiling in the room until his eyes grew heavy. A gentle shake of his shoulder by Romero woke him.

"Time to go," said Romero, as he stuffed a red scarf into his coat.

Once more, Quentin was queried by the OSS people. When they were satisfied, he was given everything he needed, including a small nine millimeter pistol and a switchblade knife used by Spaniards. "If you're stopped by the Germans, discard the pistol but keep the knife. Good luck," they told him.

It was dark when Romero and Quentin walked to their twin engine aircraft. The bulky parachute felt heavy and the harness restrictive. Romero made certain that the Cajun's chute and equipment were all in order before they entered the aircraft. Twenty minutes later, they were in the air and rendezvoused with a flight of B-25s.

"They're our cover," shouted Romero over the roar of the engines. "They'll over fly our LZ so that Jerry thinks it's some kind of raid or training flight."

An hour and a half later, Quentin and Romero parachuted into the night over southern France.

CHAPTER 19
A KNIGHT'S ERRAND

Oh, young Lochinvar is come out of the West,
Through all the wide Border his steed was the best.
Sir Walter Scott, *Lochinvar*

Marlon had called Quentin's office to learn of his whereabouts and been told that his father was on temporary duty in the United States. He left a message for Quentin to call him on his return. Marlon had numerous things to share with his father. The training program for the new flyers was nearly completed. Nine planes and five pilots were lost to bad weather and pilot error. Marlon observed carefully the performance of the new pilots, recording flying procedures that needed review and recommended modifications for the P-47. The weather over the Channel and the Continent could change quickly. Pilots needed to rely on their instruments when the ceiling dropped or when rain and fog reduced visibility. Most of all, Marlon thought that additional gunnery practice was needed and that pairing a new flyer with an experienced combat pilot was crucial. Then, there were the quirks associated with the plane they flew.

The Thunderbolt was a powerful, rugged plane that was well armored and with self-sealing fuel tanks. However, Marlon thought it needed a bubble canopy for improved visibility and additional power. The P-47's range was good but not sufficient to allow the heavy fighter to escort American bombers deep into enemy territory. The auxiliary drop tanks fitted to the Thunderbolts were a problem. The two-hundred-gallon drop-tanks would not feed fuel to the engine above twenty-one thousand feet. Yet, Marlon liked the rugged seven ton fighter. It performed very well above twenty-two thousand feet and could reach 400 mph in a shallow dive. He was eager to test the plane against Bf 109s and FW 190s. That couldn't come soon enough to please him.

As the training of new pilots in Marlon's squadron intensified and involved increasingly demanding tactics and maneuvers, there were fewer opportunities for him to get leave. Also, the weather in early March 1943 allowed few good days of flying time. Consequently, weekends and week days were all the same. When the weather was good, they flew. When it was bad, Marlon kept the pilots doing ground work and simulations. The training tended to irritate some of the pilots, especially those eager to "mix it up" with the Germans.

"Don't worry," Marlon told the new pilots, "you'll get your chance to take on the Krauts."

* * *

In America, Florence had sent a resume, documentation on flying abilities, including a copy of her pilot's license, and certificates on instrument and multiengine flying capabilities to Nancy Love at the beginning of March 1943. Two weeks later, a letter from Love arrived indicating her papers had been received and that the background materials would be examined. The last paragraph in the letter stated it might take a few weeks for her files to be reviewed.

I'll give her (Nancy Love) three weeks, Florence told herself. *If I don't hear from her by the end of the first week of April, then I'll try something else.* One way or another, Florence was determined to find a way to fly to England and be near Marlon.

The young blonde was at home practicing the piano. While doing some scales for practice, she considered contacting her father and enlisting his support and assistance to join the WAFS. However, she soon put aside that notion because Quentin might not want her to ferry military planes across the Atlantic.

I know, Father, she thought. *He'll tell me to finish up at Juilliard. He's a stickler for finishing schooling.* She did the practice scales and runs on the keyboard almost automatically while remembering how Marlon had wanted to join the French Air Service in 1939 and early 1940. Quentin had convinced her brother to finish his schooling at MIT.

No, she mused while practicing fingering techniques, *I'll do it without telling Daddy.*

Meanwhile, Nancy Love had read the material Florence sent. On paper, the young woman was an excellent flyer and someone the Women's Auxiliary Ferry Squadron could use. However, other information she had received about Florence made her hesitate. Florence Norvell was a gifted musician, considered by some a prodigy on the piano. Her father was a two star general in the army and formerly a highly successful lawyer with a top law firm in New York City. Love wondered how General Novell felt about his daughter joining the WAFS. Rather than do anything on Florence Norvell's request, Love decided to let it sit for a while. Besides, she had so many other things to do.

* * *

"Madame," Noel told Nadine when they were alone, "I have news for you." He had managed to save most of her jewels and entrust them to Millard. However, those that she kept in a bank vault would be confiscated by the Germans. He had converted several thousand Francs into bearer bonds and transferred funds Nadine had secretly set aside in case of an emergency to a bank in Lisbon. "The bearer bonds we can use anywhere," he told her. "The money in the Lisbon bank can be accessed be either of us, but only in person," he added. "Now, we must see about changing your appearance and then moving south to the Spanish border."

"I'm not leaving France," she said softly, but firmly.

"But, Madame," protested Noel, "the Gestapo—"

"I'm aware of the danger," she told him, "but there is much I can still do here."

The Frenchman looked at her with awe. He had always admired this remarkable woman and would gladly give his life for her. Even though she was a fugitive, her home, lands, enterprises, and possessions confiscated by the Boche, Nadine wanted to remain in France and fight, even though she could escape to freedom.

"You must realize the danger you pose to those around you," said Noel. "The Gestapo will seize and torture anyone they suspect of knowing you."

She knew the risks, not just for herself, but for anyone close to her. Yet, she was determined to stay. Aware she could not be dissuaded, Noel suggested Nadine change her appearance before they left. She smiled and said, "Bon! Now, a trip to the beauty parlor."

Nadine cut her hair short and put on a gray wig. Then, she had two of her teeth blackened to give the impression they were missing. She used an ointment to darken her skin and donned wire-rimmed glasses with clear lenses. The clothing given to Nadine was old and made of a rough weave used by working women in the Garonne region. It made her look older and frumpy. The shoes she was given fit loosely and looked as if they had seen hard wear. After putting a dark scarf over her head, Nadine looked in the mirror and was surprised at the reflection.

"Madame," said Noel when he saw her in disguise, "you look, well, common."

She laughed and feigned the voice of an older woman. "Come, let us go," she told Noel. They left under a cloudy sky and rode on a wagon and then walked on foot, gradually making their way south toward the town of Marmonde close to the confluence of the Garonne and Lot Rivers. They reached Marmonde in a few days and waited until nightfall to cross the river and make their way to a farmhouse just outside of the village of Tonneins, on the south side of the Garonne River. Nadine had picked this place as an alternate escape route for her network. It was a farming area with small villages and a few bastides.

The local resistance leader, an older man called Henry, recognized Noel and greeted him warmly. He welcomed Nadine politely and wondered about her. He had heard about an elegant Frenchwoman from Paris who had given large sums of money to the resistance and was now pursued by the Gestapo. The woman with Noel looked common, but something about her bearing impressed the clever French resistance leader. Henry recalled his first meeting with Noel and their discussion of Tonneins as a possible part of the Eglantine network. Henry, a school teacher, thought for a moment and wondered if the woman standing before him was the one hunted by the Gestapo. And, if so, was she a leader in the Eglantine network?

They talked for a few minutes before Henry said, "Madame, you hide your identity well. I suspect you are Eglantine. If so, we know of your work. Welcome." He kissed Nadine's hand. She smiled at Henry and gave him a hug. "You're going to the border?" he asked. Nadine shook her head and said she had other plans. "Bon," said Henry, "then we will find a place for you and Noel." In the next few days, Nadine and Noel began their plans to reconstruct the Eglantine network, albeit somewhat smaller.

They needed funds, so Nadine asked Noel to change some of the bearer bonds into currency. Noel said he would go to Agen and cash about two thousand Francs.

"Not all in one bank," Nadine warned him. Noel nodded and departed the next day.

The funds would be used for projects with Maquis groups along the reworked network. Ten days later, they began contacting friends in Spain and the Americans in Lisbon. When she thought it was safe, Nadine met with a parish priest near Casteljaloux. Through him, she sent a coded message to Christine in Lisbon.

The priest, Father Bermeo, from Casteljaloux was loyal to the Maquis and hid people sought by the Germans and sent messages through a secret network within the Catholic Church. He had heard of a well-to-do Parisian woman sought for questioning by the Gestapo. Moreover, he recognized one of the men with Nadine as a member of the local resistance. Although he did not inquire about Nadine's true identity, there was something about this woman in old clothing that intrigued him. She was well spoken, had poise, and moved gracefully. Could this be the woman the Vatican wanted to locate? Before she left, the priest asked her a simple question. "Do you like ballet?" Surprised, Nadine smiled and nodded, but she did not say anything. "Then go with God, my daughter, and take care in the eglantine," he told her.

Nadine smiled and kissed the priest's hand and in a charming voice said, "Thank you, Father."

That evening, the priest sent a coded message through his network to Rome indicating the person sought by the diplomatic arm of the Vatican might be in his area. Bishop Valderano received the secret message and forwarded the information to the Americans.

U.S. Military Intelligence in Lisbon met with Christine and asked if she had been contacted by her mother.

When she replied affirmatively, they asked if she knew Nadine's whereabouts. All Christine knew was that her mother had sent a message that she was safe. However, she believed that her mother was somewhere in southern France. That information was forwarded to the OSS in London and triggered the decision to send Crow and Robin into southern France.

* * *

The wind was like a sharp knife that cut into Quentin's face when he jumped out of the plane. It was, after all, still winter, and the weather in late March around Bordeaux was cold and damp. He felt the sudden jolt as the parachute canopy opened. Then, slowly, he drifted toward a field until he hit the soft earth and rolled to absorb the impact. He got up quickly and started to reign in the parachute but was surprised when a teenage girl and a young woman emerged from the darkness and helped him with the canopy.

"*Bienvenue â France,*" the young woman told him.

"Merci," replied Quentin, looking around to get his bearings. Then, he saw Lieutenant Romero and three men come toward him. Romero was wearing the red scarf around his neck. In excellent French, Romero, calling Quentin "Crow," asked that he help him and the others collect the two cylinders that were dropped by parachute. Inside the containers were small arms, ammunition, plastic explosives and detonators, along with French money that Romero put into his knap sack.

"This way," whispered one of the men as he motioned for them to follow him. They buried the cylinders and the parachutes and walked to a small truck waiting at the edge of the field. After loading the guns and explosives into the truck, the women and two of the men whispered "*Bonne chance* to Quentin and Romero before disappearing into the night.

"Into the back," said the Frenchman to the two Americans. They got into the truck, heard it start up and felt it move off slowly. The Cajun noticed that Romero had given something to the leader of the group. He would ask "Robin" about this later.

"Where are we?" Quentin asked Romero in French when they were alone.

"Near a place called Pineuilh. These people are from a resistance group near Bordeaux," whispered Romero. "We must not ask their names unless they reveal them."

"Are we going to Bordeaux?"

"No, were headed for Casteljaloux," replied Romero. "Stay alert," he told Quentin and motioned for him to be quiet.

They drove for several hours, stopping often to avoid detection by German patrols. It was almost four in the morning when the truck stopped and one of the men from the resistance whispered to them to stay in the truck. Waiting at the fork in the road ahead of where the truck stopped was a slight man. He and the men in the truck exchanged countersigns. Then, they walked to the back of the truck with the man waiting at the fork in the road.

"This is a friend," said the passenger in the truck. "He will take you south."

"Bring your things," said Romero, as he climbed out of the truck. Before the man from the resistance got back in the truck's cab he thanked Romero and wished both of them good luck. Romero handed him something.

Quentin and Romero followed the slight man off the dirt road and onto a path that led to a wooded area. They walked for almost an hour before he signaled a halt and motioned for them to be quiet. A few moments later, off to their left, a truck could be heard on a road.

"Boche," whispered the slight man. They waited for five minutes before resuming their trek southeast.

Romero was young and fit and easily kept up with the Frenchman. The Cajun was right with them. *He's fit and determined*, thought Romero.

The sky in the east began to show traces of light when they reached a clearing. A small farmhouse was across the clearing, and close to it was a barn that bordered on a copse of trees planted as a windbreak. They moved through the edge of the woods toward the house. When they were close to it, the Frenchman signaled for them to stay in the woods while he moved cautiously toward the structure. A few minutes later, he returned with another man.

"This way," said the Frenchman, motioning for them to follow him to the barn. Once inside, the other man raked away the straw near the back of the barn that hid a wooden floor. The farmer pulled on a hidden handle and lifted a trap door. He lit a lantern and told them to follow him into what appeared to be a root cellar. Another lantern was lit that illuminated the cellar. The dim light revealed a few wine casks, some old chests and wall shelving, cheese wheels, two barrels with apples, and three bunks. For the first time, Quentin could make out the slight man's features. He was an older man, perhaps in his late fifties.

"This is Gabriel and I am Pierre. He will look after you until I return tonight."

Gabriel was a short, stocky man, perhaps in his late forties or maybe early fifties. His shoulders were stooped, and he walked with a slight limp. He had a large moustache, and it appeared that he had not shaved in several days.

"I will bring food before starting my chores," said Gabriel in low voice. "The old woman will cook up some porridge and warm some bread. It's not much; we're poor," he said apologetically. "The little house is in the back," he told them, nodding with his head in the direction of the outhouse. Then, he moved aside a shallow set of shelves that revealed a dark tunnel.

"This goes out to the woods. If the Boche come, use it," he told them.

He gave them two signals. The first was if there was danger; the second when he was there to open the trap door.

Pierre shook their hands, said he would return at dusk, and left. Fifteen minutes later, Gabriel returned with porridge, bread, and milk.

Without the kerosene lantern, the cellar was pitch black. Gabriel gave them two large candles. "Use these and save the kerosene," he told them. "It costs money," he added before leaving them.

When Quentin woke, he looked at his watch and saw that it was almost three in the afternoon. He turned on his side and saw Romero looking at him.

Quentin and Romero talked for almost half an hour. It was the first time they were able to speak at length in private. Quentin asked Romero where he was from and was surprised to learn that he was born in a small Mexican coastal town called Mazatlan. His first name was Alejandro, but his friends called him "Alec."

"Why not Alex?" asked the Cajun. Romero chuckled and said his Jewish friends in Hollywood had given him the nickname.

"Hollywood! What did you do before the war?" asked Quentin.

Romero related living in Hollywood and working in the movies as a stunt man and stand-in. Quentin mentioned he knew about stunt men and extras. Romero added that he seldom worked as an extra. Instead, he "doubled" for movie stars like Ronald Coleman, Tyrone

Power, and Cornel Wilde in action scenes where strenuous or dangerous activities were involved.

"You know about filmmaking?" asked Romero. Quentin nodded and mentioned his association with major studio heads and helping to finance films. "Then, Crow, we have filmmaking in common," said Romero "you from the top and I from the bottom." They both laughed.

"This woman, Mrs. Desnoyers, she is special?" said Romero. Quentin nodded. "Why?" he asked.

In the next ten minutes, Quentin told Romero about his romantic involvement with Nadine, that she was the mother of their son, and his unbridled love for her. "Two more things," said Quentin. "Why the red scarf?"

Robin chuckled and said it was for good luck. "And what is it that you give to people before we leave them?" Romero grinned and said usually money, but now and then tobacco.

After their conversation, Romero's perception about the man he knew only as Crow changed. He understood why the man was risking everything, including his life, for Nadine. *This is a man to be respected and admired,* thought Romero.

At almost four o'clock they heard Gabriel knock. The trap door opened, and they saw Pierre and Gabriel looking down on them.

"Come," said Pierre, "we'll eat something and be on our way. It will be dark soon."

That evening, Romero and Quentin followed Pierre along paths that took them southeast through dark woods, cultivated fields, and narrow paths in the chaparral until they reached a river.

"Wait here," Pierre told them. A few minutes later, he returned and motioned for them to follow him. They walked along the banks of the river until they can to an inlet where a man was waiting in a row boat.

"He will take you across," said Pierre. He held the boat steady while Romero and the Cajun got in. Again, Quentin noticed that Romero gave something to Pierre. The older man thanked Romero and then pushed the bow of the boat out into the slow flowing water. As he did so, he whispered, "*Bonne chance.*"

The man rowing the boat said nothing, using strong strokes to pull the small boat across the river to a specific place on the south side. When the boat approached the bank, they saw a man waiting for them.

"*Bon jour,*" they heard the low and hoarse voice of a stocky man. They both returned the greeting and got out of the boat. Romero handed something to the boatman and heard the man whisper "*merci.*"

"This way," said the stocky man as he led them up the bank and down the other side into an orchard. They walked in silence for two hours before the stocky man whispered for them to rest for a few minutes. Quentin asked Romero about their guide.

"No names," said Romero. "Better that way for him and for us."

After a few minutes, the stocky man signaled for them to follow him. They walked cautiously through the darkness until the saw the lights of a town ahead.

"Tonneins," whispered the Frenchman. They walked cautiously around the town staying away from the low buildings until they came to a rock wall. The Frenchman motioned for them to follow. He led them to a spot that was covered in high brush. He moved the brush aside carefully to reveal an old doorway.

"Through here," he whispered. Once through the wall, they walked past a small shed and then a barn until they saw a two-story house. The Frenchman walked them toward the back of the building where he knocked softly on a wooden covering. He listened for a moment before opening a wooden door that provided access to a cellar. "Go," he pointed down.

Slowly and cautiously, Romero and Quentin made their way down some stone steps into a cellar. A single candle burned in a corner where an older man and a young woman waited with weapons at the ready, he with a rifle and she with a pistol. They heard the wooden door close behind them and the hoarse voice of their French guide say, "It's all right; they're with me."

"I'm Robin," said Romero in perfect French. This is Crow. The man and the woman lowered their weapons and greeted them.

"And I'm thirsty," said the stocky Frenchman.

"Come, Alain," said the older man, "we have coffee." They led Romero and Quentin up some stairs and into an old kitchen with a large fireplace used for cooking. The young woman motioned for them to be seated on wooden benches next to a long, carved wooden table. She offered them bread and some preserves before bringing them coffee.

"I'm Dumond," said the older man, "and this is my niece, Belda."

They sat and talked for a few minutes.

After finishing his coffee, Alain stood and said he was leaving. He shook hands with Romero and Quentin. Just before he left, Romero handed him something. Alain nodded and smiled before walking down the steps to the cellar. Belda followed him and they heard her lock the wooden door from the inside.

"I will take you to Casteljaloux," said Dumond. "Now follow me," he said, lighting their way with a lantern. They walked through the old house that once must have been a lovely home. But, now, it had an odor of dampness, the walls were bare, and the rooms they passed were sparsely furnished if at all. Dumond walked up a curved stairway and halfway up moved an arras that covered a hidden passageway. They went through it to a hidden room with small narrow windows covered on the outside by ivy. There was a small bed and a cot in the room along with two chairs and a table with an old candelabrum on it.

"You'll be safe here," said the Frenchman. "If the Boche come and search the house, go through that door," he pointed, "and take the spiral staircase down. It leads to another cellar. There is a hidden passageway that leads to the barn. Belda will show you later."

Before Dumond and Belda left them the older man said hot water would be available for them to clean up and shave. Romero offered Quentin the bed and sat down on the cot. When Quentin offered to decline the bed, Romero gave a low laugh, removed his shoes, and promptly fell asleep. The Cajun sat back on the bed, removed his shoes, and fell asleep.

* * *

"Hauptman," said Martzrek on the telephone to Captain Zollner, "good work. The bearer bonds were issued in Paris several weeks ago." The bonds cashed by Noel in Agen did not escape the attention of the Gestapo.

One of the bank clerks in Agen, a German agent, noticed the bearer bonds when they were cashed. These kinds of securities were not usually seen in Agen. Suspicious, he called two of the other banks in Agen and learned that one of them had just cashed in bearer bonds in the amount of one thousand francs. He immediately contacted Zollner and told him that bearer bonds in the amount of two thousand French francs were cashed in two separate banks on the same day in Agen. Zollner visited both banks, checked the serial numbers of the bonds, and noticed that they were contiguous. He showed the

German agent pictures of several people wanted by the Gestapo. The German agent and the other bank employee identified Noel. The Gestapo captain knew that Noel DeCloux worked for Nadine Desnoyers. *She must be near,* he thought as he called Martzrek in Paris.

"Increase your surveillance of all trains and vehicles going south," said Martzrek. "Also, I will send another Storch (Fieseler reconnaissance plane) to help with the search. The Desnoyers woman and the Frenchman will use the money to purchase passage to the Spanish border," he said before pausing. "Hauptman, I want them caught. And I want the woman alive, understood?" Zollner replied affirmatively. "By the way," said Martzrek, "Hauptman Berthold interrogated several people from Trelissac and learned the names of possible members of the resistance in Agen. His methods are crude, but effective," said Martzrek. "He'll join you tomorrow with the names of the suspects. Apprehend them and let Berthold deal with them." They talked for a few more minutes before ending the call. Zollner called in two of his subordinates and told them what needed to be done.

The following day, Berthold arrived in Agen with additional men. They quickly apprehended six people: four men and two women. A sixteen-year-old boy was among the men, and Berthold singled him out for interrogation. It took several hours before the boy cracked and admitted to working with the resistance. Berthold had broken both of his arms and legs with a metal rod. If the boy survived, he would be crippled for life. Not satisfied with breaking the boy, Berthold then interrogated the younger of the two women. She was stripped and beaten with rubber hoses and then subjected to water torture. When she hesitated answering an interrogator's question, he struck her hard across the face. Berthold immediately clubbed the interrogator and in a harsh voice said, "Not in the face or mouth, imbecile. She must be able to talk."

She too was broken and corroborated what the boy had said.

Berthold had the names of people suspected of working with the resistance in and around Agen. He called Zollner and shared what he had learned.

"Excellent," said Zollner, "I'll have these people arrested."

"What shall I do with the prisoners?" asked Berthold.

"Get rid of them," said Zollner. Berthold smiled and thought, *Yes, but first a little fun.*

* * *

After her decision to remain in France and reconstruct parts of the Eglantine network, Henry convinced Nadine to hide in a convent near Casteljaloux. He told her, "You will be safe there. The mother superior and the nuns are sympathetic to our cause and will help."

Noel agreed with Henry and said absolute caution was needed because several people in Agen had been arrested by the Gestapo.

"Were any of them with the resistance?" asked Nadine. Henry nodded and indicated that three taken prisoner had done things for the resistance. Noel shook his head in despair, a frown on his forehead. He knew the harsh methods the Gestapo used to extract information. Under such extreme duress and torture, it was just a matter of time before the person interrogated was broken.

"Madame, I wish you would reconsider and leave France," Noel told her. "The Gestapo will hunt for you and be merciless with anyone helping you. If they take you alive…" He did not finish the sentence. Henry nodded in agreement, but remained silent.

"I will stay in the convent. If it becomes necessary, we can move to Auch or Mirande," she told them. Noel nodded, and did not comment. Both places were south of

Casteljaloux and along an escape route the Maquis and the Eglantine network had used to hide people on their way to the Spanish border.

"Bon," said Henry. "I will inform our friend the priest in Casteljaloux and then the mother superior. We'll move you tomorrow," he said solemnly. Like Noel, Henry worried that the Gestapo would find Nadine and try to take her alive. He shuddered at the thought.

* * *

It did not take Zollner and Berthold long to apprehend people and learn about an older woman and a man from Paris traveling south. Two of the people interrogated volunteered information to avoid torture. One of them confessed to hearing about a man and a woman working with the resistance. When asked about the man and the woman, he said they had money and were giving it to the resistance. The second person, a woman, corroborated what the man had said and added that she believed they were somewhere north of Agen. When asked how she knew this, the woman confessed to overhearing talk about a man and a woman running from the Boche on their way to a safe house used by the resistance. When Berthold asked where the house was located, she said north of Agen, along the river. With Berthold's information, Zollner suspected DeCloux and Madame Desnoyers were hiding somewhere near Agen, perhaps on a farm north of the town.

"They must not be allowed to slip by us," he told Berthold. That afternoon, he called and reported to Martzrek.

"Excellent," said Martzrek. "They have made a serious mistake and will pay for it," he told Zollner. "Make certain that they cannot go farther south. Seal off the area and begin searching…from house to house if necessary."

Before Martzrek signed off, he told Zollner that Berthold should interrogate anyone suspected of having information about Madame Desnoyers and the Frenchman DeCloux.

"We require his skills," Martzrek said dryly.

The next day, the Germans sealed the area ten kilometers south of Agen. Checkpoints were set up to stop and search all people traveling south on foot, cart, or car. Suspects were detained. Nazi night patrols apprehended anyone caught violating the curfew that prohibited anyone out after dark without permission.

Meanwhile, squads of German soldiers began searching parts of Agen, looking for Nadine and Noel. They broke into homes ruthlessly and searched them thoroughly often bludgeoning the inhabitants. A few informants eager to receive pay from the Boche mentioned hidden rooms in suspected homes. Small accumulations of food were found. The inhabitants were arrested immediately and the food confiscated. After two days of searching without finding any trace of the fugitives, Zollner shifted the search north to Tonneins and Casteljaloux. If they found nothing there, then he would redouble his efforts to the south.

* * *

Nadine was at the convent near Casteljaloux dressed as a kitchen helper and preparing vegetables for the evening stew when the mother superior appeared and motioned for her to follow. When they were out of earshot, she whispered that German soldiers were in Tonneins, searching the area looking for a pair of fugitives from Paris.

"You must leave," warned the mother superior. "The Boche will certainly come here." Nadine nodded and went to the small room where she slept and kept her things. She packed everything, put on the wig, blackened two of her front teeth, put on the old clothes and shoes, and wrapped a dark shawl over her head and shoulders. As she walked to the back of the convent, Noel was waiting.

"We must hide in the woods," he told her. "It's not safe for us to move about in the daytime. The Boche have observation planes in the sky looking for us. Henry will come for us when it's safe." They followed a path through the high brush and slipped into the nearby woods and followed a trail to a copse of tall trees. Noel led Nadine to a large tree that provided some shelter from the wind.

"Stay here out of sight," he cautioned. "I'll climb that tree," he said, motioning in the direction of a tall tree adjacent to the trail. "If the Boche come, I'll call out like an owl," he said. "I will try to lead them away from you. You must not be caught," he warned, pointing to the pistol Nadine was carrying.

The sky overhead darkened, and a light rain began to fall. Nadine strained to hear any sound out of the ordinary. She worried what might happen if the Germans came into the woods looking for them. Ugly thoughts flooded her mind about what the Boche were doing to extract information from people in the nearby villages. She blamed herself for the harm that befell the nearby villagers. *Maybe I should leave France*, she thought remorsefully.

It was getting dark, and the rain was intensifying. Nadine was soaked to the skin and beginning to shiver from the cold when she heard someone coming. She hid behind the tree and cocked the pistol.

"Madame," said Noel from the chaparral. She saw Noel and then Henry.

"Come," said Henry, "we must hurry." They followed him through the woods to a small, well-hidden shed. "You will be safe here. Make a small fire," he told them, "but put it out once the rain stops." He handed them some food before leaving.

As Nadine and Noel sat warming themselves by the fire, she looked at him and, in a soft voice, apologized for the troubles she had caused him.

"What trouble!" he said with a smile. "I needed a vacation." She stood and hugged him, tears cascading down her cheeks.

* * *

Romero and Quentin rode into Casteljaloux on a horse-driven cart, thanked their driver as they got off, and walked toward the center of town. After making certain that no police or Germans were in the vicinity, they went to the Catholic Church. Inside, Romero whispered to Quentin to kneel in one of the pews and pretend to pray while he looked for Father Bermeo, the priest. A few minutes later, Romero and Father Bermeo appeared and motioned for the Cajun to follow through a side door. The way Romero and the priest talked, Quentin knew they had worked together before.

When they were alone, the priest greeted Crow and said the Germans were in Tonneins searching for a man and a woman from Paris.

"We too are searching for a woman from Paris," said Romero.

"Can you describe her?" asked Father Bermeo. Quentin spoke up and gave a description of Nadine, including her height, color of eyes and hair, and facial features.

"Mmm," uttered the priest, "the woman I've seen has green eyes, but appears older with gray hair. Of course she could be in disguise," he said cautiously. "There is a man with her," the priest continued, "perhaps you might know who he is."

The Cajun thought quickly and guessed that it might be Noel DeCloux. Without mentioning his name, he described Noel.

"Bon," said Father Bermeo with a smile while putting his hand on the American's arm, "they are here." Quentin took in a deep breath and, for a moment, exhibited a mixture of relief and anticipation.

"Where?" asked Romero. The priest told them Nadine was at a convent not far away and that Noel was with a Maquis member. He promised to take them to Nadine after holding church services. While Father Bermeo was occupied, Romero and Quentin were given soup, bread, and olive oil. Romero ate well while the Cajun, eager to find Nadine, just nibbled at the food.

"Patience, my friend," said Romero to assuage Quentin. "You will soon be with her."

When the priest returned, he gave them directions to the convent and cautioned against going there together. Father Bermeo would go first. Romero and Quentin would wait five minutes and make certain no one was following before leaving.

"Be careful," said the priest.

Romero made certain that no one was following the priest or them. He and Quentin walked slowly, but purposefully, in the direction of the convent. Their dress and manner suggested little more than two men walking home or to their lodging after a long day. When they arrived at the convent, they knocked on a large pair of wooden doors. They were greeted by an acolyte who bid them enter after hearing their code names of Robin and Crow. Once inside, they saw Father Bermeo standing next to the mother superior, both ill at ease.

"The Boche will come here soon," he said. "They are looking for Madame."

"Where is she?" asked Quentin.

"Gone," replied the mother superior. Quentin's heart almost caught in his throat, and he was speechless for a moment.

"Where?" asked Romero.

"Into the woods, but I do not know where." She told them a man had come to warn her about the Germans and they left together.

Quentin described Noel to the nun. The mother superior nodded and said it was him.

"Did anyone from the village come to inquire about them?" asked the priest.

"Henry, the school teacher," she said.

"Can you show us which way they went?" asked Romero. She led them to a side of the convent that faced the chaparral and a thicker wooded area behind it.

"That way," she said, pointing to a path that led into the chaparral.

"Where does that path go?" asked Romero. She replied south into a wooded area, then across a meadow before crossing a stream. Beyond that, the path narrowed until it came to a dirt road that went south.

"Then that's the way we'll go," said Romero. "But, we'll need a place to stay tonight." The mother superior said there was a barn in the back of the convent where they could stay. "Thank you," said Romero before turning to Father Bermeo. "Father, do you know this man Henry?" The priest nodded. "Can you contact him and find out if he knows where Noel and Madame have gone?"

"Of course," said the priest. "I'll go immediately. The mother superior will show you to the barn. If I find Henry, we will return this evening," he said before leaving.

"Follow me," said the mother superior to Romero and Quentin, leading them to a well tended-barn that sheltered two plow horses, two milk cows, and some nanny goats. One of the nuns showed them a hidden loft where they could stay. At almost seven, a nun came with food.

* * *

It was almost eight in the evening when the door to the barn opened and three people stepped inside out of the rain.

"We have company," Romero told Quentin as he brought his pistol to the ready.

"Robin," they heard Father Bermeo call from below.

Romero removed the false panel along the wall and stepped out cautiously. He moved to the edge of the landing, looked down, and saw the priest standing with an older man holding a lantern and next to them a young man.

"It's all right, Robin," said the priest. "This is Henry and a friend."

Romero went down the wooden ladder. He recognized Henry from a previous mission that brought him to Tonneins. The Frenchman smiled at the sight of the red scarf and the two shook hands. Romero called Crow and told him to come down.

When they were all together, Quentin noticed that the person of slight build was not a man but a young woman, and she was carrying a rifle. They exchanged greetings and introduced the young woman as Ancelin.

"You are looking for Madame?" asked Henry. Romero and Quentin nodded. "May I ask why?" he inquired.

"We will take her to Spain and then to Lisbon," replied Romero.

"But will she go with you?" Henry asked.

"See this attractive fellow," said Romero pointing to Quentin, "he will persuade her."

Henry looked at the man called Crow with a puzzled expression.

Finally, the Cajun spoke up in perfect French. "We are lovers," he told them. All of them laughed.

"If that is so," said Henry, "then you are a very fortunate man."

Henry warned them that a squad of German soldiers arrived in Casteljaloux just after dark.

"They will search every building and then come here," said Henry. He paused before telling them where Nadine and Noel were hidden. "Ancelin will take you to them. You must leave at first light." He produced a small map of the area and showed them approximately where the hidden shed was located and gave them a recognition signal to use.

"Where will you go?" Henry asked Romero.

Romero said, "South, toward Auch and Mirande, then we join pilgrims going to Lourdes."

"Of course," said Father Bermeo, "there are many pilgrims going to the shrine." They talked for a few more minutes before Henry said he and Father Bermeo were leaving.

"Do you have a wireless?" asked Romero. Henry nodded.

"Tomorrow night, send this to London." He handed the schoolteacher a coded message.

"Bon," said a puzzled Henry. "Ancelin will remain here and lead you to your friends. She will take you through the woods and show you the way south to Auch."

They shook hands, and the priest blessed them and said he would pray for their safety.

After the two men left, Ancelin mentioned she would sleep in one of the stalls. Robin informed them he would stand guard until one in the morning, followed by Quentin. Romero told the Cajun to awaken them around four in the morning.

CHAPTER 20
LOVERS REUNITED

And they are gone: aye, ages long ago
These lovers fled away into the storm.
John Keats, *The Eve of St. Agnes*

It was still dark when the Cajun woke Romero and then Ancelin. The rain had stopped, but the air was heavy and pregnant with moisture. There was a soft knock on the door to the barn, and a nun entered with food. She wished them well and left quietly. They ate in silence, Romero lost in thought while Quentin's demeanor hid the turmoil within him. The Cajun could hardly contain himself. His first instincts were to leave immediately and fly to Nadine's side, but that was not yet possible.

After finishing their food, Romero cleared away all traces of their stay. He slipped out of the barn silently to make certain no Germans were in the vicinity. He returned after a few minutes, partially opened the barn door, and motioned for Ancelin to show them the way.

The sky was overcast, and dark clouds blocked out the rays of the rising sun but not the glow that started to spread like quicksilver along the eastern horizon. It was just light enough for Ancelin to locate the path that led through the chaparral and then into the woods. She walked at a brisk pace along the narrow path stepping mainly on the wet sod to avoid the center area of earth now muddy from the rain. Their pace was slowed because of the mud, but they soon reached a place where Ancelin stopped and motioned for them to follow her in silence.

She walked slowly and cautiously through the wooded area until she signaled for them to stop and pointed to something. The light had improved enough for them to make out a small shed hidden in the woods. She cautioned them to remain where they were and slowly and silently made her way to the shed. Romero and Quentin heard her call out like an owl. Her imitation of an owl's call was so true that at first they believed it was an owl. She repeated the call; this time, something stirred in the shed. They heard what sounded like the call of another owl. Slowly, Ancelin approached the entrance to the shed and whispered the password. A moment later, a man's voice gave the countersign.

The anticipation was churning Quentin's insides. Would Nadine be there? Was she all right? He wanted to dash forward and find her. Instead, Romero motioned for him to walk slowly toward the shed. After what seemed like an eternity, the Cajun saw the figure of a man emerge from the shed, holding a pistol at the ready.

"Are you Noel?" Romero asked.

"Who are you?" replied the Frenchman.

"Cupid's helper," said the American with a smile on his face.

"What?" the Frenchman uttered, surprised by Romero's comment.

"Who is it, Noel?" asked a woman's voice from within the shed.

At the sound of the voice, the Cajun rushed forward, surprising Noel and Ancelin by how quickly he moved.

"Nadine, is that you?" the Cajun asked plaintively. Nadine could hardly believe her ears and for a moment abandoned all caution, hurried out of the shed, and stood up straight to face the tall man rushing toward her.

"Cherie," her voice filled with emotion split the moist air. Then, he was holding her fast in his arms and smothering her with kisses. She succumbed to the passion and kissed him back, her long slender fingers skewing aside his beret and smoothing their way through his hair. The others were silent for a moment, transfixed at the sight of two reunited lovers passionately embracing each other.

Romero was the first to speak. "We're glad you're well. However, the Germans are in Casteljaloux and will most certainly come this way. We must go." Ancelin, smiling as she observed the affection between the tall man and the woman dressed in the worn garb of a peasant woman, snapped out of her momentary reverie by Romero's words. She looked first at Romero and nodded before turning to the others and saying he was right. They needed to leave. The lovers embraced once more before Quentin agreed it was time to go.

Noel and Nadine packed small knapsacks, and then the five of them followed a muddy trail through the woods until they came to a stream. Ancelin led them to a shallow ford they used to cross the cold water. They walked into another wooded area and continued until Ancelin signaled for them to stop. She motioned for Romero to follow her until they came to some tall brush that she gently parted. Ahead was a dirt road.

"Follow the road south," she told him.

"Does it fork somewhere ahead?" he asked.

She was surprised by his question and replied affirmatively. "You have been here before?" she asked hesitantly.

He smiled and nodded.

"The right fork goes to Mont de Marsan," she said, a puzzled expression on her face.

"Good," he said. "You will leave us here and return to Casteljaloux?" he asked. She nodded.

Together they walked back to the others. Ancelin told them she was going back. The men shook hands with her, but Nadine hugged the young woman and said to be careful. Ancelin smiled, turned, and walked back along the trail and disappeared into the woods.

"Follow me," said Romero. The small group made its way slowly south along the dirt road. Half an hour later, they came to a fork in the road, and Romero signaled for them to follow him to the right. Confused, Noel told Romero the right fork headed west and not south.

"Yes, I know," said the American with a smile.

"Aren't we going south?" asked the puzzled Frenchman.

"Yes, but our route will take us southwest," replied the American.

* * *

A frustrated Captain Zollner called Martzrek in Paris and told him they had not found the Desnoyers woman or her assistant. There was a pause during which Zollner could hear Martzrek shifting some paper.

"Our intelligence people intercepted a wireless message a few nights ago to London from someone called 'Robin,' obviously a code name for a British agent. The transmission came from somewhere near Casteljaloux. We were able to decipher part of the message, and it mentioned something about a package, a shrine, and the name Aragon."

Zollner thought for a moment before saying, "Of course, how foolish of me. Madame Desnoyers and her accomplice are headed toward the Shrine of Lourdes and from there across the border into the Spanish province of Aragon. They will try to disguise themselves as pilgrims going to worship at the shrine."

"One moment," said Martzrek. He came back on the line and told Zollner that the road from Lourdes to Spain had a German checkpoint at Cauterets. "There is where you can intercept them," said Martzrek hesitantly.

"There is something else?" asked Zollner.

"Ja," replied Martzrek, something nagging at him. "It's too easy. This may be a diversion, something to throw us off from their real plan."

Zollner considered carefully what the colonel had said. "What do you propose, Herr Oberst?" asked Zollner.

"Look for them at Cauterets, but I will alert our people at other border crossing between Lourdes and the pass leading to Elizondo. The area west of there is too populated and well guarded by our troops." The two men talked for a while before Zollner said he would fly to Lourdes and then drive to Cauterets where roadblocks would be set up and foot patrols assigned to monitor trails that crossed from France through the Pyrenees into Spain.

"We must apprehend this woman," said Martzrek. "We have learned that she is carrying secret documents about Luftwaffe activities at Peenemünde."

"I'll do my best," said Zollner before ending the call.

* * *

Romero led the small group southwest during the next two days. They traveled overland along a route familiar to the American toward a place southwest of Mourenx.

Romero quietly observed how attentive the Cajun was to Nadine. He overheard them talk after they found a place to camp for the evening. Quentin told the Frenchwoman she had lost weight and tenderly stroked her short, cropped hair. The way the Frenchwoman touched the Cajun made a strong impression on Romero. He could see the love they had for each other. *She's lucky he loves her so,* thought Romero.

The next day, they continued south to the Spanish border. Romero noticed that the Cajun would not let Nadine carry anything. His concern for the Frenchwoman was loving and protective. They walked quickly and tried not to be in the open for long. Late in the afternoon of the second day, Romero heard a plane and motioned for them to find cover in the bracken. As he hid in the ferns, he saw the Cajun put his body over Nadine to protect her from detection.

On the third day, just before the light began to fade in the sky, they stopped at the edge of a clearing. Three wagons were in an open area with cooking fires next to them. Romero told them to wait as he walked into the clearing. A dog started to bark and then two men, each with rifles, confronted him. They recognized him and especially the bright red scarf around the American's neck. The taller of the two men patted Romero on the shoulder, and they talked for a few minutes. Robin handed them something, turned, and motioned for Noel, Nadine, and Quentin to join him.

Noel was the first to ask Romero about the people in the camp.

"They're gypsies, called Gitanos in Spanish. They're friends and will help us reach the Spanish border." He introduced them to Manolo, the leader of the group, and Hugo, his cousin. Romero said that Gitanos had migrated back and forth between southern France and northern Spain for hundreds of years. Some, like Manolo, were the progeny of intermarriage between Spanish and French Basques and gypsies. Manolo spoke the Basque tongue (Euskara), Spanish, and French and told them he was a tinker and silversmith.

That evening, Nadine slept in Manolo's wagon next to Amalia, the gypsy's woman. Amalia was youthful, exuberant, and attractive with a seductive charm. She looked carefully at Nadine and cupped the Frenchwoman's face in her hands before saying such a pretty woman should not be dressed in rags. Amalia convinced Nadine to trade her old clothes for a colorful skirt, blouse, and vest. Romero and Quentin bartered with Amalia for the clothes. Another gypsy woman showed Nadine some lovely handmade scarves and a shawl, which Quentin traded for a watch and some francs.

The food Manolo's group prepared was the first hot and delicious fare they'd eaten in several days. The dishes were hot, and Nadine's and Noel's eyes watered at the spicy food. Nadine asked for water while the Cajun and Romero laughed and ate the piquant food with gusto.

"We're used to 'hot' foods," said the Cajun, gently nudging Romero. The gypsies knew Romero well. After dinner, one of the Gitanos played a guitar, and Romero sang in a lovely voice that captivated Nadine, Quentin, and Noel.

"He may be Mexican," said Manolo, "but his heart is gypsy."

They slept soundly, with Noel, Romero, and then Quentin taking turns on guard duty. The three men slept under the wagons. They were awakened before dawn by the sounds of the gypsy women preparing for an early meal before departing. Two of the wagons were going west toward Bayonne, but Manolo would take Romero and the others overland and southwest toward St. Etienne de Bäigorry.

The first day was uneventful as Manolo's wagon, with its pots and pans clanking and drawn by two strong horses, made its way over trails that crossed the wooded areas of Southwestern France. The Cajun marveled at how the trail would often cross a well-tended farm where Manolo inquired if the farm occupants wanted pots or pans or needed repairs of any kind. At one farm, Manolo fixed a broken door and made new hinges for it. At another farm they traded two rabbits for some chickens. At any opportunity, Amalia would barter with the local women for fresh vegetables and apples.

"I'd give anything for a fresh orange," she whispered to Nadine.

They forded a cold stream that flowed west and camped on the southern side. When Noel asked Manolo how long before they reached the border, the gypsy said a day and a half, maybe two, depending on the weather and if there was work at any of the farms they'd pass.

The following afternoon, Manolo warned them about crossing a well-used dirt road. He told Romero and Quentin to leave them and split up.

"One of you go about a hundred meters west and the other the same distance east. Cross the road carefully," he cautioned. "If it's safe to cross, signal with your *eléctricas* (flashlights) one long and one short. If you spot anything, three short flashes." Manolo told Noel to walk behind the wagon while Amalia and Nadine stayed inside.

It took Romero and Quentin a few minutes to reach their respective spots. After a few minutes, both flashed the clear signal. Manolo slapped the reins and the horses started across the road. When the wagon reached the other side of the dirt road and started into the woods, a German soldier appeared abruptly out of the trees and told Manolo to halt. Noel crouched and moved toward the back of the wagon. He did not hear or see the German soldier that struck him with the butt of his rifle, knocking the Frenchman to the ground senseless.

"*Que es!*" exclaimed Manolo to the German as he reached for a rifle hidden close to his right hand. As the gypsy moved, another German came out of the underbrush with a rifle pointed at him. Four German soldiers approached the back of the wagon, one of them, a sergeant, jumped up onto the wooden landing and kicked in the door. He had a MP-40 submachine gun in one hand and a flashlight in the other.

"What have we here?" said the German as he spotted the two women. "*Raus,*" he barked and motioned with the flashlight for them to get out. When the sergeant swept the flashlight across his body, Nadine raised her pistol and shot him in the chest, causing the German to utter a cry and fall backward. Immediately, Manolo ducked as the two Germans in front of him fired. The three German soldiers in the back, alerted to the shot in the wagon and then the sergeant's cry, raised their weapons and were about to fire. Two quick shots rang out behind the wagon, then a third, and, after a moment, another. Three German troopers were lying on the ground dead. In front of the wagon, a shot from Romero's pistol caught the German corporal by surprise. The other German, a lieutenant with an MP-40, turned to fire at Romero but was hit by a bullet from Manolo's rifle. Romero dropped to the ground and rolled away to his left and fired at the German lieutenant, killing him. The sound of the shooting spooked the horses, and Manolo dropped his rifle and reached for the reins to control the frightened animals. He worried there might be more Germans. Romero checked the Germans he'd shot to make certain they were dead, then he rushed to the back of the wagon in time to see Quentin holding his pistol in one hand while helping Noel to his feet. He saw three dead Germans lying behind the wagon.

"You did this?" asked an incredulous Romero. Quentin nodded but said nothing, checking Noel to determine the extent of his injury. He motioned for Romero to hold the injured Frenchman and swung up onto the back of the wagon and peered inside. He saw the gypsy woman staring out at him from the darkness, while Nadine held a pistol in a trembling hand. The Frenchwoman was standing over the body of a German sergeant. The German groaned and moved, and Quentin, without hesitating, shot him twice. The Cajun felt Romero enter the wagon and stand behind him.

"Is he dead?" asked Romero.

The Cajun dispassionately said, "He is now." The women were stunned and stood silent while the Cajun calmly took the pistol out of Nadine's hand. In a soothing voice, he reassured her that all was well. He led Nadine out of the wagon and sat her next to Noel. She saw the dead Germans and stared in disbelief at Quentin. He knew what she was thinking and nodded his head, a sign that he'd shot all of them. He'd just killed four men in less than a few minutes. There was no hesitation and no remorse in what he'd done.

"Wait here," the Cajun told the trembling Nadine, while he went to fetch some water. She looked at the dead Germans her lover had shot, and realized he had killed four men. She was distressed by his actions. There was a dangerous and lethal side to the Cajun that unnerved her.

In the next few minutes, Manolo and Romero checked the brush to determine if there were other Germans.

"We must leave this place," warned Manolo.

"Not until we bury these Germans," said Romero. Manolo wanted to drag them into the bracken and leave them, but Romero said other Germans were certain to be along soon.

"If they find the bodies, more German troops will come to hunt us down," warned the American.

Quentin approached, wrapped a blanked around Nadine's shoulders, and said he would help bury the Germans. Manolo gave out a loud sigh, nodded, and walked to the side of the wagon where there were two shovels. They dragged the six dead Germans into the woods and began to dig a shallow grave. Amalia appeared and said Nadine was tending to Noel's head wound. She told Manolo to remove the Germans' jackets, boots, and leather goods, and to go through their pockets for valuables.

"This is good wool," she told Manolo while fingering the German lieutenant's tunic. "It can be rewoven. And the boots we can barter or sell," she added.

After the bodies were buried, Romero told Manolo he could keep the rifles, pistols, and ammunition taken from the Germans. However, he kept the two MP-40 submachine guns and contact grenades.

"If you are caught with these," said Romero, pointing at the machine guns and the grenades, the Germans will make your death a slow and painful one. "Keep whatever else you've found on the Germans."

The wagon moved slowly into the woods. Romero stayed behind to cover its tracks and make certain that they had recovered all the spent shells from their guns. Then, he trotted along the narrow trail until he caught up with the gypsy wagon.

Manolo increased the pace of the horses to put as much distance as possible from where they had killed the Germans. It was dark and starting to rain when they finally stopped for the night.

Quentin and Romero removed the bandage that Nadine used to cover the wound on Noel's head. The blow had bruised and cut the scalp on the right side of the Frenchman's head just above and behind the ear. Romero examined Noel carefully and asked him a few questions before rebandaging his head. He told the Frenchman to lie still and try to get some sleep. Outside the wagon, the others sat close together out of the rain in a lean-to shelter Manolo had fashioned from a tarp he carried.

"He has a concussion," said Romero, as he sat on a makeshift stool.

"How bad is it?" asked Quentin. Romero shook his head and said he didn't know.

"He will need to see a doctor soon," said the lieutenant. He asked Manolo if there was a town or village nearby with a doctor. The gypsy said no, but there was a small convent about a half day's ride where some of the nuns were trained as nurses.

"Can you take him there tomorrow?" asked Romero. Manolo nodded and looked at the American, waiting for him to speak. "Madame, Crow and I will leave tomorrow morning and head south into the Pyrenees. Take good care of Noel," he said, passing the gypsy some paper money. "I will arrange for you to receive gold coins when I reach Spain."

The gypsy smiled and said further payment was not necessary.

They ate a cold meal of bread soaked in olive oil, jerky, dried fruit, and nuts. Amalia and Nadine stayed inside the wagon with Noel while the others slept underneath it out of the rain. Quentin stood the first watch and was relieved by Manolo. The wind freshened and the rain intensified. Romero took the final watch. Just before dawn, they were all awake and huddled under the tarp.

"As you go higher," said Manolo, "it will snow. Amalia will give you some warm clothes." Romero thanked the gypsy, looked toward the south, and nodded.

Before they left, Nadine and Quentin informed Noel that Manolo was taking him to a nearby convent where he would be cared for properly. He smiled and told Nadine he wished her well and a safe passage to Spain.

"I'll be fine," he told Nadine. "I'll send Christine a message for you as soon as I'm able. I'll stay here and continue to fight the Boche," he added. Nadine kissed him on the cheek and squeezed his hand. The Cajun shook Noel's hand and thanked him for his friendship and loyalty to Nadine.

"When you're safe," said Quentin, "contact our military intelligence people in Lisbon." The Frenchman nodded and smiled before reclining and closing his eyes.

The rain stopped as Romero, Nadine, and Quentin headed south toward St. Etienne de Bäigorry. They reached the town a day and a half later, skirted it, and stayed at a safe house. There, Romero had a coded wireless message sent to a contact on the border with Spain. The next day they were hidden in a wagon that took them south into the Pyrenees.

It was just past the noon hour when Romero said, "The border isn't far." The American lieutenant thanked the Frenchman who had hidden them in his wagon, pressed something into his hand, and walked to join Nadine and Quentin. He motioned for them to follow him up a narrow path climbing into the mountains, the high peaks mantled in snow.

They walked for several hours, stopping twice to catch their breath. The climb, the cold, and the altitude made their passage slow. Toward the west and north, Romero made out storm clouds.

"We must hurry," he told them. "We don't want to get caught out in the open when it starts to snow.

The clouds thickened and formed a dark, gray, ominous ceiling that promised snow. The light on the western horizon was waning when Romero motioned for them to crouch behind a large boulder. They heard what sounded like a bird call. Romero imitated the sound of an owl and waited. Again, they heard the bird call, but this time Romero stood and said something that neither Nadine nor Quentin could make out. A reply came from up the trail, and two men appeared. Romero went forward to greet them and they began to talk in a language that was neither Spanish nor French. A moment later, Quentin, armed with the German submachine gun, watched Romero shake hands with the men, turn, and motion for them to come forward. The two men appeared to be in their early twenties, armed with rifles, and wearing heavy clothing, wool scarves, and berets.

"Welcome to Spain," said Romero, before introducing the two Basques who led them to a nearby cave where they would spend the night.

As they approached the cave, an old man appeared with a rifle. Romero greeted the old Basques and said something that caused the old man to chuckle. The wind was beginning to howl, and snow flurries were pecking at their faces. The old man patted Romero on the shoulder in a friendly way, tugged on his red scarf, and motioned for them to step inside the cave where two women were tending to a fire and cooking. When the younger of the two women recognized Romero, she jumped into his arms and kissed him. They spoke in a tongue that was indecipherable to either Nadine or Quentin.

Inside and out of the cold and snow, Nadine and Quentin were introduced to the Basques. They spoke Euskara, the Basque tongue. However, all but the old man could speak Spanish fluently and a bit of French. The Basque leader motioned for them to sit around the fire while the women helped Nadine get out of her wet clothes and into dry ones.

Romero motioned for Quentin to hand him one of the German MP-40 submachine guns. He told the Basques that the guns and ammunition were for them. Javier, the Basque leader, grinned as Romero handed him the machine gun, and thanked the American. He was pleasantly surprised when the American handed him several German contact grenades.

"Now don't go starting a war, Javier," teased Romero.

The food prepared by Kerena and Eskarna, the Basque women, was a rich stew that included potatoes, carrots, garlic, turnips, onion, spices, and meat. They were given freshly cooked biscuits and a hearty red wine. After they had eaten, Javier showed them where they would sleep. Nadine and Quentin talked briefly to Romero and the Basques, but soon they moved to their area and spoke to each other in hushed tones, the lovely Frenchwoman touching the Cajun's face often in a tender and loving manner.

"They are lovers?" asked Javier.

Romero nodded and said the war had separated them.

"It is good they are together again," Javier said, looking at Nadine and Quentin. "Tell them we leave early tomorrow morning. We have horses waiting in the corral down at the meadow."

Romero smiled and patted Javier on the shoulder and went to where Nadine and Quentin were sitting and talking. He informed them of the early departure.

"It will be good to ride," said Nadine with a smile, holding the Cajun's hand tightly.

"Where do we go from here?" asked Quentin, as he wrapped one arm around Nadine.

The lieutenant replied they would ride south and then west to a village on a paved road. A truck was waiting to take them to a town called Tolosa where they would board a train.

"Now, get some sleep," he said. "When we get to Tolosa, there will be new identity papers for us."

They slept soundly while outside the wind began to subside and the snow stopped falling. When they woke, it was still dark, but a glow on the eastern horizon revealed the strengthening sun. The day turned clear and crisp, with the white snow a stark contrast to the pines and rocky outcrops. The trail they used went up a bit, but then dropped quickly on the southern slope. After hiking for three hours they caught sight of a meadow and walked toward a small house with a corral. There, they met their guide, Santiago, who brought out the saddled horses. They said farewell to Javier, mounted the horses, and rode southwest. Late that evening, they arrived at a small village where Santiago turned them over to Guillermo at a safe house.

"We'll stay here tonight," said Romero. "Tomorrow, Guillermo will drive us to Tolosa." The next day, they were driven to a safe house in Tolosa where two American operatives were waiting. Romero spoke with the lead operative and then said something to Guillermo, who wished all of them well before leaving. Romero cautioned them to stay in the house.

"German operatives are in Spain, and we don't want to tip our hand to them."

"Your train leaves at six this evening," said one of the American OSS operatives. "Here are your new identities and papers. You two," he said, indicating Nadine and Quentin, "are married and on your way to Coimbre in Portugal. You, Crow" he said, motioning to the Cajun, "are going to talk with a man about a job in an orchard that harvests corks for wine bottles." Quentin smiled and looked at Nadine and winked. "Robin will be with you all the way to Lisbon. We have new clothes for you to wear and adjustable weddings rings for each of you," he said. "There is also a wedding certificate to use in case the Spanish or Portuguese authorities require it."

"You guys think of everything," said Quentin.

They talked for a while longer before the OSS operative suggested they get cleaned up and dress in the clothes provided. Quentin took a quick bath, shaved, and changed into a dark coat and trousers. The clothes were made in Spain and reflected a conservative style. The fit was remarkably good, including the shoes. Quentin noticed that Romero hid his red scarf. Nadine was radiant even though she had lost weight. The new clothes looked loose on her, but the shoes fit comfortably. Each of them had a small valise with a change of clothes. Nadine teased her short hair into something resembling a pixie style.

"It's too young for me," she said with a smile, "but there's too little hair to work with."

Romero, Quentin, and the OSS operative complimented Nadine and told her how attractive she looked.

"A hat would help," she told them, as she tied a scarf over her head.

"I'll get one for you as soon as possible," said the Cajun, as he kissed the lovely woman on the cheek.

The lead OSS operative briefed them on new developments in the war. He said the German army at Stalingrad had surrendered to the Soviets during the first week of February. The fighting in North Africa was finally turning against the Germans and their Italian allies. More convoys were reaching England from the United States, and ships, loaded with supplies for the Soviets, were going around the northern tip of Norway to the Russian port of Murmansk. American and British bombers, when the weather permitted, were striking deeper and deeper into enemy held territory on the Continent. He handed Quentin a Spanish newspaper and told him to purchase and read Spanish papers on their way to Portugal.

"Madame," he told Nadine, "we have two romance novels in Spanish for you. If you don't read Spanish, pretend you do while on the train."

While they waited until the time to depart for the train station, the OSS operatives went over Nadine and Quentin's new identities until they were satisfied the two had memorized them. At five in the afternoon, Romero, Nadine, and Quentin were driven to the train station in different cars. Quentin had traveled through Spain on trains often and was at ease. They boarded the train and found their seats. Nadine gave a sigh of relief when the train pulled away and started heading south. The Cajun sat next to her and opened a recently purchased Spanish newspaper. Seated behind them and several rows back Romero pretended to sleep.

Twice during the trip to Portugal, Spanish soldiers checked their papers. Quentin whispered to Nadine that there were still groups in Spain unwilling to accept Franco's fascist government.

"Someday, Spain will be free," he told her softly.

The train went through Vitoria, Burgos, Valladolid, and Salamanca before reaching the border two days later. It was dark when the train stopped. Portuguese authorities asked questions about their purpose in visiting Portugal and searched their luggage. An hour later, they were on a train headed to Coimbre.

Quentin was the first to notice the surveillance. *They're Krauts,* he thought. He whispered to Nadine he was getting water and asked if she wanted some. She nodded. He stood and moved to the fresh water container. As he passed Romero, he canted his head slightly in the direction of the surveillance. The lieutenant took out a handkerchief, blew his nose, got up, and walked past the Cajun as if he was going to the men's room.

"I'm on it," he whispered to the Cajun in Spanish.

Later, Quentin noticed Romero stand and say something to the conductor and press something into his hand. He wondered what was going on, but he decided to remain silent. Any furtive or nervous behavior on his part might upset Nadine. *She's been through enough,* thought the Cajun. *I just hope we get to Lisbon safely.*

At Coimbre, Romero brushed by Quentin and whispered for him to send Nadine to the restroom. After the train stopped, she was to go into the train station and wait. He motioned for Quentin to follow him. They slipped off the train on the side away from the platform. The two men watching them did not see them exit the train, and instead followed Nadine when she walked along the platform to the station office. Romero whispered to Quentin to have his pistol at the ready and they moved silently into the shadows behind the two men following Nadine.

"We have to take them by surprise," Romero told Quentin. "Can you handle it?" The Cajun nodded.

Quentin and Romero silently approached the two men and in a smooth and rapid move, the Cajun struck the bigger of the men with the barrel of his pistol hard on the right side of his head. Quentin caught him as he crumpled. Romero struck the other man hard on the head.

"Bring them over here," whispered Romero as they dragged both men to the dark end of the platform.

"What now?" Quentin asked Romero.

"I'll wait here," he replied. "You go get 'your wife' and wait on the platform facing the parking area."

Quentin walked to where Nadine was waiting and whispered that they should walk to the designated part of the platform and wait. Several minutes later, a sedan approached the train station and stopped in the parking area. A short man got out of the car and walked toward them. When he reached Quentin and Nadine, he asked them a question in Portuguese. Quentin responded in Portuguese with the countersign. The short man told them to get in the back of the car. As they pulled away, Quentin looked back and saw another car's lights turn on. A moment later, the car began to follow.

"We're being followed," the Cajun told the driver. The man nodded and said it was all right.

When Nadine asked what was going on, Quentin explained that, although Spain and Portugal were neutrals, the fascist government in Spain favored the Germans and tended to overlook some activities by Nazi operatives. In Portugal, the government had a history of working closely with the British and did not always adhere to a strict neutrality policy. However, even in neutral Portugal, Nazi clandestine operations were performed, and people wanted by the Reich often disappeared or were found dead. To assuage Nadine, he said everything was all right and "things were under control." She looked up at him and gently put her head on his shoulder. She knew that no matter what might happen, he would protect her.

Ten minutes later, they approached a small airfield and stopped near one of the hangars where a stagger wing red plane was waiting.

"You will fly to Lisbon from here," said the short man, opening the door for them to step out of the car.

The car following pulled up and Romero got out and said something to the two men seated in front before walking toward Nadine and Quentin.

"What happened back there?" Nadine asked.

"Crow helped put some curious Nazis to sleep," replied a smiling Romero. "And, while they were sleeping, someone took their money, their identity papers, pistols, and even their shoes. Tsk, tsk," continued Romero, "the black market in Portugal must be desperate." Then, he laughed and walked them to the plane.

The pilot greeted Romero in a friendly way, calling him Robin. They talked for a moment before the door to the plane was opened, and the American lieutenant told Nadine and 'Crow' to "hop in." A moment later, the pilot started the engine, and they waited until it warmed. They were airborne in a few minutes and headed for Lisbon.

The flight was uneventful, and they landed at the Lisbon airport in the dark. Quentin looked at his watch and saw that it was almost four in the morning. Nadine had slept during the flight, but she was now wide awake. The plane taxied to a hangar where several people waited. When the pilot stopped the plane and turned off the engine and the switches, Romero opened the door and stepped out. He motioned for Nadine and Quentin to follow him.

"*Hola, hombre*," came the familiar voice of Ruben Valderano. "I see you've rescued a fair maiden from the clutches of the Gestapo." The Mexican stepped forward and hugged Nadine. She kissed him on both cheeks as tears formed in her eyes.

"Don't I get a kiss?" asked Brook Hamilton Stoner standing behind Valderano.

"Yes, you too," she said, hugging the diplomat and kissing him on both cheeks.

"Hello, sport, or should I call you Crow?" Stoner teased as he extended his hand and patted Quentin on the shoulder affectionately. "Good to see you. We were a bit worried about you."

"I was in good hands," said Quentin. He motioned for Romero to join them. "Have you met Robin?" he said to Stoner and Ruben.

"Good to see you again, Lieutenant," said Stoner, extending his hand to Romero.

Valderano peered intently at Romero in the limited light. He walked up close to him and stared for a moment before saying, "What is your full name, Lieutenant?"

"First Lieutenant Alexander Romero, sir," replied the younger man.

"Your mother, her name wouldn't be Carolina Romero?" asked Valderano.

"Why yes," said a surprised Romero, studying the man in front of him carefully, a dim memory in his past suddenly awakened.

"I'm Ruben Valderano. If your mother is from Sonora, then I know her. I knew you as a boy in Mexico City."

Romero looked incredulously at Valderano and said something to him in Spanish.

"It was a long, long time ago," said Ruben. "I knew your father well. We were close friends. *Pero muchacho* (but boy) you look so much like him." They were about to pursue the conversation when Stoner told them that cars were waiting to take them to a safe place in Lisbon.

"I'll ride with the lieutenant," said Ruben. "We have much to talk about. I'll catch up with you tomorrow," he told the others. Nadine kissed Romero on the lips, called him Lieutenant Romero, and thanked him for everything before she and Stoner walked away.

"No more need for that Robin and Crow stuff now, Lieutenant Romero. Will I see you later?" asked the Cajun.

"Maybe, General" replied the lieutenant, saluting and then extending his hand to the Cajun. "May I say, sir, that you're quite a man. It's been a pleasure, sir."

Quentin shook Romero's hand and thanked him for his help and friendship. Then, he joined Nadine and Stoner.

Ruben took Romero by the arm, and, together, they walked to one of the waiting sedans.

* * *

Early in the afternoon of the following day, Quentin and Nadine were driven to the U.S. Embassy in Lisbon. They were debriefed, and Quentin was asked to prepare a report about his activities. The intelligence personnel were overjoyed when Nadine provided them with microcopies of German military projects and programs, including detailed information about Luftwaffe experiments at Peenemünde. She told them about the new Luftwaffe jet fighter, something the Germans called the "Swallow." Nadine also had information on the location of hidden munitions factories and plants in Germany. U.S. Military Intelligence officials in Lisbon could hardly believe their eyes and ears. Nadine was a treasure trove of valuable information about German war production activities. The OSS people were surprised when Nadine told them she was Eglantine.

"I still have loyal friends in France," she told them. "Let me know how I can be of assistance."

"Madame," said the senior OSS officer interviewing her, "we need you in London."

After securing permission from President Roosevelt, Quentin traveled to Switzerland to confer with Nadine's bankers and financiers. With her authorization, they would release funds to Nadine in London and New York. He received an accounting of the investments and income from the Swiss banks and brokerage houses and was pleased by the high returns. Nadine, meanwhile, stayed with Christine and Armand. Her parents greeted Nadine lovingly while tears cascaded from their eyes.

Ruben Valderano and Brook Stoner convinced U.S. Embassy staff to provide Nadine with protection while in Lisbon. Nadine teased her bodyguards by calling them "Eglantine's Musketeers."

When Quentin returned from Switzerland, he hugged Nadine and showered her with kisses and said they should marry and handed her a lovely blue diamond ring.

"Our engagement will be brief," he told her. "I'm due back in London in two days, and you're going with me."

"But, Cherie—"

Quentin pressed close to her and said, "Ruben's brother arrives tonight from Rome, and he'll marry us tomorrow. Our honeymoon will be postponed for a few days, but I'll make it up to you," he said forcefully. "If you want, we can have a big wedding in London."

When she tried to say something he shook his head and said, "I've always done what you asked, Nadine; but not now. I know what's best for us. We'll find you a lovely dress for the ceremony and have a small reception at Christine and Armand's home. Then, we'll stay in a charming hotel before leaving for London. Please marry me. I'll make you happy," he said, his eyes moist from the emotion he felt.

Nadine looked at Quentin for the longest time and thought back to when she first met him that fateful day in Paris, December 1916. He was so young and in awe of her. During the intervening years, Quentin had matured, and his love for her intensified. The passion they shared seemed endless, and she hungered to be with him. He had risked so much to come for her in France. She adored him. Now, he insisted it was time they were wed. She could feel the passion and romance within him and finally said, "*Oui, Cherie,* it is my wish too."

They were married the following afternoon by Bishop Valderano. Edmund gave her away, and Ruben was the best man. Stoner arranged a special reception at a large, plush hotel in Lisbon. Lieutenant Alejandro Romero attended the wedding and danced with Nadine during the reception. The young Mexican was as adept on the dance floor as he was an outstanding soldier. The next day, the newly married couple departed for London.

PART IV

❖

INCHING TOWARD VICTORY

CHAPTER 21
REVELATIONS

Nadine and Quentin's flight from Lisbon to London was uneventful. Ruben Valderano and Brook Hamilton Stoner accompanied them. When they arrived, even though it was early in April, the weather was cold and damp. A car was waiting for Ruben and Stoner that took them to the U.S. Embassy. The newlyweds took a cab to Quentin's flat where Thomas, Quentin's valet, was pleasantly surprised and impressed at meeting Nadine and learning about their marriage. He congratulated them and helped Nadine with her coat, gloves, and scarf. Thomas had seen her picture in Quentin's bedroom, but her hair was short now. The Frenchwoman was a beauty. Thomas pointed to various letters and messages on a table for Quentin. He handed the American an urgent message ordering him to report for duty the following morning and meet with U.S. Military Intelligence personnel. Thomas also mentioned that a sealed document had arrived by special courier for Nadine. He handed it to her. Then he told Quentin that "Master Marlon" had called several times. After showing Nadine the flat and their bedroom, the Cajun unpacked and went through his correspondence and messages.

It was almost six in the evening when Quentin called Marlon's squadron and managed to speak with him.

Marlon could not believe his ears when Nadine came on the line.

"Mother, is that really you?" he asked incredulously. She laughed in a familiar way and told him she wanted to see him as soon as possible.

"If the weather turns sour, I'll press the skipper to give me a pass," he said with exuberance. They talked for almost twenty minutes before Quentin got on the line and said he had other calls to make.

"I'll call your CO and try to get you a pass this weekend," said Quentin. Then, he teased, "Your mother and I have a surprise for you."

After completing their call with Marlon, Quentin sent a cablegram to New York informing Florence that Nadine was with him. He said he'd call as soon as he could and share a surprise. He called Geoff and told him to come by his flat the next evening for dinner.

"Come by around 7:30 tomorrow night, and please come alone. I have something important to share with you," the Cajun told him.

"What's going on?" asked a pleasantly surprised Geoff. Quentin said it was a new development that he wanted to share with the Englishman.

"By Jove!" exclaimed the Englishman, "now you've aroused my curiosity. Can you give me a hint?" Quentin laughed and said he should dress casually and bring a bright flower. "Just one?" asked Geoff.

"Yes," replied Quentin, restating that Geoff should come alone. They chatted for a few minutes before ending the call. When Quentin turned he did not see Nadine and wondered where she was. He heard soft laughter in the kitchen and followed the sound of the voices. Thomas and Nadine were seated on high stools in the kitchen talking, drinking wine, and nibbling on cheese and crackers. Quentin joined them. It struck the Cajun how natural it was for Nadine to be with him, chatting with Thomas and planning things they were going to do. With Nadine there, his flat in London seemed warmer and cheerier than before.

Quentin left early the next morning for his office. When he arrived, there were numerous messages for him, including an order to report to General Bedell Smith in the afternoon. All morning long he was debriefed, first by the OSS in London, embassy staff, and then by his superior officers. He was finally able to make some telephone calls and return messages shortly after eleven in the morning. He declined several luncheon invitations and instead worked through the noon hour responding to correspondence and prioritizing messages.

It was two in the afternoon when he arrived at General Bedell Smith's office. He waited for almost twenty minutes before the general's receptionist announced him. Quentin wondered if Smith had kept him waiting deliberately. It would be just like Smith to do something like that, he thought.

"Well, I guess congratulations are in order," said a stern Smith. Without waiting for the Cajun to say anything, the senior general continued. "I was against your decision to go to France and still think it was a dumb and dangerous thing to do. You were lucky, Norvell," he said with annoyance. "Ike and I don't appreciate your going over our heads to the president," he scolded. No sooner had the senior general said this than Quentin did something that surprised the older man. The Cajun stood up and approached Bedell Smith's desk, put his hands on the polished top edge, and leaned across it to face Smith.

"General, with all due respect to your rank, cut the crap and get to the point. If this is just a shit talk to put me in my place, skip it. We've both got more important things to do," said Quentin, staring at Smith in an ominous way.

Smith's first instinct was to stand and confront the impertinent man in front of him, but something about Norvell was intimidating. For an instant it crossed his mind that he and Norvell might come to blows. He would be no match for the aggressive younger man. Instead, he sat back and told Norvell to sit down. There was a pregnant silence as the senior general slowly regained his composure.

"Officially, your mission to France will remain a secret," said Smith, as he opened a file. "However, our embassy people and the OSS are impressed with your 'junket' behind enemy lines. And, the information provided by Madame Desnoyers is accurate and very valuable. General Marshall and the president want a copy of your report as soon as possible," he said in a desultory manner, before closing the file in front of him. "I wouldn't be surprised if the president decides to give you some kind of commendation," he added dryly. He sat staring at the Cajun for a moment before continuing.

"Ike wants to see your report. And, he wants to see you," said Smith diffidently. He muttered something under his breath that he knew Quentin could not decipher before continuing. "General Marshall will have orders for you as soon as you finish the report and clear your desk. Any questions?" asked Smith.

"No, sir," said the Cajun as he stood. "Anything else, General?" he said, staring intently at Smith with a cold, hard look on his face.

"No, that's all," said Smith. "But finish your report ASAP and then clear your desk." Quentin saluted, and the senior general returned it. The Cajun turned smartly and walked out of the office.

Goddamn that man, thought Bedell Smith.

* * *

Geoff arrived punctually at Quentin's flat and found the American ebullient.

"Well," said the Englishman, "you look bright and cheery. Now what's all this about a surprise?"

"Thomas," said a grinning Quentin to his valet, "the general needs a drink. Fix him a stiff one. What'll you have, Geoff?"

"Scotch," replied Geoff.

"Single malt, sir?" asked Thomas.

The English general smiled, nodded at Thomas, turned toward Quentin and said, "Well, my dear man, don't keep me in suspense. What's this important surprise?"

The American walked to the hall leading to the bedroom and called out, "Cherie, are you ready? Our guest has arrived." A moment later, Nadine emerged looking radiant in a black formfitting dress that accented her lovely figure. Her short hair had been teased to accentuate the lovely contours of her face. She wore a single strand of pearls and matching earrings. Her appearance completely captivated the Englishman.

"Nadine, do you remember General Geoffrey Barries-Cole Hawkins?" said the Cajun, as he held the gorgeous woman around the waist. She extended her hand to Geoff who kissed it gallantly. As he did so, the large diamond ring caught his attention.

"Geoff, Nadine and I were married recently." The words caught the Englishman by surprise, but he recovered quickly and praised the American for being so fortunate.

"Madame," said Geoff, "you are as radiant as the rising sun and as beautiful as a lovely rose in bloom."

"General," said Nadine in English with a lovely French accent, "you are so poetic. Please call me Nadine."

Thomas appeared and handed Geoff his Scotch and Nadine a glass of sherry. They sat on the comfortable divan and talked until Thomas announced that dinner was ready.

All through dinner and afterward, Geoff continued to ask Nadine questions about how she managed to escape from France and where and when she married the American. The lovely and seductive Nadine sipped her after-dinner cognac and smiled over the rim of the glass without saying anything. Quentin responded to all of the questions, saying U.S. military operatives had helped Nadine leave France and that they were married in Lisbon. They talked until almost midnight.

"Well," said Geoff, just before leaving, "you're a lovely couple, and I know you'll be very happy together."

Nadine kissed Geoff on both cheeks and thanked him for coming that evening and for his complimentary remarks. He blushed, cleared his throat and told Quentin how lucky he was. Quentin knew Geoff would call Linne and mention his marriage to Nadine. He would wait a day or two and then call Linne.

The next day, Stoner called Quentin and invited him to lunch at the U.S. Embassy in Grosvenor Square. When Quentin arrived, Stoner was waiting and escorted him to a private room where Ambassador John Gilbert Winant and three of his key aides were waiting. Quentin and Winant shared several things. Winant, like Quentin, had graduated from Princeton. The ambassador was also a flyer and had commanded the U.S. Army Air Service Eighth Aero Squadron (observation) in France during the Great War.

"Good to see you again, Quentin," said Winant, as he shook the Cajun's hand and motioned for Quentin to sit next to him. Before Quentin took his seat, the ambassador asked about Nadine. The Cajun beamed and said she was well and meeting with U.S. Intelligence personnel. The luncheon was really a business meeting and the opportunity for the ambassador to ask questions about Quentin's mission to France.

"I've heard from the president," said Winant. "He wants you and your wife to come to Washington."

"When?" asked a surprised Quentin.

"Soon," replied the ambassador. "The two of you have a few obligations here before we send you to Washington." Motioning for Quentin to come close to him, Winant whispered, "Your wife mentioned that the Nazis are arresting and systematically killing Jews. Has she told you about this?"

Quentin nodded and said, "Her information is from reliable sources. It seems the SS has special concentration camps for Jews. Nadine's sources say that at two camps, Jews are killed on a daily basis."

"Ghastly," said Winant. "We will, of course, look into this."

After the meeting, Winant told Quentin that a small reception for him and Nadine was scheduled for Friday.

"Will Lieutenant Romero attend?" asked the Cajun, expecting that his question would trigger an invitation for Romero.

Winant consulted with an aide and listened for a moment before saying something the Cajun could not hear. He looked at Quentin and indicated that if Lieutenant Romero was available, he would be invited. They talked awhile longer until the ambassador was reminded of another appointment.

"I'll look forward to meeting your wife," said a smiling Winant. "Until Friday, then," he said, extending his hand to Quentin.

The remainder of the day passed quickly for Quentin. He completed the report and began to empty his in-basket. It was just after six when he called Nadine and said he was on his way home.

"Cherie," said a smiling Nadine as she greeted Quentin at the flat. "We have a dinner invitation for Thursday evening."

"With whom?" he asked.

"With Charles de Gaulle," she said with élan. Quentin smiled at his lovely wife and asked how this had come about. Nadine mentioned speaking with Etienne and Argentina on the telephone and, a few hours later, receiving a call from General de Gaulle's aide inviting them to dinner at the general's residence in London.

"You are absolutely remarkable," he said, embracing Nadine and kissing her first on the lips and then finding a favorite spot on her neck. She moaned at their passion and pressed herself against him, enjoying the warmth of his body. Thomas appeared and asked when they would like to have dinner. Nadine turned and smiled at him and said eight o'clock.

That evening, Quentin called Florence in New York and shared the news of Nadine's escape from France and their marriage. Florence was overjoyed and asked to speak with Nadine immediately. The two women talked for over five minutes until Quentin asked for the telephone. When he spoke to Florence, she was excited and wanted to know if she could come to London. He informed her that they would be in Washington soon and make arrangements for them to be together.

"When will you be here?" asked an excited Florence. He said probably in a week and that once their schedule was confirmed, he would like her to join them in Washington. "Oh, Daddy, that will be super." They talked for a while longer before ending the call.

"I've never had so many social obligations," said the Cajun with alacrity.

Nadine, helping Thomas set the table, shot him a knowing look and said married life had its share of obligations. Then they both laughed.

In the next three days, Nadine and Quentin attended a dinner that Geoff arranged for them. Over twenty people were present, including Linne and Erleen. Both Englishwomen were impressed with Nadine. She was glamorous in a recently purchased cocktail dress that accentuated her lithe figure. A malachite necklace, matching earrings, and bracelet added to her image and highlighted her lovely green eyes. When Nadine and Linne were alone, she complimented the lovely Frenchwoman.

"I'm more than fond of Quentin," said Linne, "and envious of you for being married to him. I hope we will become good friends," she added sincerely.

Nadine responded graciously and hugged Linne, saying, "I know we will become good friends."

The dinner with General de Gaulle was all about Nadine. Quentin realized that once Nadine was identified at Eglantine, she became a celebrity and a source of pride among the Free French. She'd fought the Boche in her own way and escaped their attempts to apprehend her. De Gaulle was visibly taken with the beautiful Frenchwoman, and impressed by her wealth and dedication to the defeat of the Nazis. When Nadine recited passages from his *Appeal of June 18,* the leader of the Free French forces was impressed and captivated by the beautiful woman's patriotism. All through dinner Charles de Gaulle and Nadine sat next to each other and spoke exclusively in French. De Gaulle was entranced by the lovely Frenchwoman. He wanted her to work with some of his staff.

Etienne nudged Quentin after dinner when de Gaulle insisted on escorting Nadine to a sitting room where cognac and brandy were served.

"I'm afraid you've lost your lovely wife to the general," he teased the American.

Quentin smiled and mentioned he had a plan to steal Nadine away from her admirers. "Besides," quipped the

Cajun, "I have your charming wife to console me," he said, as Argentina took his arm.

That evening, in their bedroom at the flat, Nadine and Quentin shared each other's bodies. His lovemaking was slow and passionate, and she savored every moment of the ecstasy.

Marlon arrived Friday afternoon and was surprised to learn from Thomas that Nadine was at the Free French headquarters in London. When she arrived at four in the afternoon, Marlon took her in his arms and literally swept Nadine off her feet. She hugged and kissed her son as tears streamed down her cheeks.

"I can't believe you're here," he uttered, his words pregnant with emotion. "How did you manage to leave France?"

"Marlon, your father came for me," she said while wiping the tears that continued to flow.

He said he would, thought Marlon, remembering what Quentin had told him about getting Nadine out of occupied France. "I will always remember and thank Dad for bringing you to us," Marlon said with admiration. "Where is he?"

She told Marlon that they would meet Quentin at the reception. They sat and chatted for a few minutes before Thomas informed them that their car was waiting.

The reception was anything but small. Nadine estimated that there were at least fifty or sixty people present. She looked for Quentin and saw him standing next to Lieutenant Alexander Romero. She caught Romero's eye and motioned for him to nudge Quentin. The handsome Mexican American smiled and whispered something to the Cajun. The Cajun turned and drank in the sight of his gorgeous wife and their son. Romero whispered something to him and cleared a way through the crowd to where Nadine and Marlon were standing. But, by now, Nadine was surrounded by admirers, including several generals and colonels.

During a lull in the reception, Ruben and Stoner cornered Quentin and teased him about Nadine eclipsing him as a celebrity. The Cajun laughed and said it was wonderful.

"But tell me," Stoner inquired of Ruben, "you seem to know Lieutenant Romero."

"Yes, I know his mother. His father and I were close friends in Mexico," answered Ruben, looking at Romero busily engaged with several young and very attractive women. He briefly mentioned knowing Romero's father before he was killed in Mexico for his political beliefs. Then, he praised the lieutenant's mother, Carolina. Just as he was sharing information about Romero's family, Argentina de Gavrelac approached and kissed Ruben on the cheek. The older Mexican smiled at her in a paternal way.

"Ruben," Stoner mentioned with a smile, "the two most beautiful women in this room, Argentina and Nadine, lavish attention on you. What is your secret?" Valderano chuckled and said it had to be his Latin charm.

That evening, Marlon, Nadine, and Quentin talked until almost one in the morning. The young pilot was overjoyed that his mother was safe and now married to his father. *Dad couldn't have given me a better present than getting Mother out of France,* thought Marlon, with a lump in his throat. *She seems so happy and relaxed,* thought Marlon trying hard to hold back his emotions. When Nadine left the two of them, Marlon whispered to his father how much he loved and appreciated him for "saving mother." With his voice near to cracking, Marlon said, "Bringing her here is the best gift you could give me." The Cajun looked at his son and smiled. Quentin was more content that night than he had ever been.

A few days after the reception, Quentin left for Washington with Nadine for a meeting with President Roosevelt. They stopped in New York to pick up Florence before continuing to Washington. Florence and Nadine talked almost nonstop before Quentin's plane cleared the tarmac at La Guardia, bound for National Airport.

Quentin met first with General Marshall. They discussed in detail his analysis of the process he underwent preparing for and then making his way out of France. Marshall listened carefully to what the Cajun said and took notes. After almost an hour of questions and discussions, Marshall asked Quentin if he wanted something to drink.

"Coffee," replied the Cajun.

"Quentin," Marshall addressed him informally, "the information your wife provided is extremely valuable. We've suspected that the Germans were building a jet fighter. It appears they have a workable model and will make it operational soon. As for the flying bombs, our British friends are divided over whether or not the Germans are capable of building such a thing. The schematics and other details provided by your wife are solid proof that they're experimenting with such a weapon. Now that we know what they're up to and where they're doing testing, we'll try to learn how far along they are."

There was a knock on the door, and a black servant entered the room with a carafe of freshly brewed coffee and sugar cookies. Marshall motioned for him to put down the tray and pour each of them a cup. When they were alone, Marshall continued.

"Quentin, Bedell Smith is furious with you. I'd like to hear your side of it," said the chairman of the Joint Chiefs. Quentin explained his encounter with Smith and the exact words and tone he had used.

"Well, we can't have you intimidating senior generals," said Marshall with a deadpan expression. "So, I guess we'll have to change your assignments." He did not elaborate. "We're due at the White House soon. You might want to freshen up," he suggested.

When Marshall and Quentin arrived at the White House, they were escorted to where someone was playing a piano. The Cajun recognized the music and surmised it was Florence. Their escort knocked on the door and opened it. Florence was at the piano, and Eleanor Roosevelt and Julia Valderano were seated next to each other. The president and Harry Hopkins, with Nadine between them, were facing the attractive pianist.

The Cajun smiled when he saw Roosevelt patting Nadine's hand. He could tell they had talked and enjoyed their conversation. Nadine was a lovely woman who dazzled men and women with her beauty, poise, and intelligence. Now, she was known as a member of the French resistance and a favorite of General Charles de Gaulle.

"Your daughter is a talented musician," said Roosevelt, with Hopkins nodding in agreement.

"She's a lovely and gifted young woman," added Eleanor Roosevelt.

"Harry and I would like to stay," Roosevelt announced, his comments intended for the women in the room, "but I need to discuss some matters with George and Quentin. Ladies, please join us for lunch," the president offered.

In the Oval Office, Roosevelt praised Quentin for the report and for the success of his mission.

"Your report reads like a novel," said Roosevelt with a smile.

Quentin noticed how tired the president appeared. There were more lines in his face than he remembered and dark shadows under his eyes. *He's not well,* thought the Cajun.

"George will fill me in on the specifics of your mission," said Roosevelt. "And your charming wife has told me about your 'adventures' in France. I got a message from Charles de Gaulle. He's quite taken with Nadine." The men in the room looked at each other and nodded. "But, there are some other things we need to discuss," said the president. In the next twenty minutes, Quentin went over in detail what Nadine had provided and what he thought the Germans were planning.

"It's just a matter of time before they make their jet fighter operational. It's faster than any plane we have," said the Cajun. "They'll use it against our bombers."

The president glanced at Hopkins and Marshall with a worried expression. He fitted a cigarette into his long holder and lit it, taking a long drag before saying anything. "We've got to go deeper into Germany to bomb their factories," said Roosevelt. "Our bombers will have to go on to their targets without fighter protection. Our losses are high now, but they will get worse. Hap (General Arnold) says our fighters must carry extra fuel tanks to stay with the bombers. Still, our losses are mounting. Quentin, I want you to look into this and find out what's going on," Roosevelt told him.

Quentin nodded and remained silent. Marshall opened a file and handed the Cajun data on Eighth Air Force bomber and fighter losses. After glancing at the numbers, he concurred with the president.

"Quentin, I want you to work directly with George," said the president. "You'll serve as liaison to Ike and Hap Arnold. And, you'll also work closely with the British and the Free French and their air arm. It's going to be a tricky assignment," he cautioned. "You'll be considered George's spy. If you handle this assignment like I think you can, I'll get you a third star," Roosevelt proffered.

"I'll do my best," replied the Cajun.

"Good," said the president with a smile. "Now, I have something else for you. It seems an insistent first lieutenant has pestered Bill Donovan about a "badge" for you. George, you want to do the honors?" asked Roosevelt.

Marshall stood, approached the Cajun, and motioned for him to stand. He produced a blue infantryman's combat badge and pinned it on Quentin's tunic.

"Lieutenant Romero mentioned in his report that you 'dispatched' three German soldiers in close combat, and a fourth. In his eyes, you earned this badge," said Marshall, shaking the Cajun's hand.

"I wish we could give you a medal," said Roosevelt, extending his hand. "But, for the time being, your mission to France must remain a secret." Hopkins congratulated Quentin. The four men chatted until there was a knock on the door, and Roosevelt was reminded of an appointment.

"I'll see you for lunch," said the president. "George, stay a moment," Roosevelt told Marshall.

The lunch hosted by Franklin and Eleanor in the White House was attended by about twenty people. Ruben and Julia Valderano sat close to Quentin and Nadine, and Florence sat next to Eleanor. After the meal, Eleanor asked Florence to play, and she complied, her first selection *andante grazioso* from Mozart's "A Major Sonata" (K.331), followed by a Chopin Polonaise. She finished with a medley from George Gershwin's "An American in Paris."

Nadine, Florence, and Quentin returned to New York that evening. The newlyweds stayed overnight at the apartment that was now their daughter's. They invited Kathleen and the Vandersteels to join them and talked until almost eleven. Kathleen mentioned being busy training new nurses. When Quentin inquired about Florence's progress at Juilliard and her plans for the summer, she told them about a summer tour to Canada and

Great Britain. Florence changed the subject adroitly and asked about Marlon. Nadine and Quentin shared what they knew about Marlon and his assignment as an executive officer of a fighter squadron.

"Have you heard from Healy?" asked Quentin. Florence beamed as she rushed to her room, yelling back that she had something for them to see. A few minutes later, she returned with a large album. In it were photographs and carefully preserved stories by the photojournalist. In Healy's pictures and stories about the war in the Pacific, she skillfully depicted the battle-weary expressions of U.S. Marines and pilots on Guadalcanal. She had an uncanny ability to capture soldiers in highly evocative images reflecting the ravages of combat. Her photos of nurses weary after long hours working in hospitals at forward bases touched Kathleen deeply, and her eyes clouded over. Another section of the album was devoted to the war in North Africa. The pictures conveyed so much about the desert that it was almost possible to feel the grit and the coarseness of the sand in her photos. Images and symbolism literally leaped off the pages she wrote and the photographs that accompanied the stories.

"Someday she'll put all of this into a book," said Florence, a faraway look in her eyes.

"Well," said the Cajun, "it's late, and Nadine and I leave for England early tomorrow morning. I'll have someone drive you home," said Quentin, giving Kathleen a hug and a kiss on the cheek. Harold Vandersteel said they would take Kathleen home. Nadine embraced the nurse and whispered something to her the Cajun could not hear. Then, she hugged and kissed the Vandersteels.

The next morning, Nadine and Quentin returned to England and began a new life together. But, new challenges awaited each of them in England.

* * *

The days and weeks passed quickly for Quentin and Nadine. Before they knew it, the spring of 1943 gave way to summer in London. They saw Marlon often, and Quentin learned much from him about the mounting losses of American pilots and planes.

"Dad, a Thunderbolt saddled with a hundred-gallon auxiliary tank's no match for a Bf 109, let alone a FW 190," he said with frustration.

"When you're jumped by the Krauts, don't you drop your tanks?" asked Quentin.

Marlon shook his head and said no.

"Why not?" asked the Cajun.

Marlon mentioned that their orders were to stay with the bombers as long as they could, even if enemy fighters attacked them.

"That's ridiculous," Quentin fumed.

Quentin made a mental note to review the U.S. Air Force standard operating procedures for bomber escorts. What Marlon shared puzzled and angered him. *I can't see a logical reason for our pilots to risk their lives escorting bombers to the target with orders that prevent them from jettisoning auxiliary tanks when the Krauts jump them,* he thought angrily.

When the Cajun began to examine the air force operations orders and policies, he learned that Marlon was telling the truth about staying with the bombers and not dropping their extra tanks. Annoyed, he began to trace back the operational plans to determine the origin for the policy. After several long and tedious weeks of research, he learned that efficiency experts in Washington were responsible for the policy. It would take time for the Cajun to review the data and the discussions that had led to the establishment of the policy before he could challenge it. *Meanwhile,* he thought, *Americans are getting shot down and killed.*

* * *

In America, Florence had not heard from Nancy Love, and her efforts to reach the American flyer failed. Frustrated, Florence finally telephoned Julia Valderano and asked if she would arrange a private meeting with Eleanor Roosevelt. Julia asked about the topic for the meeting, and Florence said increasing the role of women in the war effort. They talked at length until Julia finally agreed to contact Eleanor. A few days later, Julia called and said Eleanor had set a time and date for them to meet in Washington.

"Florence, it wasn't easy to get an appointment with Eleanor. She's very busy," said Julia. "I told her you had something very important to ask of her. She agreed to this meeting because of our friendship." Florence was silent for a moment before saying,

"Thank you, Julia. I appreciate what you've done for me. I'll fly down."

When Florence met with Eleanor Roosevelt, she wasted little time asking the president's wife to assist her with Nancy Love.

"Are you a good pilot?" asked Eleanor, trying to determine Florence's flying abilities.

"Yes," replied Florence, mentioning that she had her pilot's license, was certified to fly multiengine planes, and was rated to fly on instruments. She also volunteered that she had flown across the United States and the Atlantic, often in her father's plane.

"Why don't you take me up," Eleanor challenged.

"Let's go," said Florence. An hour later, they were at the airfield and sitting in the twin engine plane while the motors warmed. Once everything was in order, Florence got clearance from the tower, taxied to the end of the runway, and advanced the throttles. They were airborne quickly. Florence did several maneuvers with the twin engine plane that elicited a big grin from the first lady.

After they landed, Florence helped Eleanor out of the plane. The older woman smiled at the lovely young blonde and said she had some questions.

"You are such a talented musician. Are you really willing to put aside your musical studies to become a pilot?"

Florence nodded and reached across to touch the older woman's hand.

"I want to do this for my country and for me too!" Florence said emphatically.

They chatted for a few more minutes until Eleanor smiled at the younger woman and said she would contact Nancy Love. A few days later, Love called Florence and offered her a place in the next class of women recruits for the Women's Auxiliary Ferry Squadron (WAFS).

A determined Florence took a leave from Juilliard and moved to Sweetwater, Texas, where she completed her training in July 1943. By then, the WAFS were merged with other women's air groups to become the Women Airforce Service Pilots (WASP). From Texas, Florence went to Lockbourne Army Air Force Base in Ohio where she trained to fly and ferry B-17 Flying Fortresses.

It was during the second week of Florence's training at Lockbourne that Quentin learned of her enlistment in the WASP. He was in Washington for meetings and could not believe that his daughter had joined the WASP. He flew to Lockbourne to confront Florence.

"Mind telling me why you're doing this?" he said when they were alone.

"I want to do something for my country," she replied hesitantly. When he asked about her musical studies, she answered that she would resume them after the war.

"What you're doing is risky," he told her. "And ferrying B-17s across the Atlantic is very dangerous," he said, a hard look on his face.

"I know," she replied, trying to sound resolute. "But I can do it and I want to do it," she added, trying to muster courage.

"You realize I could pull strings and ground you," he told her with an edge to his voice.

At first, Florence wanted to challenge her father and tell him she had already made up her mind and she could do whatever was required, but there was intensity and determination within her father that made the young woman decide to adopt a different tactic.

"Please, Daddy," said Florence, throwing her arms around his neck, her body tense. "It's what I want to do. There's a big job to do, and I want to do my part. Oh, please, Daddy, don't stop me from doing this. If you love me, please…" She wanted to cry, but instead pleaded in way that washed away the hardness in the Cajun.

"If it means that much to you," he said softly, comforting her, "then so be it. But Goddamn it, Florence, next time you want to do something like this, at least let me know before you do it!" he scolded. She showered him with kisses and promised to be careful.

In the weeks that followed, Florence finished her training and flew her first mission as a copilot on a new B-17 bound for England. She arrived in London wearing the uniform of a WASP second lieutenant. Her first call was to Marlon's squadron. He was not available, and she guessed that he was probably on a mission. Florence left him a message with a telephone number where she could be reached. The next day, he called. His voice sounded down. *He must be tired*, she speculated.

"Hello, Funny Face," Marlon baited her. "What brings you to London? You doing a recital?"

"I'm in the WASP," she replied, "and ferrying B-17s from the U.S. over here."

"What?" he exclaimed incredulously. "Does Dad know about this?"

"Yes, and it's OK with him," she said bravely.

"Well I'll be damned," he blurted. "I would never have thought—"

"I don't have much time. I'd really like to see you," Florence said insistently.

"I can't get leave," he said. "We'll be in the air tomorrow. Will you be back soon?"

"Soon as I can get a B-17 to bring over here," she replied. "Are you sure you can't get away for a few hours?" She heard him pause before saying it was impossible. "OK, I understand. There is a war on, but when I return I want to see you," she insisted. They chatted for a few more minutes before Marlon mentioned he had to go and said good-bye.

Florence sat and looked forlornly at the black telephone on the desk, wanting it to ring and hear Marlon's voice say that they could be together. Instead, the black instrument was mute and the room quiet. That evening, Florence dined with Nadine and Quentin. The day before she departed for the United States, she wandered around London. No matter where the beautiful young woman walked, men admired her and several introduced themselves and handed her their cards. She was polite and smiled at her admirers but later discarded their cards. The following day she arrived at an American air base and boarded a transport for the return trip to the United States. On the plane were several injured flyers returning to America for medical treatment. She said a little prayer for the wounded and pleaded to the heavens that Marlon not be injured or killed.

The proximity to the wounded men had a profound effect on Florence. These men had fought in the air and been badly wounded. Now they were returning to America, some of them permanently maimed and others scarred emotionally. She felt pity for them and reproached herself for being selfish and doing things only to be close to Marlon. Yet, wretched as she considered herself, Florence continued to be driven by the desire to be with her brother. She wanted desperately for him to love her the way she loved him. *Am I so awful?* she asked herself over and over again on the flight.

* * *

The days and weeks quickly accumulated into months as Nadine worked closely with the Free French. Charles de Gaulle asked for her assistance to contact and organize resistance groups in France. Nadine managed to contact Noel DeCloux. After convalescing for a few days at a convent in the South of France, Noel joined the Maquis along the Spanish border. When he learned that Nadine was safe and needed his assistance, he sent a message by courier. During the summer of 1943, with American assistance, the Free French dropped weapons, ammunition, and explosives to the Maquis for use against the Germans. The Americans sent demolition experts to train the French resistance in the use of explosives. One of the Americans sent to assist the Maquis was Lieutenant Alexander Romero. The intrepid American always carried messages from Nadine to Noel.

Gradually, the Free French enlisted the support of people in France willing to risk their lives to sabotage Nazi installations and gather military intelligence for the British and the Americans. Nadine continued to use the code word Eglantine, and her voice was heard over the radio and wireless exhorting the French to resist the Boche. Her messages were filled with hope and the promise of victory. In several of her talks, Nadine mentioned the valor of Free French forces and the leadership of General de Gaulle. Her voice became an inspiration to the enslaved people of France and a hated adversary for the Boche.

Although Nadine and Quentin were married and living together in London, his schedule and frequent trips to America and elsewhere left her alone often. She busied herself with social activities that resulted in frequent contact with Argentina de Gavrelac. And, she also saw more of Linne Kidsgrove. They worked together to assist English families displaced by the bombings. Gradually, Argentina, Linne, and Nadine became good friends and helped to provide for the welfare of children from London sent to safe locations. They provided food and entertainment for the children and did what they could to help parents visit their children.

Nadine's wealth increased because of Quentin's prudent investment and financial decisions. While a substantial portion of her wealth was confiscated by the Nazis, the Cajun had sheltered large sums of money and investments in Switzerland, the United States, and Canada.

"Even though you've lost a 'ton' of money to the Boche," Quentin told her, "you're very well off financially."

Nadine smiled and said she wanted to channel large sums into two projects.

"Yes, what are they?" asked the Cajun.

She replied helping English children separated from their families and funds for the Free French to organize the French resistance.

"You're so special," said Quentin, as he wrapped his arms around the lovely Frenchwoman's waist, drinking in the light aroma of her perfume and personal civet. However, he could sense something bothering his partner. When he asked what it was, she told him.

"I'm worried about Marlon. He's often despondent and angry. He let slip frustration with 'air force protocols.' But, when I asked him to elaborate, he internalized his anger and resentment." She hugged and kissed the

Cajun passionately and asked him about Marlon and his squadron.

"I can't really talk about what's happening," he told her.

"But something is wrong, Cherie," she insisted.

"Yes," he said, running his left hand through his hair, "Marlon and his squadron are facing difficult challenges."

"Then you must help him, Cherie," she told him. He nodded and kissed her softly.

CHAPTER 22
TURNING THE TIDE

Victory at all costs, victory in spite of terror,
victory however long and hard the road may be;
for without victory there is no survival.
Sir Winston Spencer Churchill, *First Statement*
As Prime Minister, House of Commons
[May 13, 1940]

The days and weeks turned to months, and the end of November1943 approached. Quentin's varied duties were often interrupted by orders to work on high priority developments such as the establishment of new air bases in the Mediterranean. For several weeks in October and early November, he traveled to Sardinia regularly to monitor construction of bases for American planes. The fighter squadrons on Sardinia received new models of the P-47. The powerful and well-armed Thunderbolts were ideal for the types of low-level ground attack missions they were scheduled to fly against German forces in Northern Italy.

While in the Mediterranean, the Cajun met with Kendall Valderano, who was stationed in Malta with the RAF. The young pilot asked Quentin if he might intercede and help with a transfer to a British base in England.

"I'll do better than that," said Quentin. "How would you like to transfer to the U.S. Air Force and come work for me?"

"Doing what?" asked a surprised Kendall.

"I'll need an aide for about two or three months," said Quentin. "And I can promise you promotion to captain."

"You can do that?" asked the excited younger pilot. The Cajun nodded.

"Will I get a chance to fly with a fighter squadron?' he asked excitedly.

"Yes," replied the Cajun. "I'll need you to do some things before that happens. But, I promise you'll be assigned to an American fighter squadron by no later than February of next year."

Kendall smiled, and they shook hands. A month later, Kendall received orders to report to Quentin in London.

A steady flow of new U.S. pilots and planes reached England every month. One of Quentin's assignments was to work in tandem with headquarter groups to evaluate pilots for leadership roles. The establishment of new squadrons required seasoned officers ready for leadership roles. He spent long hours reviewing air force personnel jackets and efficiency ratings of pilots at the rank of captain and above. On several occasions, Quentin met with squadron leaders and senior officers in fighter groups. He was not surprised to find Marlon's personnel file among the list of officers singled out for promotion. After examining his son's file, the Cajun whispered that it was time for Marlon to be promoted to lieutenant colonel and given command of a fighter squadron. But, first, he needed to visit Marlon's squadron and talk with his CO. *This might be a good time to find out what's bothering Marlon,* he thought.

The Cajun had not forgotten his promise to Nadine about Marlon. Even though he was working long hours and traveling extensively between England, the Mediterranean, and the United States, Quentin continued to investigate and analyze air force policies that required U.S. fighters to stay with the bombers even if attacked. German pilots had significant advantages under such circumstances. American pilots unable to drop their auxiliary tanks lost speed and maneuverability and were easy prey for the speedier and more maneuverable German Bf 109s and FW 190s. The Luftwaffe realized the American disadvantage and gave orders for U.S. planes to be engaged shortly after they crossed the Channel. American fighter escorts that managed to avoid attack by enemy fighters and stayed with the bombers all the way to the target, or close to it, were the target of murderous flak.

Kendall, now a captain in the U.S. Air Force, was Quentin's aide-de-camp. The Cajun had Kendall organize and analyze all the materials he'd gathered on fighter squadron policies that included the use of auxiliary gas tanks, staying with the bombers, and restrictions against leaving high altitude and going "down on the deck" (close to the ground) in pursuit of enemy planes. One evening, late in November, the two of them sifted through the materials and discussed the problems involved.

"These op (operation) orders don't make sense anymore," said a serious Kendall. "We're losing too many planes and good pilots because of these outdated tactics."

"What would you do?" asked the Cajun.

"Well, the first thing is to drop the extra fuel tanks the moment Jerry jumps our fighters," said Kendall.

Quentin nodded, but he could see other opportunities. "Kendall, we have enough new fighter squadrons to do a better job of escorting our bombers."

"What have you got in mind, sir?" asked Kendall.

Quentin mentioned sending several squadrons to escort the bombers. Some of the squadrons would drop their tanks and engage the enemy no matter where they made contact. The others would stay with the bombers as long as possible. Then, he mentioned sending Mitchell B-25s supported by fighter squadrons to attack and bomb Luftwaffe bases and planes on the ground.

"It doesn't matter where we destroy German planes," Quentin told his aide. "The more planes we destroy, the better. If they're on the ground or just taking off, they'll be easier to destroy."

"I'm with you, sir," said an enthusiastic Kendall. "But, can you convince the top brass around here? The attrition rate for planes that go down on the deck is much higher than for planes that stay up with the bombers," he added.

"That's true," said Quentin, "but staying with the bombers doesn't necessary result in shooting down German fighters. We have enough planes and seasoned pilots to start attacking Luftwaffe air bases and still protect our bombers." Kendall smiled and nodded at what the older pilot recommended. In the few short days that he worked for Quentin, his respect and admiration for the general grew. *He's quite a guy,* thought Kendall.

The following day, Quentin asked Kendall to find a time when they could meet with Marlon at his squadron. Kendall met the Cajun just after four in the afternoon and said that Marlon's squadron was assigned to escort duty the following day.

"Call the squadron CO and let him know we'll be at the base tomorrow," said Quentin. "And bring along a cameraman. I'm going to headquarters," the Cajun told him as he put on his tunic and prepared to leave. "I'll go home from there. I'll see you tomorrow morning."

Dark, ominous clouds were building from the west when Quentin and Kendall arrived at Marlon's squadron, a part of the Fifty-sixth Fighter Group. Lieutenant Colonel Tully Kilmer, with a worried expression, greeted them in front of the control tower.

"What's up, Colonel?" Quentin asked.

"Your son and another pilot are overdue. We've heard radio chatter about one of them being shot up," Kilmer replied cautiously.

"Sir," called the duty officer, "we've got Major Norvell on the horn." Immediately, Quentin, Kendall, the cameraman, and Tully Kilmer raced to the top of the control tower.

"Put it on the speaker," Kilmer told the radio operator. From the speaker they heard Marlon use his call sign, "Cobra leader to haystack, do you read me, over?"

The controller replied affirmatively.

Marlon's voice came over the speaker again saying he was escorting an injured "chick" (P-47 Thunderbolt) to base. He requested landing instructions and "the meat wagon" (ambulance). He was given the number of the runway and wind direction. Quentin was handed large binoculars by Kilmer who pointed toward the northeast.

A few moments later, Quentin saw the two planes approach the field. One was trailing smoke. From the speaker, the Cajun heard his son encourage the other pilot, patiently repeating things for the flyer to do.

"I want this on film," Quentin told the cameraman.

"We're almost home," they heard Marlon say. Then, he instructed the other pilot to lower his flaps and landing gear. There was a burbling sound on the speaker from the injured pilot.

The two planes slowed as they approached the runway, their canopies open. Ever so slowly, the P-47s, flying in tandem, came closer and closer to the ground. They seemed to float in the air, like an aerial ballet, until the smoking plane touched down. Then everything changed. The starboard landing gear on the damaged plane crumpled, and the stricken fighter skidded off the runway, its propeller bending as it dug deep into the earth, causing the plane to spin and suddenly nose into the ground.

Marlon's plane seemed to race by the crash and land safely.

"Let's go," said Quentin to Kilmer, Kendall, and the cameraman. They ran down the stairs to a waiting jeep and drove quickly to the crashed P-47. They arrived just after the fire crew and ambulance. "Film it," barked the Cajun, as the fire crew and the medics undid the injured pilot's harness and began to carefully extricate him from the damaged plane. The pilot was bleeding badly from chest wounds. He was gently placed on a stretcher, a frail, frightened boy, coughing blood, barely able to keep his eyes open.

Quentin remembered a time during the Great War when he was flying for the French Twenty-seventh Escadrille and escorted a damaged plane back to their aerodrome. The pilot crashed his Nieuport on landing, and Quentin and another man risked their lives to pull him from the burning wreckage. Blood from the injured pilot rubbed off on Quentin as they dragged the injured pilot to safety. It was a scene he would never forget. Now, it was happening again.

Kilmer and Kendall helped the medics lift the stretcher into the ambulance. As they did so, the Cajun bent low and whispered something to the injured flyer and tenderly patted his head. Kendall noticed the general was fighting to control his emotions, and there were tears in his eyes.

When the ambulance pulled away, Quentin regained his composure and told the cameraman to photograph the damaged plane.

"I want you to show that it still has its auxiliary tank," he insisted. Just as the cameraman was completing his filming, Marlon arrived.

"Sir," said Marlon to his father, "how's Lieutenant Brinkley?"

"He's pretty badly shot up," said the Cajun, while Colonel Kilmer shook his head. "Let's go to debriefing," said Quentin. They drove to a Quonset hut where Marlon gave his report. They were escorting B-17s and were on the return trip when German fighters attacked.

"Brinkley never had a chance," said Marlon, running a trembling hand through his hair. "They hit us before we could jettison our tanks. Brinkley tried to cover for his wingman, but they knocked Lieutenant Owens down, and then an FW 190 hit Brinkley. By the time I got there, another FW was shooting at Brinkley."

"Did you still have your auxiliary tank?" asked Quentin.

"No, sir. The moment they jumped us I dropped it," he said. Quentin nodded.

"Good work," Kilmer told Marlon as he patted him on the shoulder.

Quentin noticed that Marlon's hands were shaking. He stood, poured some coffee into a thick white mug and handed it to Marlon. Then he took off his trench coat and placed it over his son's shoulders.

"That'll be all," said Kilmer to the debriefing officer. "General, I think the major should see the doc." Quentin nodded and watched as Kendall and another officer walked Marlon toward the infirmary.

"General," Kilmer addressed Quentin as they walked to the squadron leader's office, "may I speak freely?" Quentin nodded. "We're getting the shit kicked out of us by the Krauts."

"Speak your mind, Colonel," said Quentin.

Kilmer took in a deep breath and then began a diatribe against the operations policy calling for the fighters to stay with the bombers and not drop their auxiliary gas tanks. He took Quentin into a Quonset hut that was used by the pilots as a ready room and showed him slogans on wooden placards.

"See this crap?" said Kilmer, now red faced with anger, pointing to the slogans and operations orders from Group. "They're from a bunch of desk-flying jerks and pencil pushers."

He continued to rant until Quentin touched him on the forearm and told him he was "swinging after the bell."

"All right, General," said Kilmer, trying to regain his composure. "But, my boys are getting shot to pieces, and all the brass at Group does is lecture us and send more slogans. Sir, can't you do something about this?"

Quentin tried to reassure Kilmer. *Even if I have to raise some hell,* thought an angry Quentin, *I'll try to stop this slaughter.*

"Who's your superior officer at Group?" asked the Cajun.

"General Gilbert Milner," replied Kilmer desultorily.

"Thank you," said Quentin. Then, he asked Kilmer about Marlon and whether he was ready to head a squadron.

"I'd hate to lose him, sir," said Kilmer. "But, he's ready. I'm going to put him up for a DFC (Distinguished Flying Cross). He's earned it!"

Quentin shook hands with Kilmer, saluted him, and said he was going to stop by the infirmary and say goodbye to his son.

"The doc's given Marlon a sedative," Kendall told Quentin in the infirmary.

"Get the cameraman and wait for me in the car," the Cajun told Kendall, as he walked to where Marlon was. When he approached Marlon, a nurse touched his arm gently and handed him his trench coat and said not to stay too long.

"Marlon," whispered the Cajun to his son, "I'm leaving now. Get some rest. I'll call you tomorrow. We'll talk then. What you did today was special, son." He leaned down and kissed Marlon on the forehead and walked away.

* * *

"Take us to Group headquarters," Quentin told his driver. They arrived at Group headquarters, and Quentin asked to meet with General Gilbert Milner.

"He's in with General Fanning," said the adjutant standing at attention.

"Where?" asked the Cajun sternly. The adjutant motioned to a door with the name of General Lucius Fanning on it. Quentin knocked, opened the door, and walked into the office. There were three men in the room, a two star general that Quentin thought was probably Fanning, a brigadier he supposed was Milner, and a full colonel. The three men were drinking coffee and eating chocolate cake.

"Well," said General Fanning, "do you always burst into a room without waiting?"

Quentin disregarded the admonition and introduced himself. He turned to Milner and said he wanted a report on squadron policies and op orders for escort duty, and losses of planes and pilots for the last two months.

"See here," said Fanning irately, "you can't come in here and start giving orders..."

The Cajun ignored his remarks, walked to the telephone, and picked it up. "Get me General Matthews at Pinehurst," he barked into the telephone. General Kurt Matthews was a three star general at Pinehurst, the code name for Fighter Squadron Command at Eighth Air Force Headquarters.

"You question my authority, General?" said Quentin to Fanning, while Milner and the colonel looked on in awe. "Then you'll want to speak with General Matthews," he added.

"I'll just do that," said a red-faced Fanning.

Quentin knew the general was trying to save face. Just then, the operator said General Matthews was on the line. Quentin spoke to Matthews. A few moments later, he handed the telephone to Fanning.

The general spoke into the telephone and started to complain about Quentin, stopped abruptly, and listened. Then, he began saying, "Yes, sir…of course, sir…yes, sir." His expression turned from anger to obsequiousness.

He handed the telephone to Quentin, who spoke with Matthews and mentioned dropping by his offices the following day. Then, he hung up the telephone and looked sharply at the three other men in the room.

"General Fanning, what's your combat experience?" asked the Cajun with asperity. Fanning confessed he had none. "And, you, General?" Quentin asked Milner. Again, the answer was none. "Colonel?" asked the Cajun. The man shrugged and said five missions. "I see," said Quentin dryly, trying to hide his disgust. "General," the Cajun told Milner, "I want that report on my desk in two days. Gentlemen," he said, saluting the three officers as he left the room.

* * *

Three days later, Quentin met with the senior officers in charge of Fighter Command for the Eighth Air Force, General Bedell Smith and two senior officers from Bomber Command. There were nine men in the room when Quentin called the meeting to order and mentioned the purpose of the "briefing." He was the junior officer in the room. The other men were either three or four star generals. Quentin handed out copies of the operations orders for escort duty by fighter squadrons, including directives that the fighters stay with the bombers and not drop their auxiliary fuel tanks. He also added

some of the outdated slogans that General Milner distributed to the squadrons in the Fifty-sixth group.

"I have a film for you to watch," said the Cajun,
as the lights dimmed and the projector ran the film of the
crippled P-47 crash landing at Marlon's air base. The camera caught the entire sequence of events from the time
the P-47 crashed landed until it panned over the stricken
and badly damaged plane that revealed the auxiliary
fuel tank still attached. He stopped and rewound the
film to show the bleeding pilot being removed from the
Thunderbolt.

"Unfortunately, Lieutenant Brinkley died on the
operating table," said the Cajun in a somber voice.
Quentin shut off the projector and turned on the lights.
"Gentlemen, the information in front of you include the
most recent data for fighter and bomber losses, along
with pilots and crews wounded or killed. They're depressing," he said slowly and for effect.

In the next ten minutes, Quentin mentioned the
challenges American bombers and fighters faced as they
flew deeper and deeper into enemy territory. He carefully
presented the types of fighters and flak that the Germans
were using to knock down American planes.

"Gentlemen, our losses are mounting. It's getting to
a point where we are losing men and equipment faster
than they can be replaced. Unless we do something soon,
we might have to reconsider precision daylight bombing," he cautioned. The men in the room started to talk
among themselves.

Quentin glanced at Bedell Smith, who was focusing
intently on the data. Smith looked up for a moment with
a serious expression and nodded at the Cajun. Quentin
spoke up and asked for their attention.

"General," said General Matthews, "I think most of
us have seen these data. So, just what do you propose?"
Quentin had previously spoken with Matthews and was

prepared for the question. He began by outlining needed changes for fighter squadrons and new tactics for the air force to use against the Germans. Among them were putting more fighter squadrons in the air to escort bombers and designating some of them to drop their auxiliary tanks the moment enemy fighters attacked. He also recommended low-level attacks against Luftwaffe airfields by B-25 bombers supported by flights of Thunderbolts. Finally, he mentioned developing new squadrons that would use the most current version of the P-51 Mustang. A discussion quickly ensued about the dangers involved in some of what the Cajun proposed. Finally, Bedell Smith spoke up.

"General Norvell, we're aware of the problems, and I, for one, think we need to do something about them. What guarantee do we have that your proposed solutions will turn the tide of the air war for us?"

It was exactly what Quentin wanted. He quickly mentioned support for the strategy by several well-regarded fighter squadron leaders and added, "The British would like to hit German airfields as often as possible. They just don't have the planes and crews to do so and carry out their night campaigns. But, if we do, and start destroying enemy planes on the ground, General Barries-Cole Hawkins at the RAF promises their full support," he said, and waited for them to respond.

Finally, Bedell Smith spoke up. "Gentlemen, I think we should give General Norvell's plans a try. If things don't work out, well, at least we tried," he said, looking directly at Quentin. Matthews agreed with Smith. Soon, all of the senior officers concurred.

As they were leaving the "briefing," General Matthews and Smith approached Quentin and praised him for his initiative.

"That film you showed is disturbing," said Smith, "and very effective. However, keep it in the can. We don't want it to go public. That's the kind of bad press we don't need right now." Quentin nodded and thanked them for their help.

A few weeks later, new operational orders for fighter squadrons were prepared at Eighth Air Force assigning additional fighter squadrons for escort duties, with the stipulation that if they or the bombers were attacked, designated sections would drop their auxiliary tanks and engage the enemy. In addition, attacks on German air bases with large concentrations of fighters were ordered. The attacks would be carried out by B-25 bombers and P-47 fighters armed with bombs.

The sloppy weather in early December 1943 allowed just a few sorties against Luftwaffe airfields. However, the results were positive, and numerous German planes were destroyed on the ground. A week later, Quentin was called to Washington.

* * *

Nadine and Quentin managed to catch the same flight on which Florence was returning to the United States. She looked tired and distant to the Cajun. When he asked how she was, Florence said "busy" and little else.

"You still a copilot?" asked the Cajun. She nodded and looked away.

"Be patient," he told her solicitously. "You'll soon be a first lieutenant and then a plane commander," he added to encourage her.

"Have you see Marlon?" asked Nadine. The lovely Frenchwoman asked the question to determine something that puzzled her. When Florence blushed and hesitated before responding, Nadine confirmed something that she suspected. After Florence responded, Nadine smiled and remained silent. Before she said anything to Quentin, she needed to speak with Marlon. However, she underestimated the Cajun. He was already far ahead of her.

In Washington, Quentin met with George Marshall, Hap Arnold, and some of his top staff. Arnold was pleased by the new data and the increasing number of German planes destroyed on the ground and in the air.

"Our new P-51 is ready," said Arnold. "It still has a few bugs. Can you recommend someone to work out the wrinkles?" asked Arnold.

Quentin nodded and said he had just the man.

"OK, give me his name and unit, and we'll cut orders for him to work on the project," said Arnold, while Marshall watched the Cajun carefully.

"Let's sweeten the pot," said Quentin. "The man I have in mind is an experienced combat pilot, an engineer by training, and ready to become a squadron leader."

"What do you propose?" asked Marshall.

"Give the man I designate two months to get the P-51 ready for combat, offer him promotion to lieutenant colonel and command of a new squadron equipped with P-51s," he told them.

"You've got it," said Arnold. "Who do you have in mind?" he asked.

"My son, Major Marlon Norvell," the grinning Cajun replied.

Arnold laughed out loud while Marshall remained impassive. After the meeting, Marshall accompanied Quentin to the White House. On the way, he praised the Cajun's initiative and mentioned he supported Marlon's appointment and promotion to lieutenant colonel.

When they met with Roosevelt in the White House, Quentin was taken aback by how tired and stressed the president appeared. *Either this job is killing him or something bad is happening,* thought the Cajun.

Roosevelt tried to appear upbeat and praised Quentin for his proposals and the new operations against German airfields. They talked about Quentin's activities for a few minutes before Roosevelt looked at Marshall and asked, "Isn't it's about time we give him the news?"

Quentin glanced first at the president and then at Marshall who produced a letter and said, "With the concurrence of the Senate, you are hereby promoted to the rank of lieutenant general." Marshall handed the Cajun the letter of promotion and shook his hand.

"Quentin, you've earned that third star," said the president, extending his hand for the Cajun to shake. They talked for a few more minutes about new duties for Quentin. "We're almost ready for the second front," said Roosevelt. "I want you to help with plans for the air campaign. George will fill you in on the details." The president used the intercom and called for the "guests" to enter. Nadine, Julia and Ruben Valderano, and Florence entered the room, along with Stoner and his wife, much to the Cajun's surprise.

"Let's have lunch," said Roosevelt, "so we can grill the new three star general."

On their return to London, Nadine put her head on Quentin's shoulder and said she loved him very much. "You are so special to me," she told him softly and affectionately. "I owe you my life, and I love the way you have protected our son. You are a marvelous father."

"I wonder…," said the Cajun softly, as he contemplated the disturbing attraction he suspected between his son and daughter. He did not want to share his concerns and suspicions with Nadine. *Better if I talk first with Marlon and then Florence,* he thought.

In London, the weather turned cold and bitter, and it was not long before Nadine and Quentin were celebrating the coming of the New Year, 1944.

* * *

In January 1944, Marlon went to the North American factory in Texas where he met the team working on the P-51. He befriended test pilot, Captain Kevin Corbet. The two worked closely with the production heads to add the modifications to correct the Mustang's minor problems. The plane was a hybrid: an American design fitted with the powerful English-made Merlin engine. By mid-February, Marlon was satisfied with the progress on the new Mustang and contacted Quentin. The Cajun arrived in Dallas and flew the modified Mustang. He agreed with Marlon and Corbet that the plane was ready and should be mass produced.

"All right, Dad," Marlon told his father. "You said I could head a new squadron." Quentin smiled and said he would arrange the promotion to lieutenant colonel and ensure that his squadron had the new Mustangs.

"Just one more thing," said Marlon. "Captain Corbet wants to join a combat squadron. I think he'd make a great exec." Quentin asked about Corbet's background and was surprised to learn that the captain had flown P-38s in the Pacific and was an ace. He wondered why Corbet had not been assigned to a fighter squadron instead of test pilot duties.

On his return to Washington, Quentin made inquiries about Corbet. To his surprise, Hap Arnold asked to meet with him. When they met, Arnold explained that Corbet had been part of a dangerous assignment in the Pacific and had earned a medal for his performance. But, because the mission involved American deciphering of the Japanese Naval Code, Corbet and other members of the raid could not be allowed to fall into enemy hands.

"But, that was in the Pacific, almost a year ago," said the Cajun. "He's a damn good pilot, and we need men like him in England," he added.

After considerable back-and-forth comments, Arnold finally relented.

"What do you propose?" Arnold asked Quentin. The Cajun recommended promoting Corbet to major and making him the executive officer in the new squadron of P-51s that Marlon would command. Arnold chuckled, nodded his head, and said OK.

Two months later in England, Marlon and Kevin Corbet greeted the arriving pilots for the new squadron. As Quentin had promised, they flew the up-to-date version of the P-51. Marlon and Kevin worked long and hard hours training and preparing the new pilots. By the time the Allies landed in Normandy, their squadron was a top-performing unit in the U.S. Air Force.

* * *

Between February and June 1944, final preparations for air force missions to support Operation Overlord, the invasion of France, took place. On that fateful day, June 6, 1944, the Allies landed in force on the shores of Normandy. They gained a bloody foothold on the beaches, and, by the end of a long and punishing day, they pushed the Germans back and moved inland. The second front had begun. In a few months, Paris was liberated, and the German army retreated north and east to defensive positions along the Rhine River.

The war in Europe was not over, and the Germans unleashed new weapons that were destructive and murderous. The first German jet fighter, the Messerschmitt 262, appeared and attacked American bombers. Quentin convinced Allied leaders that the Luftwaffe jet was faster than any Allied fighter and a dangerous weapon in the hands of an experienced pilot. He also brought attention to the intelligence that Nadine had provided about the new flying bomb that began to hit London and kill innocent civilians. The V-1, or Buzz Bomb, as it was called, was unmanned and powered by a turbojet engine. The

British people learned to cope with the new deadly warfare unleashed by the Germans. As late as September 1944, the V-1 bombs were indiscriminately killing people in London.

Quentin recommended three new priorities for the air force. He told Marshall that squadrons equipped with P-51s should be the main escorts for the bombers attacking targets deep in Germany. The powerful and heavily armed P-47s should be used for low-level and ground-support missions.

"We have to cut German supply lines and strangle their units," he told Marshall and Ruben Valderano. When asked what he had in mind, the Cajun replied destroying key bridges and major roads along with rail centers and as much rolling stock as possible.

"We'll attack during the day," said the Cajun, "and encourage the resistance to bomb supply columns at night and sabotage German supply centers and radar installations."

His second priority was to destroy the launching sites for the V-1s. "This will be tough," he told Marshall and Ruben. "The Germans use prefabricated components for their launch sites. The moment we or the British attack a site, the Germans set up others elsewhere. So, we need to keep blowing them up wherever they appear." The other two men nodded.

"And your third priority?" asked Marshall.

"Keep hitting and destroying German airfields and planes on the ground," he told them.

* * *

Paris was liberated at the end of August 1944 when Free French armored units under the command of General Philippe Leclerc fought their way into the City of Lights. The following day, General Charles de Gaulle entered

Paris. Nadine was emotionally overwhelmed by the news and asked Quentin when she could travel to Paris.

The Cajun smiled and said, "In a few weeks."

Nadine returned to Paris and to her home at the end of September 1944. Her identity and role as Eglantine with the resistance and her work and support for the Free French made her a heroine. But, the return to Paris was bittersweet. Her property had been trashed by the fighting, and the Germans had stripped her home and buildings of furniture, fixtures, and artwork. It would take time and money to rebuild her properties and wealth.

The war continued, and Quentin was occupied with new developments and demands.

In early September, Quentin learned that Field Marshal Montgomery convinced Churchill of a plan to conduct a daring thrust into Germany from Holland and gain control of the Ruhr, the industrial heart of Germany. Montgomery called his plan Market Garden. The plan required precision and the capture of strategic objectives: the key bridges across the Rhine. A massive airdrop was involved, something that bothered Quentin and other U.S. military leaders. Churchill's persistence caused President Roosevelt to relent and support Montgomery's plan. It was one of the few times Quentin heard Ruben Valderano grumble.

"This operation is too risky," said the Mexican. "Any delay in seizing the bridges can be calamitous," he warned.

The attack, the largest airdrop of the war, began on September 17. The British First, the American Eighty-second, and One Hundred First Airborne Divisions, and a Polish Paratrooper Brigade were parachuted well behind enemy lines. The Americans attacked and captured the bridges at Eindhoven and Nijmegen, while the British tried to capture the easternmost bridge at Arnhem. The Polish Brigade, delayed by fog, arrived late and sustained heavy losses. By September 24, 1944, over seven thousand British troops were killed, wounded, or captured by the Germans. First British Airborne Division effectively ceased to exist.

The German victory at Arnhem coupled with the continual bombardment of London by buzz bombs was a bitter blow for the English people and the Allies.

When General Marshall met with Ruben, Quentin and senior representatives from Eisenhower's staff were present to discuss the outcome of Market Garden. Marshall turned to the Mexican and, in a solemn voice, said, "We took a risk, and it proved a bad one. Ruben, we should have listened to you and the Dutch underground."

From October through early December 1944, Quentin and Ruben worked together in Eisenhower's headquarters. The Germans were retreating. The Luftwaffe was slowly being cleared from the sky. On the Eastern Front, the Red Army was inexorably pushing toward Berlin. It seemed as if the war was over, but the Whermacht was not yet defeated.

On December 16, under the cover of bitterly cold weather and snow, the Germans launched an attack in the Ardennes against thinly spread American forces. The winter weather "grounded" Allied planes, preventing reconnaissance and attacks on advancing German armor and mechanized units. Quentin and Ruben read the reports of the German advances. By Christmas, the Whermacht had pushed the Americans back and surrounded Bastogne, a strategically important town in Belgium. The resolute One Hundred First U.S. Airborne Division prevented the Germans from taking Bastogne. When the weather cleared on December 26, Quentin and other air force tacticians ordered missions to support the Americans trapped at Bastogne and attack enemy positions. By early January 1945, the Wehrmacht's advance into Belgium was stopped, and the Allies were back on the offensive.

"It's just a matter of time, now," said Ruben to Quentin and others in Eisenhower's headquarters in late January. He was right. Hitler would commit suicide on April 30, 1945, and Germany would surrender unconditionally on May 8, 1945.

* * *

As American and British forces advanced into Germany, a horrifying discovery was made. Concentration camps were liberated where Jews were held captives, the inmates starving and emaciated. Moreover, two major death camps in Germany were found, where thousands of Jews had been systematically killed by the SS.

When Quentin heard about the death camps, and the slaughter of innocent Jews, he wondered what kind of people could do this. He told Nadine that she had been right about the information on the Nazi death camps and said,

"Every last German responsible for these atrocities should be hunted down and brought to justice. We must punish the despicable people who ruthlessly killed millions of Jews, and see that nothing like this ever happens again."

When the war ended, the extent of what came to be known as the Holocaust staggered the imagination of people around the world. Investigations by the Allies revealed barbaric acts of cruelty by the Nazis against the Jews, Gypsies, and others. The Holocaust was a grim reminder of how educated and cultured men and women could be so savage in killing innocent men, women, and children.

CHAPTER 23
PEACE

*The legitimate object of war
is a more perfect peace.*
William Tecumseh Sherman, *Speech at St. Louis*
[July 20, 1865]

Quentin and Ruben met with George C. Marshall in Washington at the beginning of March 1945. They carried important dispatches for the chief of staff and for the president. When they met with Roosevelt, Quentin was shocked by his appearance. *He's dying,* thought the Cajun. But, Roosevelt, confined to his wheelchair, managed a brave front and handed the Cajun a letter that promoted him to the rank of general.

"The Senate concurs with my recommendation that you deserve a fourth star," said Roosevelt, his features and skin tone evidencing serious illness. Quentin thanked the president and shook the extended hand that was offered. There was no strength in the president's grip, and his skin felt cold to the touch. They talked about the war in Europe, and the president smiled when Ruben and then Quentin told him that the fighting would soon be over.

"How soon?" asked Roosevelt.

"Late April, maybe early May," said Ruben, with Marshall nodding in agreement.

"Thank you," said the president, his eyes heavy and showing signs of fatigue.

They talked for a while longer before a presidential aide knocked and entered. The aide whispered something to Roosevelt, who nodded, his movement revealing discomfort. The president congratulated Quentin again on his promotion and thanked Ruben and Marshall for their hard work.

"I've another matter that needs attention," said the president as he was wheeled out of the room.

"He's a very sick man," said Ruben to Marshall and Quentin as they were leaving the White House. Marshall, a worried expression on his face, remained silent, but his eyes betrayed him.

On April 12, 1945, President Franklin Delano Roosevelt died in Warm Springs, Georgia. He did not live to see the defeat of Nazi Germany in Europe and the surrender of Japan in August 1945. Roosevelt's death had a profound impact on the Cajun. America had lost a great leader, and he had lost a special friend.

* * *

When Nadine returned to Paris at the end of September 1944, she busied herself hiring a new staff to help reconstruct her enterprises. Noel joined her in early October 1944 and resumed his duties as her executive assistant. Most of her immediate staff had scattered when Nadine fled from the Nazis. Those who delayed leaving fell into the hands of the Gestapo and were killed. But, gradually, and with Noel and Millard's help, a few of her previous employees returned to Paris. They found her waiting with open arms.

In February 1945, Nadine arranged for her parents to move back to their home in Paris. Desirée and Bertrand stayed in Switzerland until the end of February 1945. At the beginning of March, Nadine arranged for Christine and Armand to return to Paris from Lisbon.

Quentin flew into Paris as often as he could to be with Nadine and her family. But, his duties with Marshall and in Eisenhower's headquarters kept him away often, as did his frequent trips to the United States.

General Marshall introduced the Cajun to President Harry Truman in late April 1945. Truman had read Quentin's file and discussed him at length with George C. Marshall. He confessed to Marshall liking the Cajun for his "gutsy style." When they met, there was something about Truman's manner that appealed to Quentin.

"He's so different from President Roosevelt," Julia said during dinner one evening with Quentin and Ruben. The two men smiled.

"There is something very honest and direct about Truman," Ruben volunteered.

"He's a little rough around the edges," added the Cajun. "But, I think he's conscientious and capable."

"When will we see Nadine again?" asked Julia. Quentin said that as soon as the Germans surrendered, he would bring her to Washington.

On a lovely spring day in mid-May 1945, Quentin and Nadine met with President Truman and Bess, his wife. Ruben and Julia, George Marshall, Stoner and his wife, Healy Rohwer, and Florence were also present. It was an enjoyable and entertaining evening. Truman played the piano and even did a duet with Florence. The president was gracious and yielded the piano to the beautiful young woman still wearing the uniform of a WASP, now a first lieutenant. Healy, looking thin and tired, complained to Quentin about a travel schedule that was demanding and exhausting. Her stories and photographs about the war were syndicated and she mentioned leaving in a few days for the Pacific.

Try as Quentin might to speak privately with Florence, she skillfully avoided being alone with him. The more she kept him at arm's length, the more the Cajun was convinced about something serious between her and Marlon. *She's afraid I might ask about her and Marlon*, mused the

Cajun. *Well,* he thought, *she can't avoid me forever.* Quentin decided, instead, to meet first with Marlon. Talking with him might clarify matters and confirm his suspicions about Florence and her feelings toward Marlon.

Two days after the Germans surrendered, Quentin invited Marlon to dinner. They met in London at an exclusive club where they could speak privately. The meal started quietly, but Marlon, sensing his father had an agenda, made small talk about what might happen now that the Germans had surrendered. After they had finished the main course, Quentin spoke up.

"Marlon, what's going on between you and your sister?"

The question did not seem to surprise the younger pilot. He looked at his father for a moment before saying, "What do you mean?"

A question for a question, thought Quentin, *he's being evasive.* "Marlon, don't play games with me. I know something is happening between you and Florence. I can see it in her eyes," he stated firmly. He waited for his words to take their effect before continuing. "Marlon, don't put me off. I can see and feel the stress and tensions in Florence and in you."

After a long pause, during which Marlon barely glanced at his father, trying to avoid eye contact with him, he decided to relent. It was time to tell his father about him and Florence. "Dad, Florence is in love with me."

"Romantically?" asked the Cajun. Marlon nodded and continued to look down at the tabletop. "Have you done anything about it?" asked the Cajun. Marlon shook his head. Quentin released a barely audible sigh before continuing. "Tell me about it," said Quentin in a soft voice, as he extended his left arm and touched the younger man's hand.

In the next twenty minutes, Marlon told his father about the way Florence began to demonstrate and vocalize her romantic affection for him.

"Heaven knows I didn't do anything to encourage it. I try to see Flo only when other people are present and avoid being alone with her. This thing, these strong emotions, my feelings toward Flo, they're driving me crazy," Marlon confessed.

Quentin could see the turbulence and emotional struggle within his son, and it moved him to reach out and touch him again.

They sat quietly for several minutes before a waiter came by and asked if everything was all right. Quentin, still holding Marlon's hand, replied, "Yes. Just the check, please."

"Walk with me," said the Cajun, as he took Marlon's arm. They wandered through the streets of London, the cool night air a welcome elixir that calmed both men. Finally Quentin spoke.

"What are you going to do?"

"I don't know, Dad," replied a sober Marlon.

"I know how difficult this is for you," said the Cajun in a soft and supportive tone, "but sooner or later you and Florence will have to decide how to deal with this."

"Are you going to talk with Flo?" asked Marlon, shooting a quick glance at his father.

The Cajun said yes and didn't say any more.

"Have you told any of this to Mom?" asked the younger pilot.

Quentin shook his head. "I'm going to talk with Florence first," said the Cajun, his jaw firm and his lips tight. "After that, I'll talk with your mother. I'm pretty sure she'll want to talk with you then."

They continued to walk and occasionally talk. Toward the end of their stroll, Marlon stopped and hugged his father. He began to sob. The Cajun felt enormous compassion for Marlon and his predicament.

"We're not always in control of our lives and masters of our emotions and passions," Quentin said, as he embraced Marlon. "We must know how to act with conviction and honesty when a difficult choice is required. I'm not going to tell you what to do. You know the difference between right and wrong. But, in matters of the heart, love is paramount, and the will too often succumbs to passion. You must do what you think is right. I love you, Marlon, and will always stand by you. Don't forget that," said the Cajun, as he took his son's arm and they walked together slowly into the night.

Ten days later, Quentin confronted Florence in New York. He made certain they were alone in the apartment and asked if she wanted some tea. She nodded, and he made a pot and asked her to join him in the spacious living room. They sat and sipped tea, Florence guarded and the Cajun calm and determined to get his daughter to share her feelings with him. He finally mentioned his talk with Marlon. She stiffened and looked away from him. There was a long pause before Quentin finally spoke.

"Florence, please talk to me. I need to know what you're thinking and how you feel."

Florence jumped to her feet and snapped, "Why?"

"Why!" he exclaimed. "Because your feelings and behavior toward Marlon are hurting him."

"That's not true!" she shot back, her eyes flashing and avoiding his.

"Florence, stop and think for a moment," said the Cajun standing to face his daughter. "Marlon loves you as a sister, and perhaps more, but your love is causing him pain." She rejected this and tried to turn away from him. He moved close to Florence and stood in front of her, his eyes examining her face carefully. "Can't you see what you're doing to him?"

"You don't know anything," she said angrily. "You can't understand my feelings for Marlon. Besides, I know he loves me," she told him haughtily.

"Granted, I don't know exactly how you feel," he said in a controlled voice, "but, unless you tell me, I'll never understand your affections for Marlon."

"I know what you want. You're just like all the others, smug, narrow, and caught up in your precious morals and conventions," she spat.

"That's not true and you know it," he said softly and deliberately. She stood in a confrontational pose, uncertain what to say or do, ready to bolt out of the room if necessary.

"Florence," he told her, while searching for her eyes, "you're my daughter. We're blood kin, and I know the passion and determination within you. Before she died, your mother told me she wanted you to have her qualities and my strength. If she were here now, she'd tell you to talk to me."

Florence was momentarily caught off guard by the mention of her mother and what her father had said.

"Florence, Florence," the Cajun said softly and slowly, "don't keep this thing locked up inside of you. Be courageous as I know you are and trust me," he implored.

She was caught between the terrible emotions of love and hatred and considered for a fleeting moment striking out at her father, the person tormenting her. But, something from deep within her surfaced and washed away that anger. In its place emerged a vulnerability and a need for understanding and compassion. She hesitated for a moment before lunging at her father and bursting into tears. Quentin caught Florence and held her in a strong and loving embrace.

"I can't help it, Daddy. I love him, I love him," she sobbed, burying her head into his shoulder.

Quentin held Florence and patted her affectionately while he kissed the back and side of her head, tenderly fingering the golden, silky strands of her hair. He remembered a time many years before in Central Park when Florence erupted in anger and frustration. His business trips and visits to Nadine in Paris had left the young girl alone too often. Florence's emotional outburst and her momentary rejection of him convinced the Cajun that she needed him. Now, he had to do whatever necessary to reestablish the bond between them. He wanted to help his daughter, and he needed to keep a promise to Ione he'd made on her deathbed.

"Tell me, honey, please," he pleaded. She cried hard for a long time before calming down. She sighed before telling Quentin about her love for Marlon and how much she wanted to be with him. He remained silent, but his supportive touch and manner encouraged her to continue. When she finished and he said nothing, she pulled back slightly and looked up into his face. She saw tears in his eyes and only love for her.

"Oh, Daddy, I love you so much," she said between sobs.

He held Florence tightly in his arms and did his best to comfort her before saying, "No matter what you and Marlon decide, I'll always love you. It's not my place to tell you what to do or how to behave," he said in a reassuring voice. "Just remember that as long as I live, you can always count on me."

Florence felt relieved and safe in her father's arms. She finally stepped back from his embrace and asked if Nadine knew anything about her feelings toward Marlon.

"No, but she suspects something," he told her.

"Do you have to tell her?" she asked, hoping against hope that he would say no.

"I'll have to tell her," he said, looking deeply into her lovely blue eyes. "Better that she find out from me than someone else."

Florence's eyes dropped, and her shoulders slumped, the thought of sharing her secret with Nadine weighing heavily on her.

In a soothing voice, he said, "It'll be all right. Let me handle it."

"Thank you," Florence whispered.

* * *

On his return to Paris, Quentin sat with Nadine in the privacy of her study and related his conversations with Florence and Marlon. As he spoke, he examined carefully the lovely woman's face and body language for reaction to his comments. Nadine sat still and emotionless, waiting for him to finish his remarks. It seemed like such a long time, but it was just a few minutes.

"This must stop," he heard her utter firmly in a low voice.

"Nadine?" inquired the Cajun, wanting her to speak to him. She looked away from Quentin, preoccupied in deep thought before speaking.

"I must talk with both of them and tell them to stop this awful thing," her voice was a mix of disappointment with traces of annoyance. The Cajun stood, walked to Nadine's side, and took her hand in his.

"That may not be desirable," he cautioned her gently.

"Why not?" she said emphatically. "What Florence wants is a sin. It's incest!"

Quentin listened patiently to Nadine, now and then asking her to clarify something she said or implied. She was angry and thinking aloud as she examined and reexamined in her mind the attraction between her son and his half sister. Something within Nadine surfaced that was new to the Cajun. He probed slowly and cautiously to determine the importance of this orientation in his wife. Abruptly, Nadine decided to end their conversation.

"Enough," she told Quentin. "No more talk. I must speak with Marlon." At that moment, Quentin knew that any attempt on his part to influence Nadine's perceptions of the strong attachment between their children was futile.

I hope that when she meets with Marlon it goes well, he thought.

In the next two days, Quentin noticed a tension in Nadine as she grappled with the situation between Marlon and Florence. She called Marlon and arranged to meet with him in London. Quentin offered to join her, but she refused.

"I must speak with him alone," she told the Cajun forcefully.

When Nadine returned to Paris and the Cajun picked her up at the airport, she was distraught, and he could tell she had been crying.

"What happened?" he asked solicitously. She refused to say anything about her meeting with Marlon.

That evening, Nadine stayed up late, and Quentin thought he could hear her crying in the study. The next day, he called Marlon and asked what happened.

"Mother told me to break it off with Florence," said the younger man.

"And?" probed the Cajun.

"Dad, she was calm and icy and insisted that what Flo and I were doing was a sin. When I told her we hadn't done anything, she started to lecture me." Quentin listened as Marlon told him more about the meeting. "I guess I lost it, Dad," said the younger man sorrowfully.

"What do you mean?" asked Quentin.

"I lost my cool and told mother that Flo and I were adults and would deal with the situation. She was surprised by my outburst, Dad."

"What happened then?" probed the Cajun.

"She told me I was making a big mistake and that what Florence and I were doing was sinful and ruinous for us and the family. I guess that's when I told her I didn't care what others and the family thought."

Wow! Quentin thought. "What happened then?"

"She did a slow burn and started to pace," said Marlon. Quentin encouraged him to continue. "I'm afraid I put my foot in it, Dad."

"What do you mean?" asked the Cajun.

"I told mother she should be as understanding as you are," Marlon said apologetically.

"I bet that didn't go over well with her," Quentin volunteered.

"No, Dad, it didn't. That's when she really got sore and said I was making a big mistake."

"Did she walk out on you?" asked Quentin. Marlon replied affirmatively. They talked for a few more minutes before Quentin said he would try to get to London and meet with him. Before they ended the call, the Cajun told Marlon, "You did the only thing you could, son. I'll talk with your mother. She'll come around."

"Thanks, Dad," he heard Marlon say with resignation but deep affection. Quentin sensed that he and Marlon had never been closer. He loved his son and had to find a way to mend the relationship between Marlon and Nadine.

* * *

The warm weather at the beginning of July 1945 held Paris fast, but the discomfort from the heat and humidity could not dampen the happiness the people of Paris exhibited. The war in Europe was over, and the fighting in the Pacific would end soon. Yet, for Nadine, another unresolved conflict remained.

It had been over ten days since Nadine and Marlon met in London. Quentin had been called to Washington for meetings, been to New York City to see Florence, and then ordered to Rome for meetings. When he returned to Paris, he told Nadine they needed to talk.

Shortly after dinner, they sat to talk. Nadine was tense, convinced that their conversation would be unpleasant. He began by asking, "Have you talked with Marlon since you returned from London last month?" She shook her head and remained silent. "It's not good for the two of you to be at odds," he said softly. She did not reply, but her eyes searched his, probing. "Why don't you talk to me?" he implored. Still, she remained silent, but her expressive green eyes could not hide the anguish she felt. "Nadine, please don't do this. Talk to me," he pleaded. He approached and sought to embrace her. She tried to resist by turning her back to him. The Cajun reached out and grasped her shoulders with his hands to prevent her from escaping. He whispered in her ear how much he loved her and how important it was to share their thoughts and emotions about their children. He told her a few other things in a soothing voice and gradually felt the tensions within her subside. Quentin turned Nadine around to face him and, again, asked her to talk to him. This time she relented.

She told him about her meeting with Marlon and how it had ended badly. "He must hate me," she confessed. He shook his head and said no. "Oh, Cherie, we must make them stop before they do something wicked," she said, her eyes moist.

Quentin mustered his courage and resolve before responding. Nadine was wrong, and it was now up to him to find a way to defuse the impasse between her and the children.

"My dear," he told Nadine, "they are adults. If we try to tell them what to do, it will drive them away." She looked surprised by what he said. "We cannot order them like children." When she tried to say something, he tenderly touched her lips with his left index finger and shook his head.

"Nadine, I've always done what you wanted," he said softly. "You've taught me so much about love, about fulfilling the needs of a partner, and about growing as a person. I was wrong to avoid you after Ione died and to question why you had kept secret that Marlon was our son. You were right then. And, you were right to stay in France and fight the Boche in your own way. But, now, I cannot stand by and watch our family be torn apart. We must let Marlon and Florence decide what they think is best for them." She looked into his eyes. "We may not approve of what they decide," he said solemnly, "but it must be their choice. If we love them, we must abide by their decision and do what we can to help."

"But it's a sin," she said tenuously.

"We don't know what they will decide," he said. "Trying to use church dogma to condition their choice will not work." They continued to debate the matter until Quentin again pressed his index finger to Nadine's soft lips.

"You must trust me, my dearest," he told her. "It's hard to watch them struggle with their feelings, but, ultimately, it's their choice and their lives. All we can do is trust in what we taught them as children and young adults, and hope they have become responsible adults because of the examples we set for them."

As Quentin talked, Nadine's love for him intensified. She had taught him so much and helped him become the wonderful man he was. Now, he was taking the lead in their dyad. She knew he did not want to control their relationship. All he asked was for them to be equals and love each other. They went to bed that evening and held each other without saying a word. As the days passed, she relented and told Quentin he was right and that she would abide by the decision of the children.

* * *

Quentin was in Washington when the first and the second atomic bombs were dropped on Japan. He had been informed by Marshall about the super bomb the United States was developing but told little more. Unlike many Americans, he understood in theory the potential of nuclear fission. However, the devastation caused by the bombs was overwhelming and staggered the imagination. Shortly after the Japanese surrendered on the deck of the *USS Missouri*, he, Marshall, and Ruben had a long lunch in Washington. They were about to go in separate directions. Ruben was preparing to move his family back to Santa Barbara, and Quentin was ready to leave the army.

"What will you do?" Ruben asked Marshall.

"I'm career military," replied the chairman of the Joint Chiefs, "and will stay in my job."

"And you, hombre," Ruben nodded in Quentin's direction.

"I'll leave the army and try to convince Barston, Marwick, Fowler, and Peterson to open an office in Paris," said the Cajun with a chuckle. They all laughed.

Marshall looked at the Cajun and said, "Quentin, if I call on you in the future, I hope you'll reply favorably."

The Cajun smiled, and said, "George, all you have to do is ask."

EPILOGUE

Try as Quentin might to leave the U.S. Army, Generals Eisenhower and Marshall convinced him to remain and help with the occupation and reconstruction of Germany. He remained a general and worked out of Paris to be with Nadine. But, late in 1946, President Truman and General Marshall asked him to participate in a large-scale effort to rebuild the European states devastated by the war. He agreed and served for many years as a civilian leader within the Marshall Plan. The Plan to rebuild Europe was successful. Quentin expanded his fortune while working with the postwar army and the Marshall Plan. He retired at fifty-eight as a multimillionaire.

When Quentin heard about Nicholas von Kleist's situation, he contacted him. The von Kleist ancestral home and estates in East Prussia were lost. Some of the properties and holdings were in the reestablished Polish state, and others were confiscated by the East German Communist government. Nicky was living with Lorelei's parents in Bavaria. Late in 1945, Quentin hired Nicky to help with the German reconstruction, and, in 1946, arranged a senior management job for him with the Bavarian Motor Works. Nicky and the Cajun continued a long and enjoyable friendship.

Nadine, with Quentin's help, reacquired her holdings in France and elsewhere and rebuilt her wealth. She invested prudently and modernized the industries and production facilities for her products. By 1948, her fortune had nearly doubled. She and Quentin continued to live in Paris, but they often stayed at her modernized home near the Normandy Beach, or at La Croisiere, the estate Louis Bondurant willed to her.

Marlon was discharged as a full colonel in September 1945 and returned to America. He worked for an architectural firm until the following year when he entered the Master of Fine Arts program at Yale University. He graduated from Yale two years later and joined a large architectural firm. He met and married a former New York debutant and Wellesley graduate. They had two children, a boy and a girl. With Quentin's help, he became a highly successful architect and builder.

Florence returned to New York and completed her studies at Juilliard. She moved to Cambridge to study music at Harvard and earned an advanced degree. A highly regarded pianist, she was much in demand and toured the United States, Canada, England, Europe, and South America before settling in Connecticut. She married a well-known conductor fifteen years her senior. They had a son. Five years later, Florence divorced him and raised the boy on her own.

Florence and Marlon saw each other secretly two and sometimes three times a year. They rendezvoused away from prying eyes, sailing together in the Caribbean, skiing in British Columbia, sharing a bungalow on a secluded beach at Bora Bora near Tahiti, or traveling together incognito through remote parts of Argentina and Chile. Quentin knew about their meetings, but he never mentioned it to Nadine. He gave them substantial portions of his wealth and would often arrange for private aircraft they could fly to their undisclosed destinations. If Nadine suspected that Marlon and Florence met secretly, she never revealed it.

Two or three times a year, Quentin visited Ione's grave on Long Island. He often went alone. But, as the years passed, he and Florence visited the grave together.

Nadine died shortly before her eighty-first birthday. Quentin buried her at La Croisiere next to her parents and Louis Bondurant. The Cajun continued to live an active and productive life sharing time with his children and grandchildren at the summer home in Normandy that he and Nadine loved, and the colorful and bountiful La Croisiere. He died peacefully in his sleep at ninety-three. He was cremated and his ashes interred in Nadine's grave.